Splatoon™

VOL. 4

STORY AND ART BY

Sankichi Hinodeya

CONTENTS

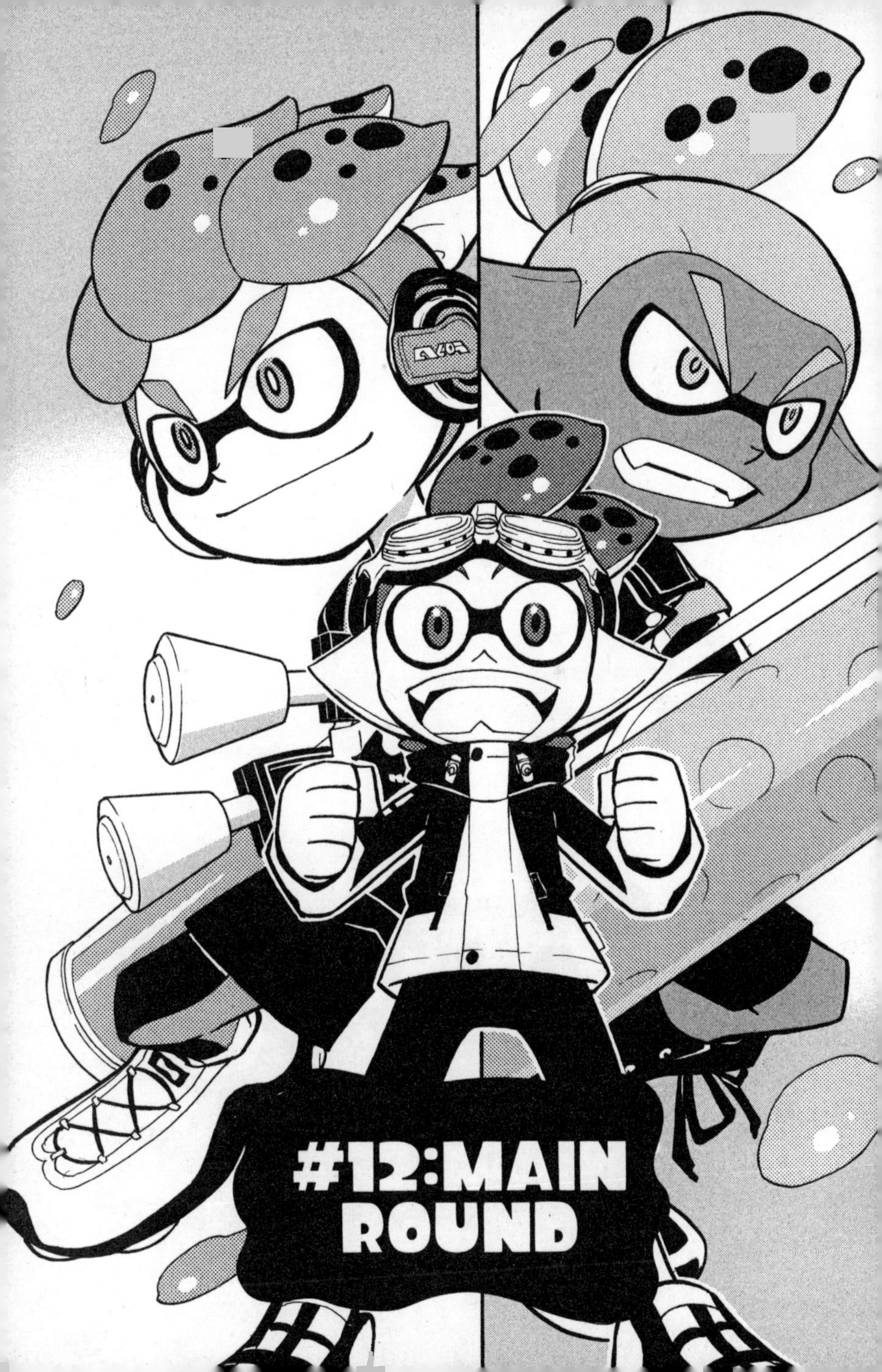
#12: MAIN
ROUND

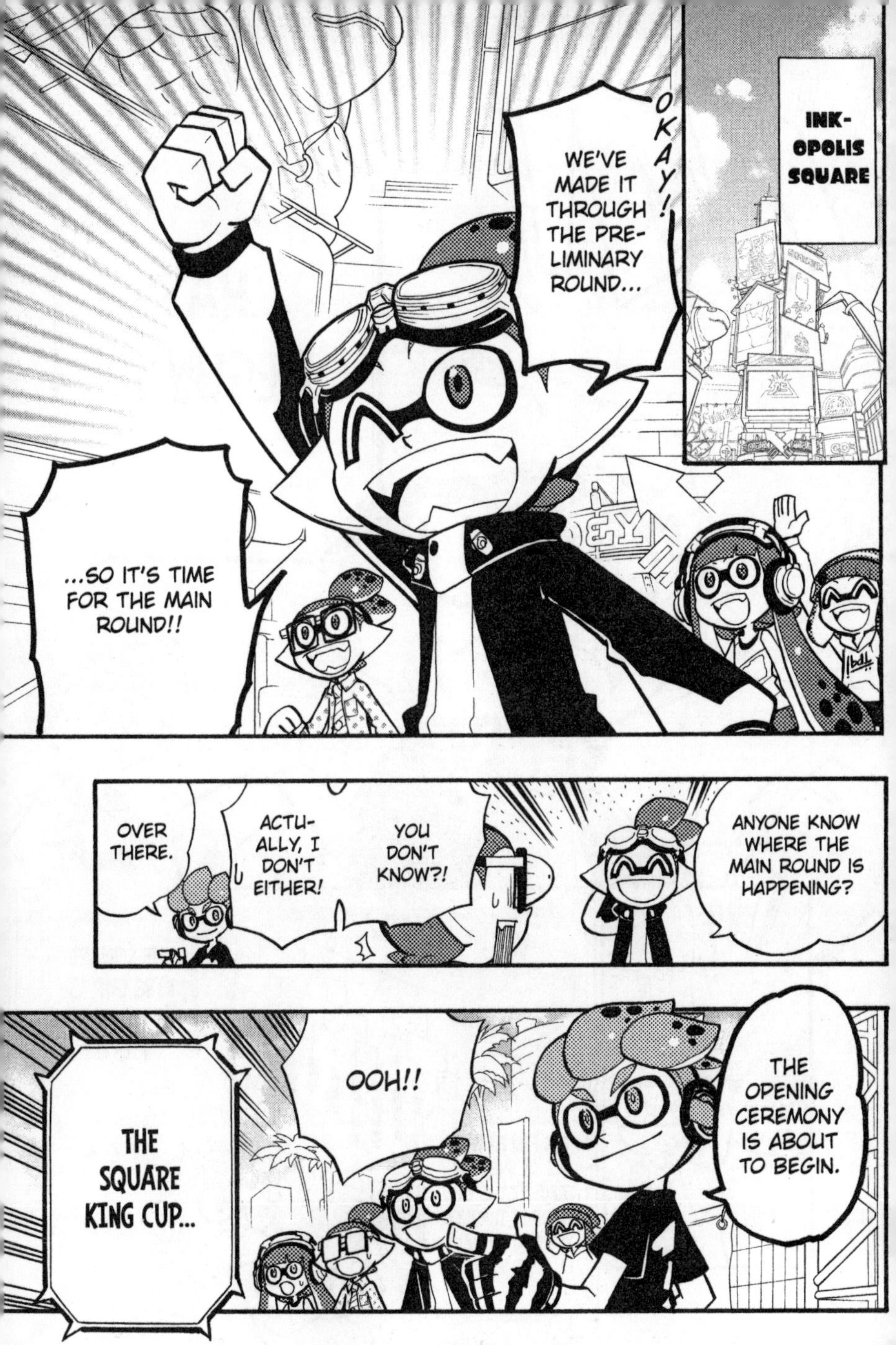
INK-OPOLIS SQUARE
OKAY!
WE'VE MADE IT THROUGH THE PRE-LIMINARY ROUND...
...SO IT'S TIME FOR THE MAIN ROUND!!
ANYONE KNOW WHERE THE MAIN ROUND IS HAPPENING?
YOU DON'T KNOW?!
ACTU-ALLY, I DON'T EITHER!
OVER THERE.
THE OPENING CEREMONY IS ABOUT TO BEGIN.
OOH!!
THE SQUARE KING CUP...

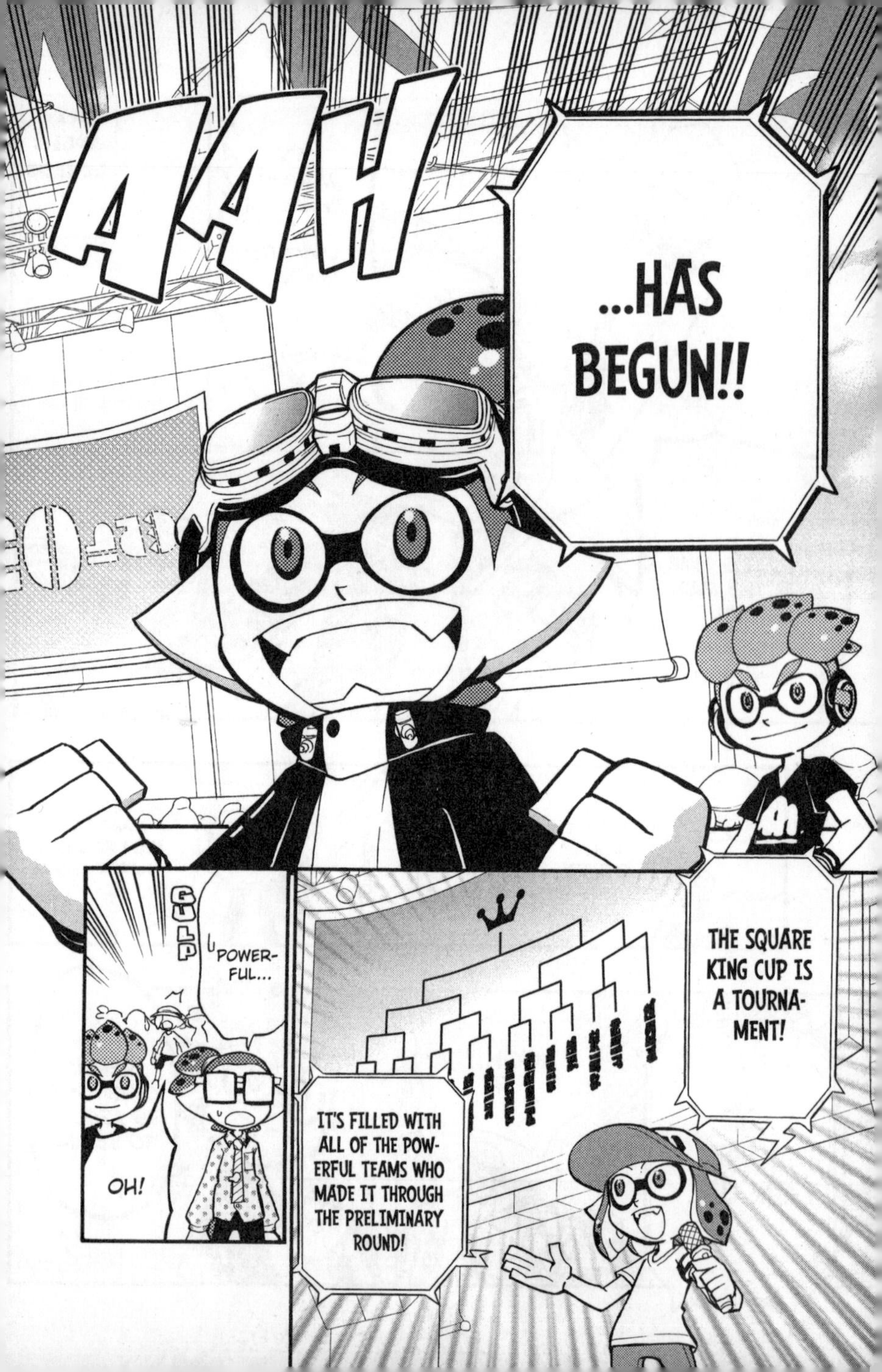
...HAS BEGUN!!
AAH
THE SQUARE KING CUP IS A TOURNA-MENT!
IT'S FILLED WITH ALL OF THE POW-ERFUL TEAMS WHO MADE IT THROUGH THE PRELIMINARY ROUND!
GULP
POWER-FUL...
OH!

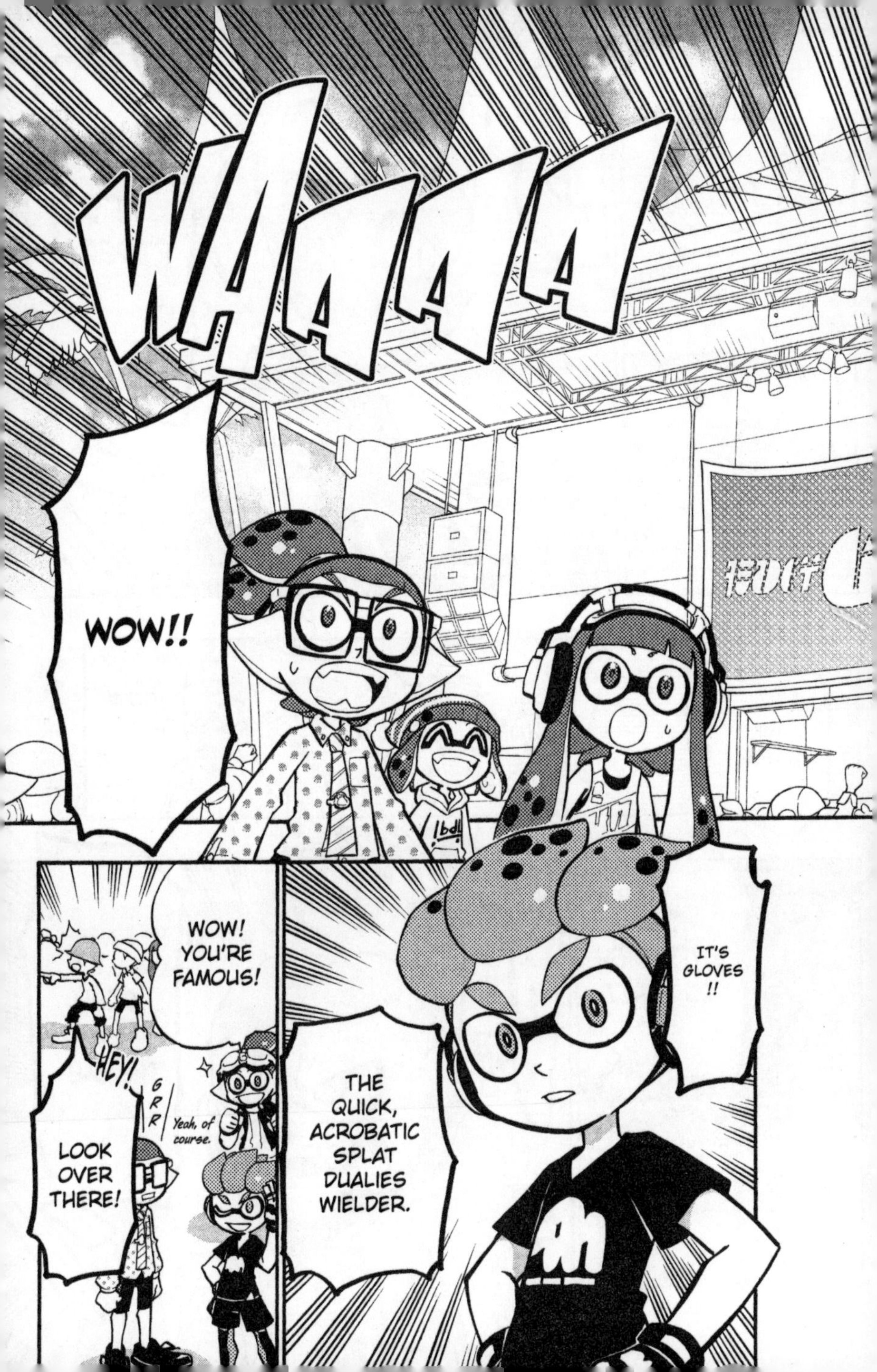
WAAAA
WOW!!
IT'S GLOVES!!
THE QUICK, ACROBATIC SPLAT DUALIES WIELDER.
WOW! YOU'RE FAMOUS!
HEY!
GRR
Yeah, of course.
LOOK OVER THERE!

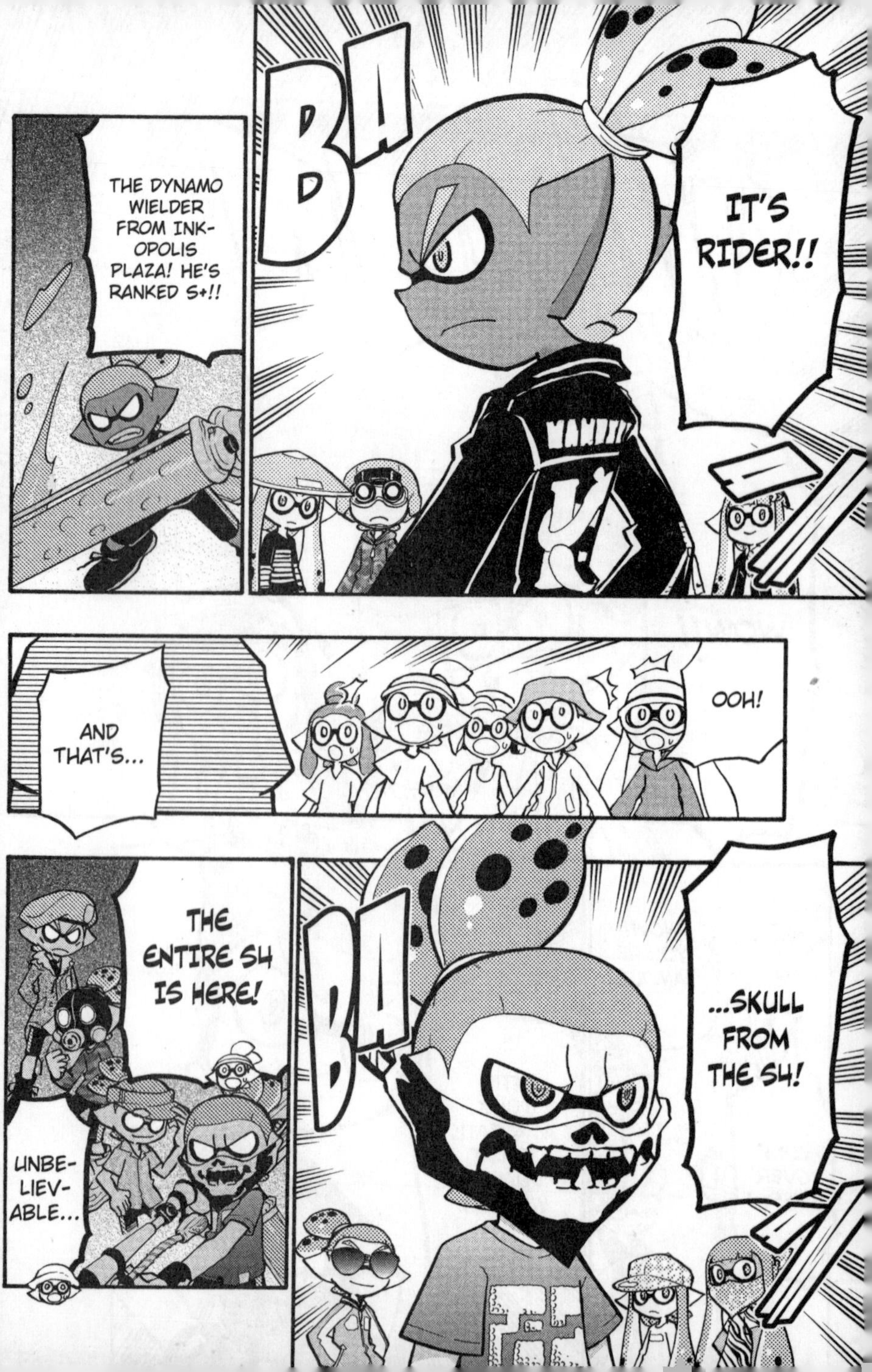
BA
IT'S RIDER!!
THE DYNAMO WIELDER FROM INK-OPOLIS PLAZA! HE'S RANKED S+!!
OOH!
AND THAT'S...
BA
...SKULL FROM THE S4!
THE ENTIRE S4 IS HERE!
UNBE-LIEV-ABLE...

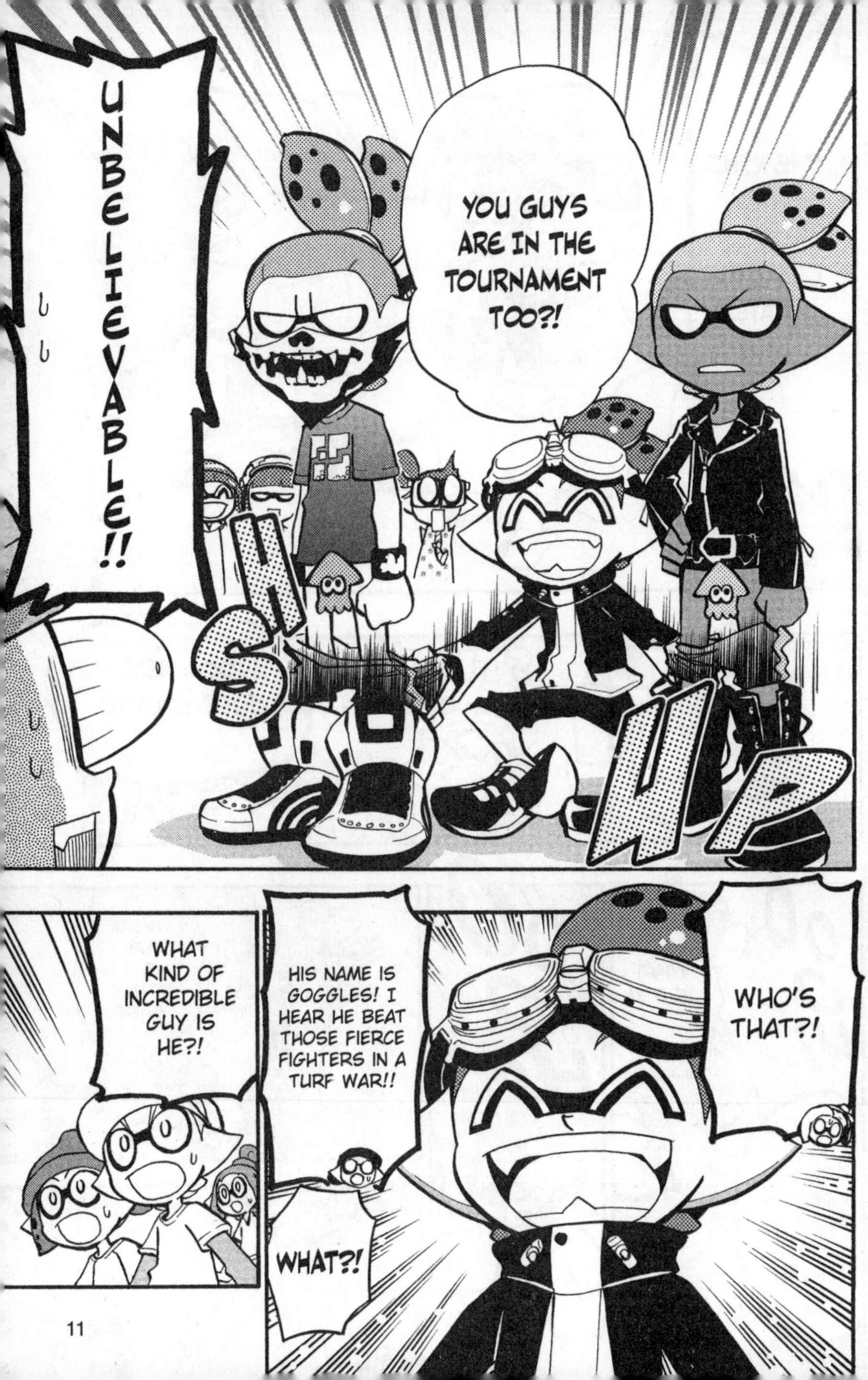
YOU GUYS ARE IN THE TOURNAMENT TOO?!
UNBELIEVABLE!!
UP
SH
WHO'S THAT?!
HIS NAME IS GOGGLES! I HEAR HE BEAT THOSE FIERCE FIGHTERS IN A TURF WAR!!
WHAT?!
WHAT KIND OF INCREDIBLE GUY IS HE?!

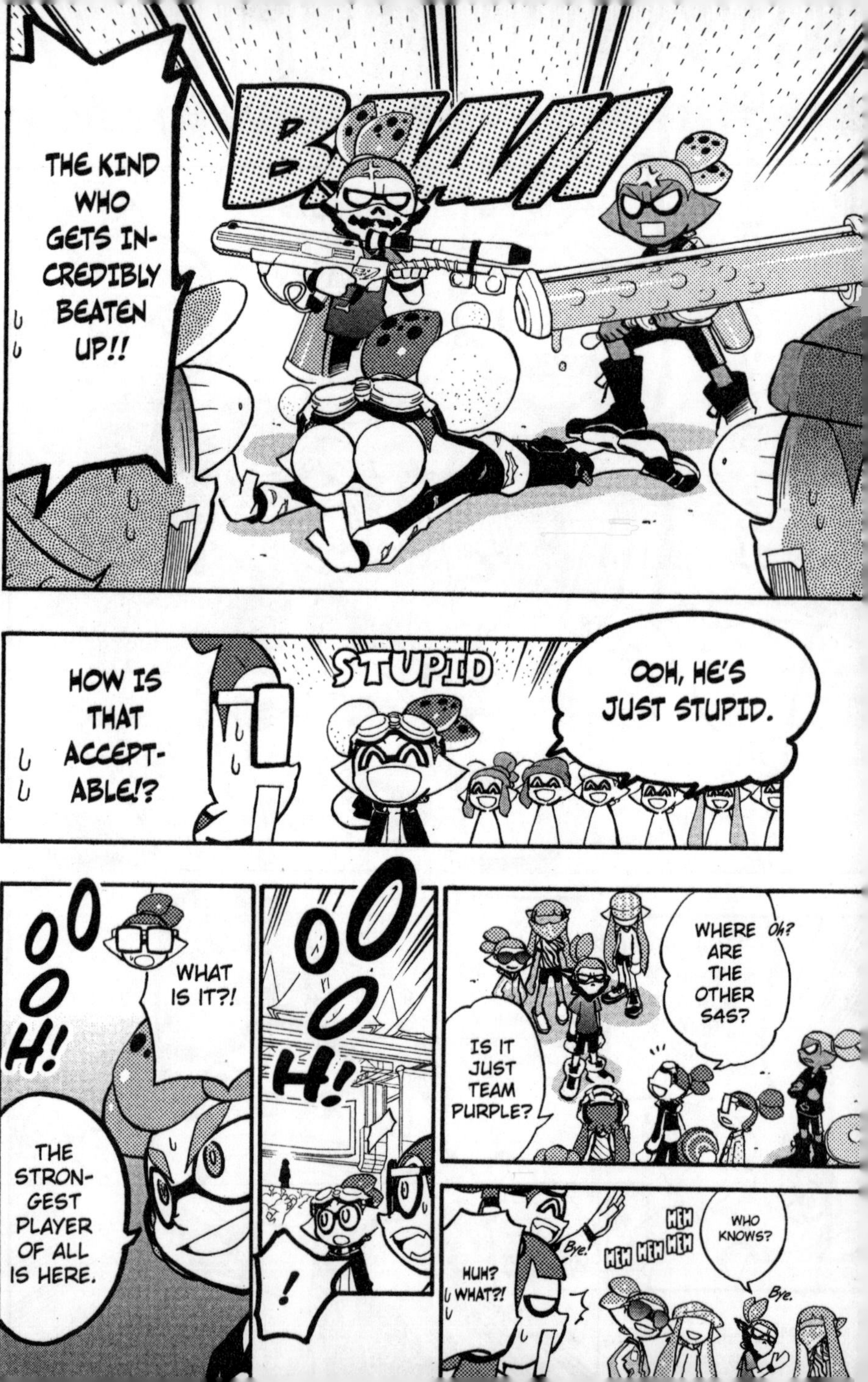
BAM
THE KIND WHO GETS INCREDIBLY BEATEN UP!!
OOH, HE'S JUST STUPID.
STUPID
HOW IS THAT ACCEPTABLE!?
Oh?
WHERE ARE THE OTHER S4S?
IS IT JUST TEAM PURPLE?
WHO KNOWS?
Bye.
MEH MEH MEH MEH
Bye!
HUH? WHAT?!
OOOH!
!
OOOH!
WHAT IS IT?!
THE STRONGEST PLAYER OF ALL IS HERE.

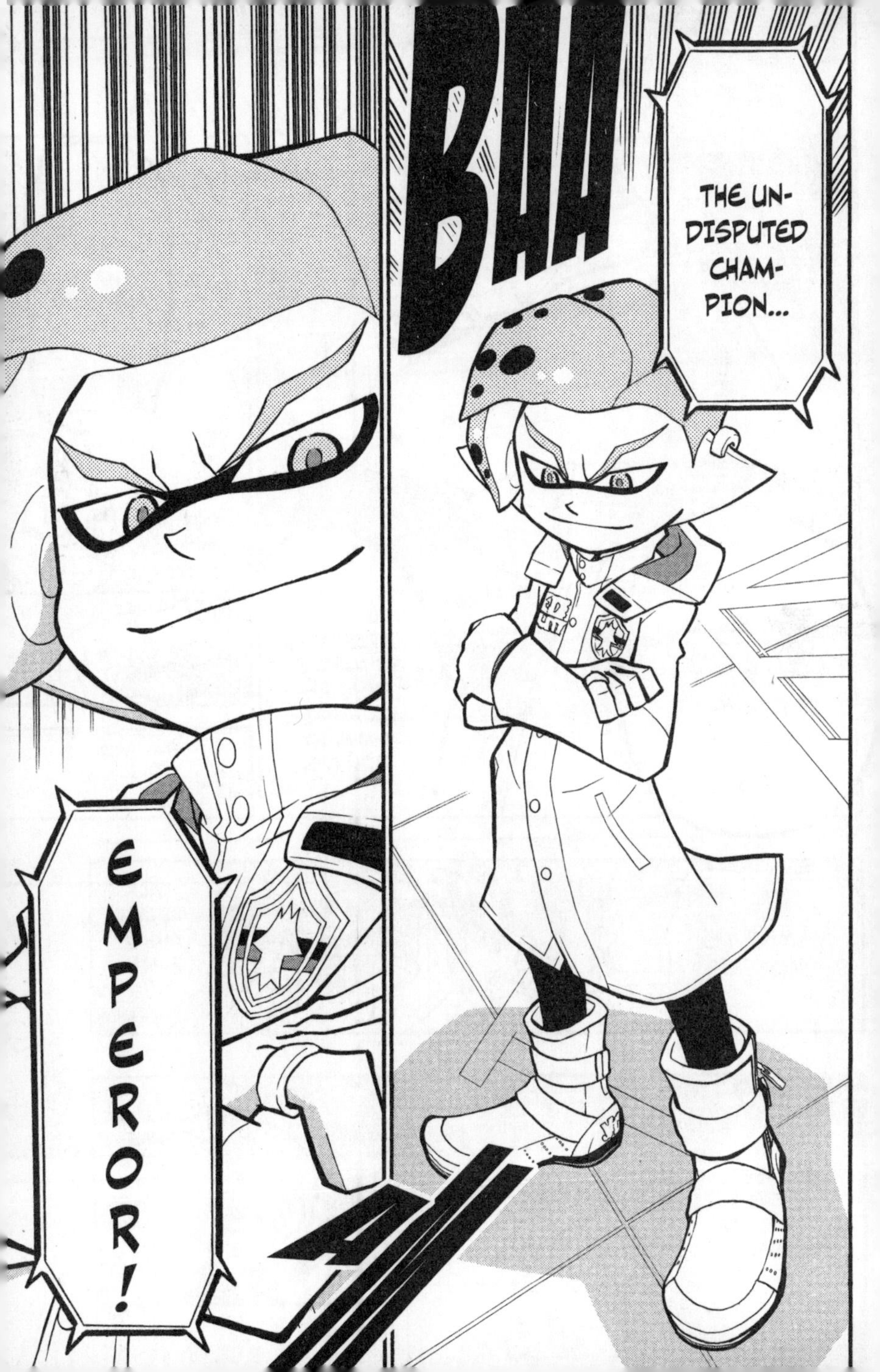
THE UN-DISPUTED CHAMPION...
EMPEROR!

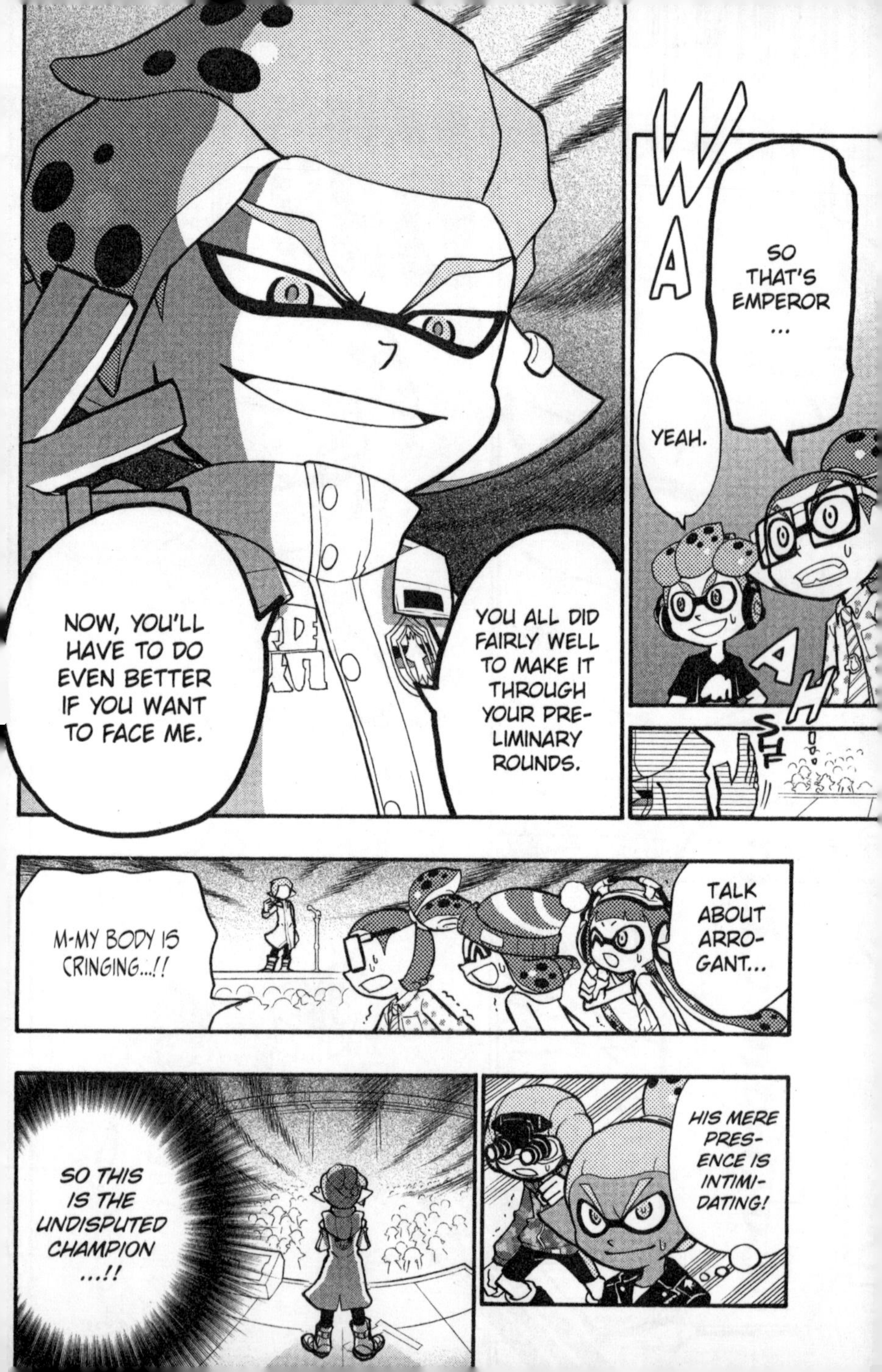
WA
SO THAT'S EMPEROR...
YEAH.
AH
SHH
!
YOU ALL DID FAIRLY WELL TO MAKE IT THROUGH YOUR PRE-LIMINARY ROUNDS.
NOW, YOU'LL HAVE TO DO EVEN BETTER IF YOU WANT TO FACE ME.
TALK ABOUT ARRO-GANT...
M-MY BODY IS CRINGING...!!
HIS MERE PRES-ENCE IS INTIMI-DATING!
SO THIS IS THE UNDISPUTED CHAMPION...!!

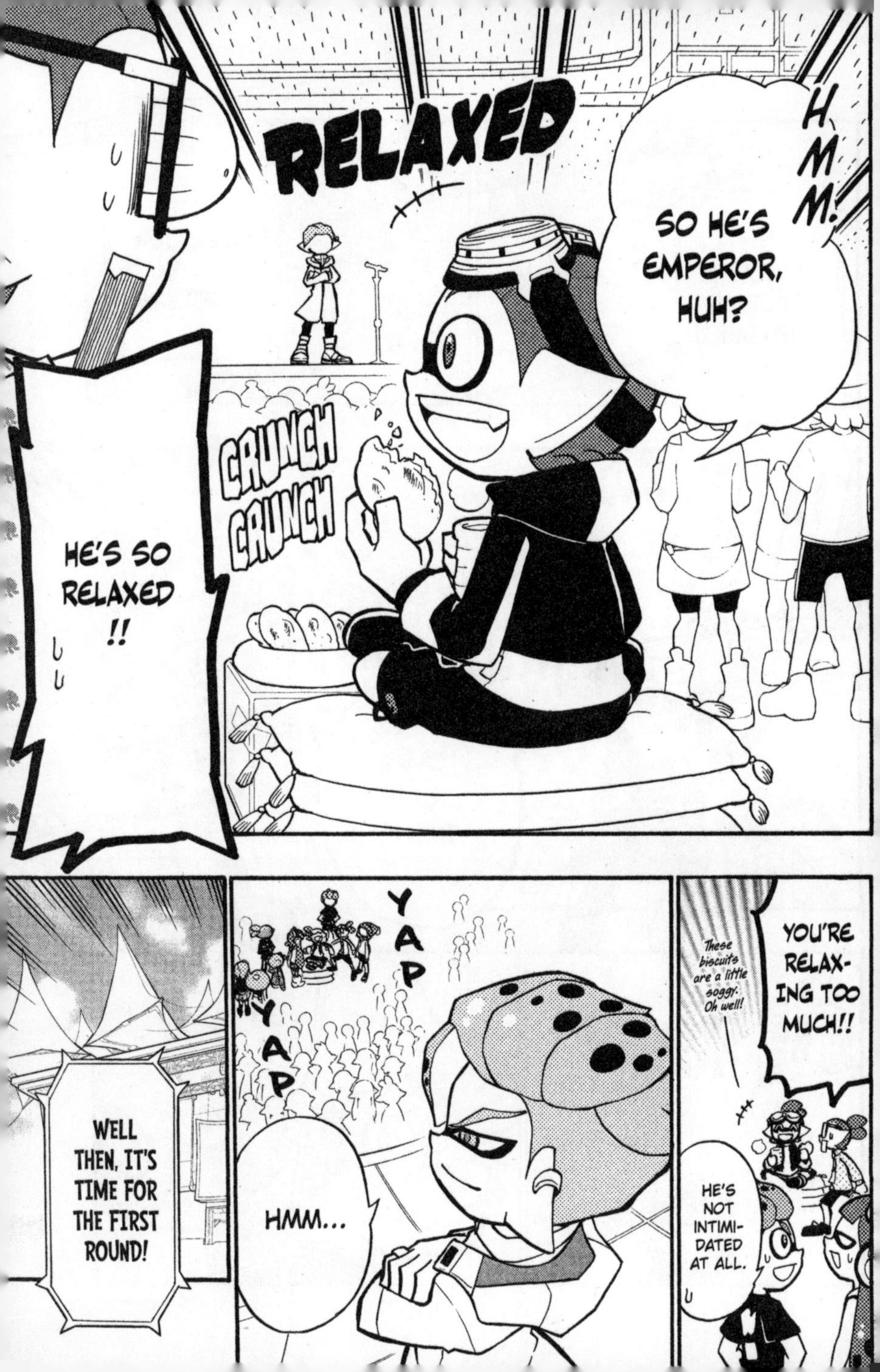

HMMM!
SO HE'S EMPEROR, HUH?
RELAXED
CRUNCH CRUNCH
HE'S SO RELAXED!!
YOU'RE RELAXING TOO MUCH!!
These biscuits are a little soggy. Oh well!
HE'S NOT INTIMIDATED AT ALL.
YAP
YAP
HMM...
WELL THEN, IT'S TIME FOR THE FIRST ROUND!

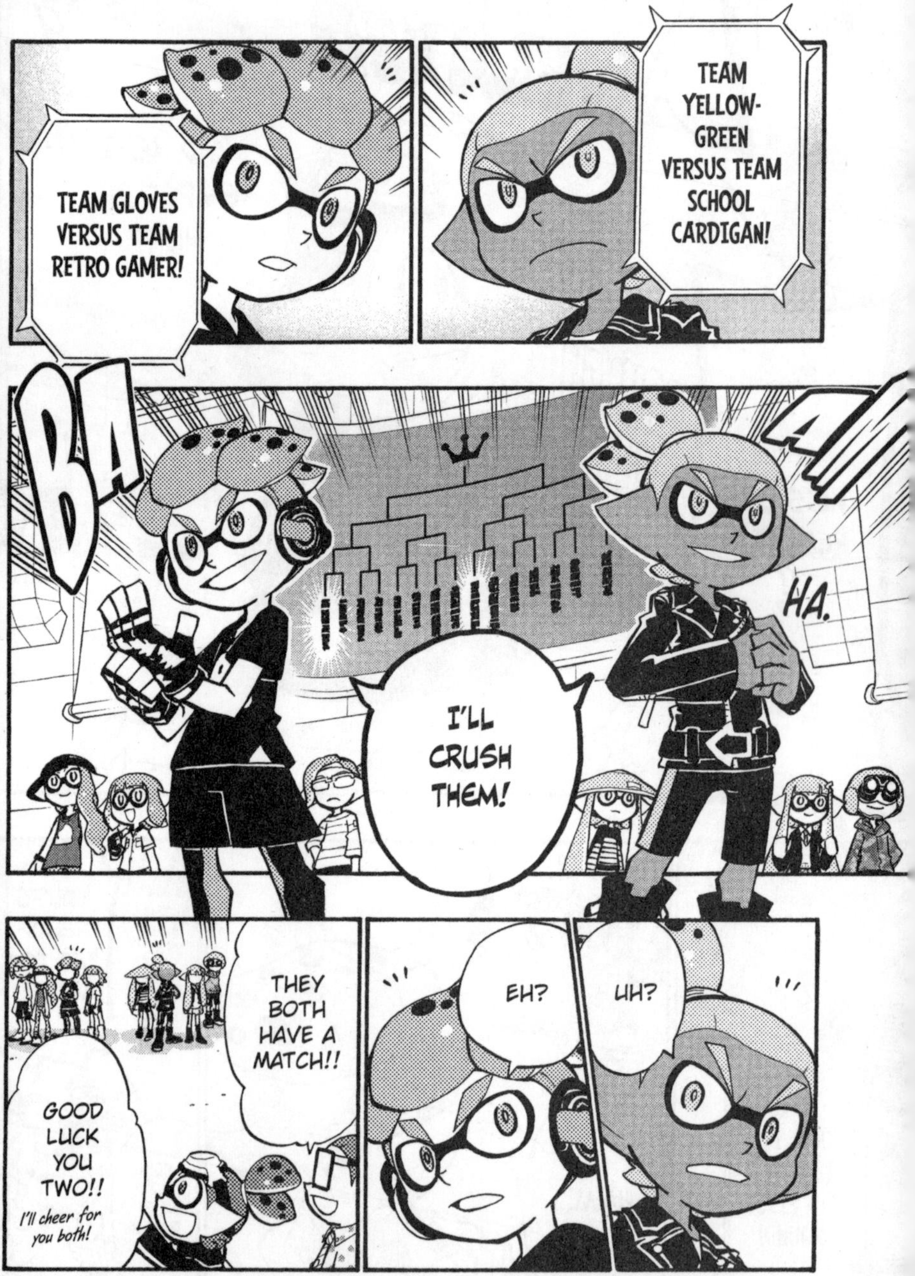
TEAM YELLOW-GREEN VERSUS TEAM SCHOOL CARDIGAN!
TEAM GLOVES VERSUS TEAM RETRO GAMER!
BA
A
HA.
I'LL CRUSH THEM!
UH?
EH?
THEY BOTH HAVE A MATCH!!
GOOD LUCK YOU TWO!!
I'll cheer for you both!

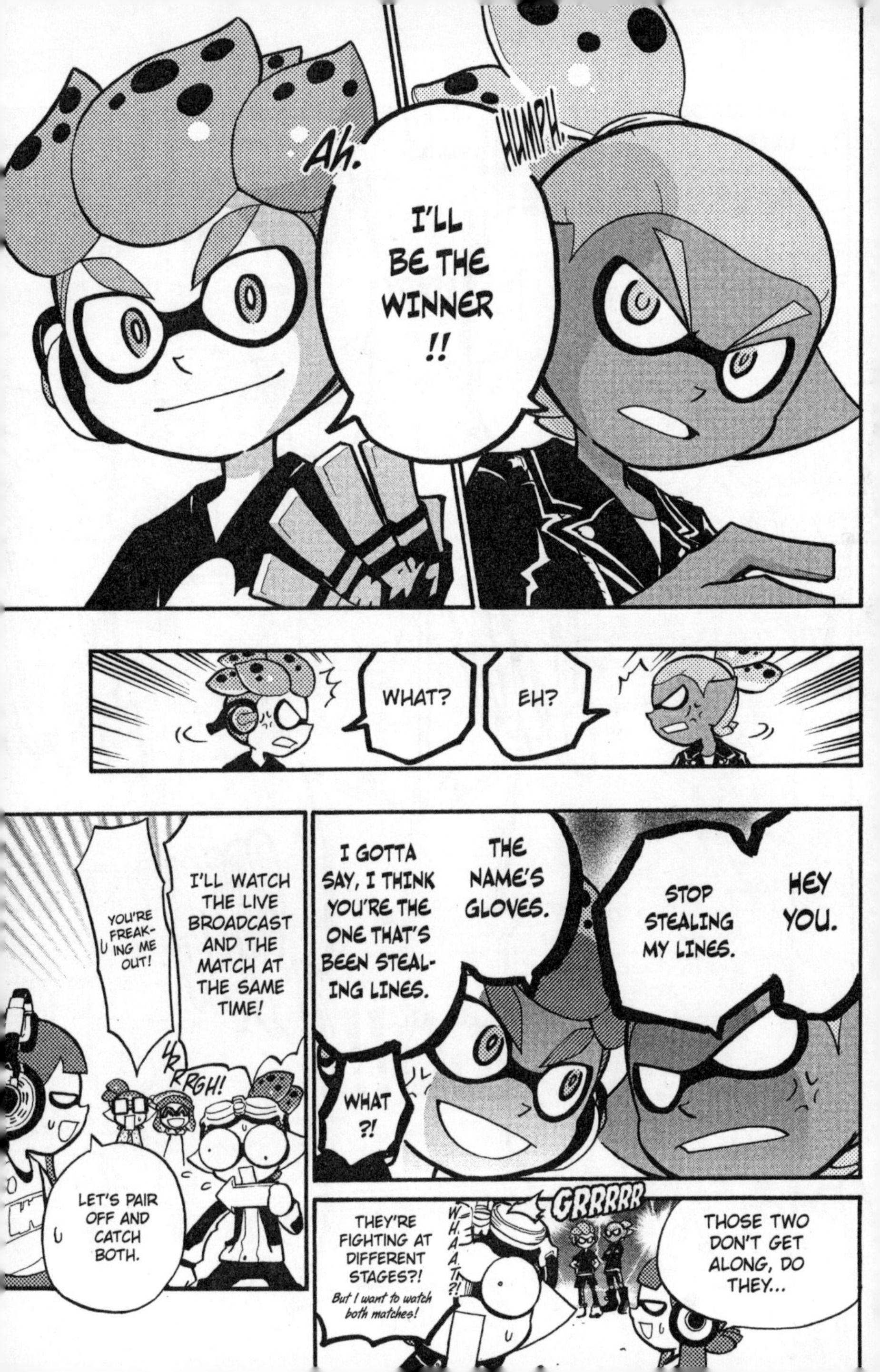
HUMPH.
Ah.
I'LL BE THE WINNER!!
EH?
WHAT?
HEY YOU.
STOP STEALING MY LINES.
THE NAME'S GLOVES.
I GOTTA SAY, I THINK YOU'RE THE ONE THAT'S BEEN STEALING LINES.
WHAT?!
THOSE TWO DON'T GET ALONG, DO THEY...
GRRRRR
WHAAT?!
THEY'RE FIGHTING AT DIFFERENT STAGES?!
But I want to watch both matches!
I'LL WATCH THE LIVE BROADCAST AND THE MATCH AT THE SAME TIME!
YOU'RE FREAKING ME OUT!
RRGH!
LET'S PAIR OFF AND CATCH BOTH.

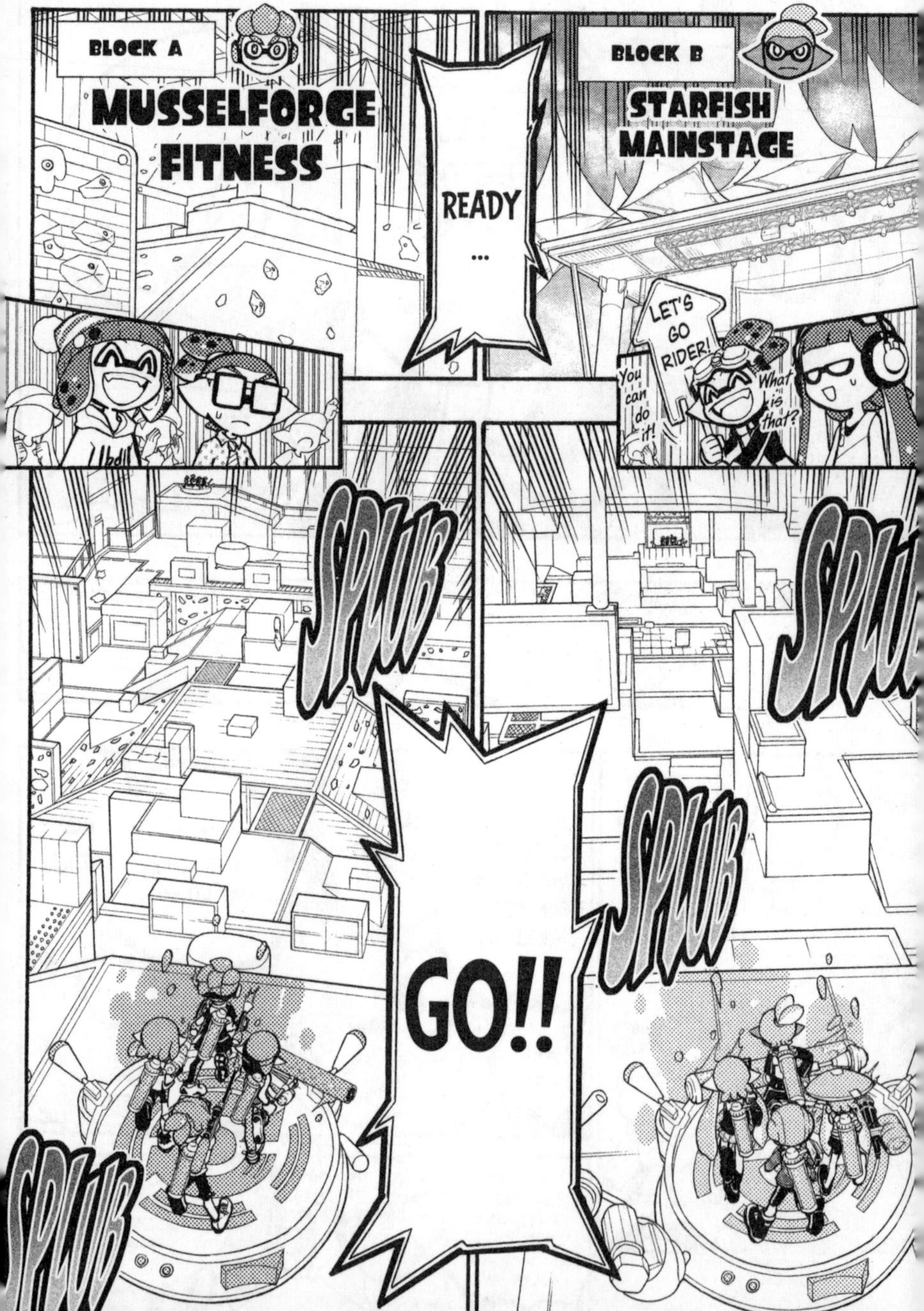
BLOCK B
STARFISH MAINSTAGE
READY
...
BLOCK A
MUSSELFORGE FITNESS
LET'S GO RIDER!
You can do it!
What is that?
SPLUB
SPLUB
GO!!
SPLUB
SPLUB

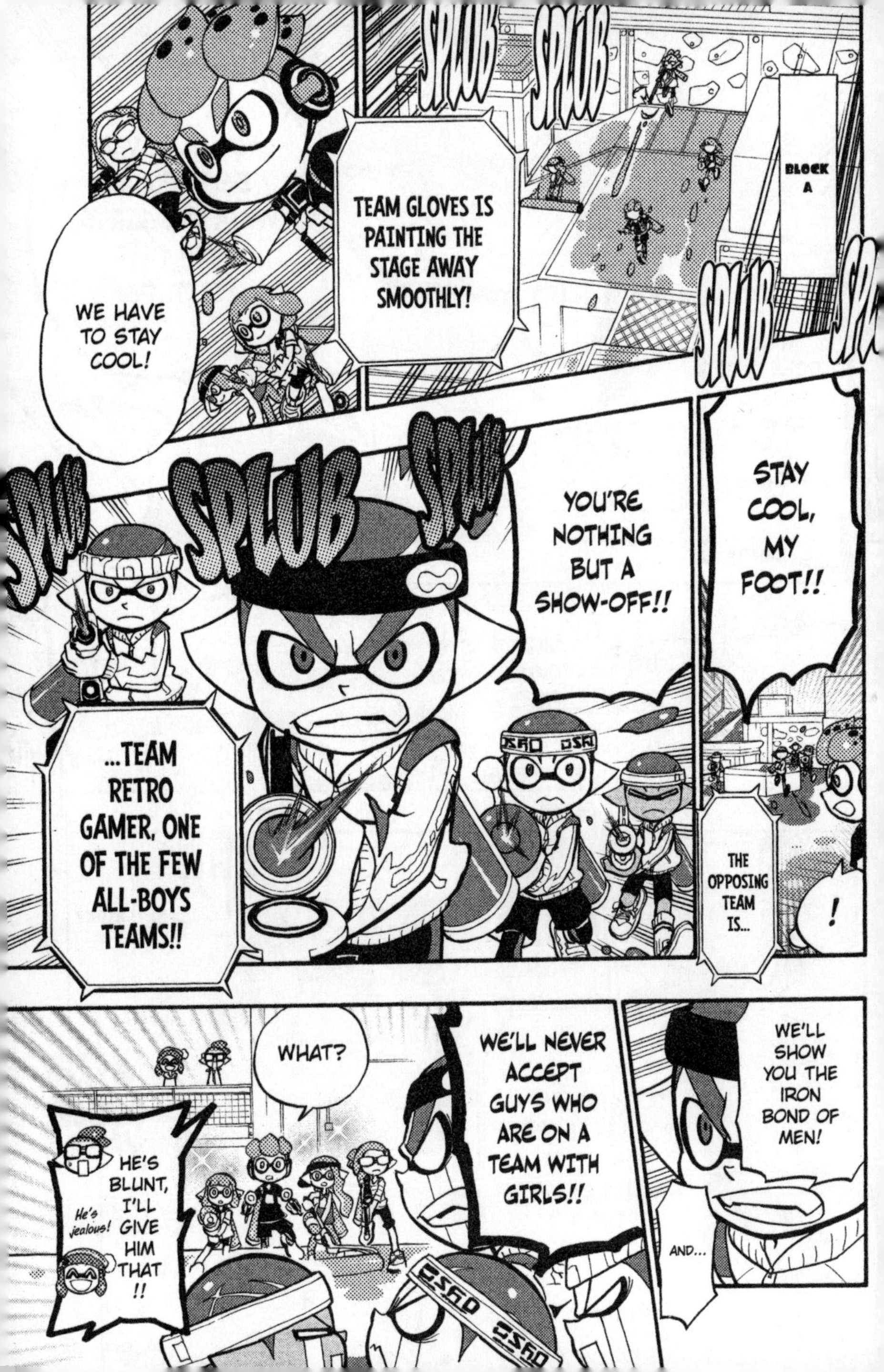
SPLUB
SPLUB
BLOCK A
TEAM GLOVES IS PAINTING THE STAGE AWAY SMOOTHLY!
SPLUB
SPLUB
WE HAVE TO STAY COOL!
STAY COOL, MY FOOT!!
THE OPPOSING TEAM IS...
!
SPLUB
SPLUB
SPLUB
YOU'RE NOTHING BUT A SHOW-OFF!!
...TEAM RETRO GAMER, ONE OF THE FEW ALL-BOYS TEAMS!!
WE'LL SHOW YOU THE IRON BOND OF MEN!
AND...
WE'LL NEVER ACCEPT GUYS WHO ARE ON A TEAM WITH GIRLS!!
WHAT?
HE'S BLUNT, I'LL GIVE HIM THAT!!
He's jealous!

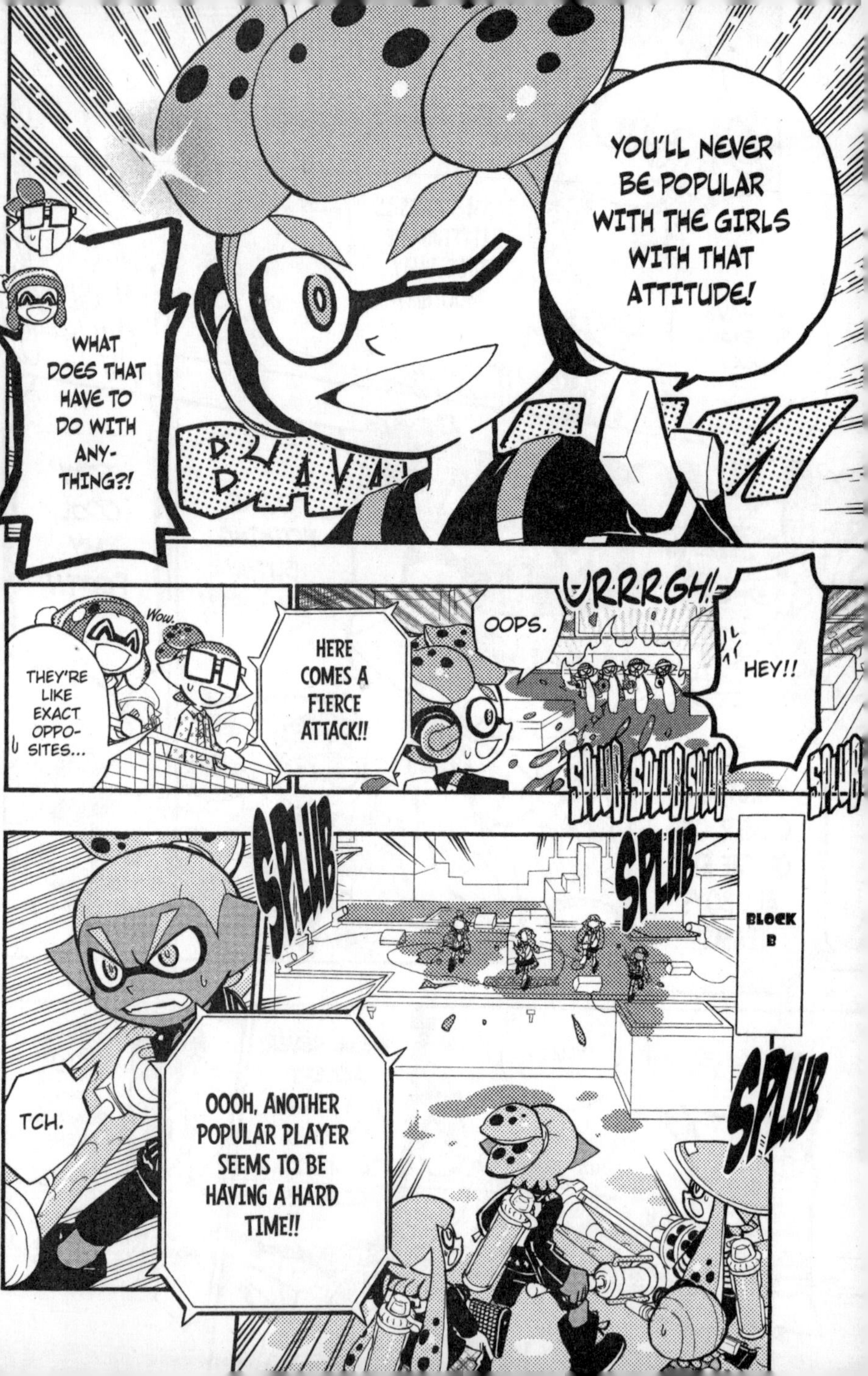

YOU'LL NEVER BE POPULAR WITH THE GIRLS WITH THAT ATTITUDE!
WHAT DOES THAT HAVE TO DO WITH ANY-THING?!
URRRGH!
HEY!!
OOPS.
SPLUB SPLUB SPLUB
SPLUB
HERE COMES A FIERCE ATTACK!!
Wow.
THEY'RE LIKE EXACT OPPO-SITES...
BLOCK B
SPLUB
SPLUB
SPLUB
SPLUB
OOOH, ANOTHER POPULAR PLAYER SEEMS TO BE HAVING A HARD TIME!!
TCH.

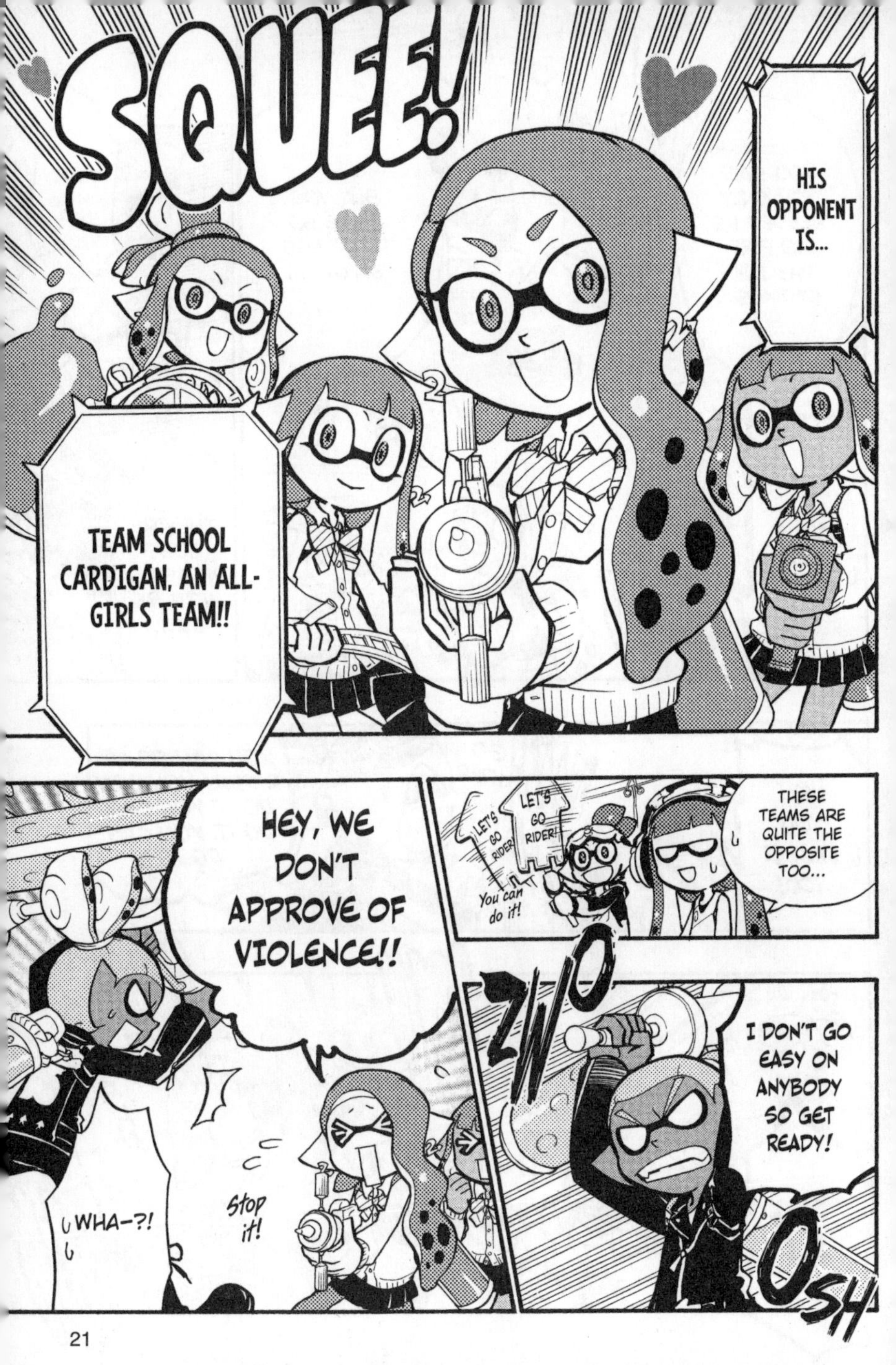
HIS OPPONENT IS...
SQUEE!
TEAM SCHOOL CARDIGAN, AN ALL-GIRLS TEAM!!
THESE TEAMS ARE QUITE THE OPPOSITE TOO...
LET'S GO RIDER!
LET'S GO RIDER
You can do it!
I DON'T GO EASY ON ANYBODY SO GET READY!
ZWOOSH
HEY, WE DON'T APPROVE OF VIOLENCE!!
Stop it!
WHA-?!

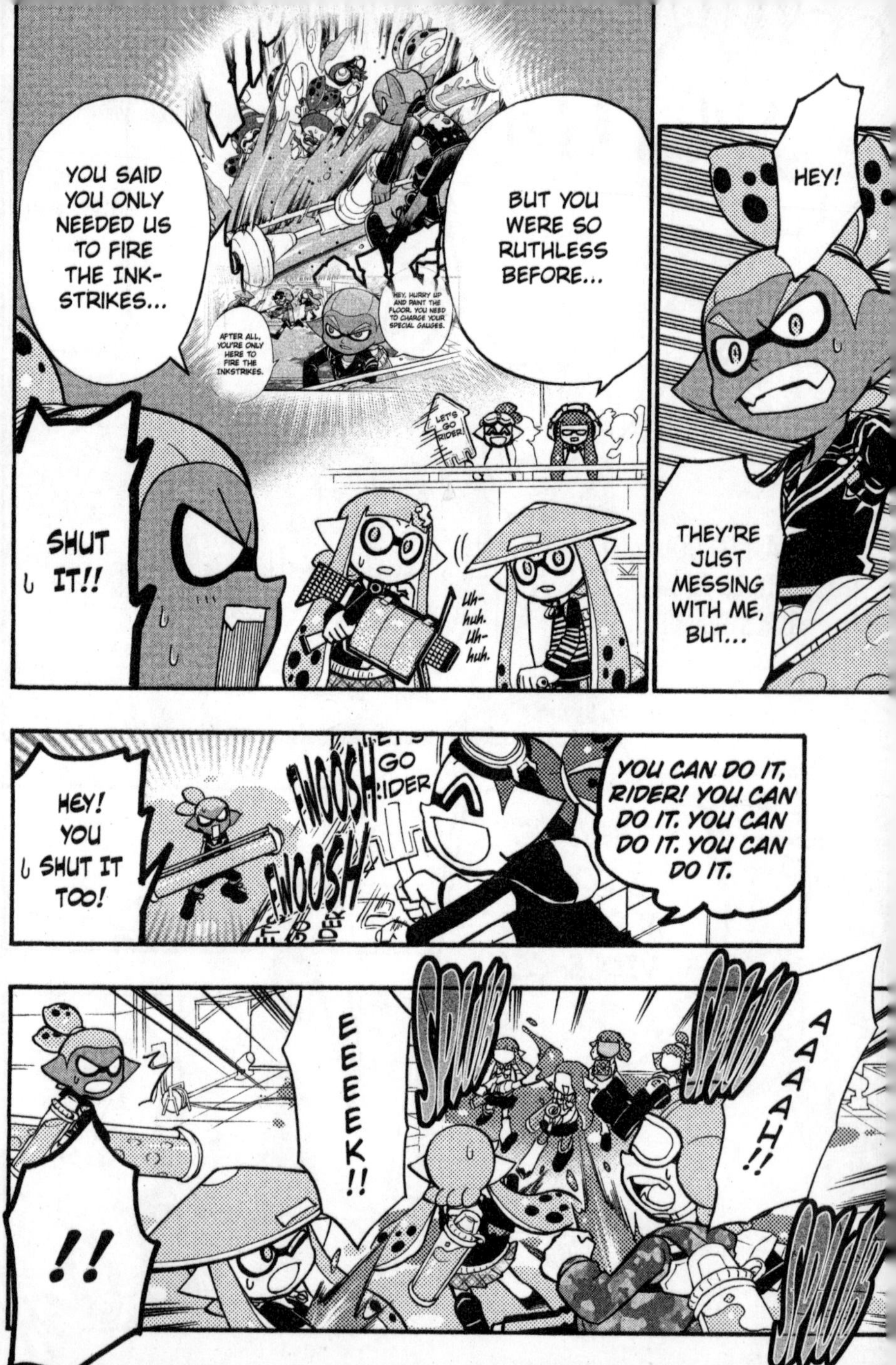
HEY!
THEY'RE JUST MESSING WITH ME, BUT...
BUT YOU WERE SO RUTHLESS BEFORE...
HEY, HURRY UP AND PAINT THE FLOOR. YOU NEED TO CHARGE YOUR SPECIAL GAUGES.
AFTER ALL, YOU'RE ONLY HERE TO FIRE THE INKSTRIKES.
YOU SAID YOU ONLY NEEDED US TO FIRE THE INK-STRIKES...
LET'S GO RIDER!
Uh-huh. Uh-huh.
SHUT IT!!
YOU CAN DO IT, RIDER! YOU CAN DO IT. YOU CAN DO IT. YOU CAN DO IT.
FWOOSH
FWOOSH
GO RIDER
HEY! YOU SHUT IT TOO!
AAAAAH!!
EEEEEK!!
!!

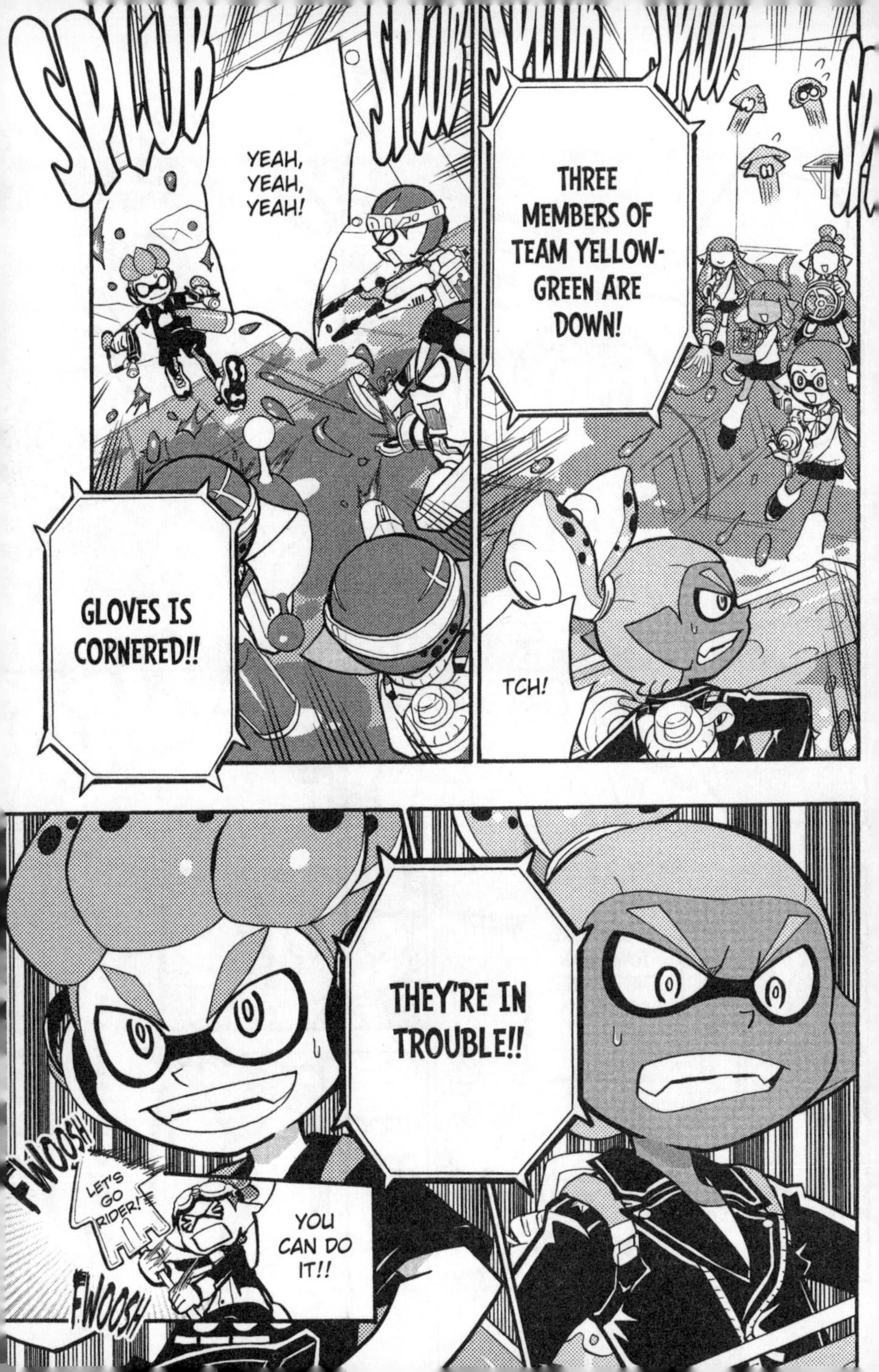

SPLUB
THREE MEMBERS OF TEAM YELLOW-GREEN ARE DOWN!
TCH!
SPLUB
SPLUB
YEAH, YEAH, YEAH!
GLOVES IS CORNERED!!
THEY'RE IN TROUBLE!!
FWOOSH
LET'S GO RIDER!
YOU CAN DO IT!!
FWOOSH

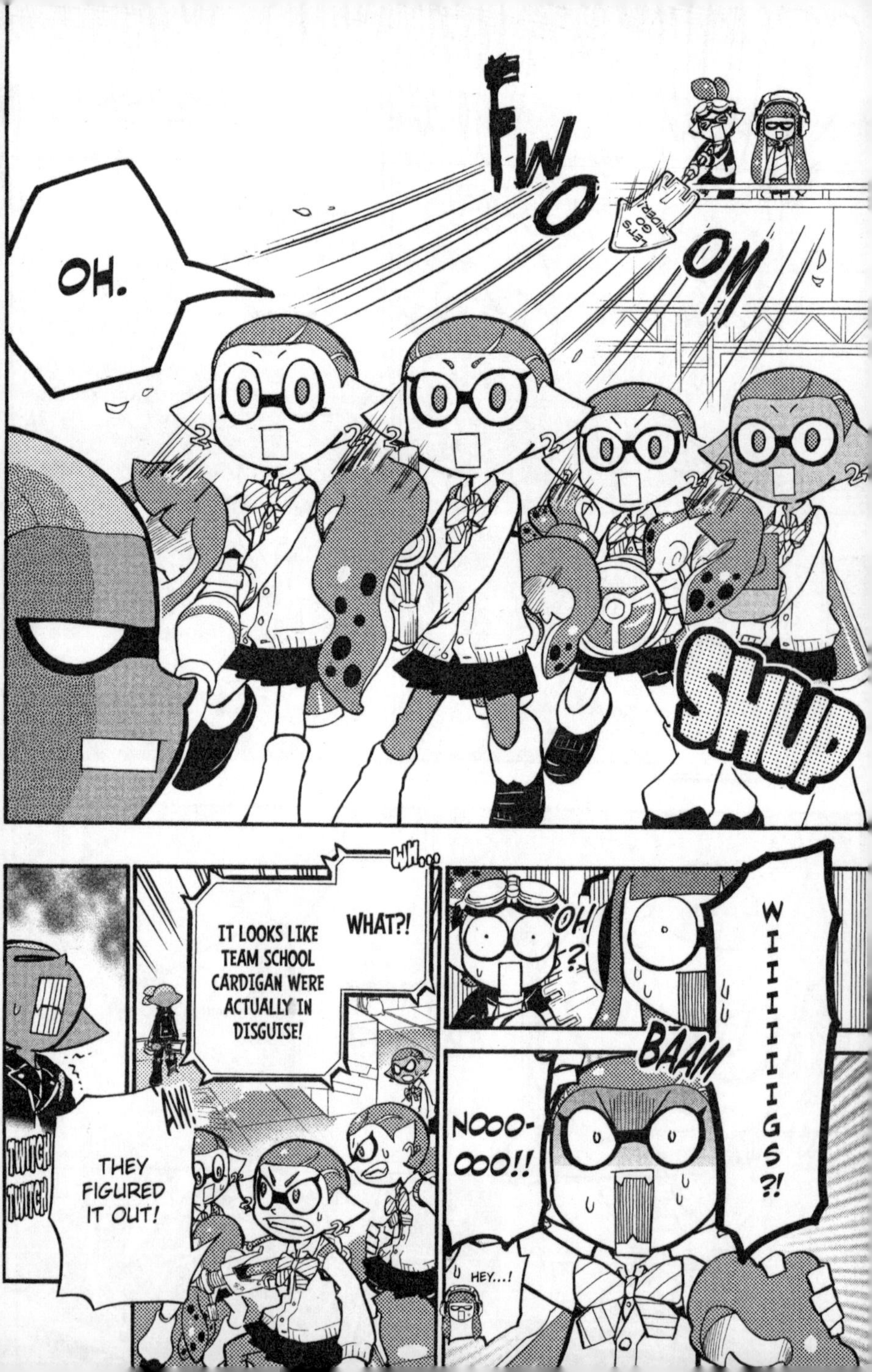
LET'S GO RIDER!
FWOOOM
OH.
SHUP
WIIIIIIGS?!
OH?
BAAM
NOOO-OOO!!
HEY...!
WH...
WHAT?!
IT LOOKS LIKE TEAM SCHOOL CARDIGAN WERE ACTUALLY IN DISGUISE!
AW!
THEY FIGURED IT OUT!
TWITCH TWITCH

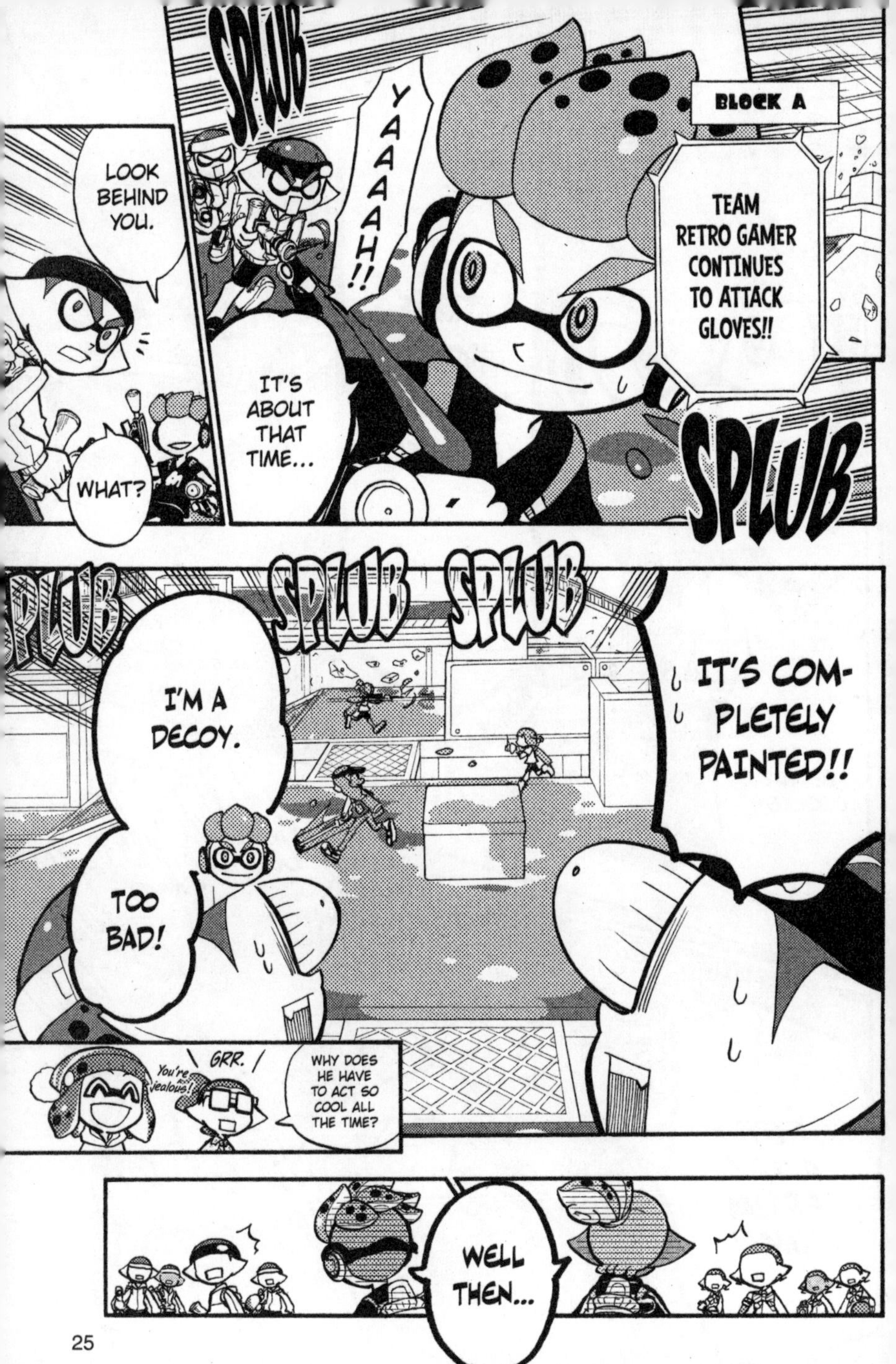
BLOCK A
TEAM RETRO GAMER CONTINUES TO ATTACK GLOVES!!
SPLUB
SPLUB
YAAAAAH!!
IT'S ABOUT THAT TIME...
LOOK BEHIND YOU.
WHAT?
SPLUB SPLUB
SPLUB
IT'S COM-PLETELY PAINTED!!
I'M A DECOY.
TOO BAD!
WHY DOES HE HAVE TO ACT SO COOL ALL THE TIME?
GRR.
You're jealous!
WELL THEN...

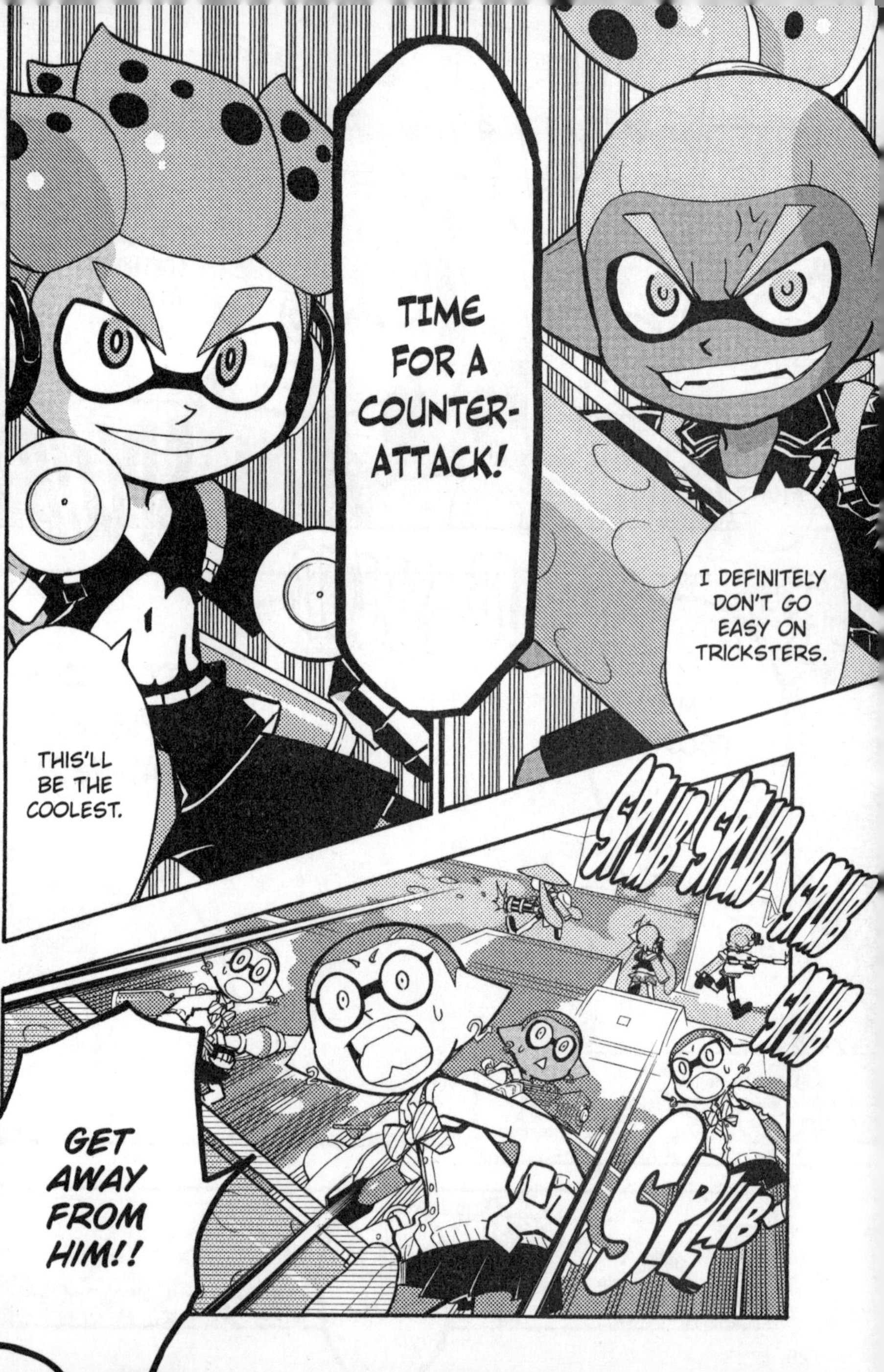
I DEFINITELY DON'T GO EASY ON TRICKSTERS.
TIME FOR A COUNTER-ATTACK!
THIS'LL BE THE COOLEST.
GET AWAY FROM HIM!!

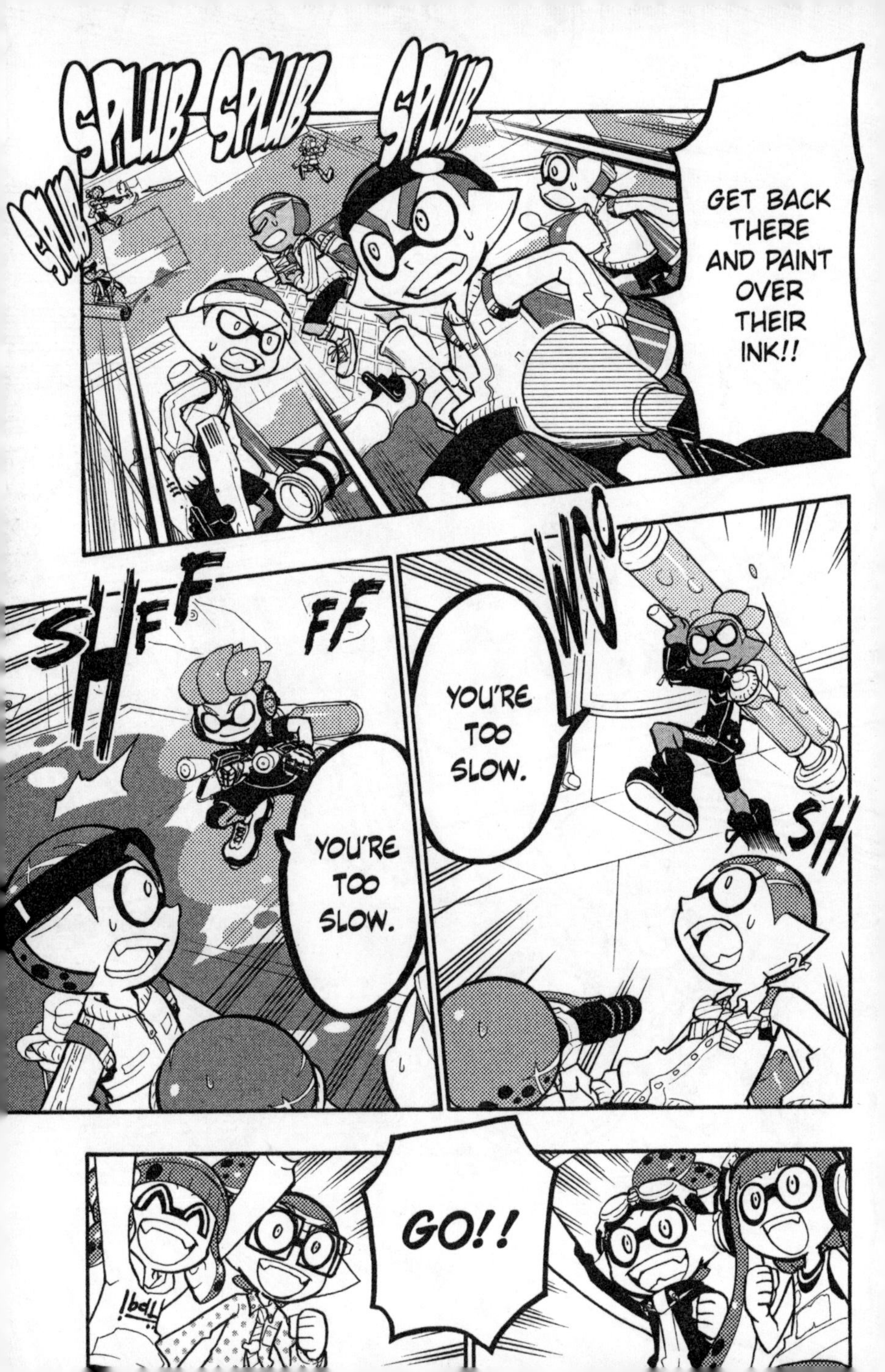
GET BACK THERE AND PAINT OVER THEIR INK!!
SPLUB SPLUB SPLUB SPLUB
WO
YOU'RE TOO SLOW.
SH
FF
SHFF
YOU'RE TOO SLOW.
GO!!

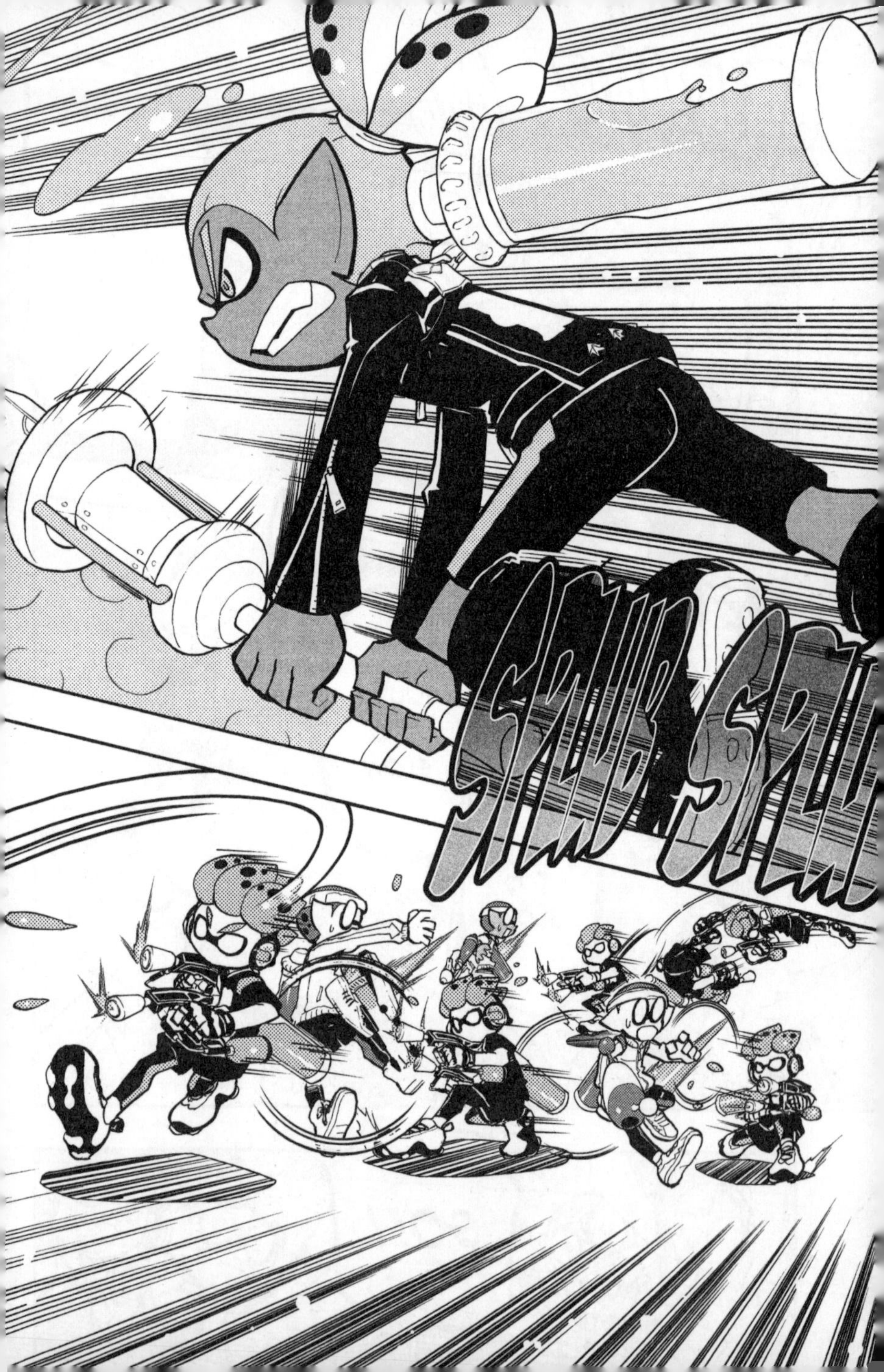
SPLUB SPLU

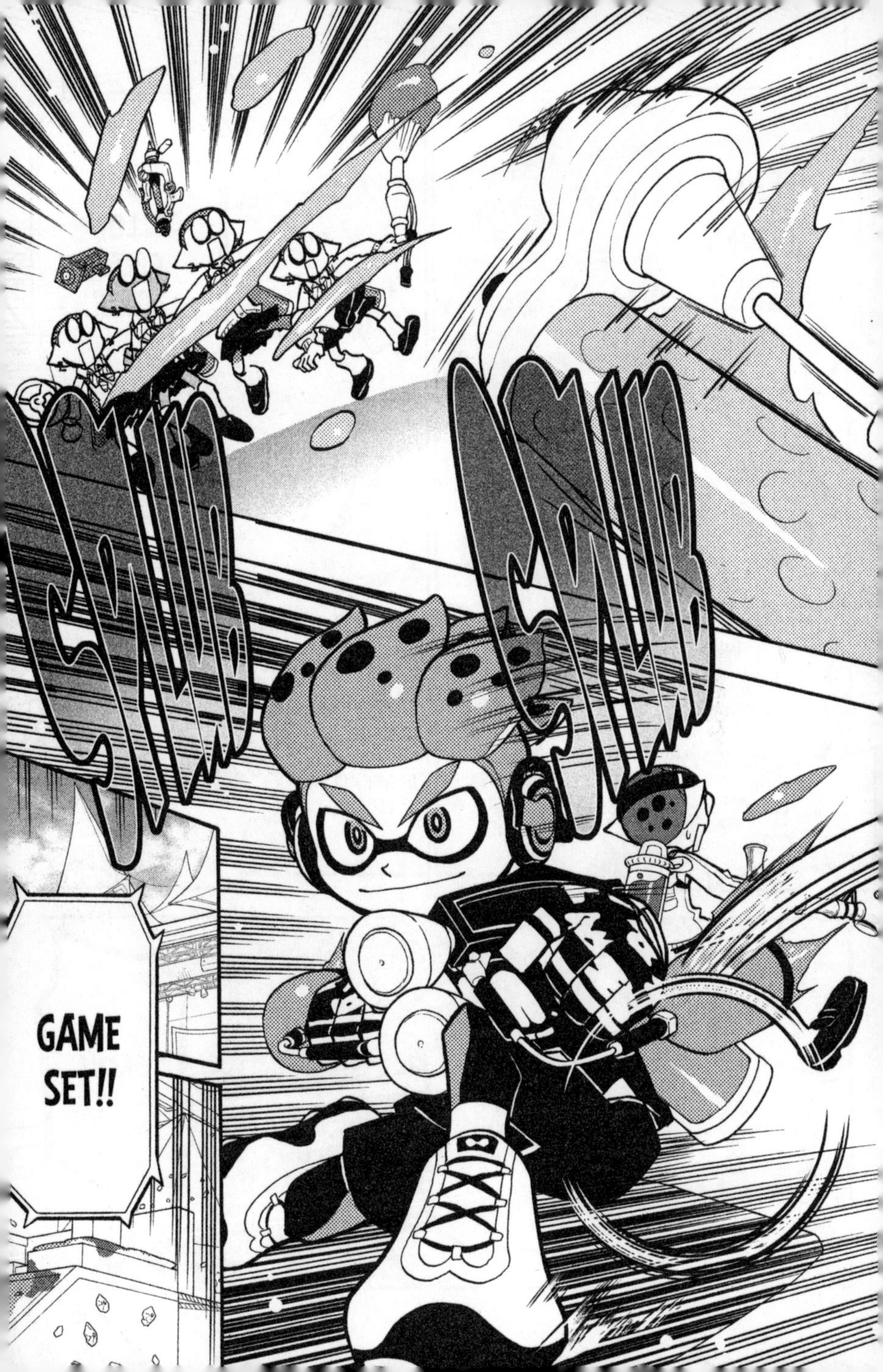
GAME SET!!

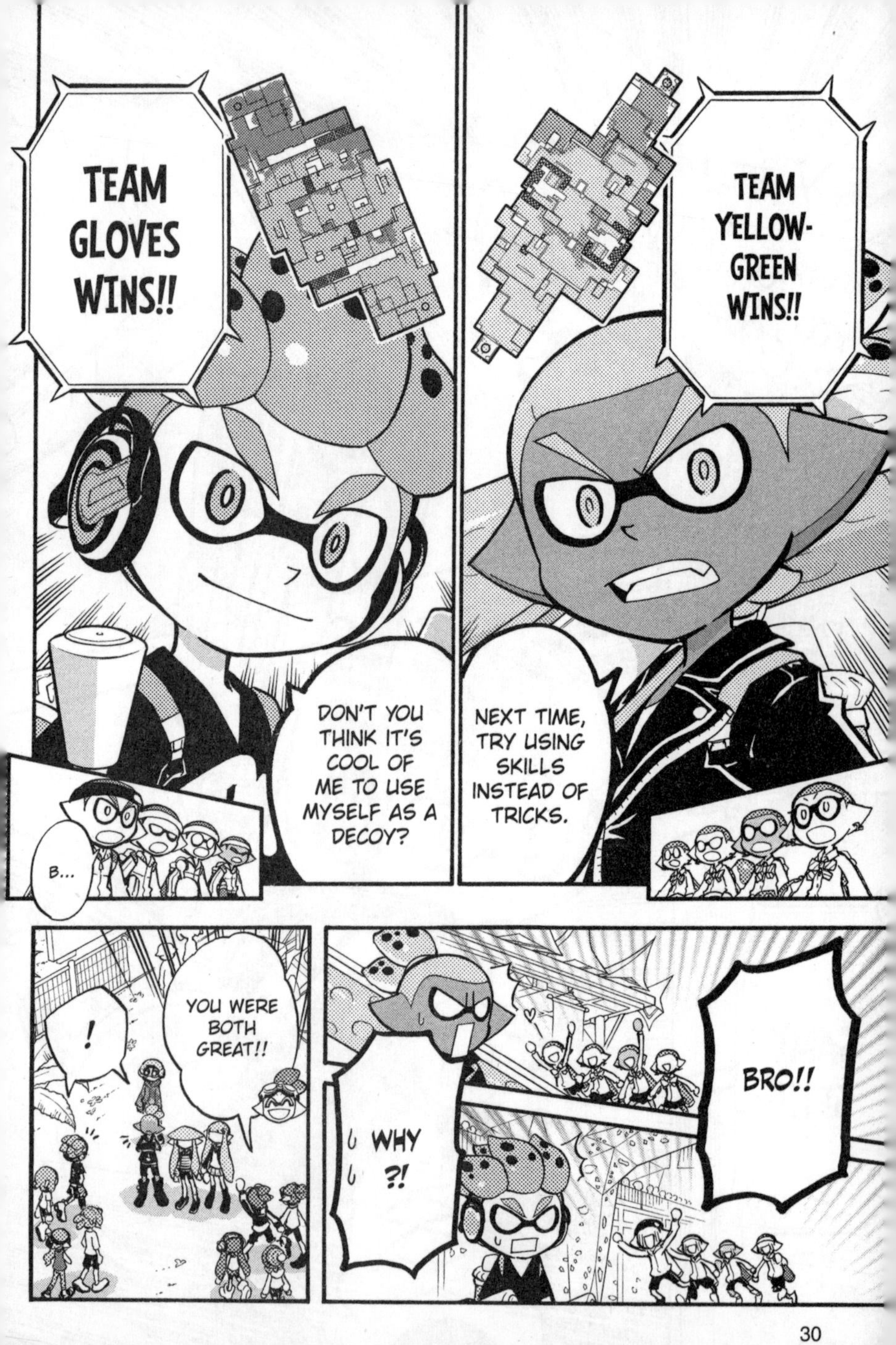
TEAM YELLOW-GREEN WINS!!
NEXT TIME, TRY USING SKILLS INSTEAD OF TRICKS.
TEAM GLOVES WINS!!
DON'T YOU THINK IT'S COOL OF ME TO USE MYSELF AS A DECOY?
B...
BRO!!
WHY ?!
YOU WERE BOTH GREAT!!
!

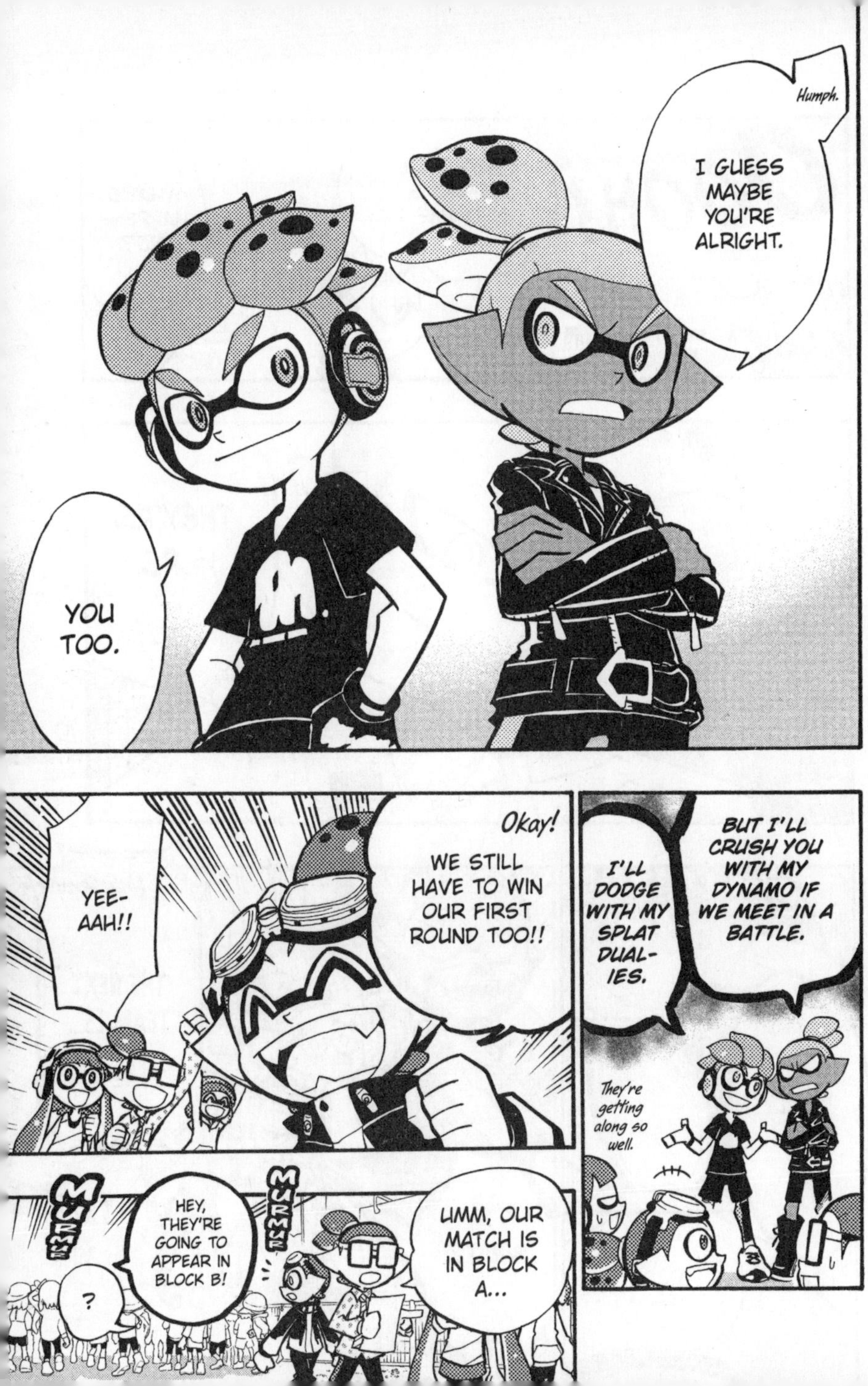
Humph.
I GUESS MAYBE YOU'RE ALRIGHT.
YOU TOO.
BUT I'LL CRUSH YOU WITH MY DYNAMO IF WE MEET IN A BATTLE.
I'LL DODGE WITH MY SPLAT DUAL-IES.
They're getting along so well.
Okay!
WE STILL HAVE TO WIN OUR FIRST ROUND TOO!!
YEE-AAH!!
UMM, OUR MATCH IS IN BLOCK A...
MURMUR
HEY, THEY'RE GOING TO APPEAR IN BLOCK B!
?
MURMUR

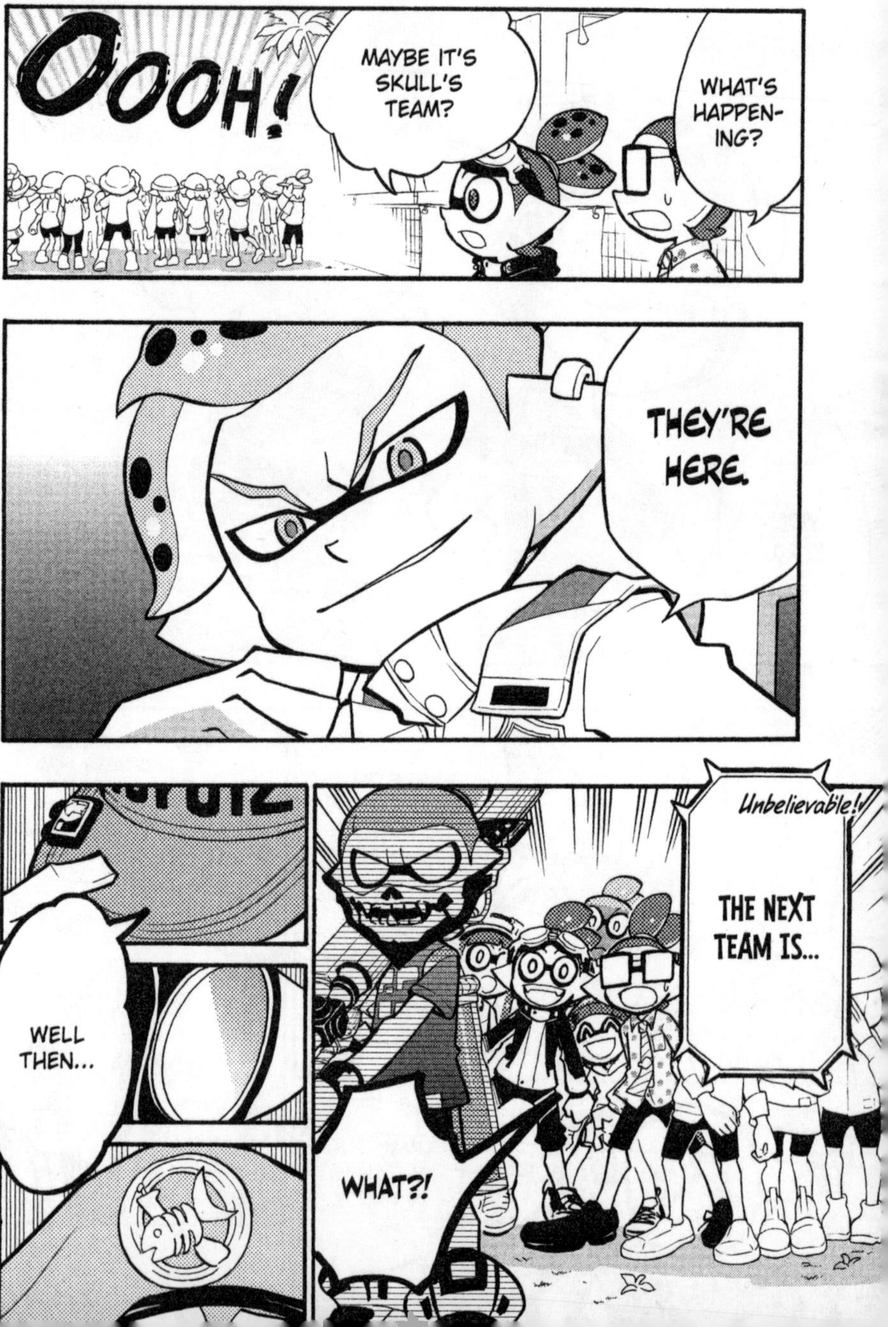
WHAT'S HAPPEN-ING?
MAYBE IT'S SKULL'S TEAM?
OOOH!
THEY'RE HERE.
Unbelievable!!
THE NEXT TEAM IS...
WHAT?!
WELL THEN...

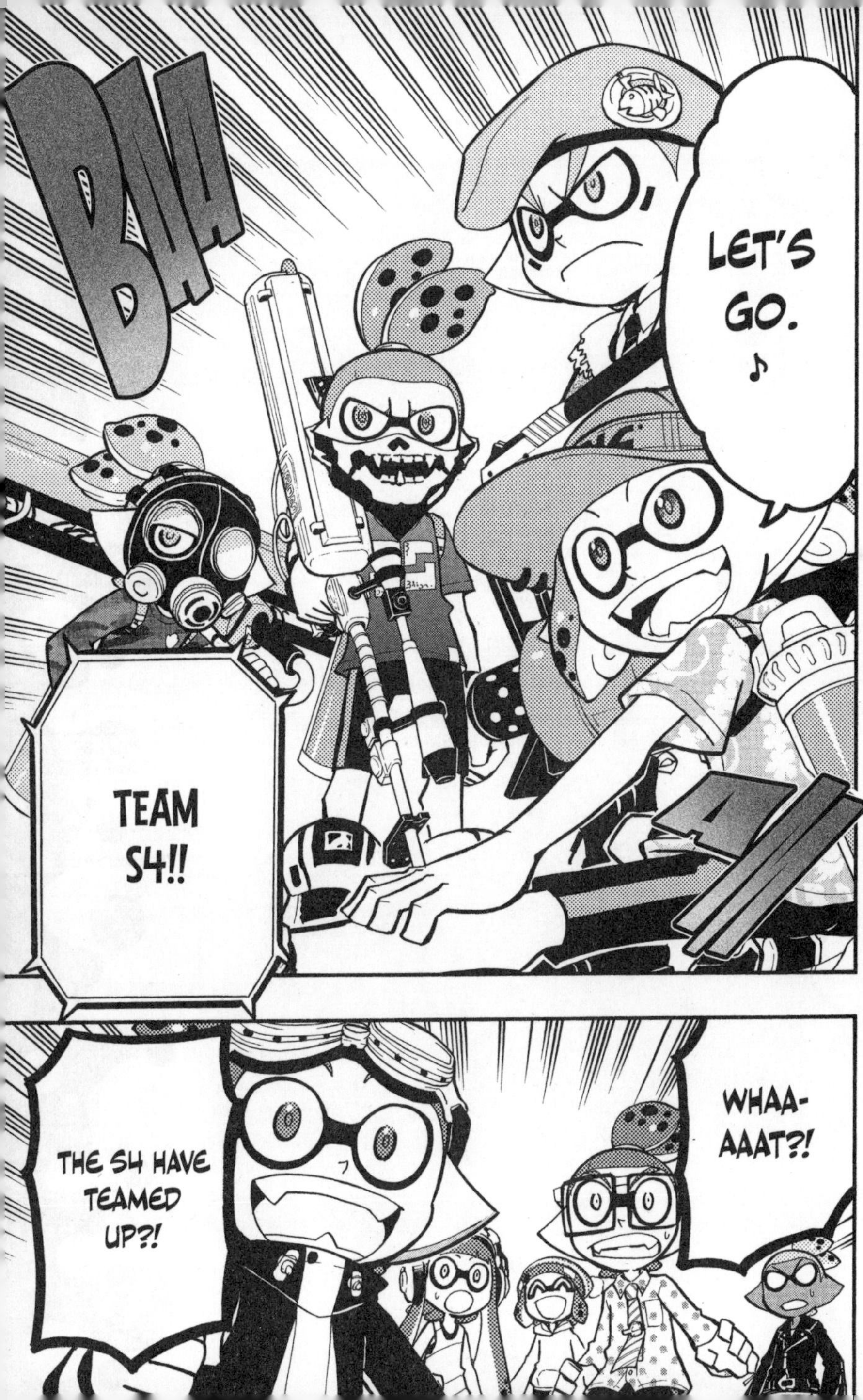
LET'S GO. ♪
BWAH
TEAM S4!!
WHAA-AAAT?!
THE S4 HAVE TEAMED UP?!

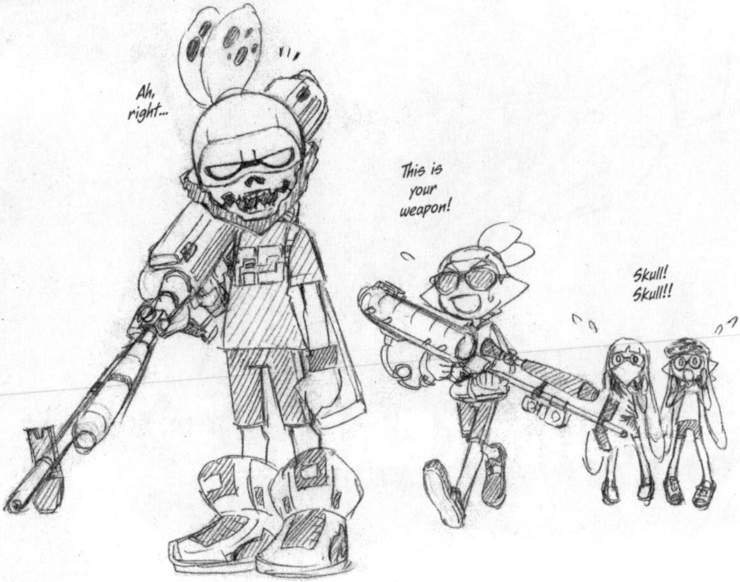
This is your weapon!
Ah, right...
Skull! Skull!!

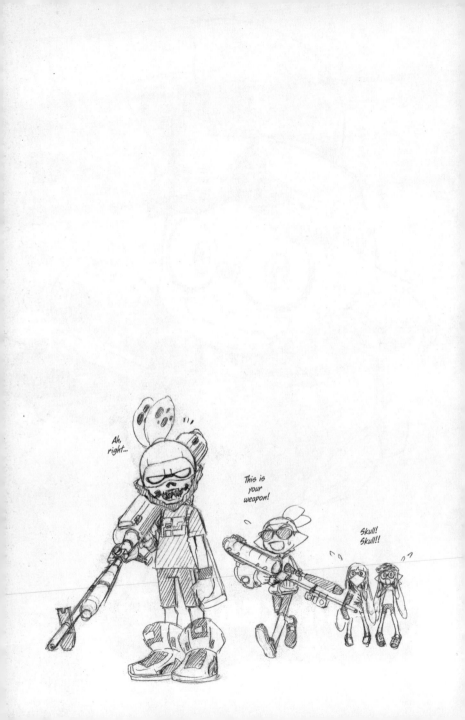

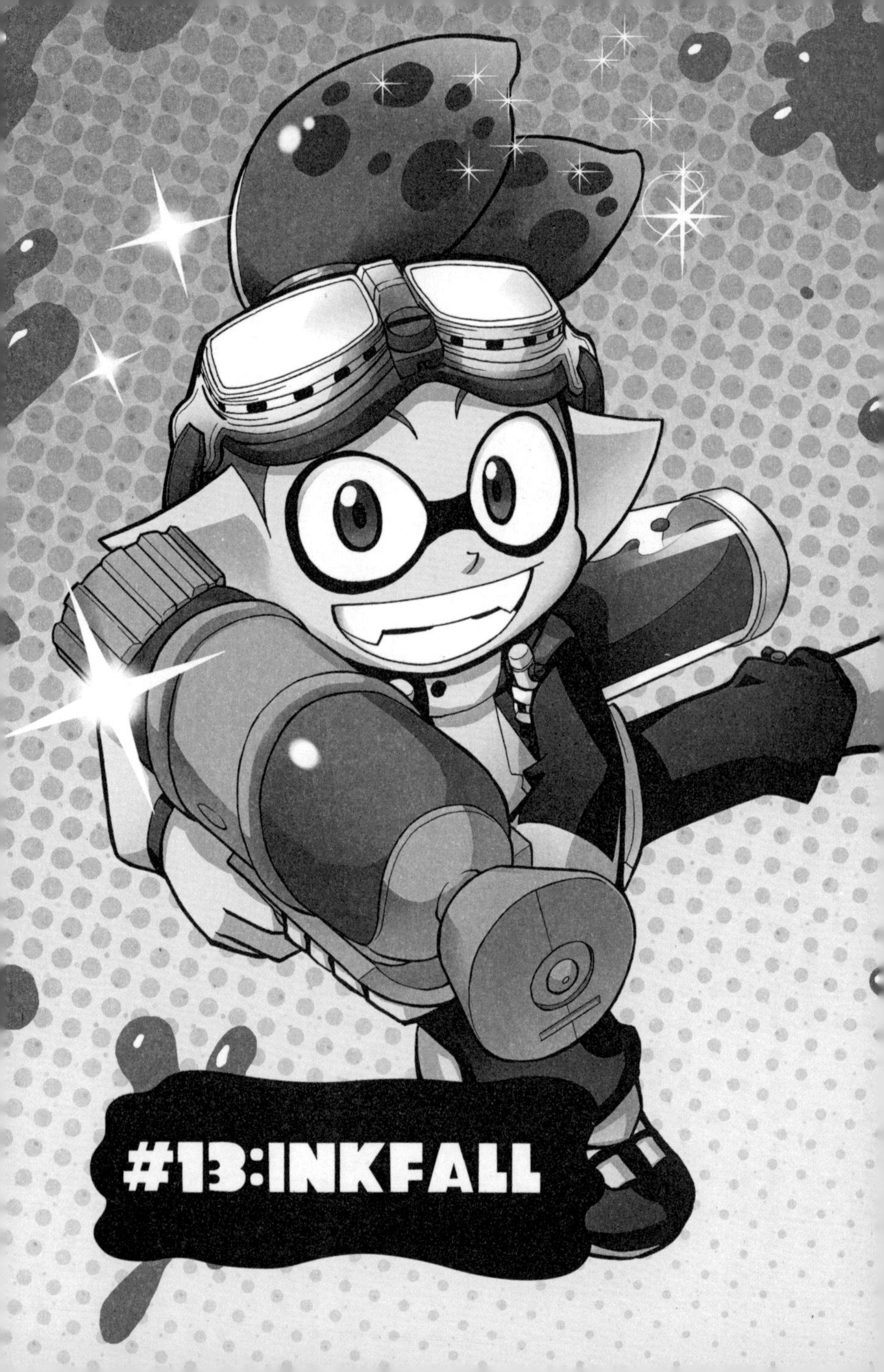
#13:INKFALL

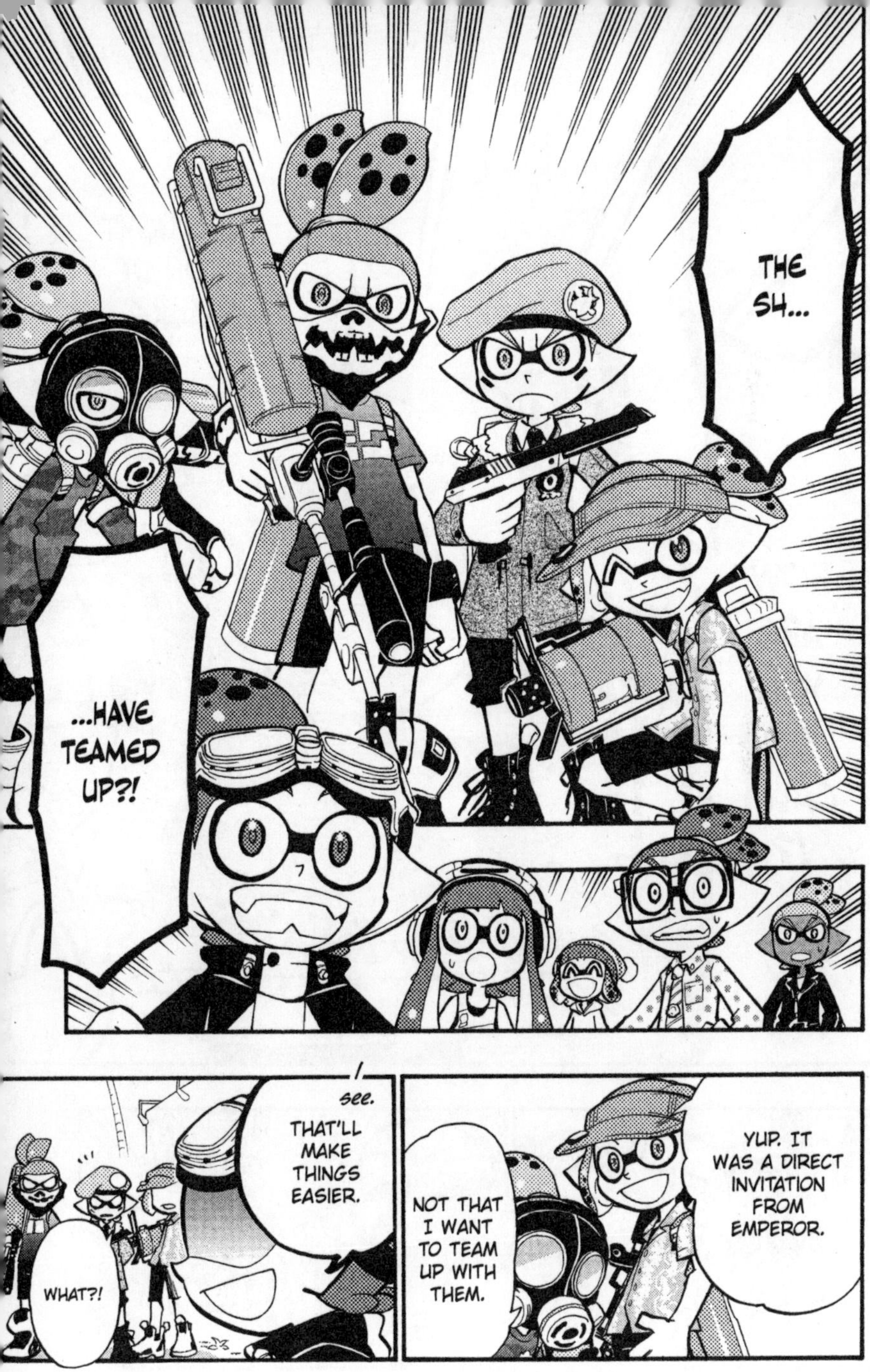
THE S4...
...HAVE TEAMED UP?!
YUP. IT WAS A DIRECT INVITATION FROM EMPEROR.
NOT THAT I WANT TO TEAM UP WITH THEM.
I see.
THAT'LL MAKE THINGS EASIER.
WHAT?!

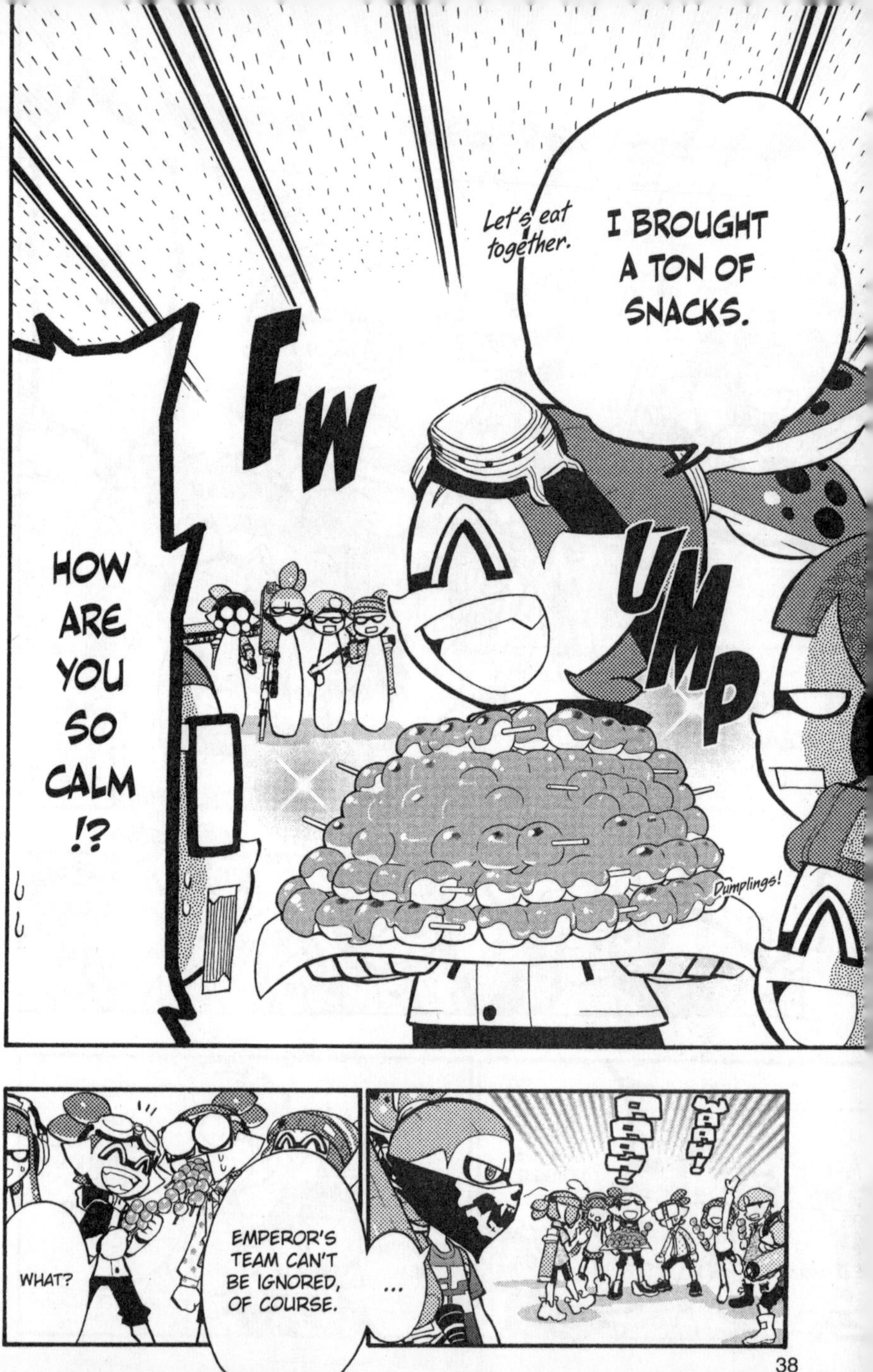
I BROUGHT A TON OF SNACKS.
Let's eat together.
FWUMP
Dumplings!
HOW ARE YOU SO CALM !?
WAAH!
AAAH!
...
EMPEROR'S TEAM CAN'T BE IGNORED, OF COURSE.
WHAT?

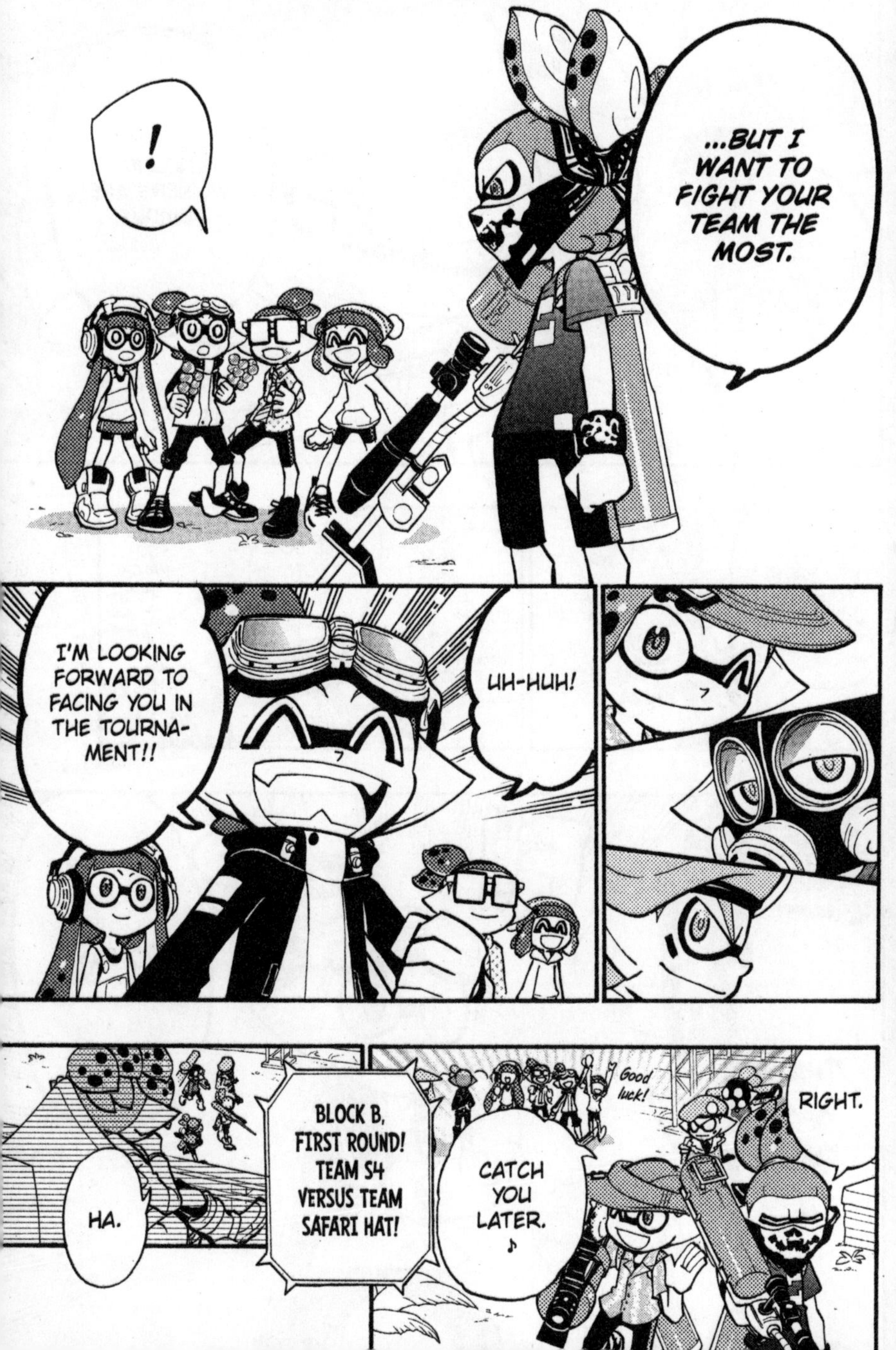
...BUT I WANT TO FIGHT YOUR TEAM THE MOST.
!
UH-HUH!
I'M LOOKING FORWARD TO FACING YOU IN THE TOURNA-MENT!!
RIGHT.
Good luck!
CATCH YOU LATER. ♪
BLOCK B, FIRST ROUND! TEAM S4 VERSUS TEAM SAFARI HAT!
HA.

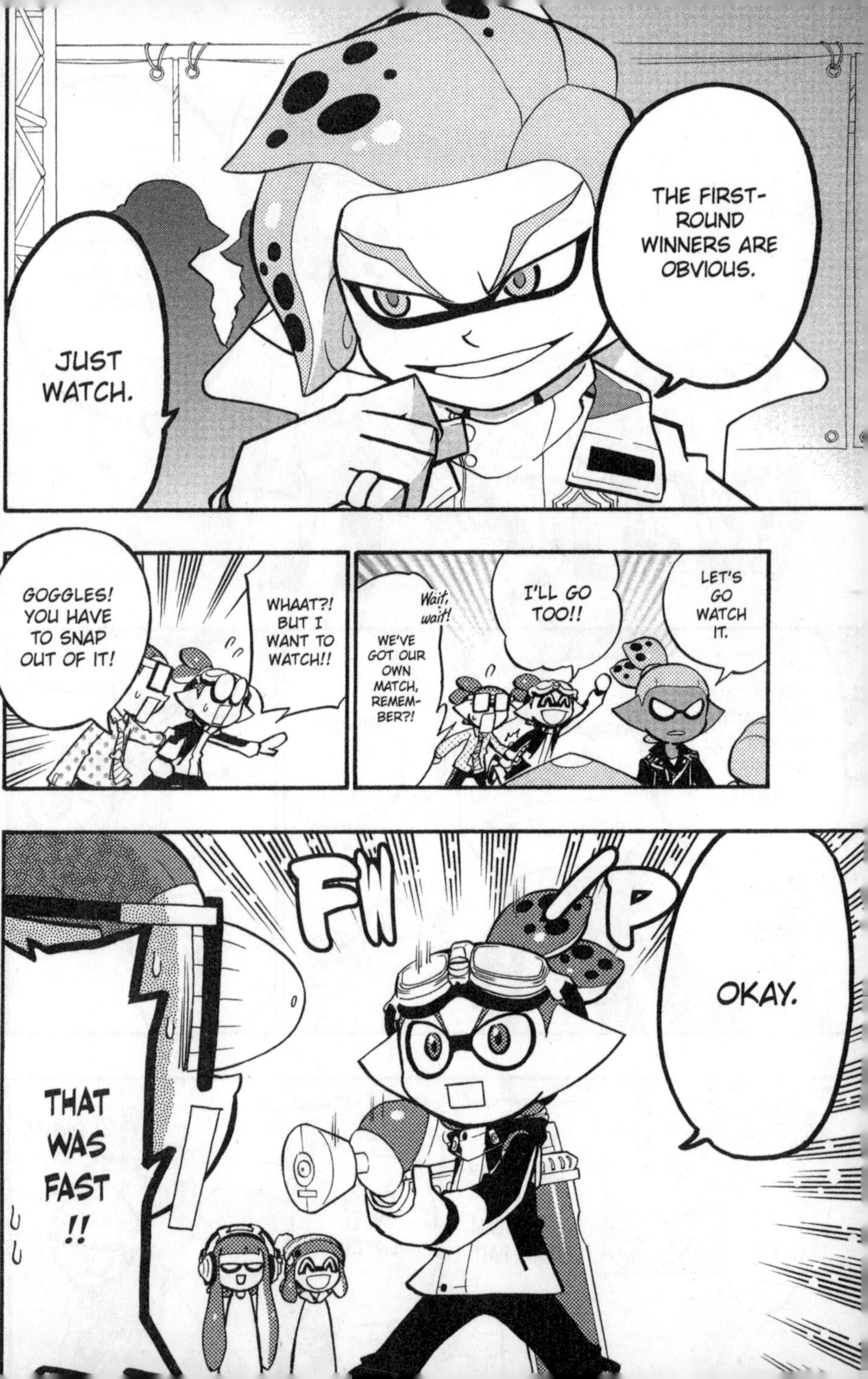
THE FIRST-ROUND WINNERS ARE OBVIOUS.
JUST WATCH.
LET'S GO WATCH IT.
I'LL GO TOO!!
Wait, wait!
WE'VE GOT OUR OWN MATCH, REMEMBER?!
WHAAT?! BUT I WANT TO WATCH!!
GOGGLES! YOU HAVE TO SNAP OUT OF IT!
OKAY.
FWIP
THAT WAS FAST!!

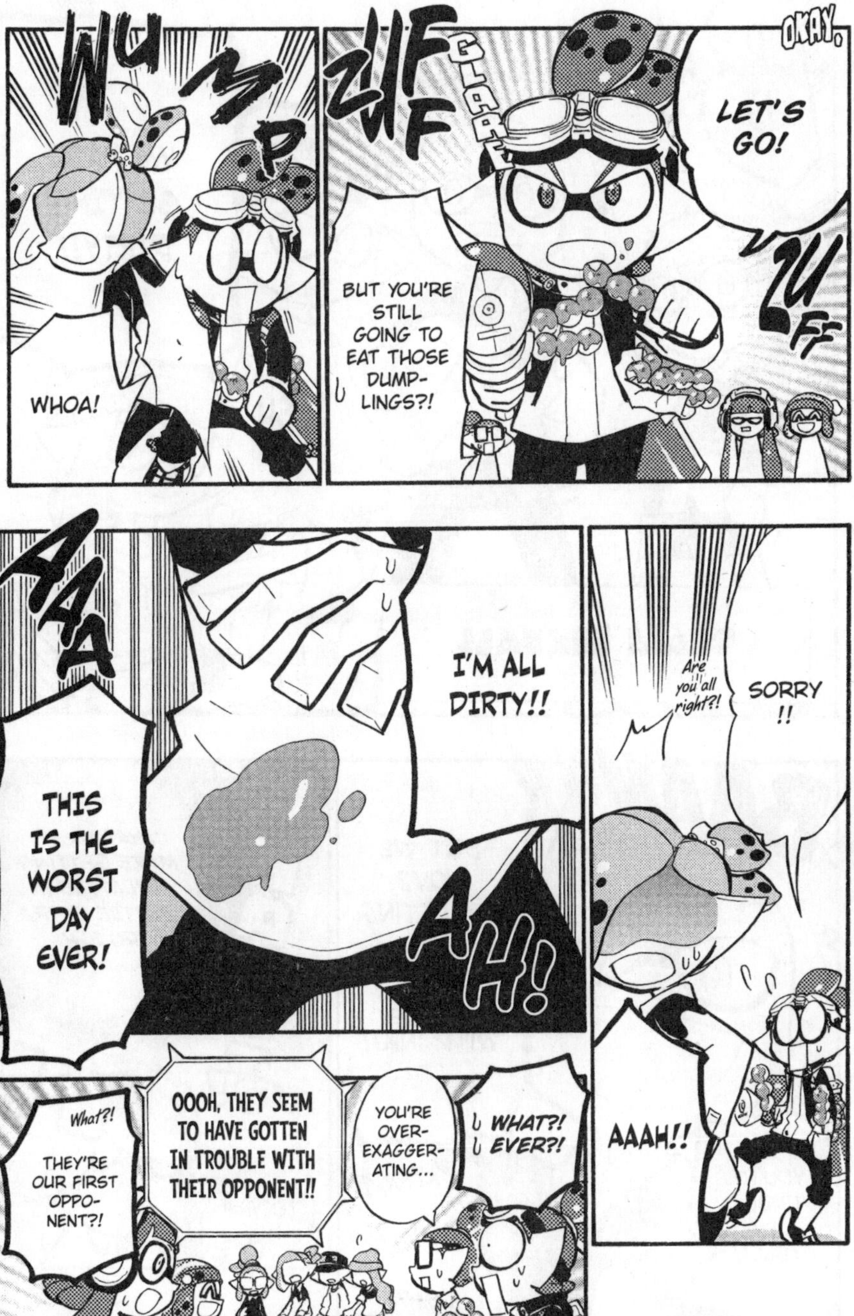
OKAY,
LET'S GO!
ZUFF
GLARE
ZUFF ZUFF
BUT YOU'RE STILL GOING TO EAT THOSE DUMP-LINGS?!
WUMP
WHOA!
SORRY!!
Are you all right?!
AAAH!!
AAA
I'M ALL DIRTY!!
AH!
THIS IS THE WORST DAY EVER!
WHAT?! EVER?!
YOU'RE OVER-EXAGGER-ATING...
OOOH, THEY SEEM TO HAVE GOTTEN IN TROUBLE WITH THEIR OPPONENT!!
What?!
THEY'RE OUR FIRST OPPO-NENT?!

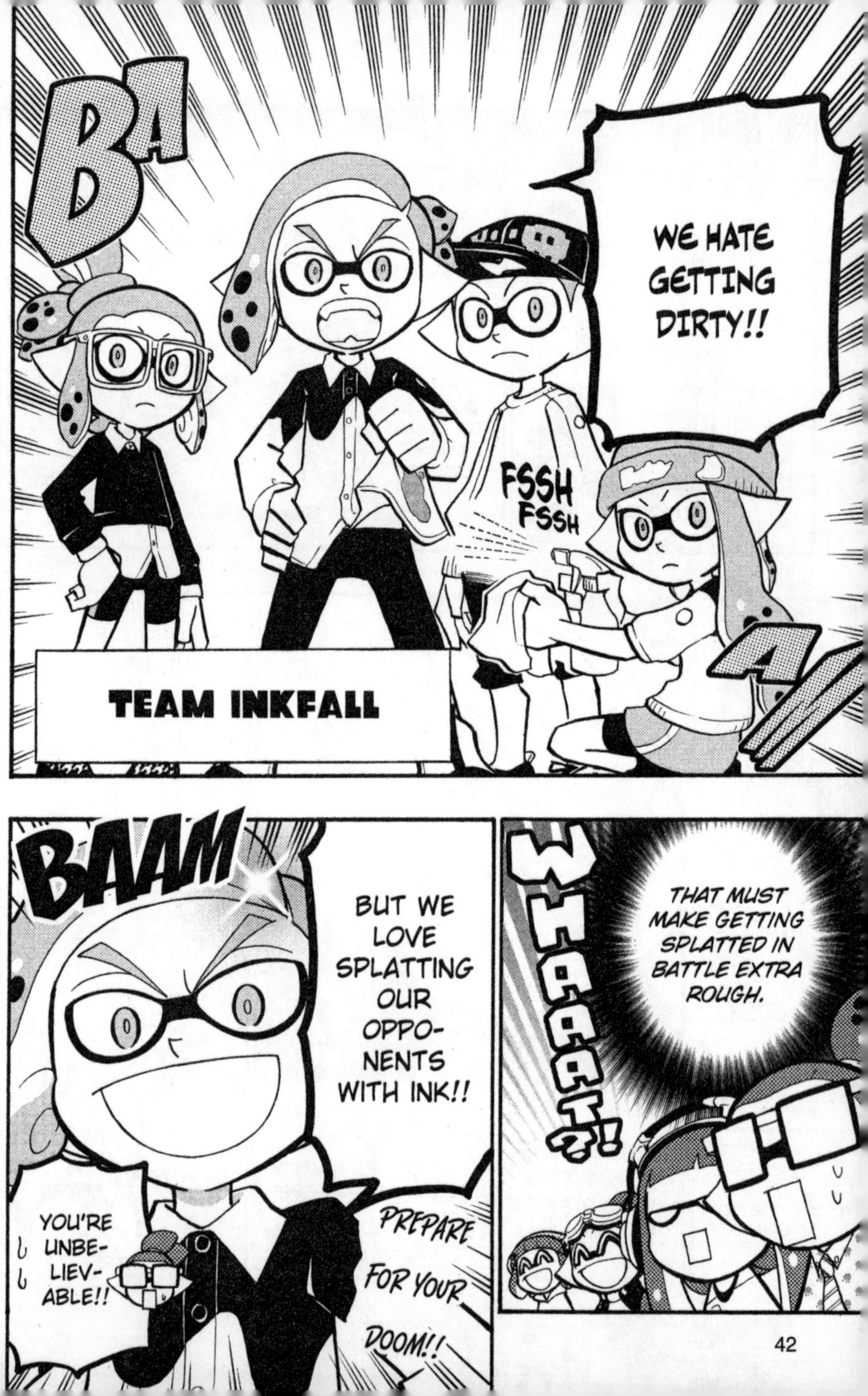
WE HATE GETTING DIRTY!!
BA
FSSH FSSH
TEAM INKFALL
THAT MUST MAKE GETTING SPLATTED IN BATTLE EXTRA ROUGH.
WHAAAT?!
BAAM
BUT WE LOVE SPLATTING OUR OPPO-NENTS WITH INK!!
PREPARE FOR YOUR DOOM!!
YOU'RE UNBE-LIEV-ABLE!!

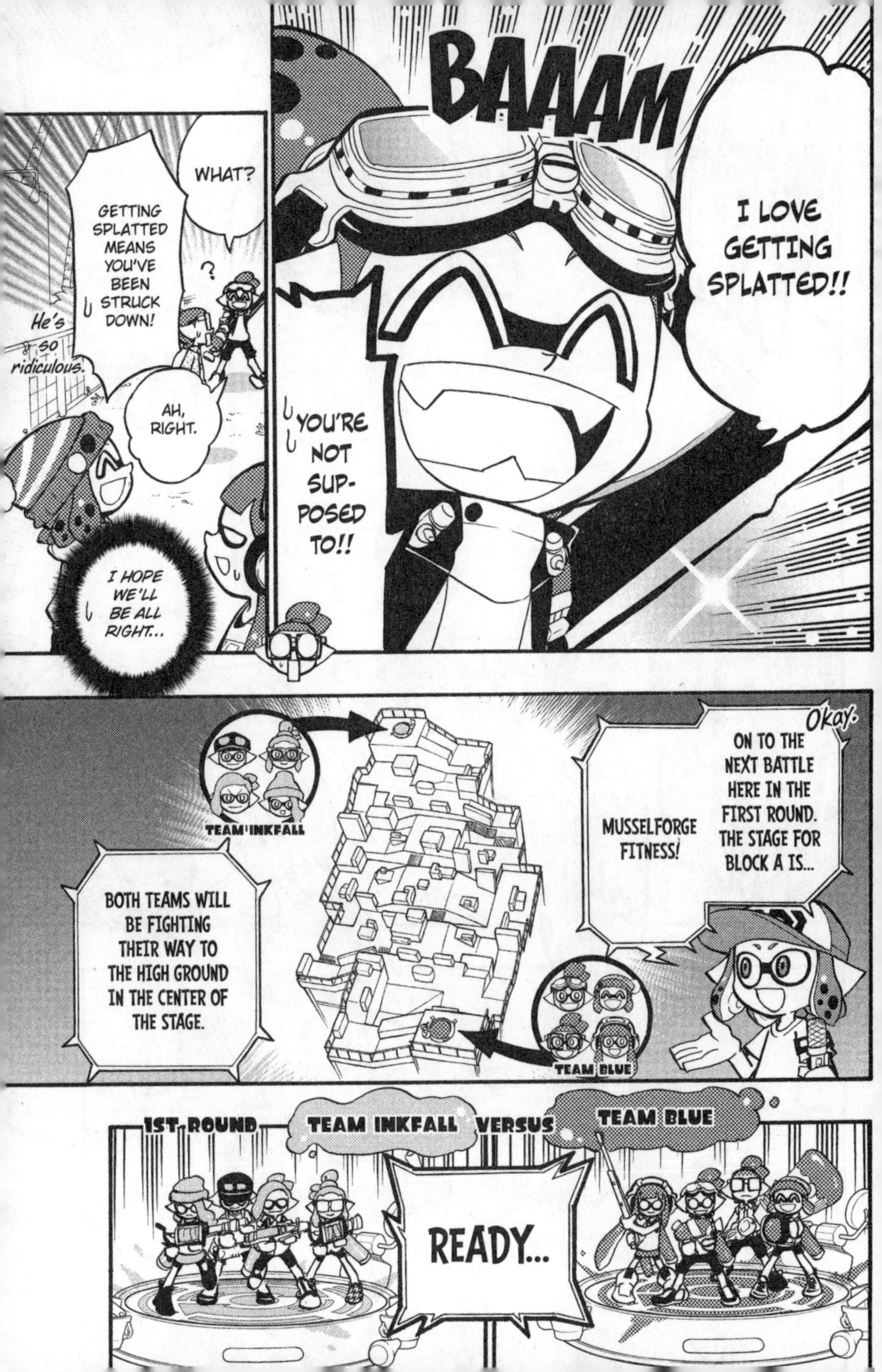
BAAAM
I LOVE GETTING SPLATTED!!
YOU'RE NOT SUP-POSED TO!!
WHAT?
GETTING SPLATTED MEANS YOU'VE BEEN STRUCK DOWN!
He's so ridiculous.
AH, RIGHT.
I HOPE WE'LL BE ALL RIGHT...
Okay.
ON TO THE NEXT BATTLE HERE IN THE FIRST ROUND. THE STAGE FOR BLOCK A IS...
MUSSELFORGE FITNESS!
TEAM INKFALL
BOTH TEAMS WILL BE FIGHTING THEIR WAY TO THE HIGH GROUND IN THE CENTER OF THE STAGE.
TEAM BLUE
1ST ROUND
TEAM INKFALL
VERSUS
TEAM BLUE
READY...

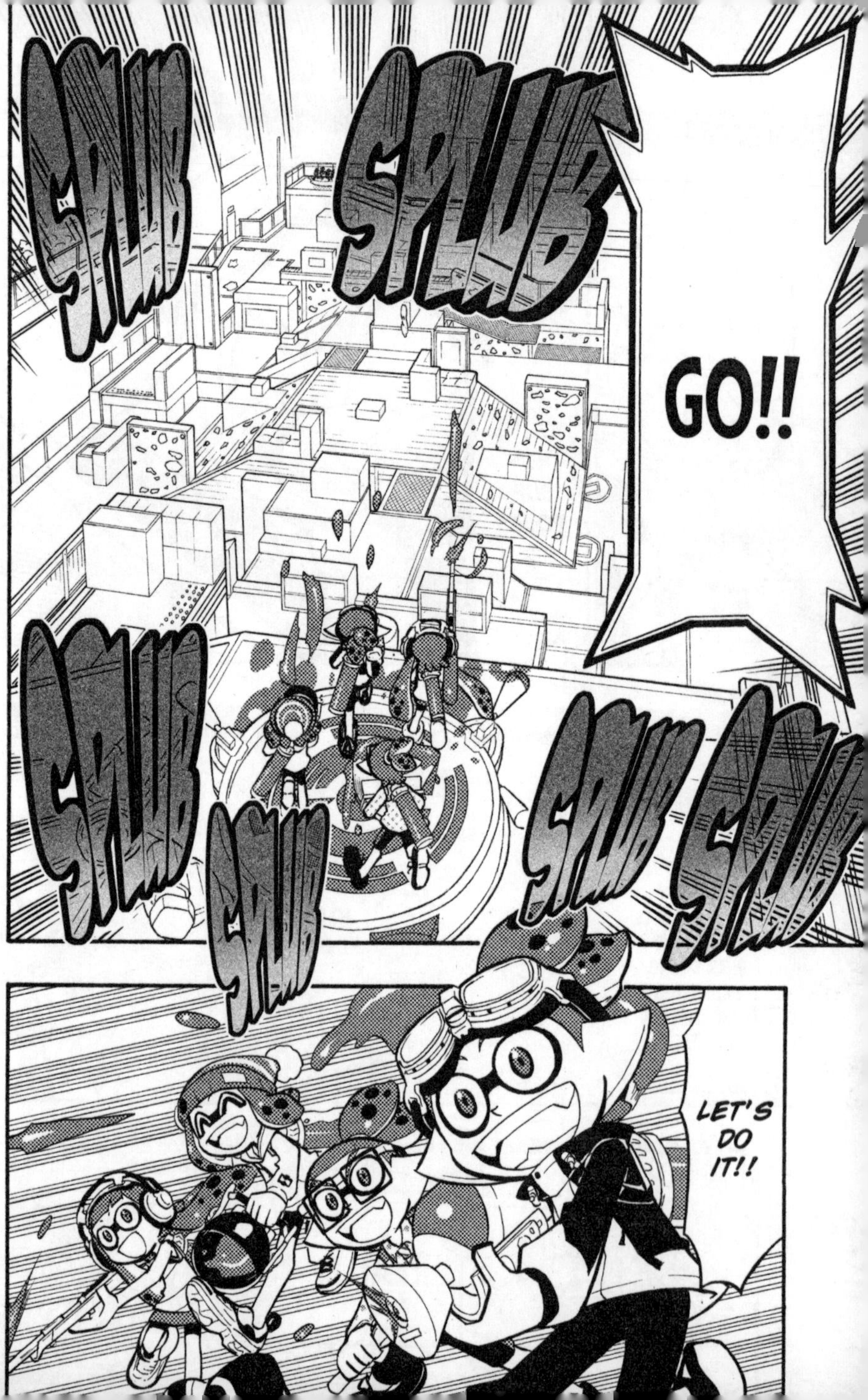
GO!!
SPLUB
SPLUB
SPLUB
SPLUB
SPLUB
SPLUB
LET'S DO IT!!

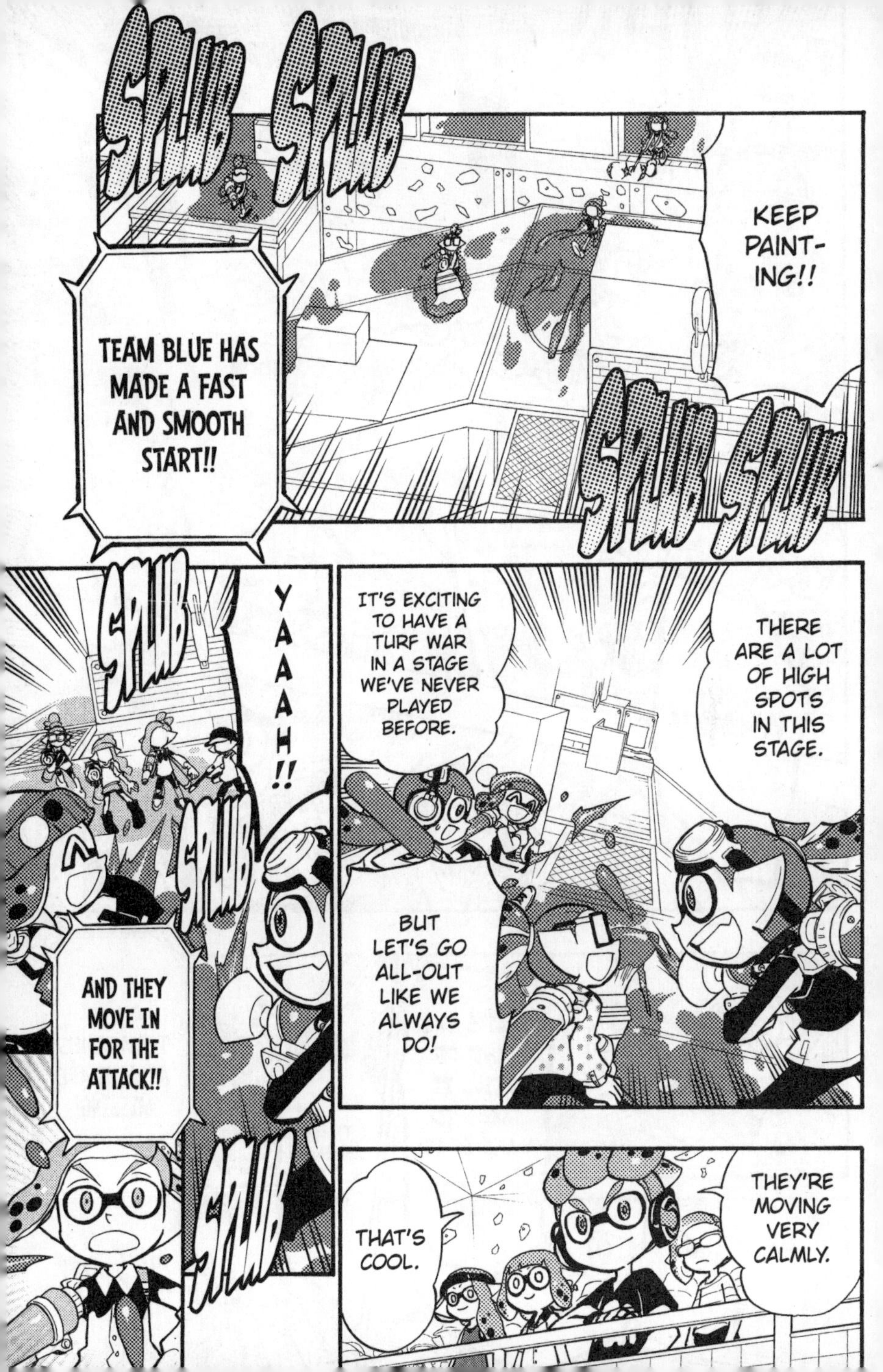
KEEP PAINTING!!
SPLUB SPLUB
SPLUB SPLUB
TEAM BLUE HAS MADE A FAST AND SMOOTH START!!
THERE ARE A LOT OF HIGH SPOTS IN THIS STAGE.
IT'S EXCITING TO HAVE A TURF WAR IN A STAGE WE'VE NEVER PLAYED BEFORE.
BUT LET'S GO ALL-OUT LIKE WE ALWAYS DO!
THEY'RE MOVING VERY CALMLY.
THAT'S COOL.
SPLUB
YAAAAH!!
SPLUB
AND THEY MOVE IN FOR THE ATTACK!!
SPLUB

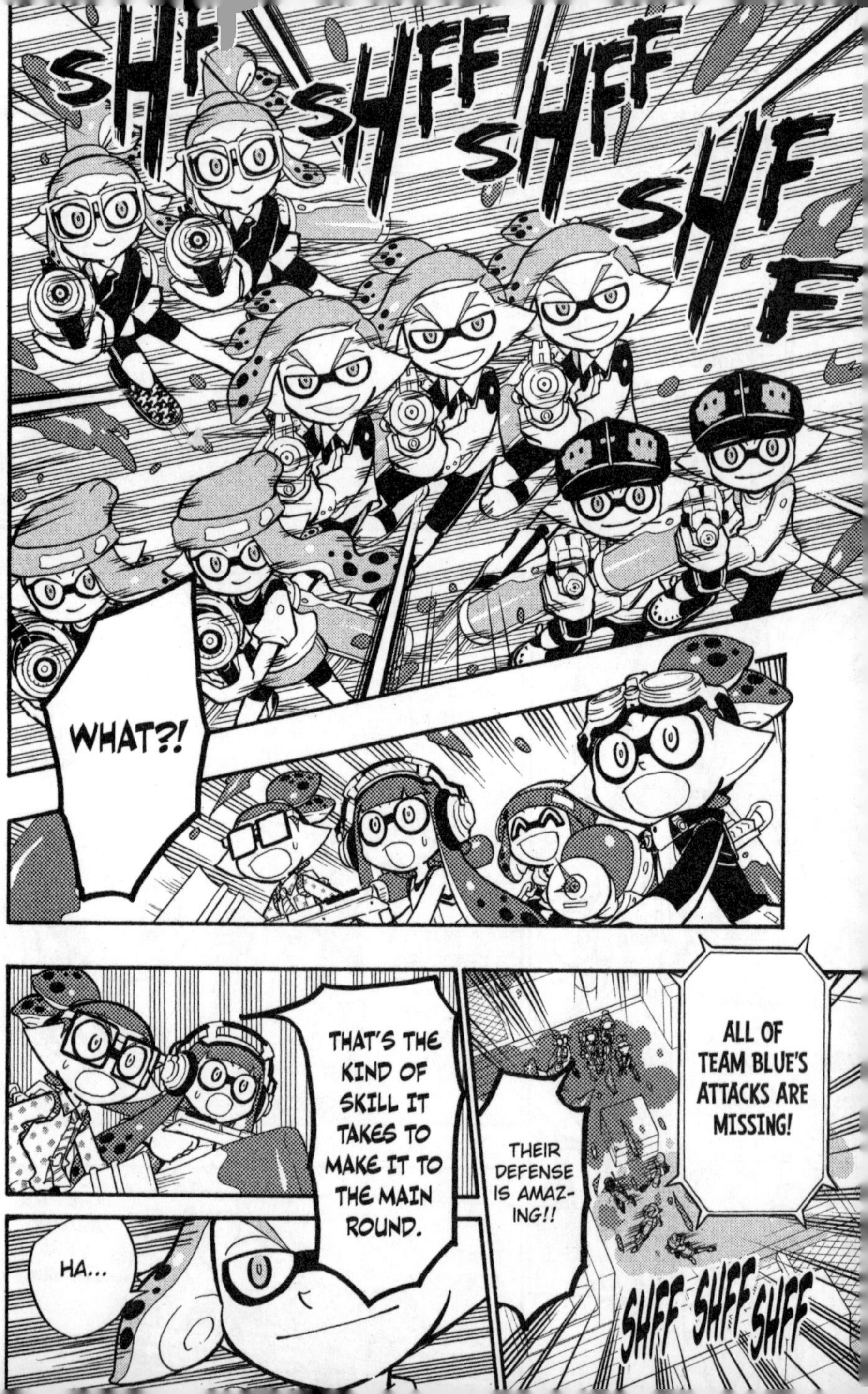
SHFF
SHFF
SHFF
SHFF
SHF
WHAT?!
ALL OF TEAM BLUE'S ATTACKS ARE MISSING!
THEIR DEFENSE IS AMAZ-ING!!
SHFF SHFF SHFF
THAT'S THE KIND OF SKILL IT TAKES TO MAKE IT TO THE MAIN ROUND.
HA...

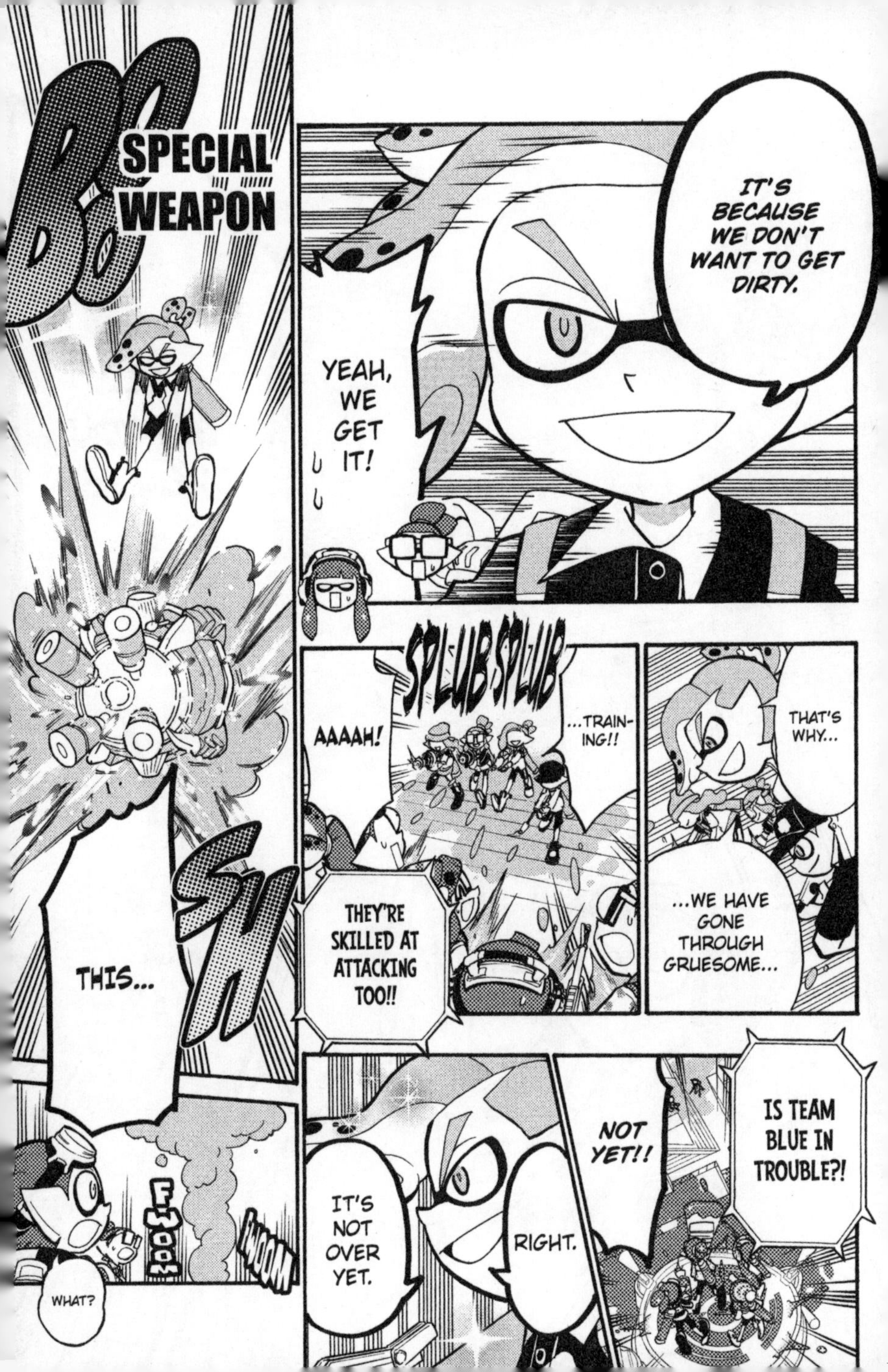
IT'S BECAUSE WE DON'T WANT TO GET DIRTY.
YEAH, WE GET IT!
THAT'S WHY...
...WE HAVE GONE THROUGH GRUESOME...
...TRAINING!!
SPLUB SPLUB
AAAAH!
THEY'RE SKILLED AT ATTACKING TOO!!
IS TEAM BLUE IN TROUBLE?!
NOT YET!!
RIGHT.
IT'S NOT OVER YET.
SPECIAL WEAPON
THIS...
SH
FWOOM
WHAT?

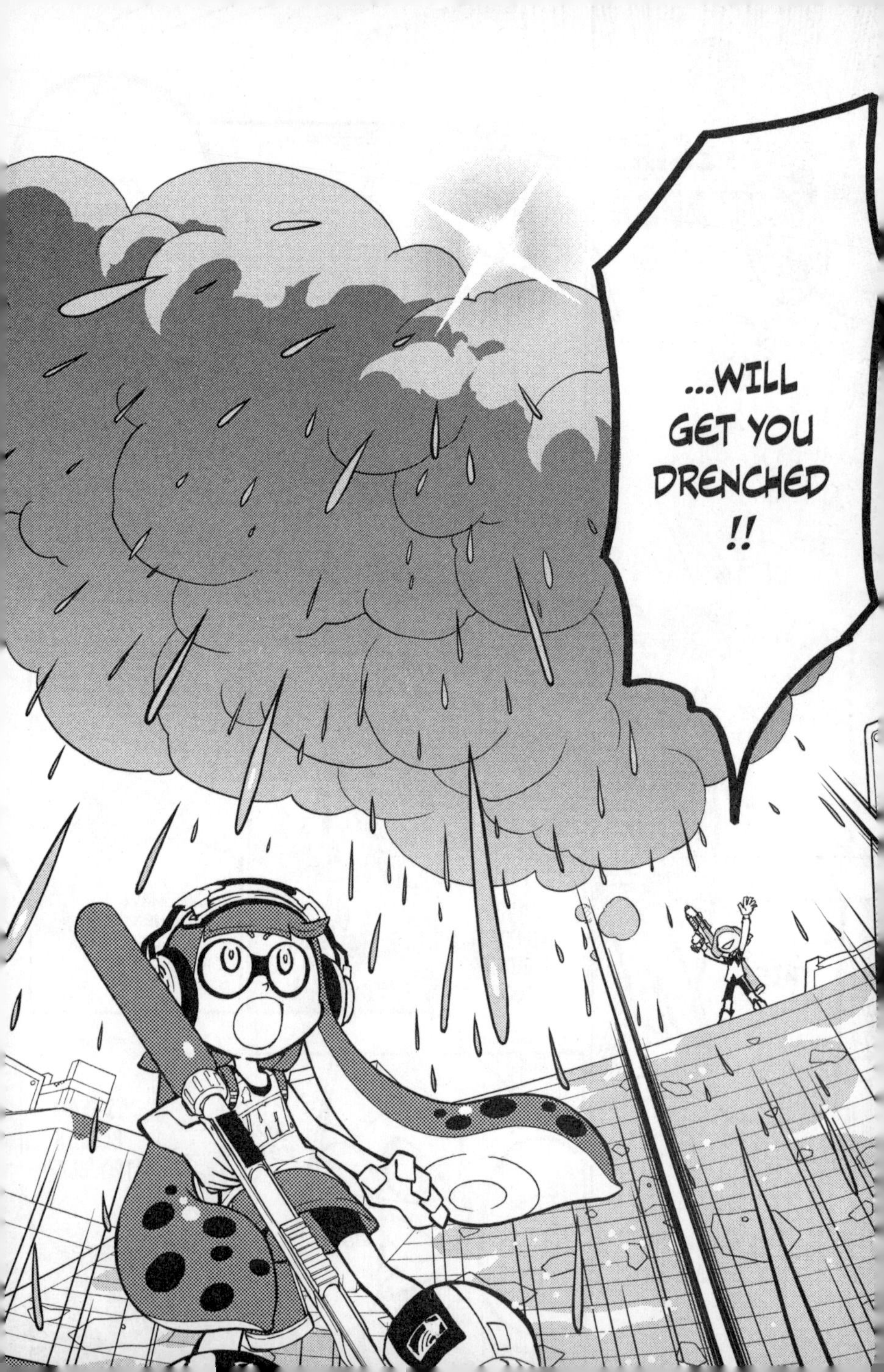
...WILL GET YOU DRENCHED !!

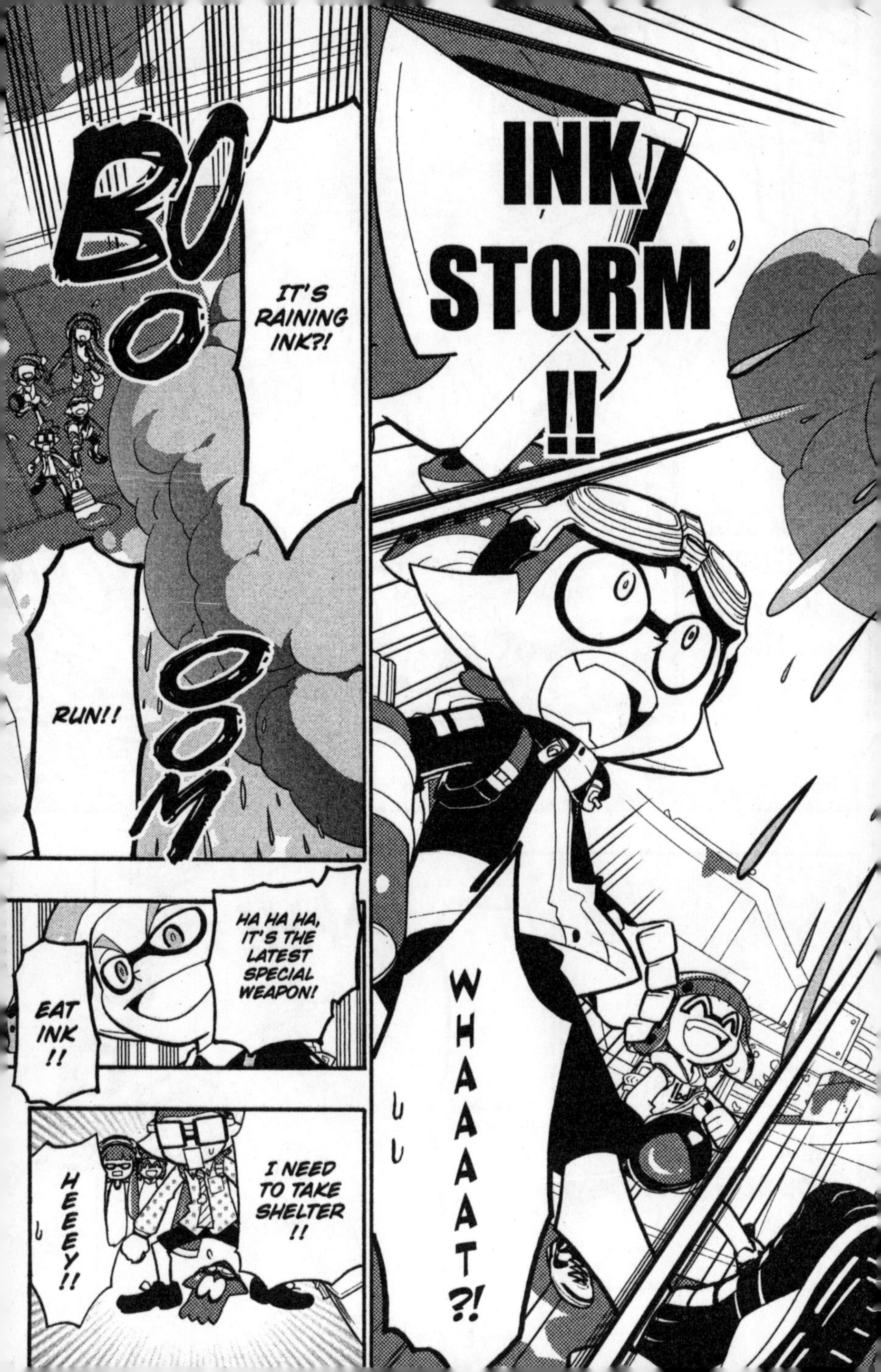

INKY STORM !!
WHAAAAT ?!
IT'S RAINING INK?!
BOOOOM
RUN!!
HA HA HA, IT'S THE LATEST SPECIAL WEAPON!
EAT INK !!
I NEED TO TAKE SHELTER !!
HEEEY!!

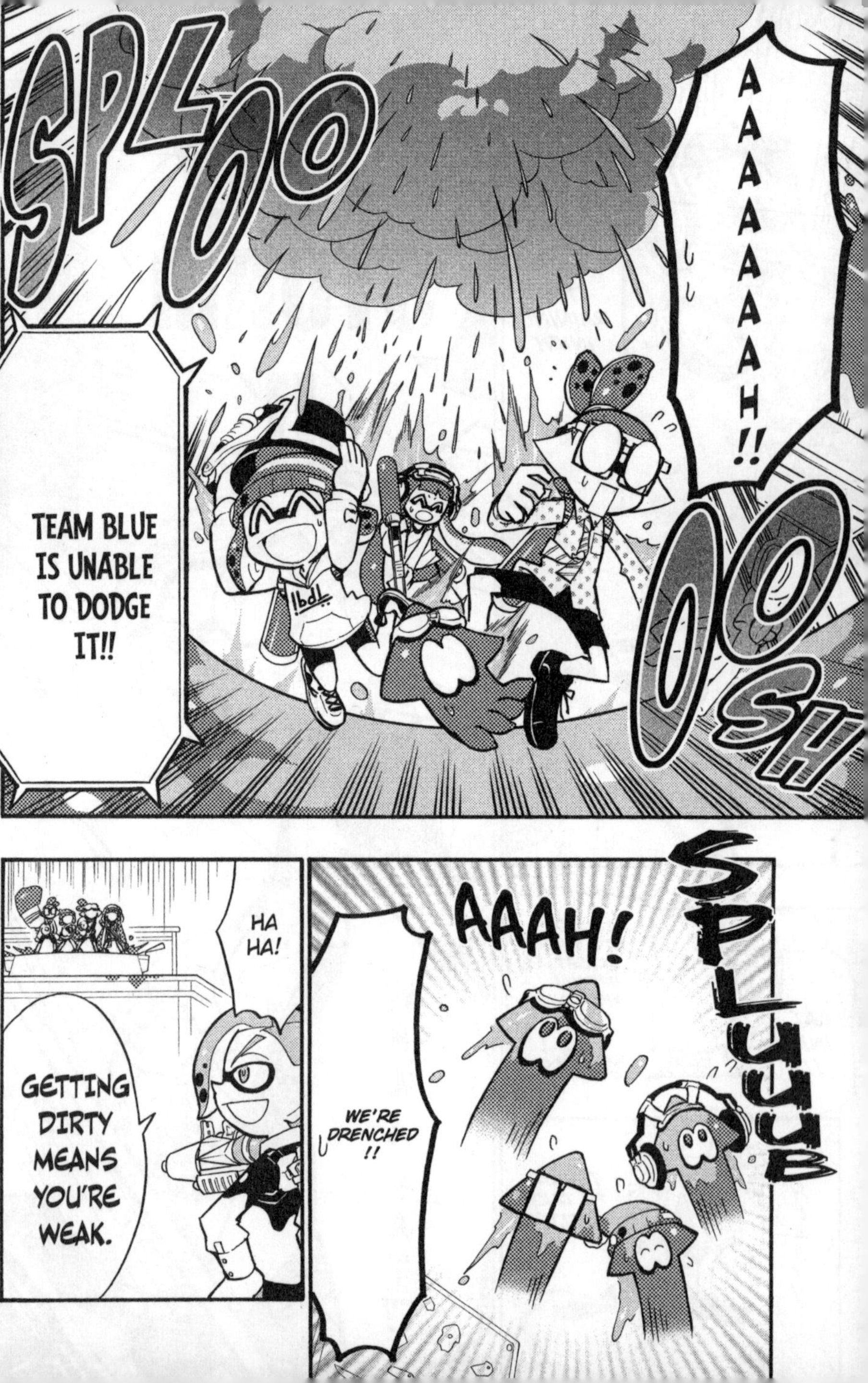
AAAAAAAAH!!
SPLOOOOSH
TEAM BLUE IS UNABLE TO DODGE IT!!
SPLUUUUB
AAAH!
WE'RE DRENCHED!!
HA HA!
GETTING DIRTY MEANS YOU'RE WEAK.

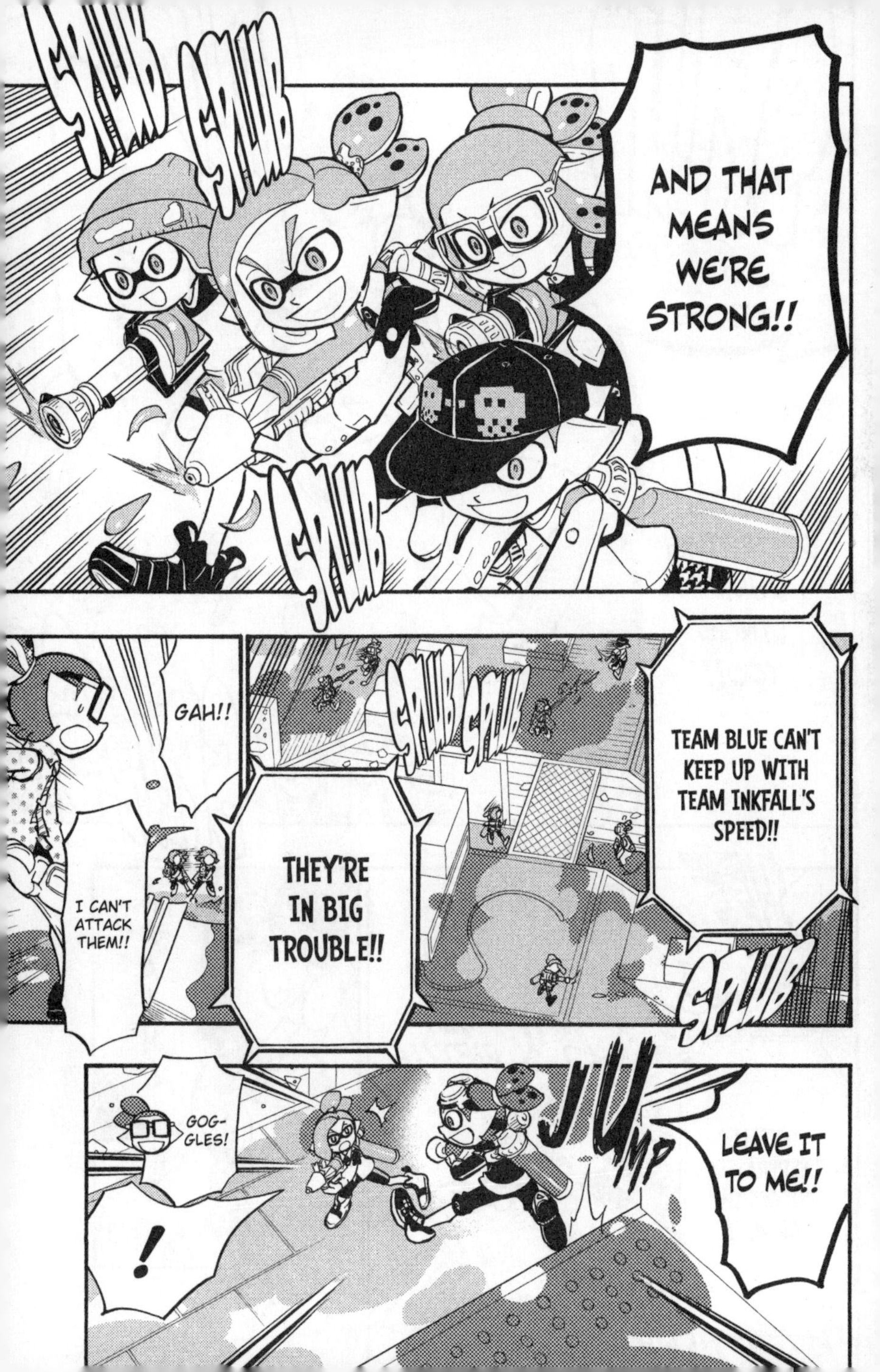
AND THAT MEANS WE'RE STRONG!!
SPLUB SPLUB
SPLUB
TEAM BLUE CAN'T KEEP UP WITH TEAM INKFALL'S SPEED!!
SPLUB SPLUB
THEY'RE IN BIG TROUBLE!!
SPLUB
GAH!!
I CAN'T ATTACK THEM!!
LEAVE IT TO ME!!
JUMP
GOG-GLES!
!

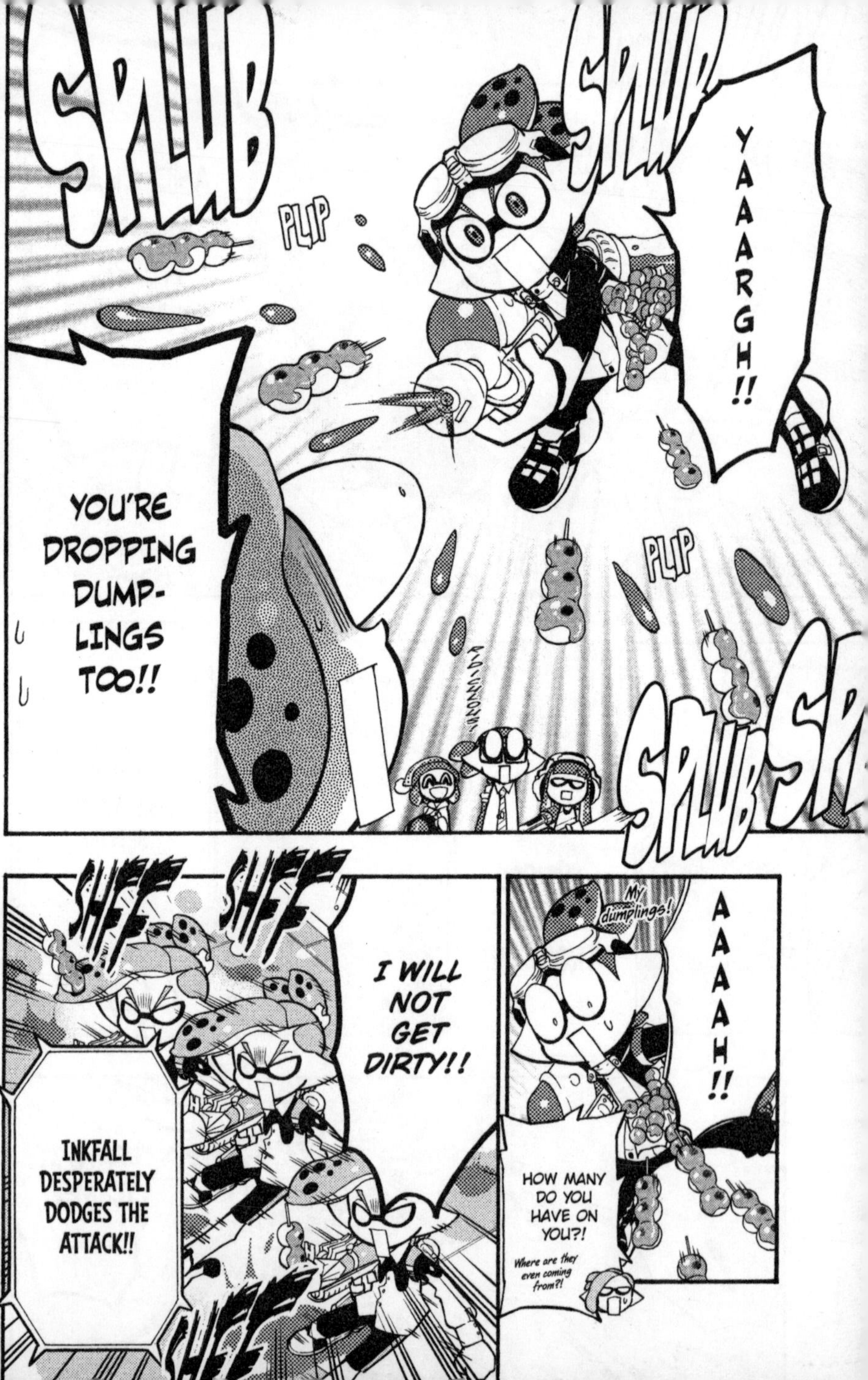
SPLUB
YAAAARGH!!
SPLUB
PLIP
YOU'RE DROPPING DUMP-LINGS TOO!!
PLIP
SPLUB SPL
My dumplings!
AAAAAH!!
HOW MANY DO YOU HAVE ON YOU?!
Where are they even coming from?!
SHFF SHFF
I WILL NOT GET DIRTY!!
INKFALL DESPERATELY DODGES THE ATTACK!!

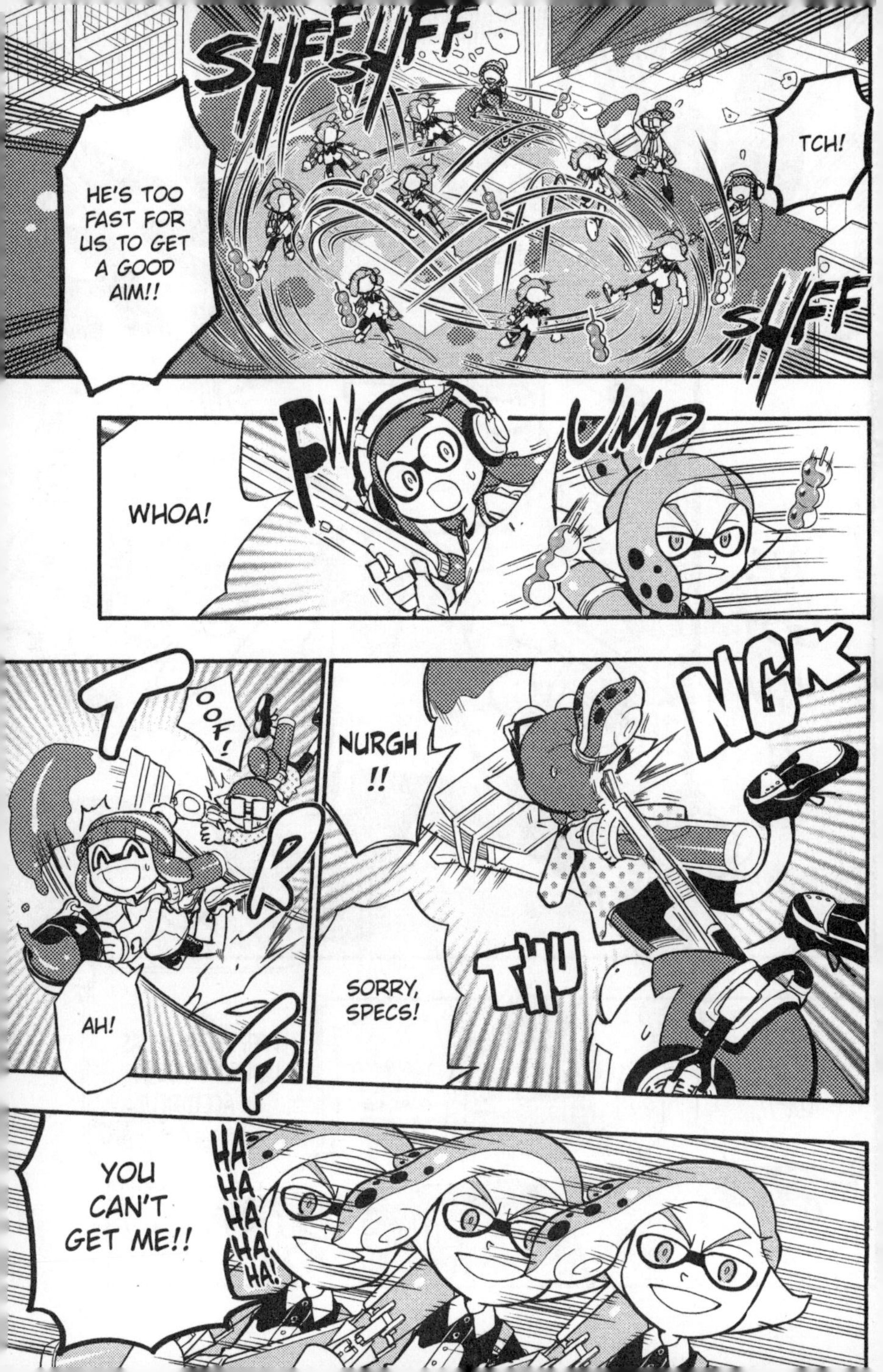
SHFF SHFF
TCH!
HE'S TOO FAST FOR US TO GET A GOOD AIM!!
SHFF
FWUMP
WHOA!
NGK
NURGH!!
THU
SORRY, SPECS!
OOF!
TRP
AH!
YOU CAN'T GET ME!!
HA HA HA HA HA!

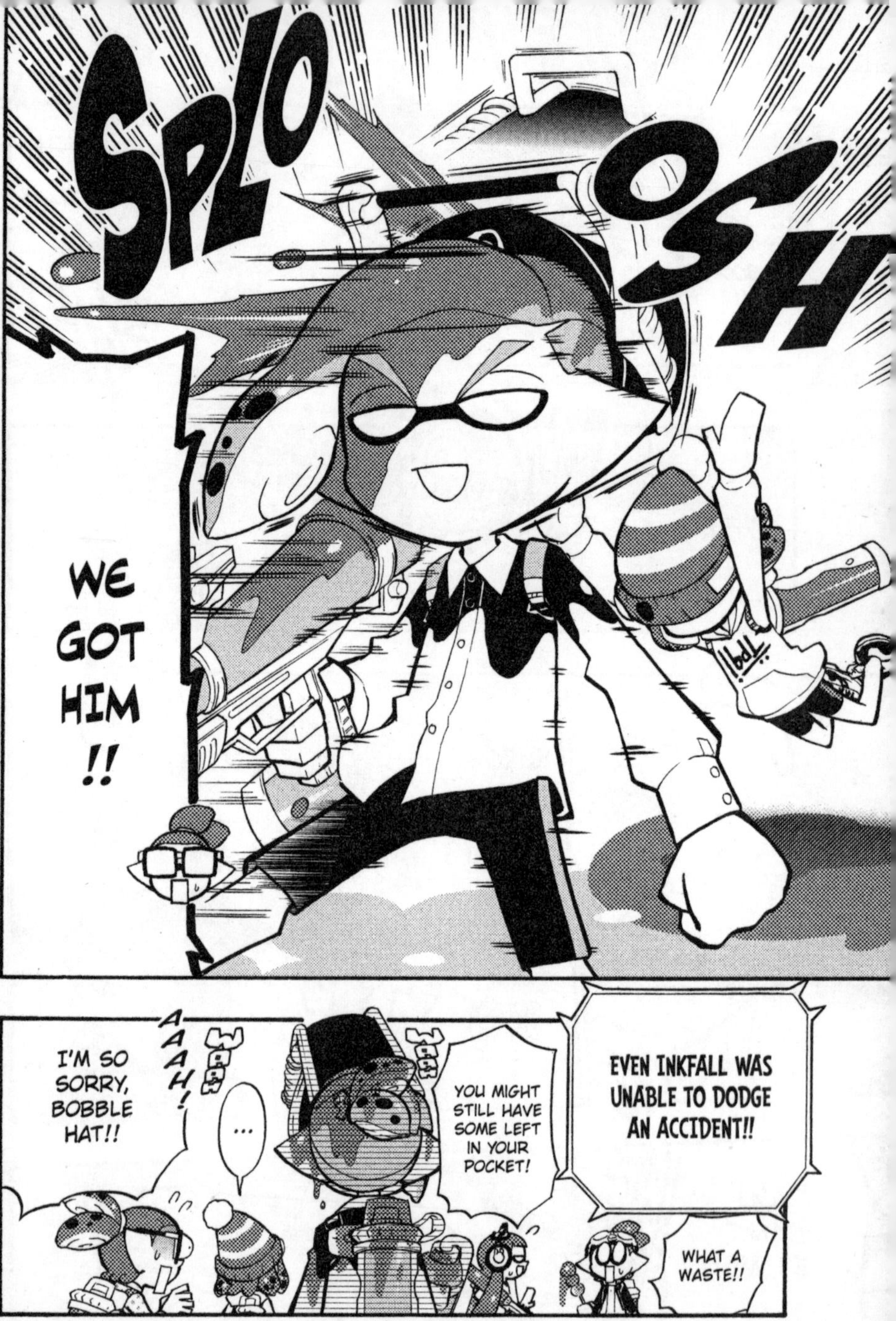
SPLOOSH
WE GOT HIM !!
EVEN INKFALL WAS UNABLE TO DODGE AN ACCIDENT!!
WHAT A WASTE!!
YOU MIGHT STILL HAVE SOME LEFT IN YOUR POCKET!
...
AAAH!
I'M SO SORRY, BOBBLE HAT!!

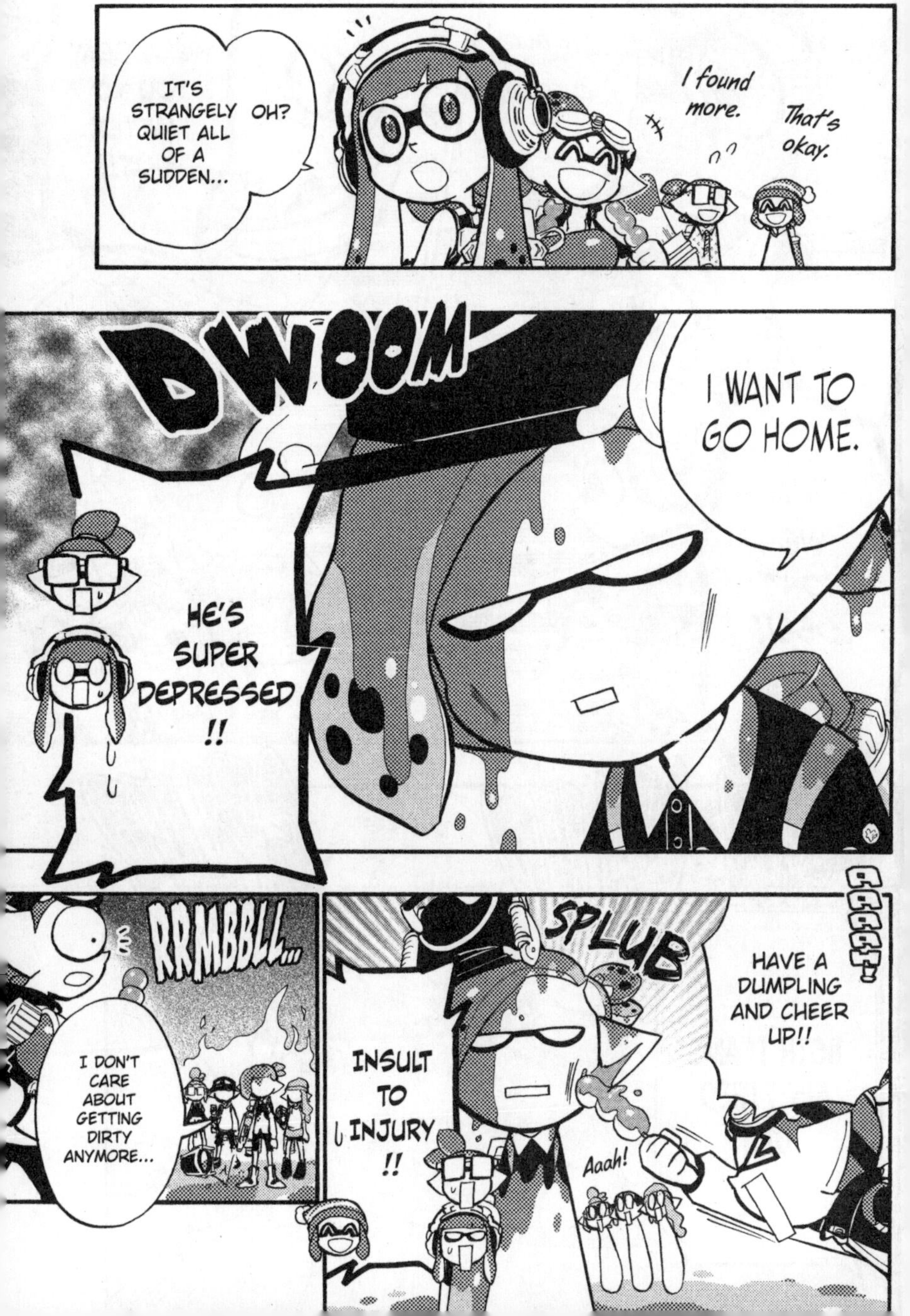
That's okay.
I found more.
OH?
IT'S STRANGELY QUIET ALL OF A SUDDEN...
I WANT TO GO HOME.
DWOOM
HE'S SUPER DEPRESSED!!
AAAAH!
HAVE A DUMPLING AND CHEER UP!!
SPLUB
INSULT TO INJURY!!
Aaah!
RRMBBLL...
I DON'T CARE ABOUT GETTING DIRTY ANYMORE...

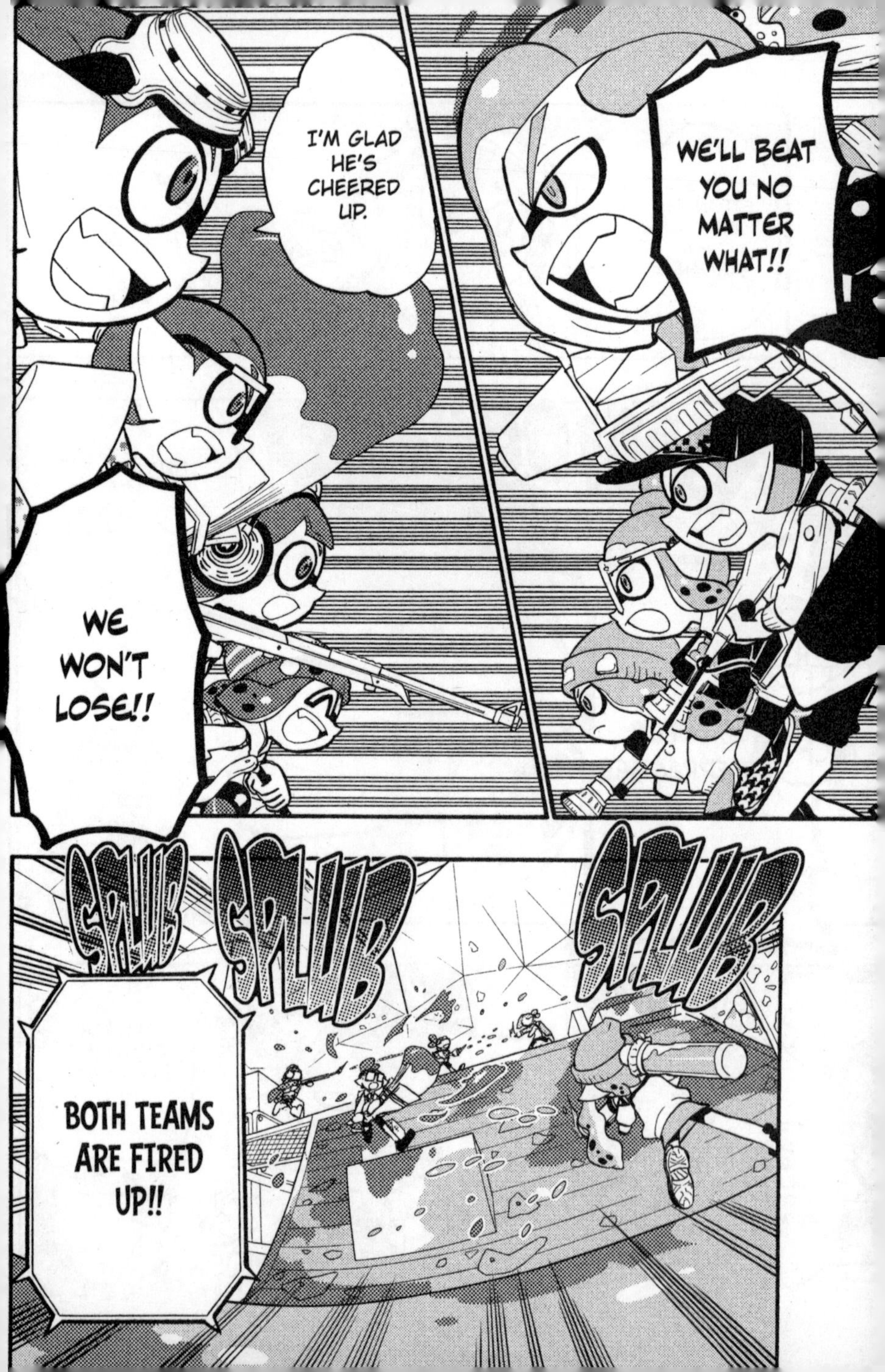
WE'LL BEAT YOU NO MATTER WHAT!!
I'M GLAD HE'S CHEERED UP.
WE WON'T LOSE!!
SPLUB
SPLUB
SPLUB
BOTH TEAMS ARE FIRED UP!!

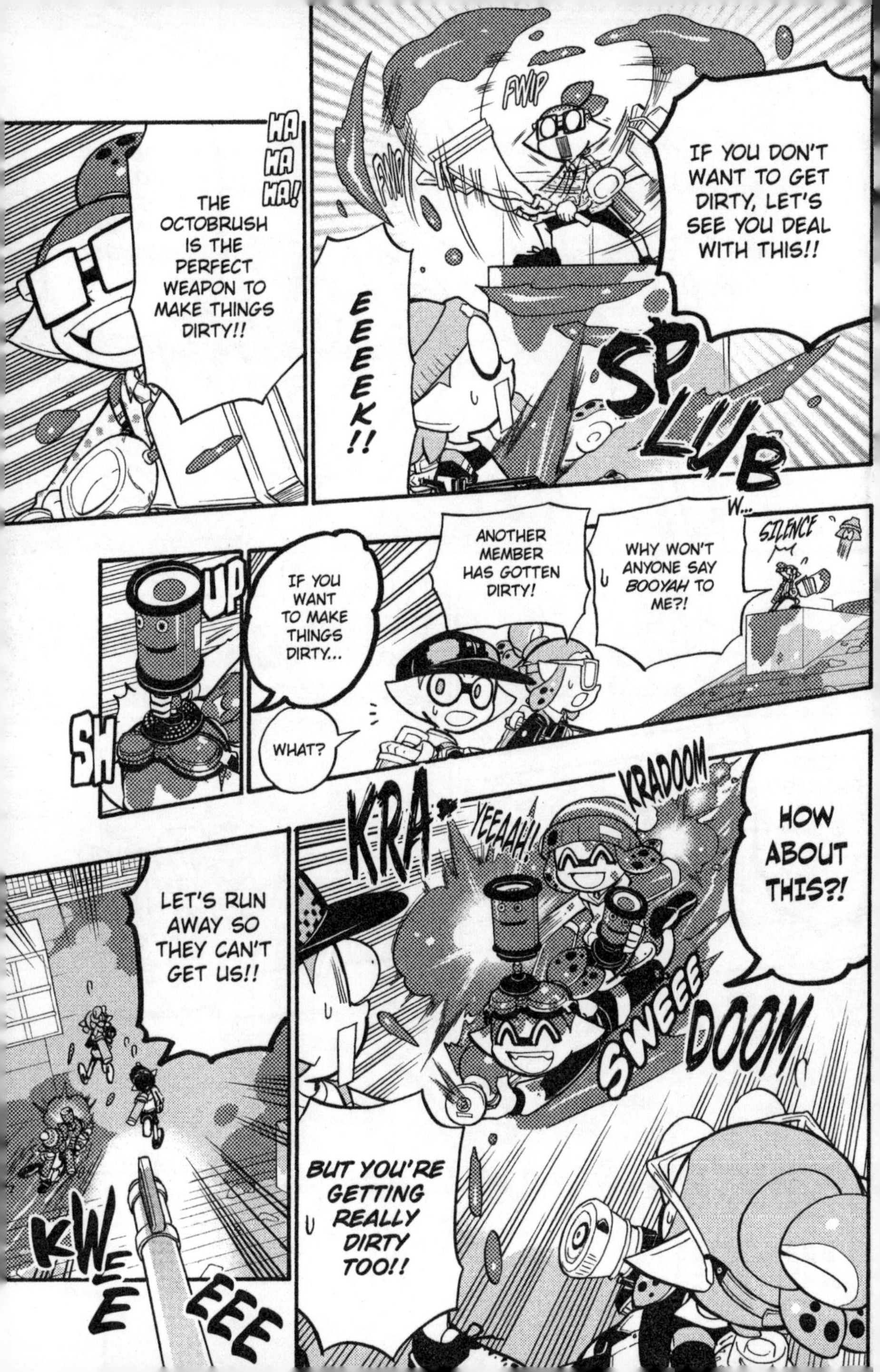
FWIP
FWIP
IF YOU DON'T WANT TO GET DIRTY, LET'S SEE YOU DEAL WITH THIS!!
EEEEEK!!
SPLUB
HA HA HA!
THE OCTOBRUSH IS THE PERFECT WEAPON TO MAKE THINGS DIRTY!!
W...
SILENCE
WHY WON'T ANYONE SAY *BOOYAH* TO ME?!
ANOTHER MEMBER HAS GOTTEN DIRTY!
IF YOU WANT TO MAKE THINGS DIRTY...
WHAT?
UP
SH
HOW ABOUT THIS?!
KRADOOM
YEEAAH!
KRA
SWEEE
DOOM
BUT YOU'RE GETTING REALLY DIRTY TOO!!
LET'S RUN AWAY SO THEY CAN'T GET US!!
KWEEEEE

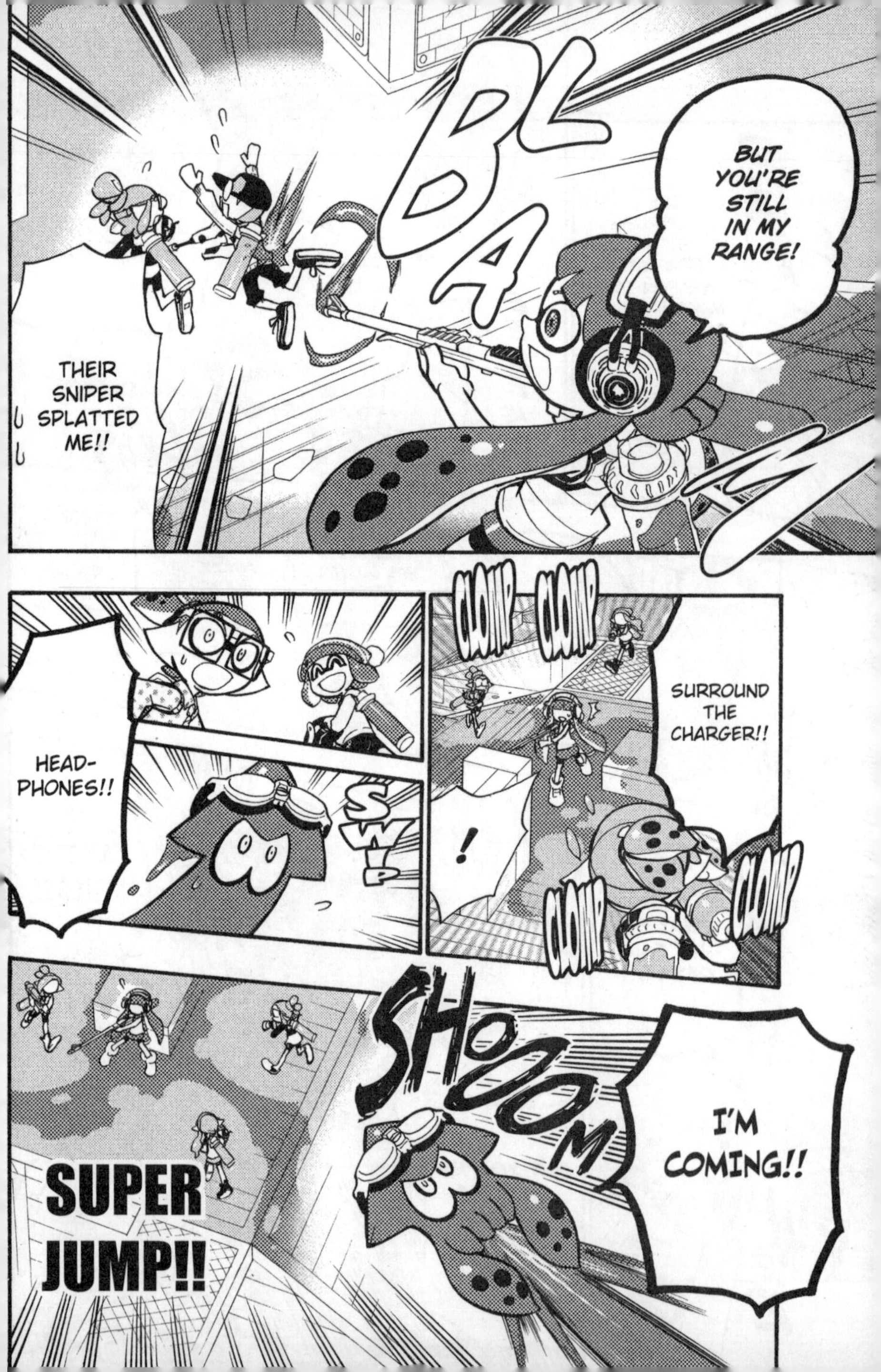
BUT YOU'RE STILL IN MY RANGE!
BLAM
THEIR SNIPER SPLATTED ME!!
CLOMP CLOMP
SURROUND THE CHARGER!!
!
CLOMP CLOMP
HEAD-PHONES!!
SWIP
I'M COMING!!
SHOOOM
SUPER JUMP!!

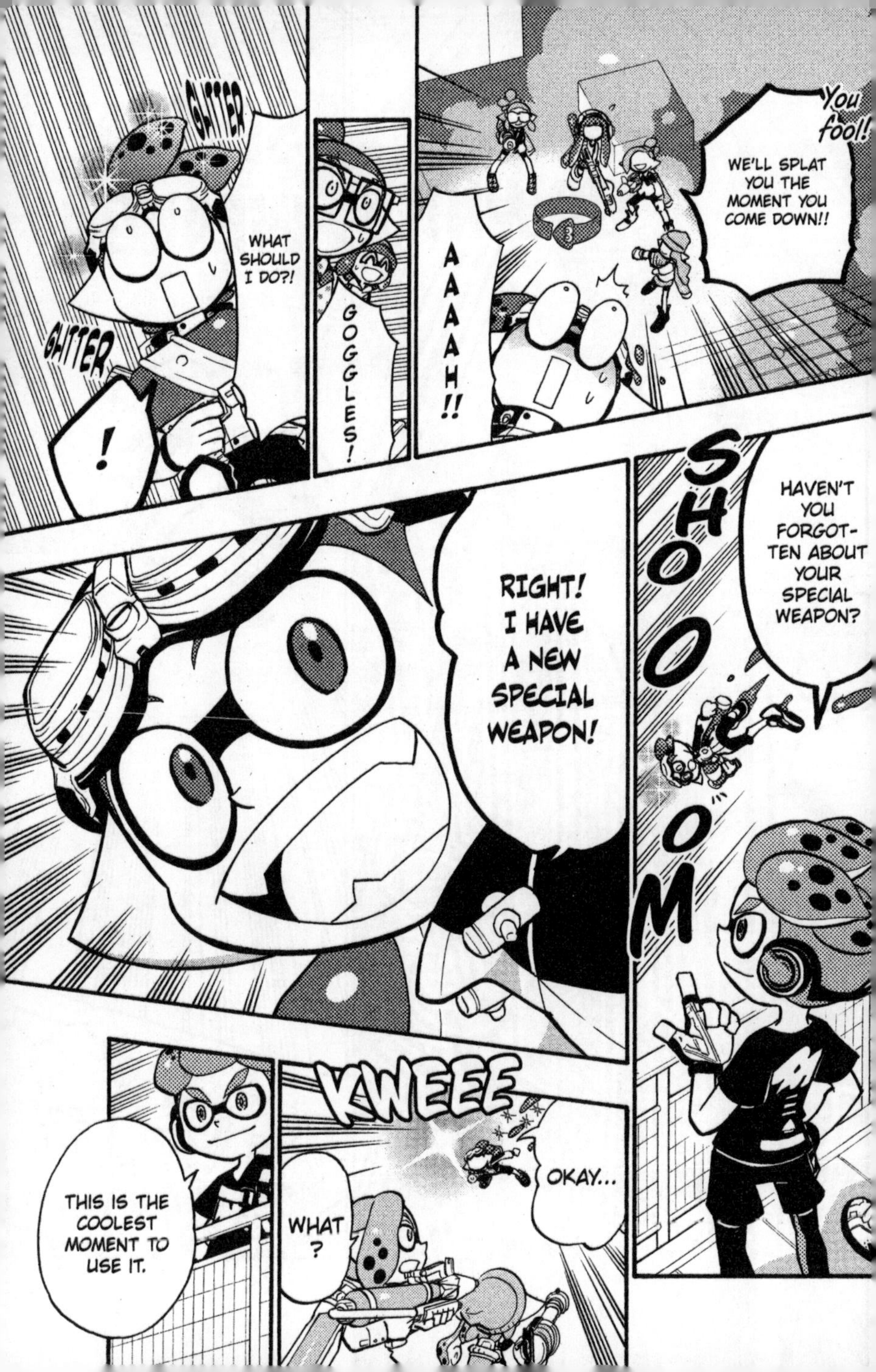
You fool!
WE'LL SPLAT YOU THE MOMENT YOU COME DOWN!!
AAAAAH!!
GOGGLES!
GLITTER
WHAT SHOULD I DO?!
GLITTER
!
SHOOOOOM
HAVEN'T YOU FORGOT-TEN ABOUT YOUR SPECIAL WEAPON?
RIGHT! I HAVE A NEW SPECIAL WEAPON!
KWEEE
OKAY...
WHAT?
THIS IS THE COOLEST MOMENT TO USE IT.

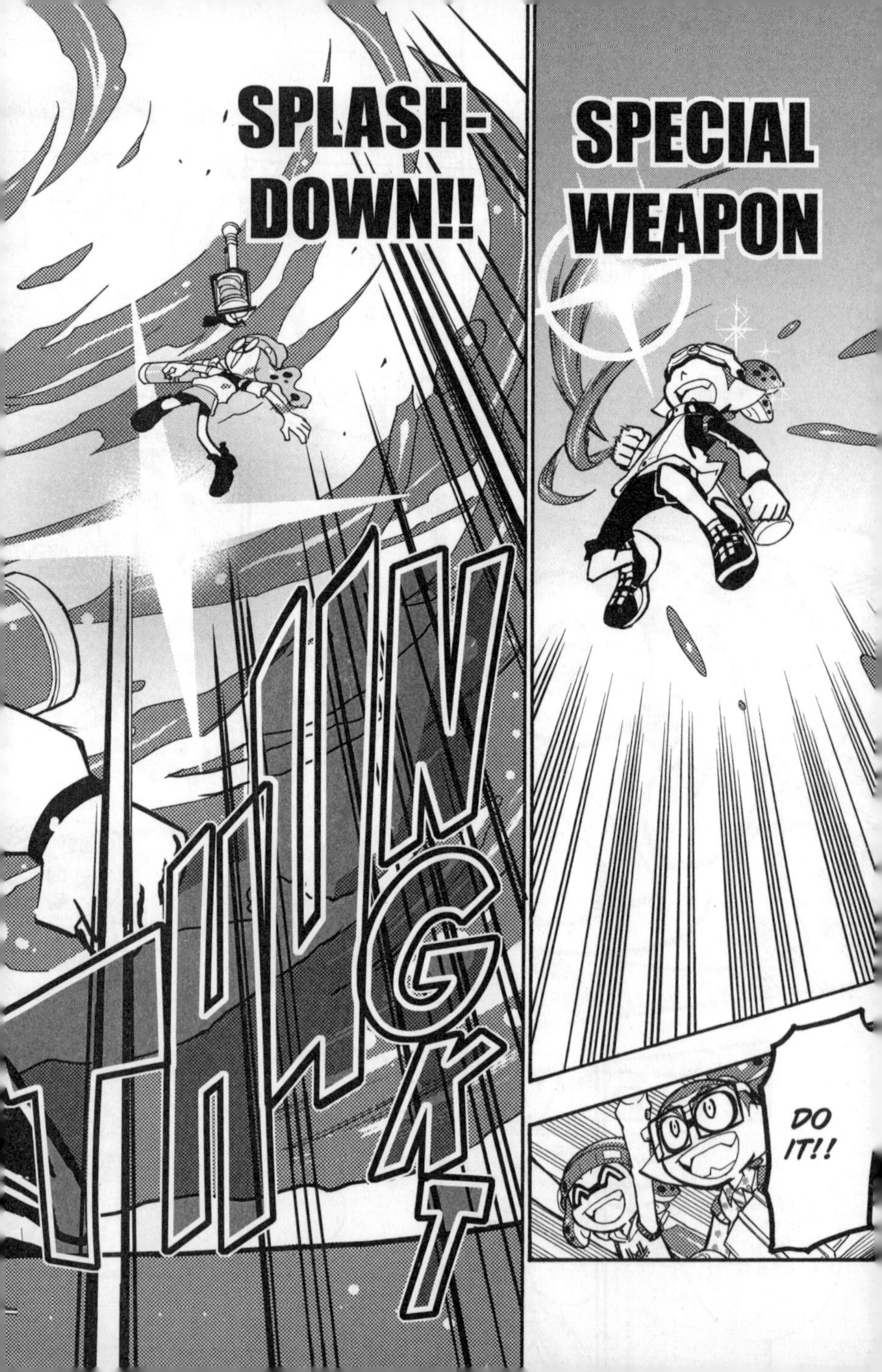
SPECIAL WEAPON
DO IT!!
SPLASH-DOWN!!

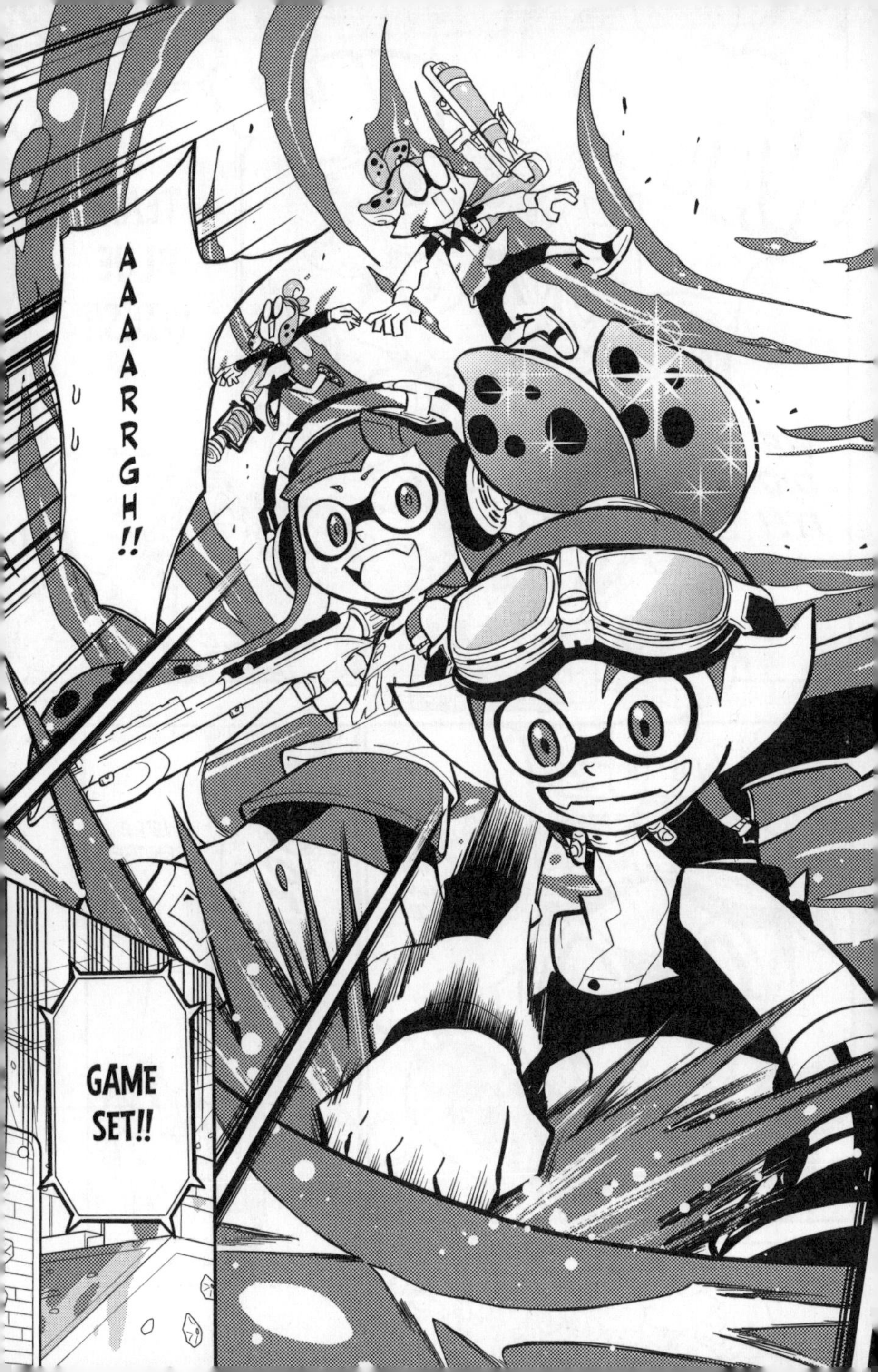
AAAARRGH!!
GAME SET!!

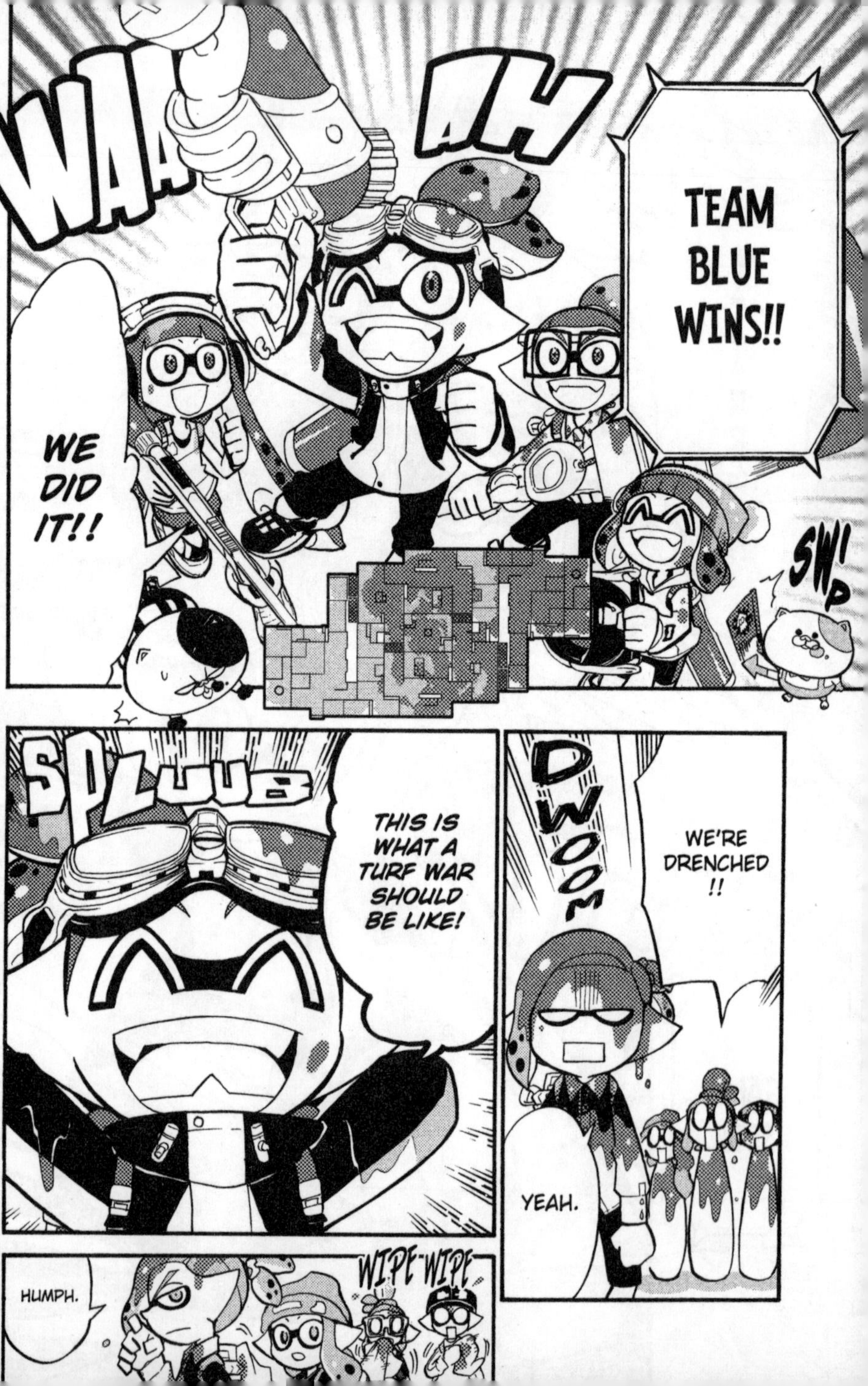
TEAM BLUE WINS!!
WAA AH
SWIP
WE DID IT!!
DWOOM
WE'RE DRENCHED !!
YEAH.
SPLUUB
THIS IS WHAT A TURF WAR SHOULD BE LIKE!
WIPE WIPE
HUMPH.

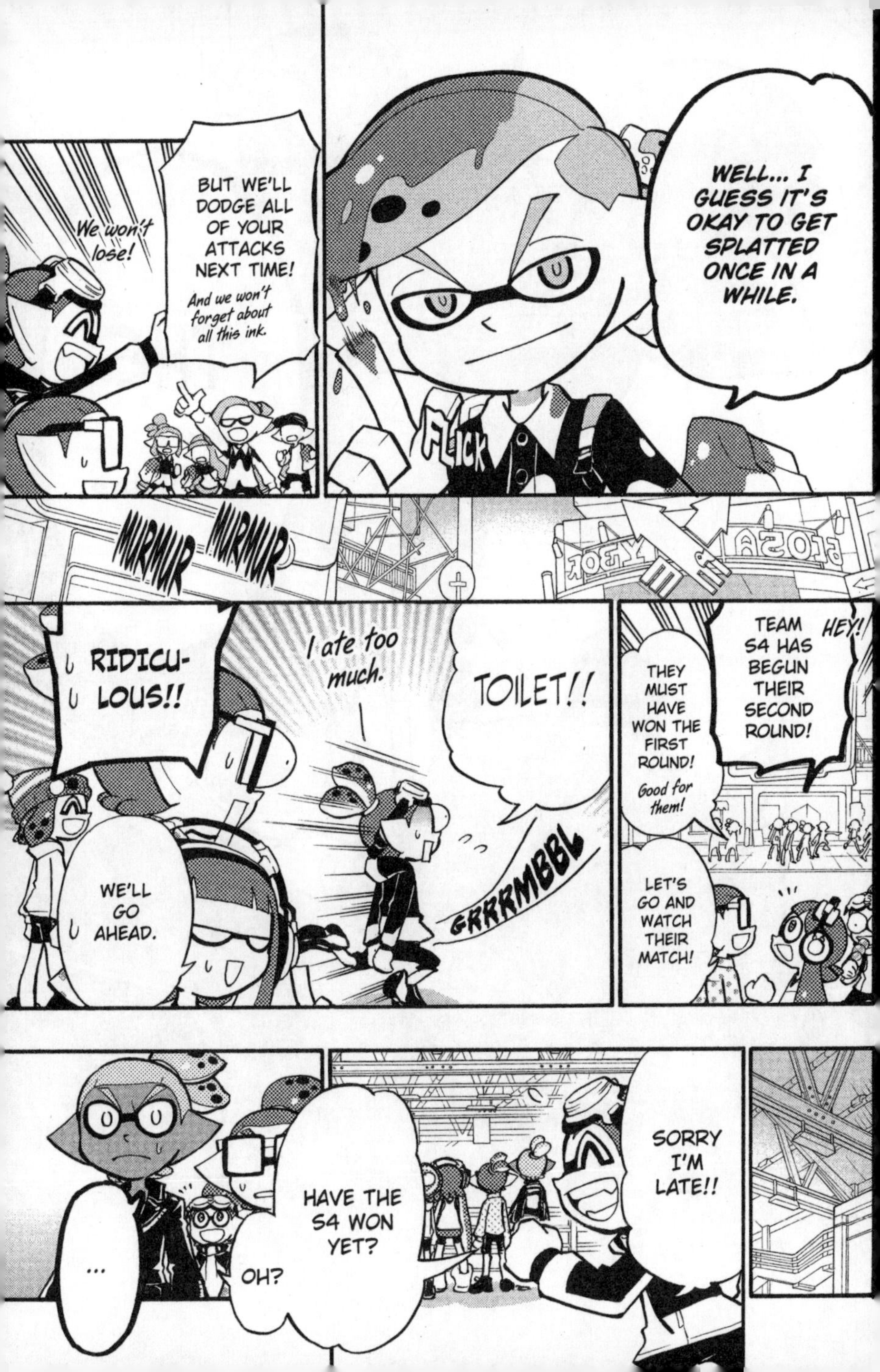
WELL... I GUESS IT'S OKAY TO GET SPLATTED ONCE IN A WHILE.
FLICK
BUT WE'LL DODGE ALL OF YOUR ATTACKS NEXT TIME!
And we won't forget about all this ink.
We won't lose!
MURMUR
MURMUR
HEY!
TEAM S4 HAS BEGUN THEIR SECOND ROUND!
THEY MUST HAVE WON THE FIRST ROUND!
Good for them!
LET'S GO AND WATCH THEIR MATCH!
TOILET!!
I ate too much.
GRRRMBBL
RIDICU-LOUS!!
WE'LL GO AHEAD.
SORRY I'M LATE!!
HAVE THE S4 WON YET?
OH?
...

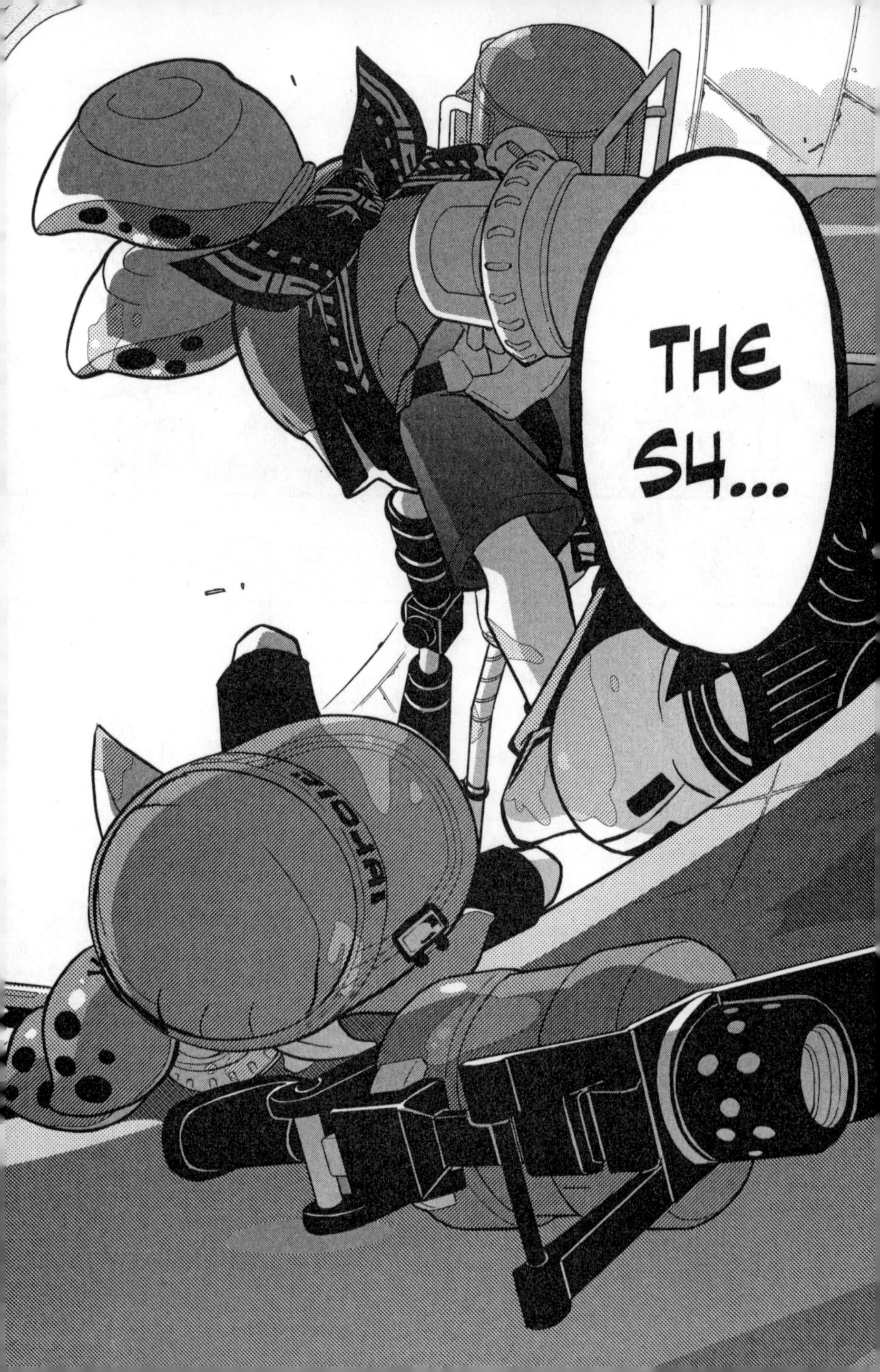
THE S4...

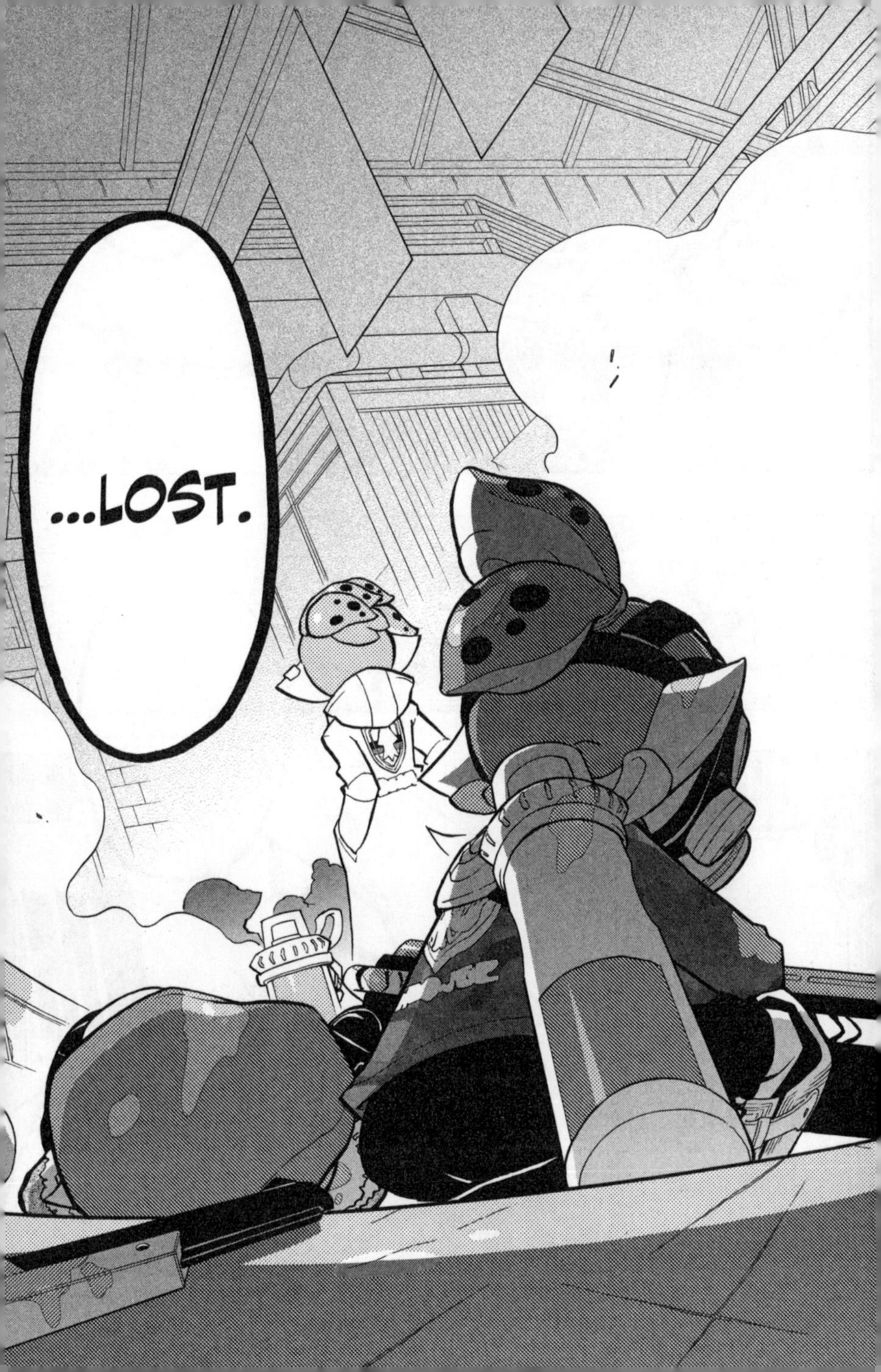
...LOST.

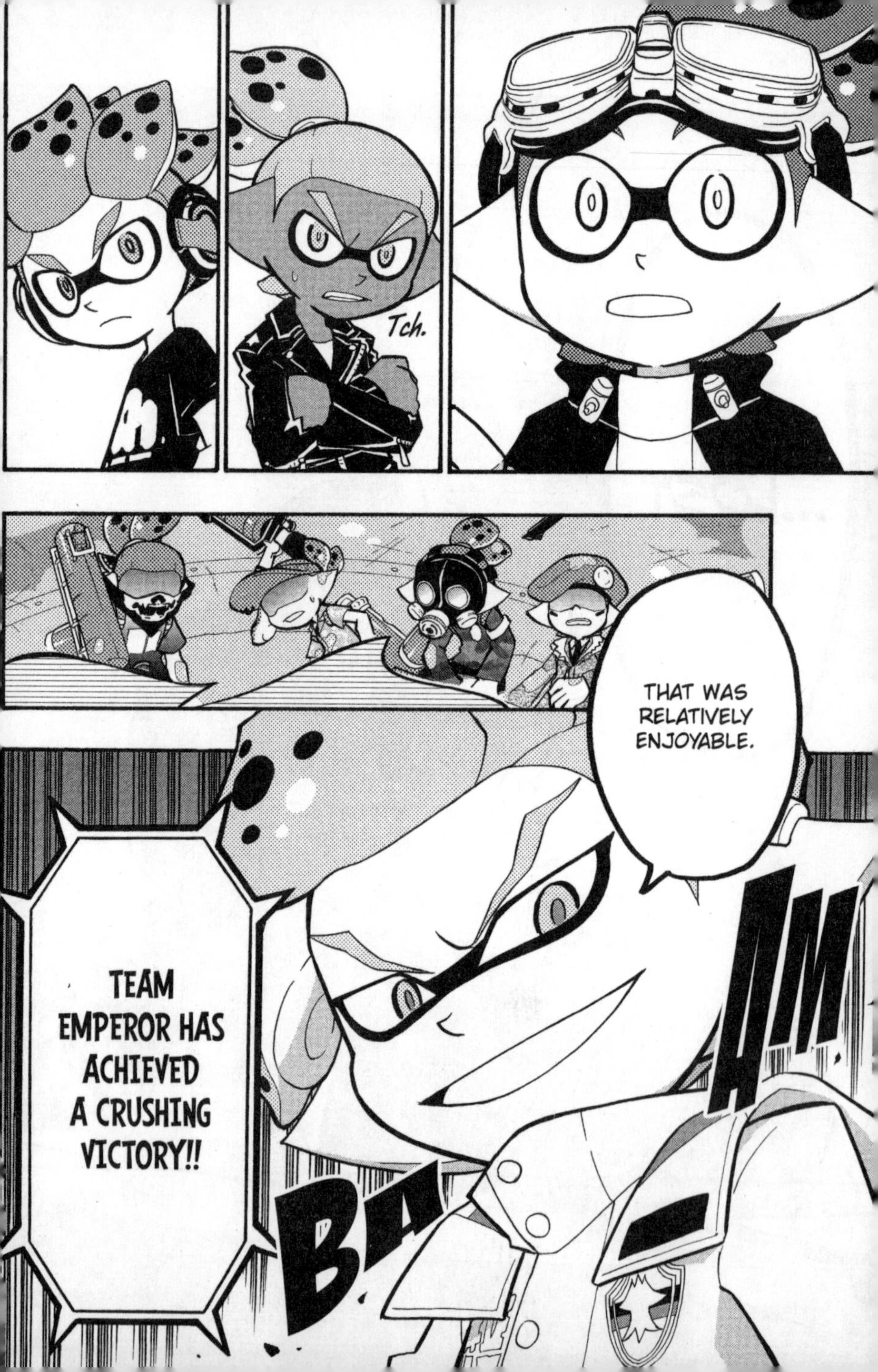
Tch.
THAT WAS RELATIVELY ENJOYABLE.
BAAM!
TEAM EMPEROR HAS ACHIEVED A CRUSHING VICTORY!!

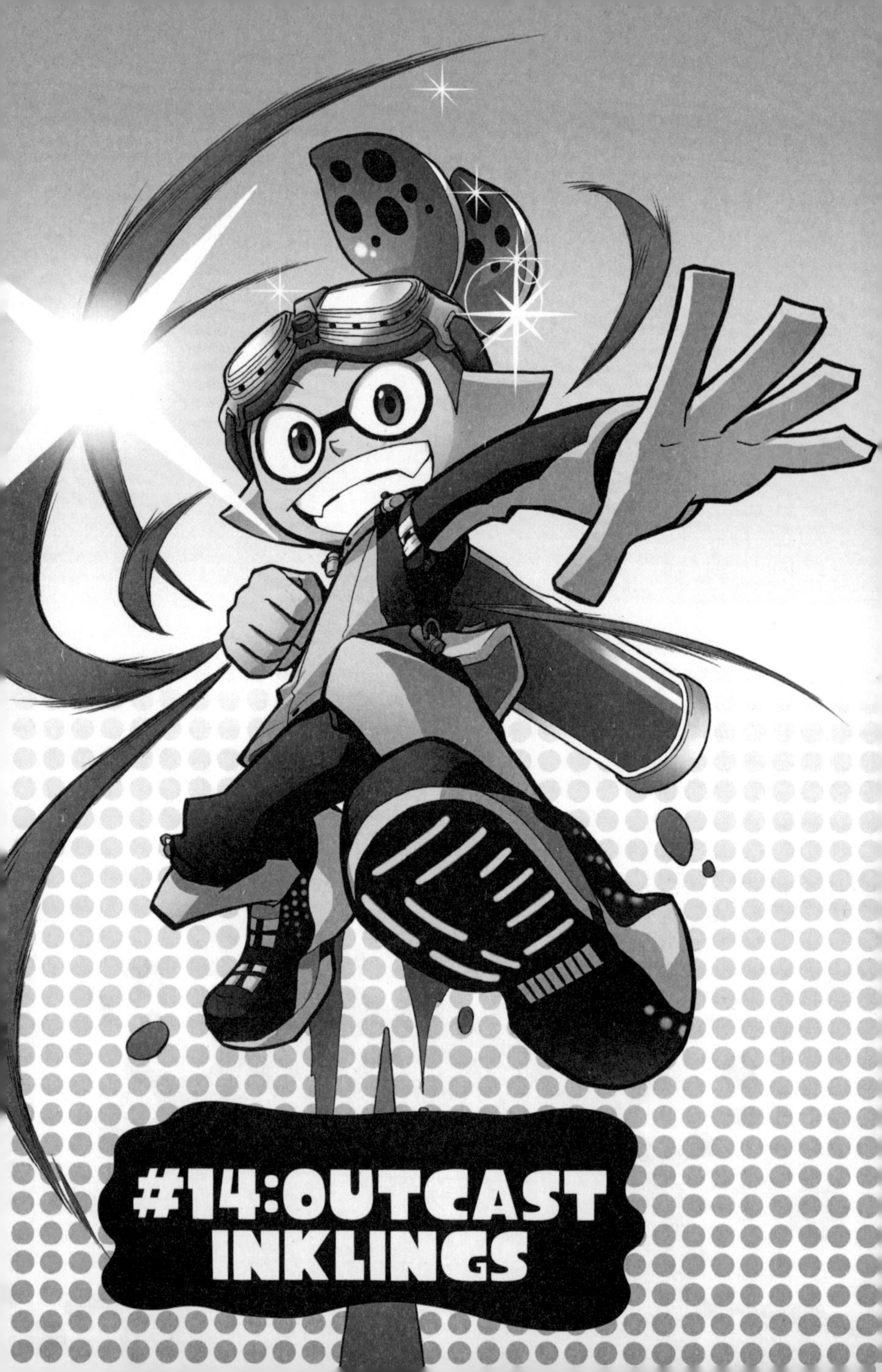
#14: OUTCAST INKLINGS

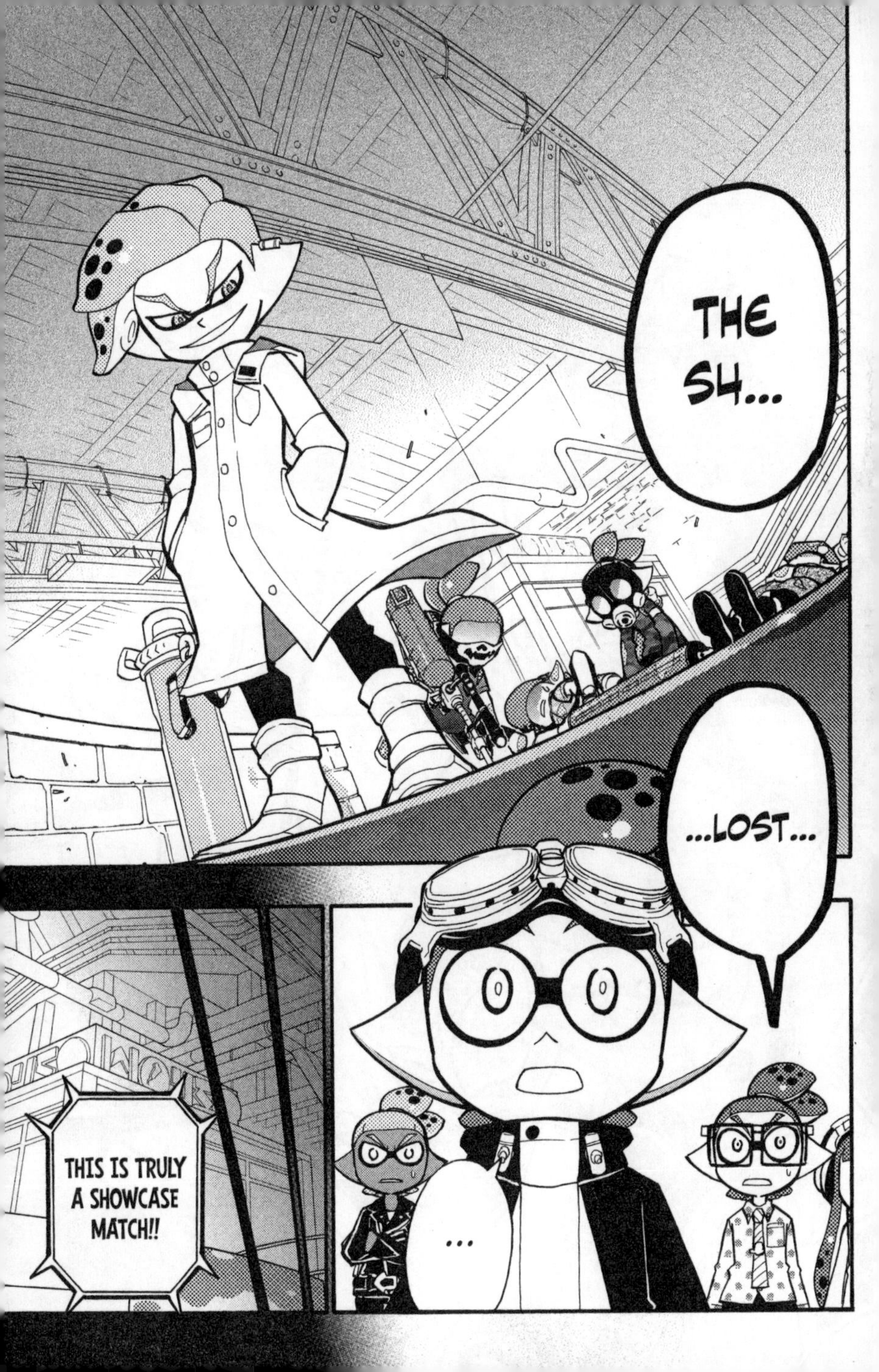
THE S4...
...LOST...
...
THIS IS TRULY A SHOWCASE MATCH!!

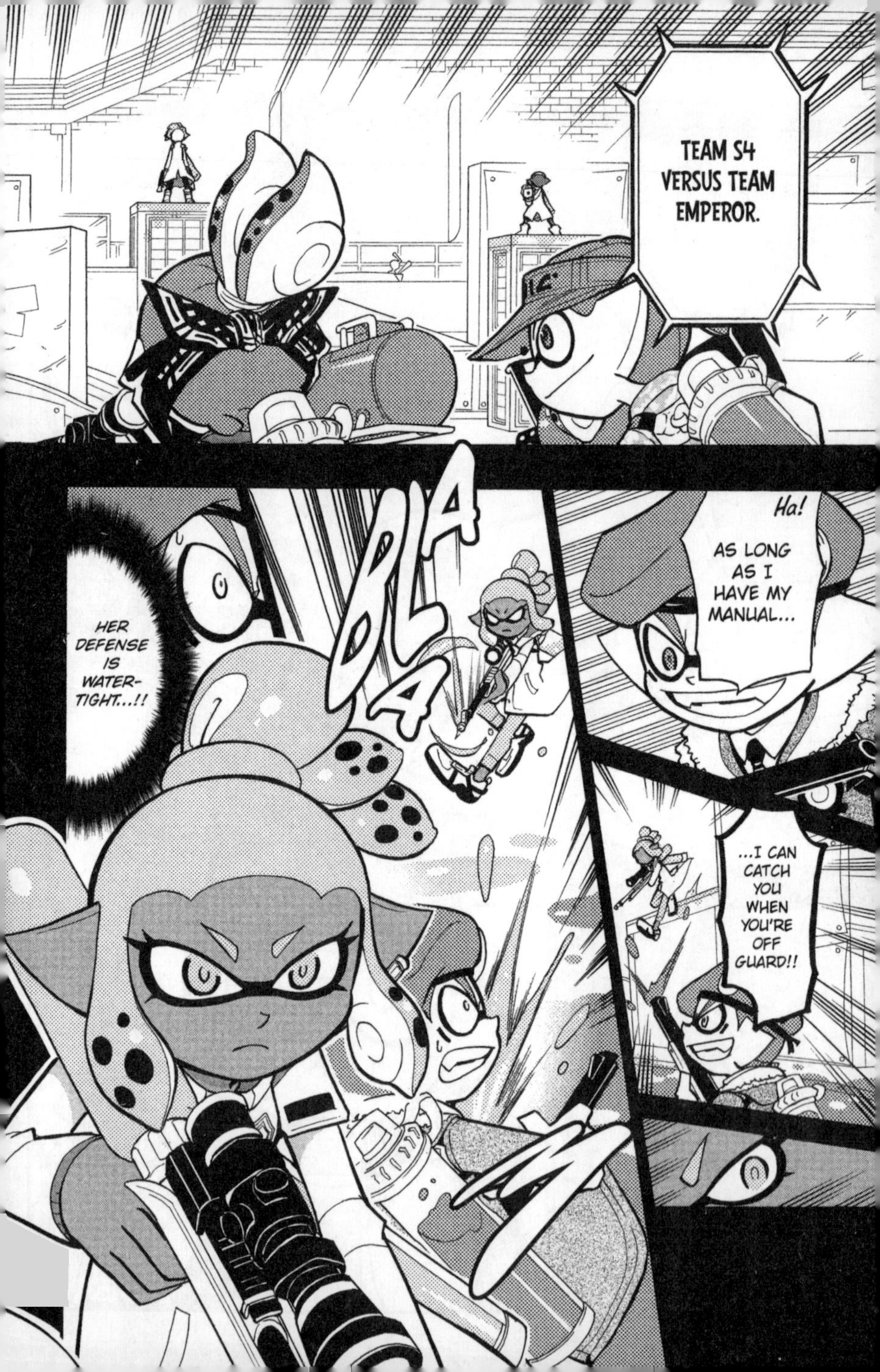
TEAM S4 VERSUS TEAM EMPEROR.
Ha!
AS LONG AS I HAVE MY MANUAL...
...I CAN CATCH YOU WHEN YOU'RE OFF GUARD!!
BLAA
HER DEFENSE IS WATER-TIGHT...!!

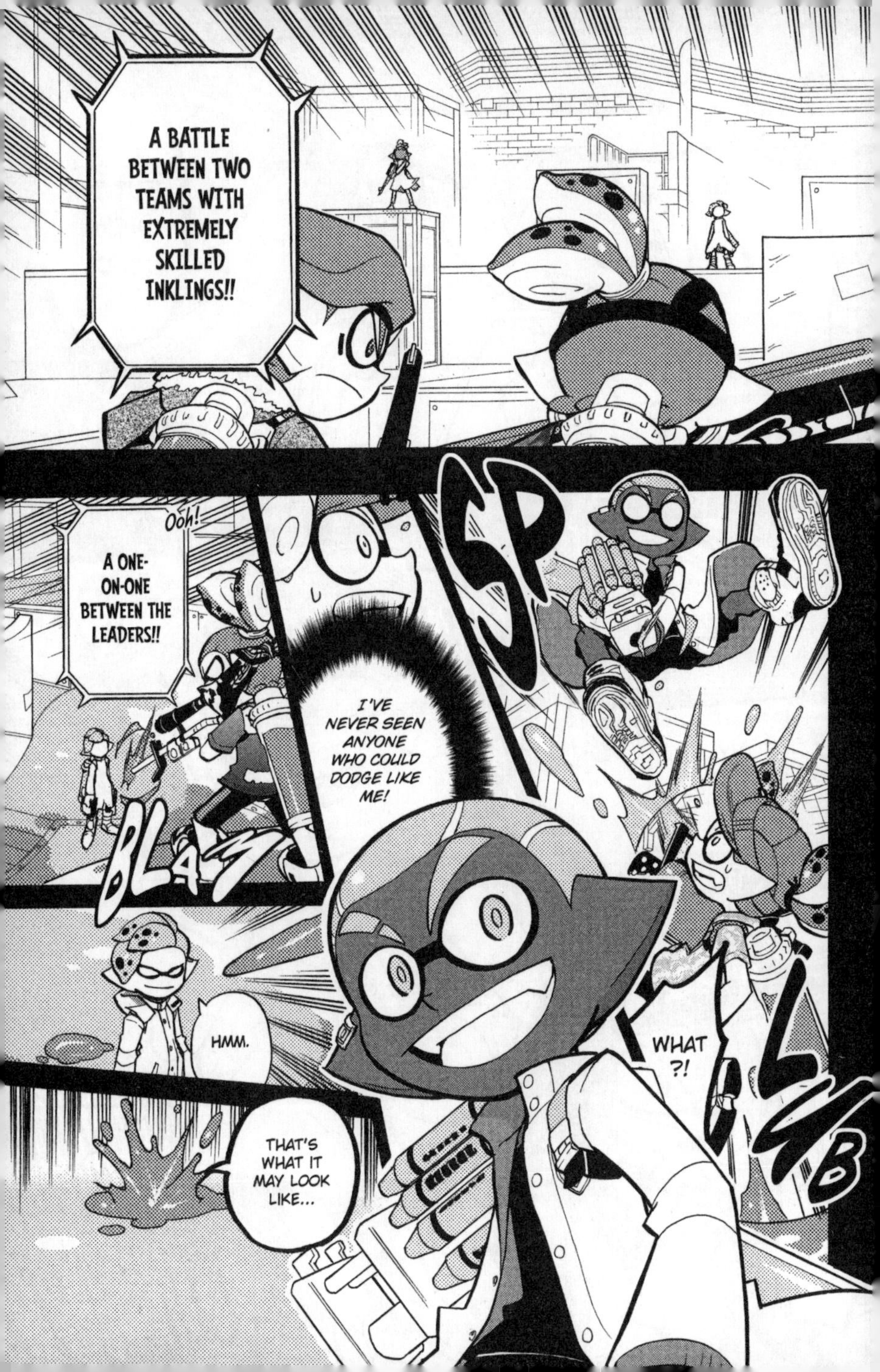
A BATTLE BETWEEN TWO TEAMS WITH EXTREMELY SKILLED INKLINGS!!
SP
I'VE NEVER SEEN ANYONE WHO COULD DODGE LIKE ME!
Ooh!
A ONE-ON-ONE BETWEEN THE LEADERS!!
BLAM
WHAT?!
HMM.
THAT'S WHAT IT MAY LOOK LIKE...

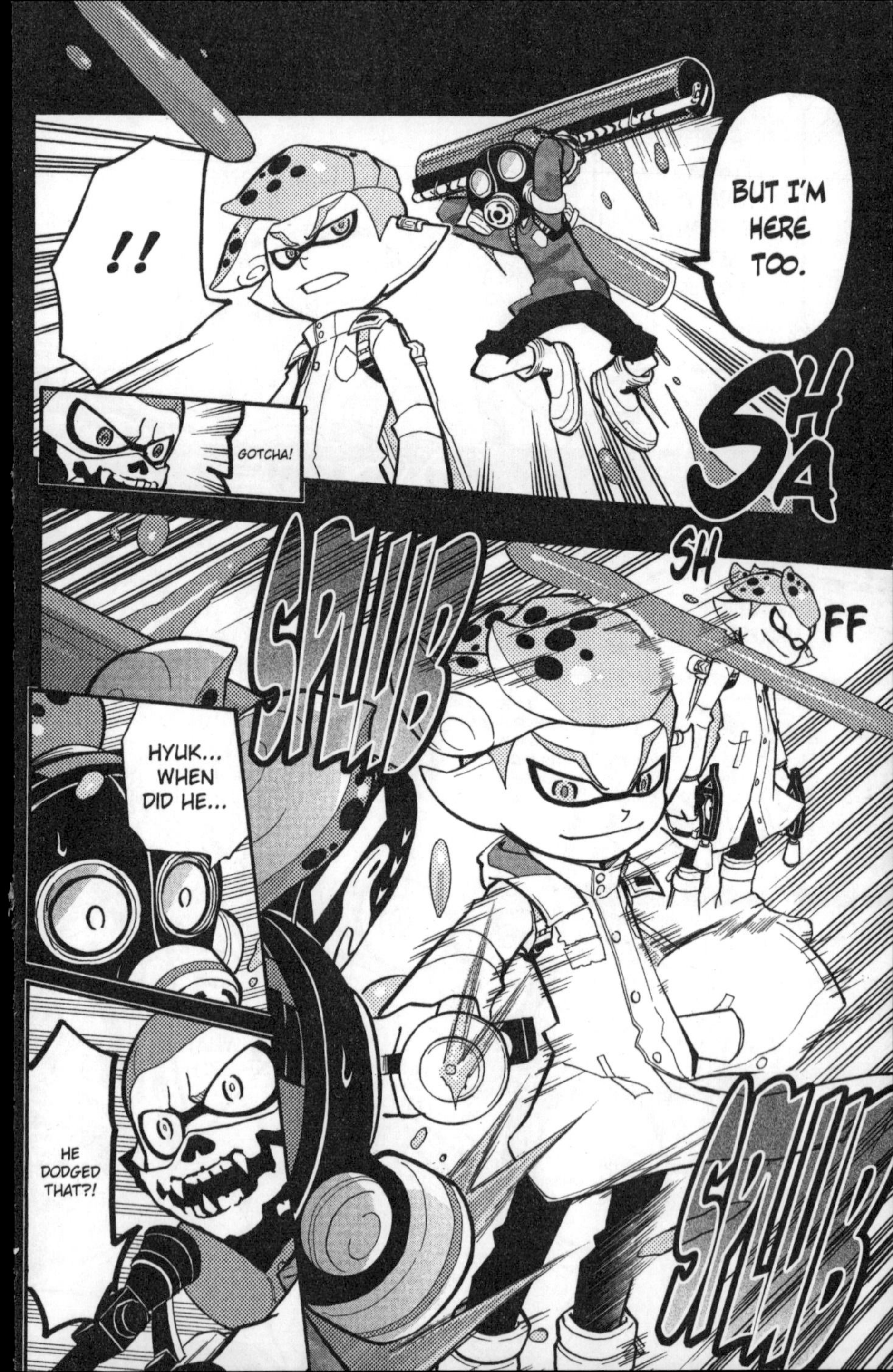
BUT I'M HERE TOO.
SHA
!!
GOTCHA!
SH FF
SPLUB
HYUK... WHEN DID HE...
SPLUB
HE DODGED THAT?!

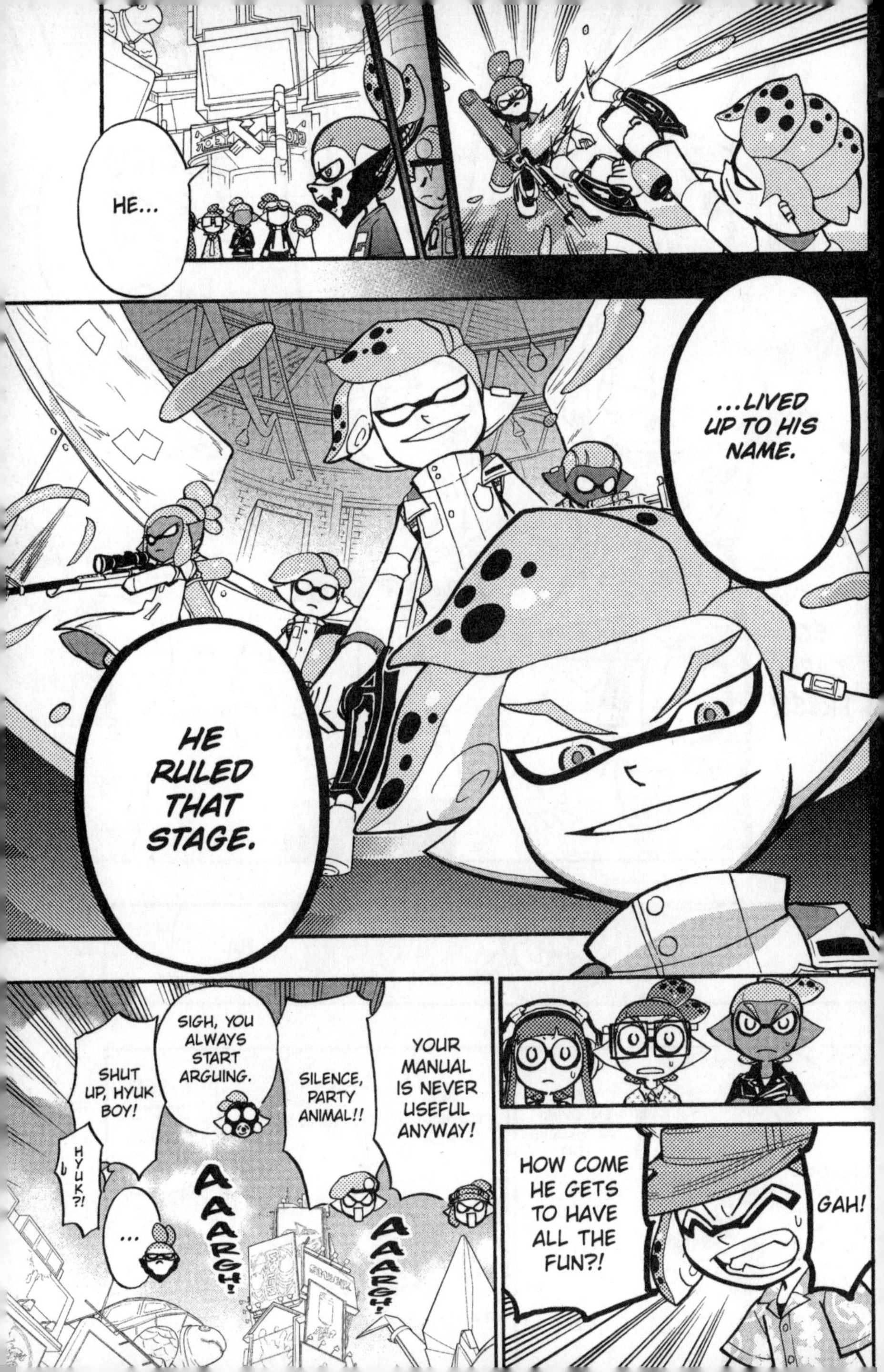
HE...
...LIVED UP TO HIS NAME.
HE RULED THAT STAGE.
GAH!
HOW COME HE GETS TO HAVE ALL THE FUN?!
YOUR MANUAL IS NEVER USEFUL ANYWAY!
SILENCE, PARTY ANIMAL!!
SIGH, YOU ALWAYS START ARGUING.
SHUT UP, HYUK BOY!
AAAARGH!
AAAARGH!
HYUK?!
...

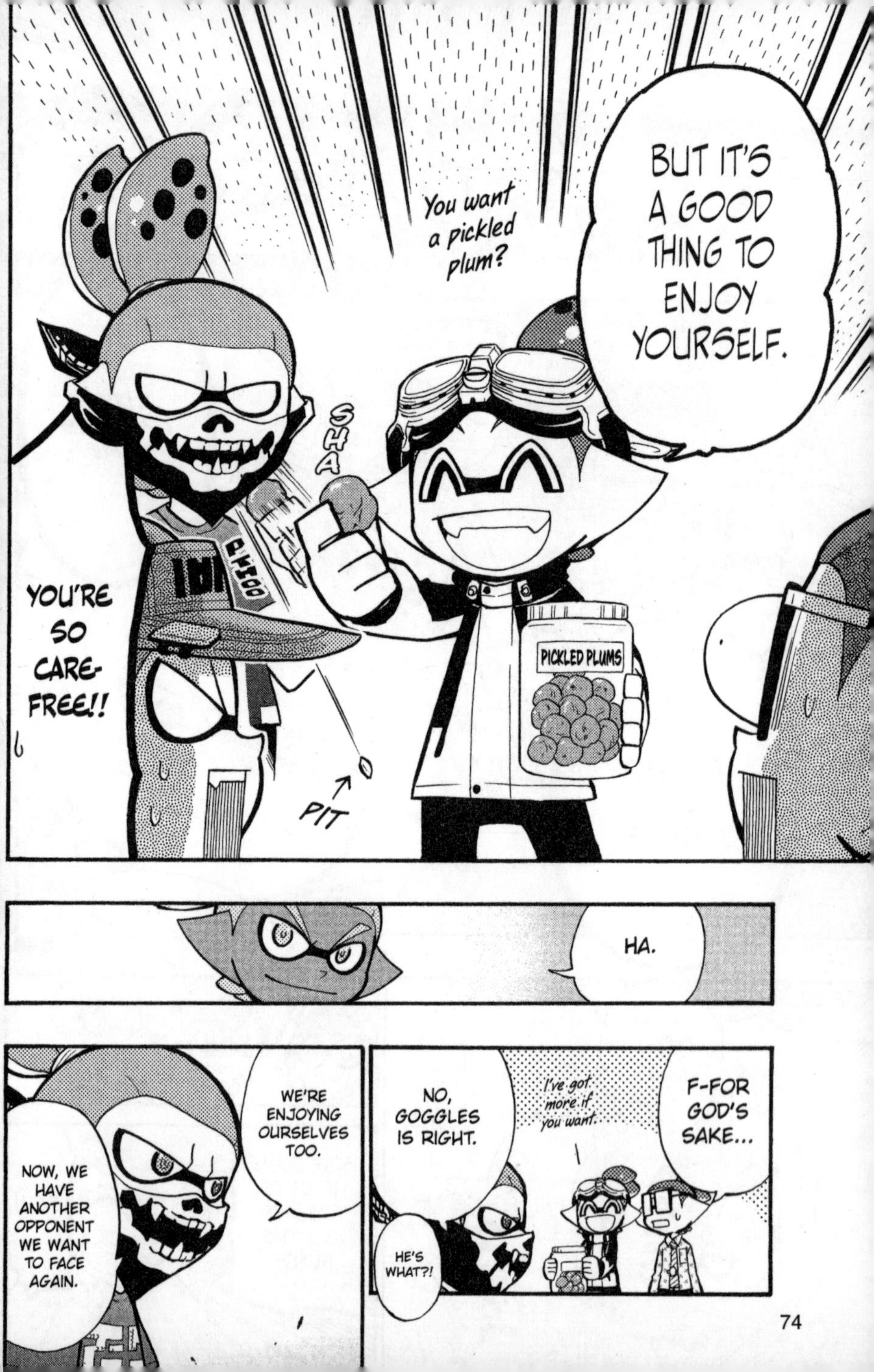
BUT IT'S A GOOD THING TO ENJOY YOURSELF.
You want a pickled plum?
SHA
PICKLED PLUMS
YOU'RE SO CARE-FREE!!
PIT
HA.
F-FOR GOD'S SAKE...
I've got more if you want.
NO, GOGGLES IS RIGHT.
HE'S WHAT?!
WE'RE ENJOYING OURSELVES TOO.
NOW, WE HAVE ANOTHER OPPONENT WE WANT TO FACE AGAIN.

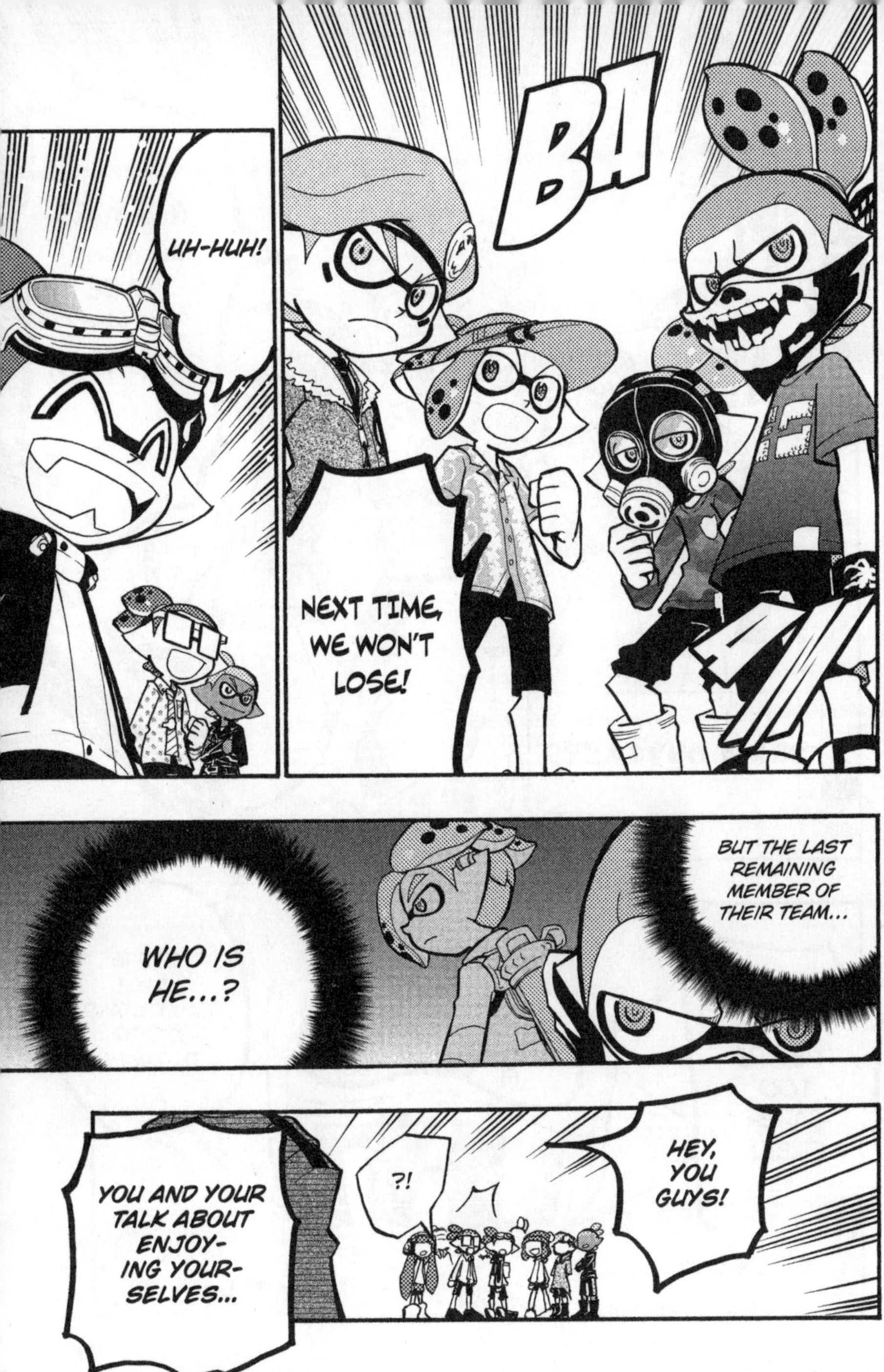
BA
NEXT TIME, WE WON'T LOSE!
UH-HUH!
BUT THE LAST REMAINING MEMBER OF THEIR TEAM...
WHO IS HE...?
HEY, YOU GUYS!
?!
YOU AND YOUR TALK ABOUT ENJOY-ING YOUR-SELVES...

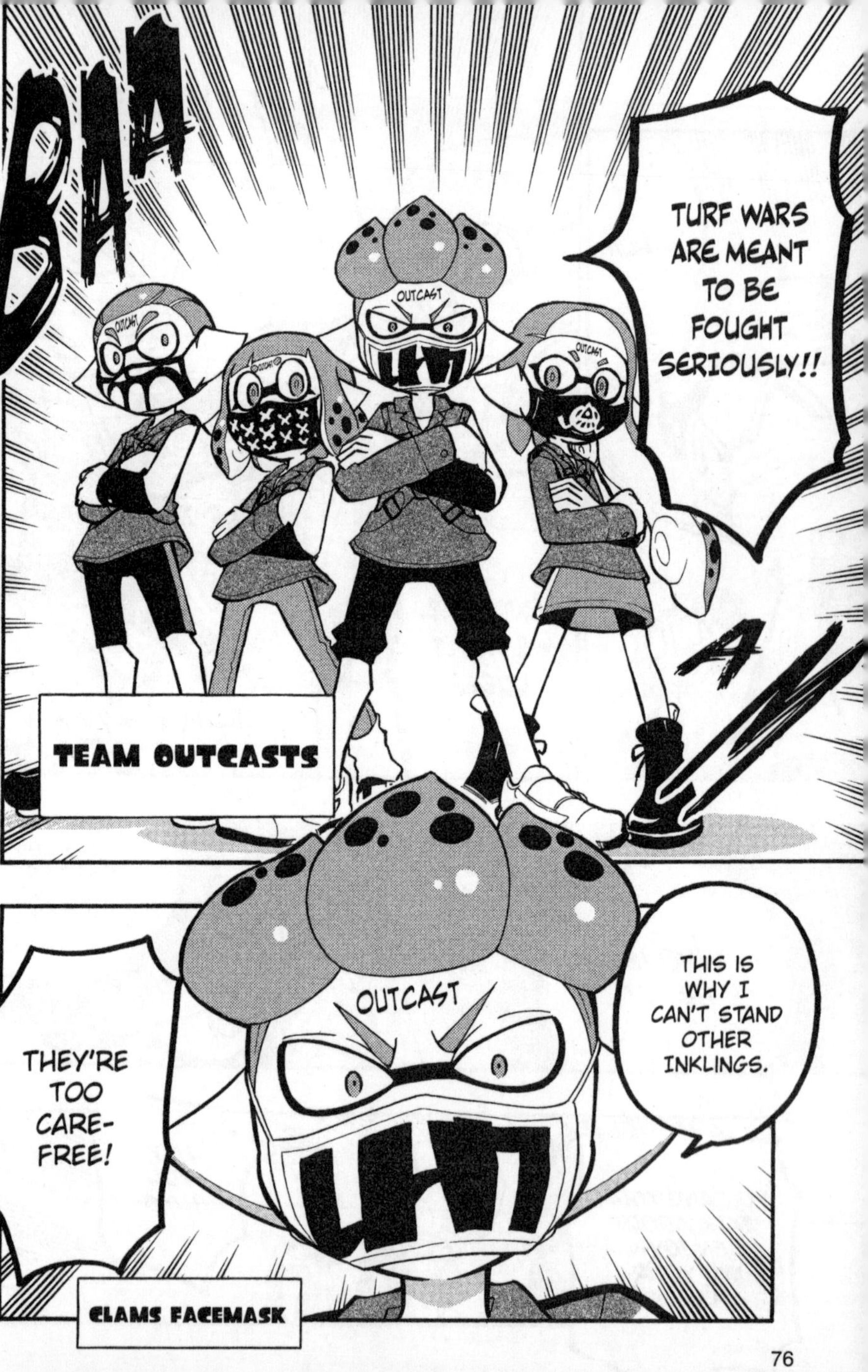
TURF WARS ARE MEANT TO BE FOUGHT SERIOUSLY!!
BA
AM
TEAM OUTCASTS
THIS IS WHY I CAN'T STAND OTHER INKLINGS.
OUTCAST
THEY'RE TOO CARE-FREE!
CLAMS FACEMASK

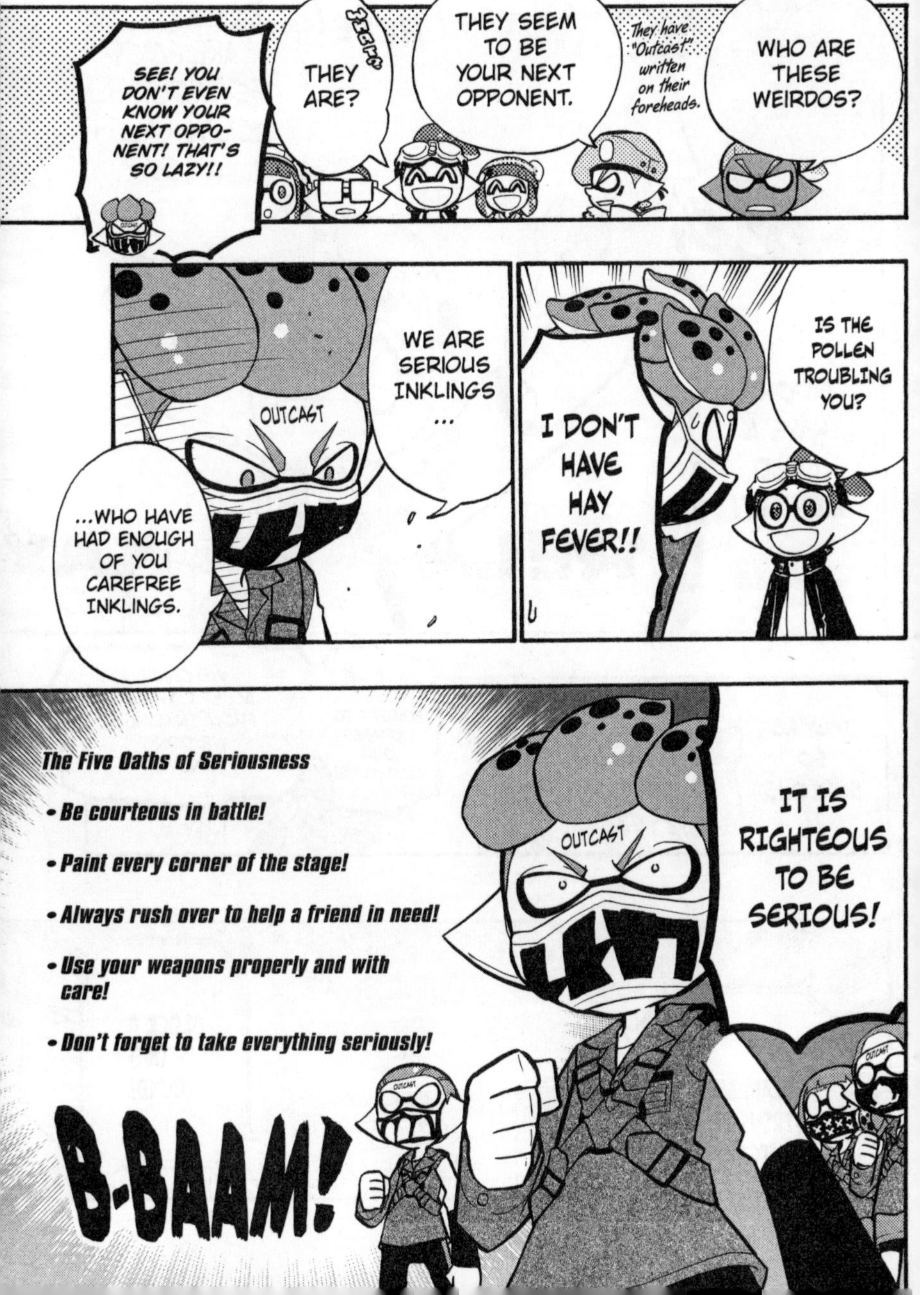
WHO ARE THESE WEIRDOS?
They have "Outcast" written on their foreheads.
THEY SEEM TO BE YOUR NEXT OPPONENT.
THEY ARE?
SEE! YOU DON'T EVEN KNOW YOUR NEXT OPPO-NENT! THAT'S SO LAZY!!
OUTCAST
IS THE POLLEN TROUBLING YOU?
I DON'T HAVE HAY FEVER!!
OUTCAST
WE ARE SERIOUS INKLINGS ...
...WHO HAVE HAD ENOUGH OF YOU CAREFREE INKLINGS.
IT IS RIGHTEOUS TO BE SERIOUS!
OUTCAST
The Five Oaths of Seriousness
• Be courteous in battle!
• Paint every corner of the stage!
• Always rush over to help a friend in need!
• Use your weapons properly and with care!
• Don't forget to take everything seriously!
B-BAAM!

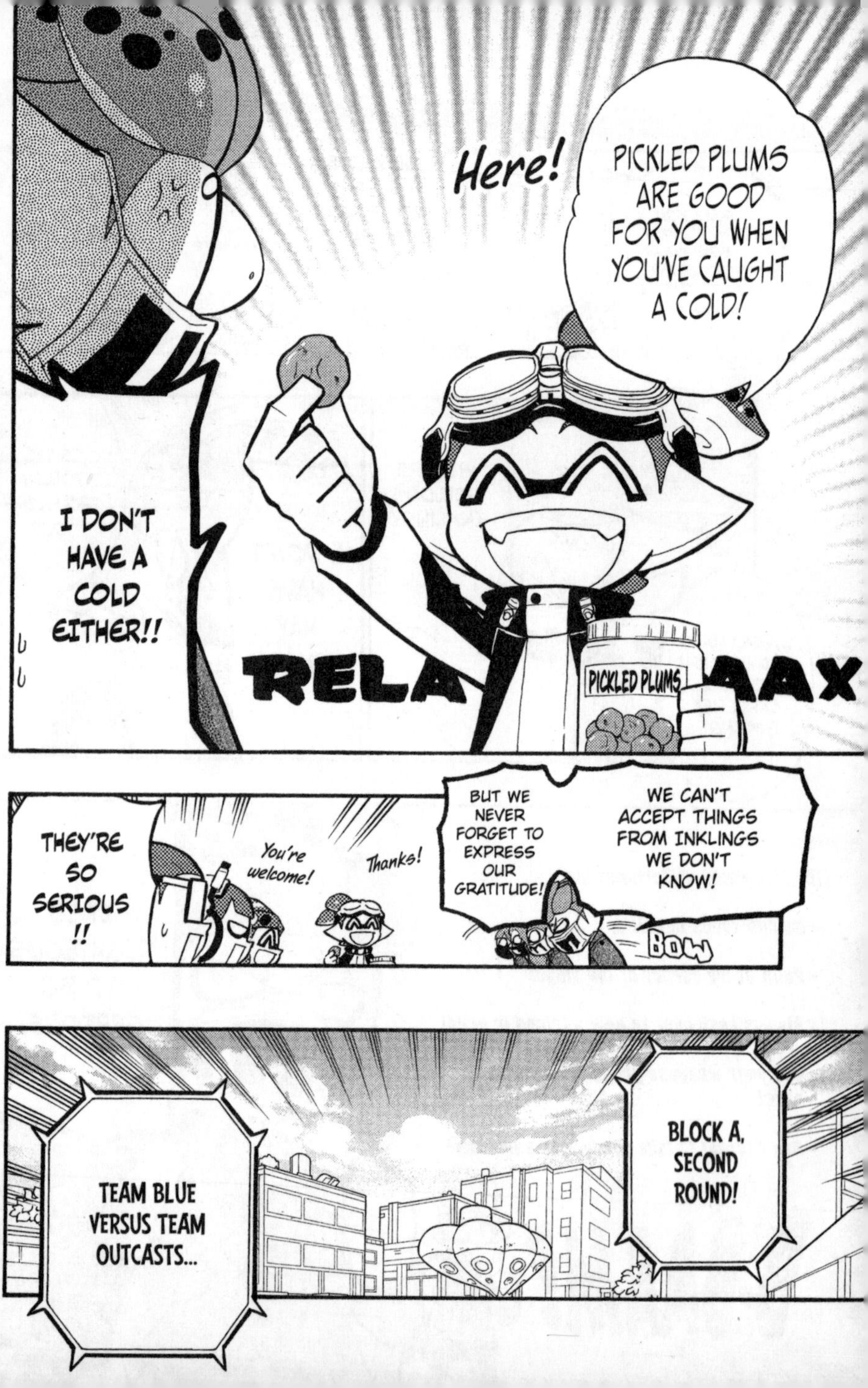
PICKLED PLUMS ARE GOOD FOR YOU WHEN YOU'VE CAUGHT A COLD!
Here!
RELA
AAX
PICKLED PLUMS
I DON'T HAVE A COLD EITHER!!
WE CAN'T ACCEPT THINGS FROM INKLINGS WE DON'T KNOW!
BUT WE NEVER FORGET TO EXPRESS OUR GRATITUDE!
BOW
Thanks!
You're welcome!
THEY'RE SO SERIOUS!!
BLOCK A, SECOND ROUND!
TEAM BLUE VERSUS TEAM OUTCASTS...

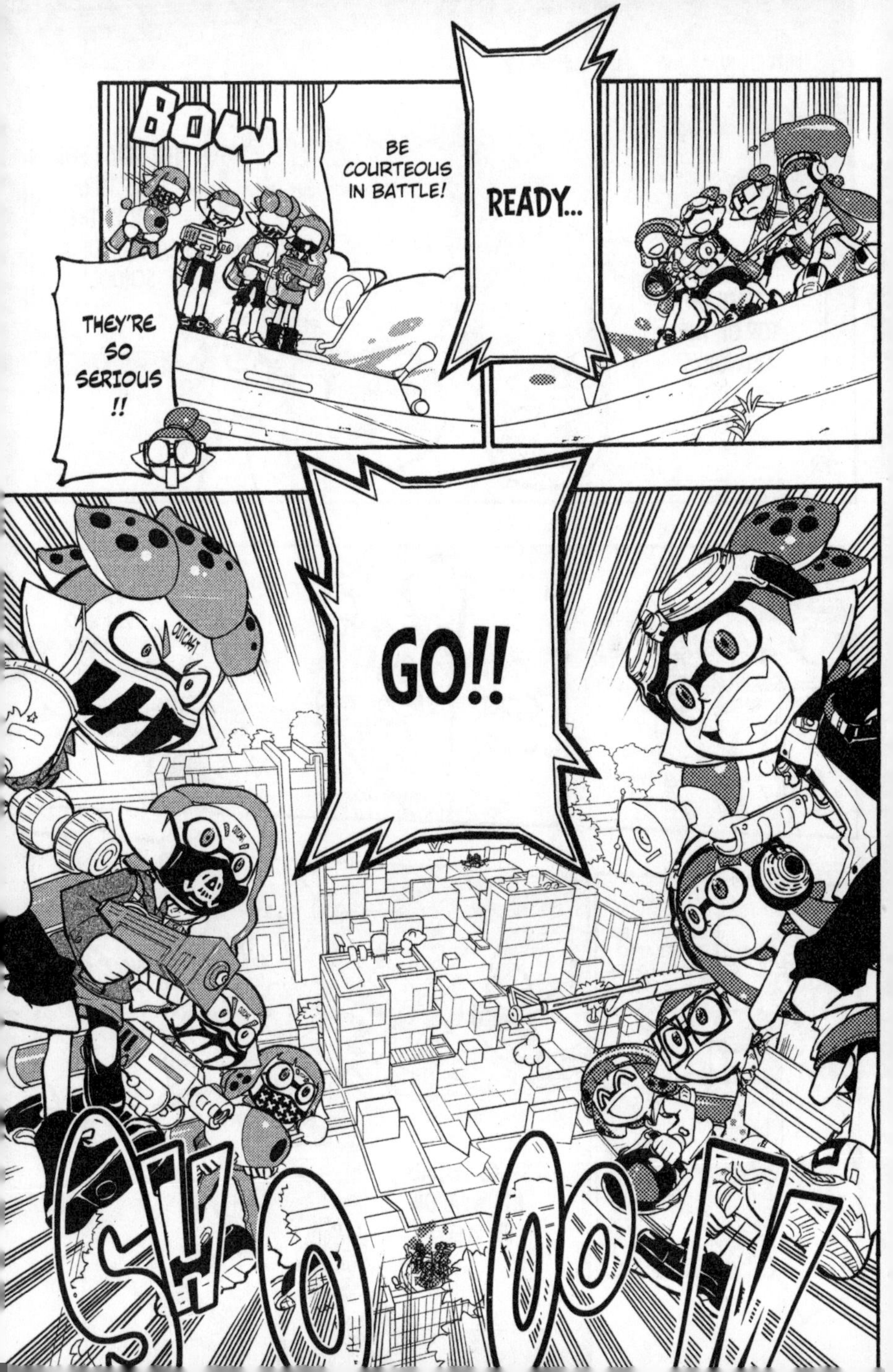
BOW
BE COURTEOUS IN BATTLE!
THEY'RE SO SERIOUS!!
READY...
GO!!

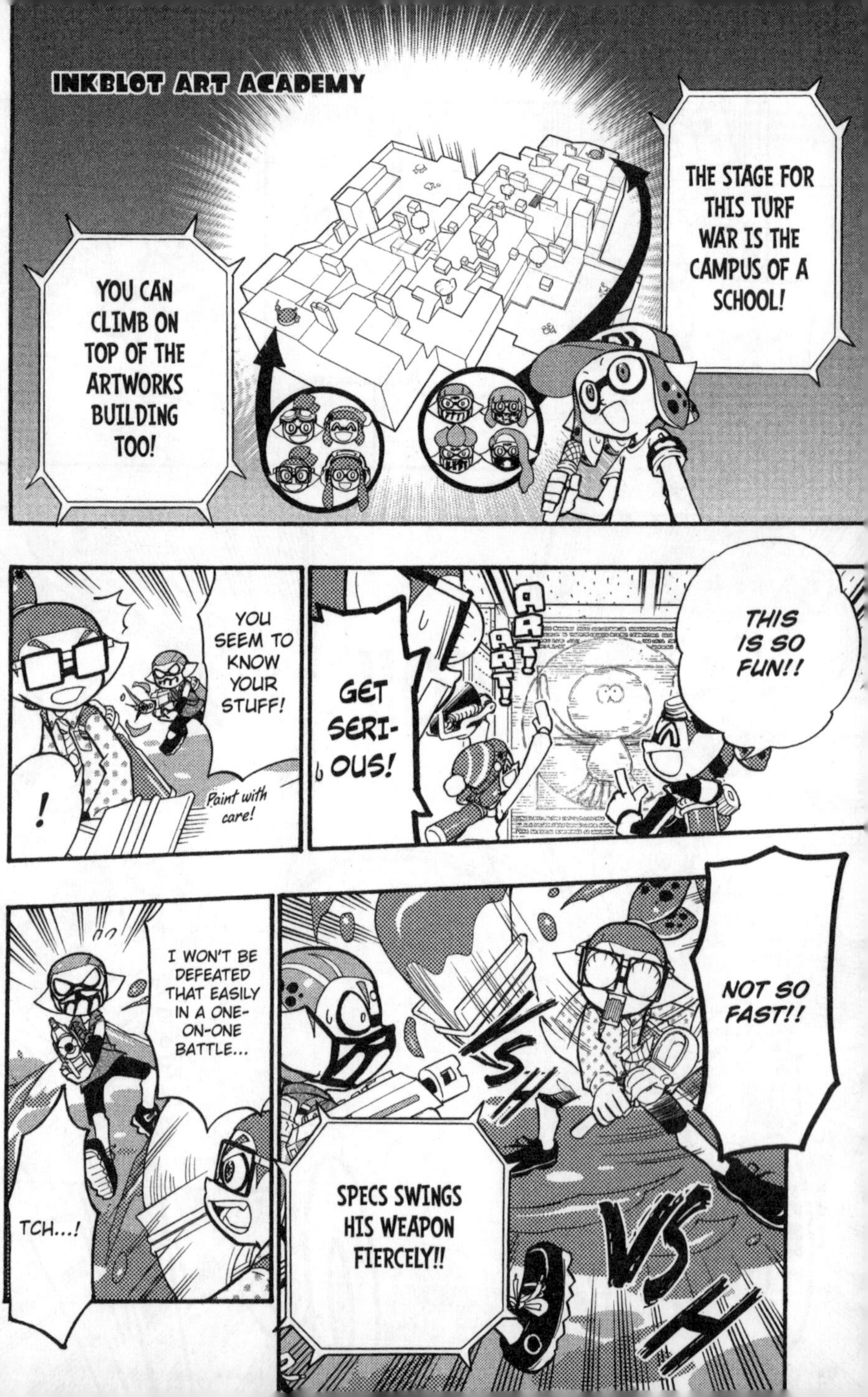
INKBLOT ART ACADEMY
THE STAGE FOR THIS TURF WAR IS THE CAMPUS OF A SCHOOL!
YOU CAN CLIMB ON TOP OF THE ARTWORKS BUILDING TOO!
THIS IS SO FUN!!
ART ART
GET SERI-OUS!
YOU SEEM TO KNOW YOUR STUFF!
Paint with care!
!
NOT SO FAST!!
VSH
SPECS SWINGS HIS WEAPON FIERCELY!!
VSH
I WON'T BE DEFEATED THAT EASILY IN A ONE-ON-ONE BATTLE...
TCH...!

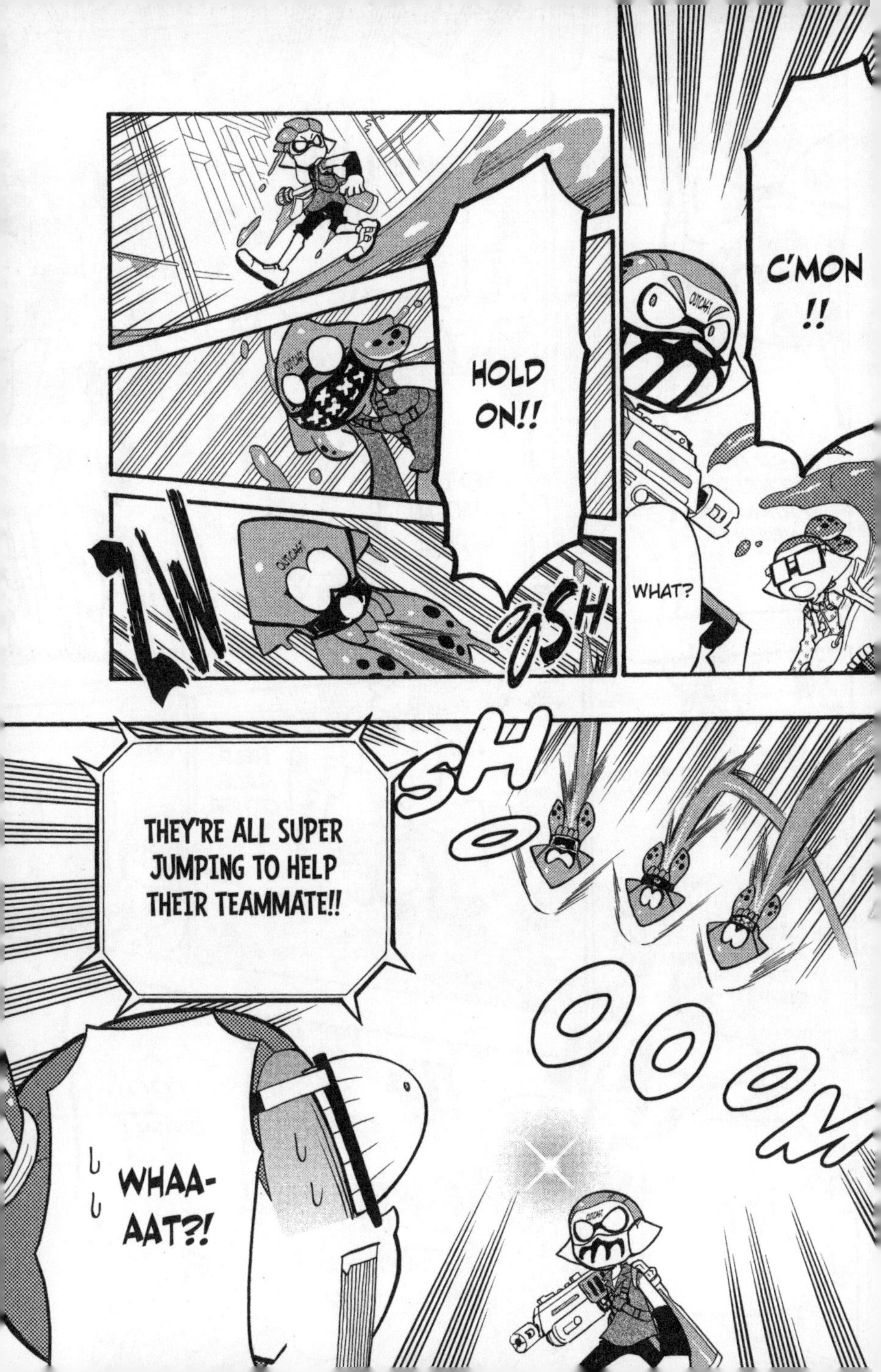
C'MON!!
HOLD ON!!
WHAT?
ZW
OSH
SH
O
OOOM
THEY'RE ALL SUPER JUMPING TO HELP THEIR TEAMMATE!!
WHAA-AAT?!

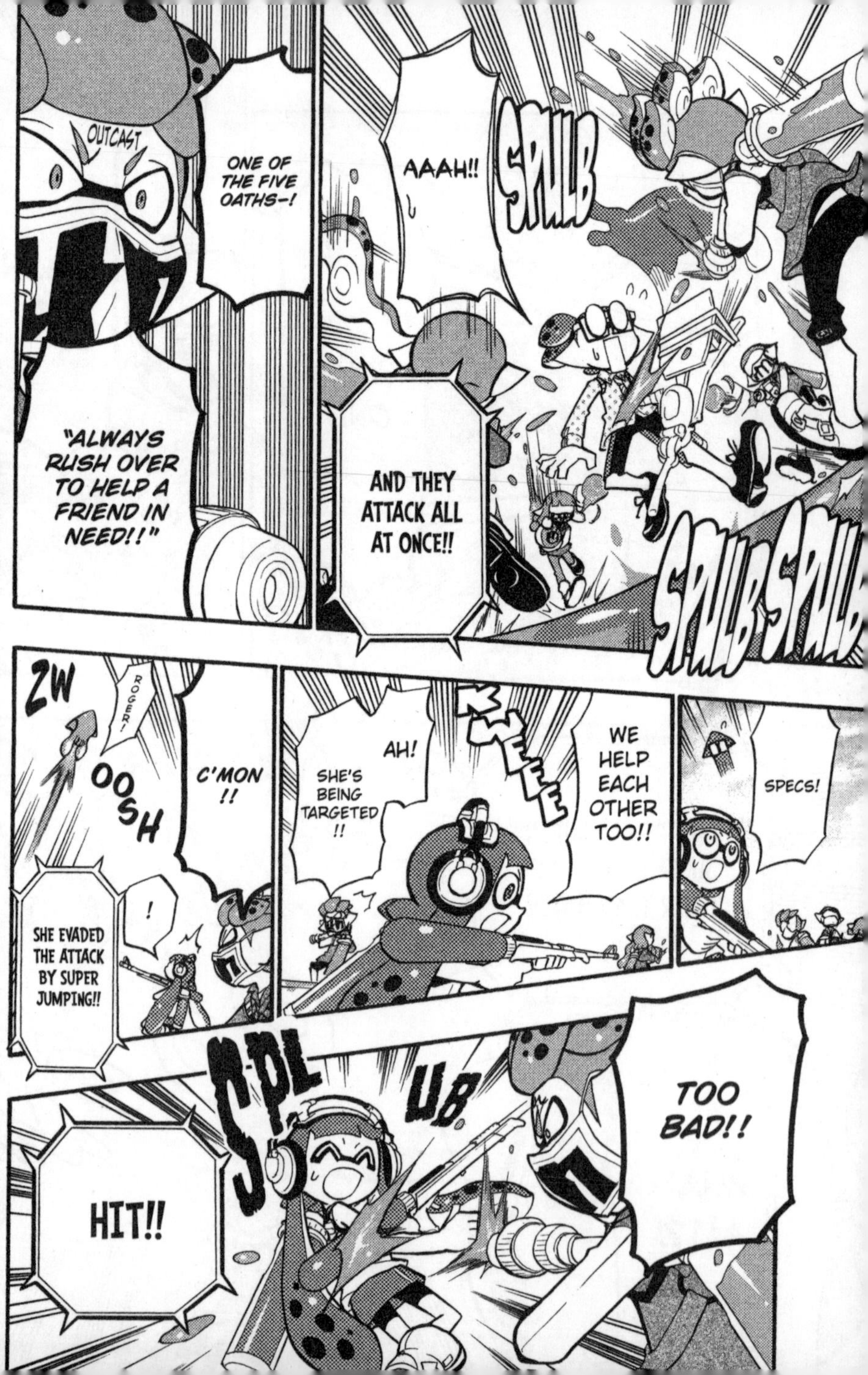
AAAH!!
SPULB
AND THEY ATTACK ALL AT ONCE!!
SPULB SPULB
OUTCAST
ONE OF THE FIVE OATHS-!
"ALWAYS RUSH OVER TO HELP A FRIEND IN NEED!!"
SPECS!
KWEEE
WE HELP EACH OTHER TOO!!
AH!
SHE'S BEING TARGETED !!
C'MON !!
ROGER!
ZW
OOSH
!
SHE EVADED THE ATTACK BY SUPER JUMPING!!
TOO BAD!!
S-PL UB
HIT!!

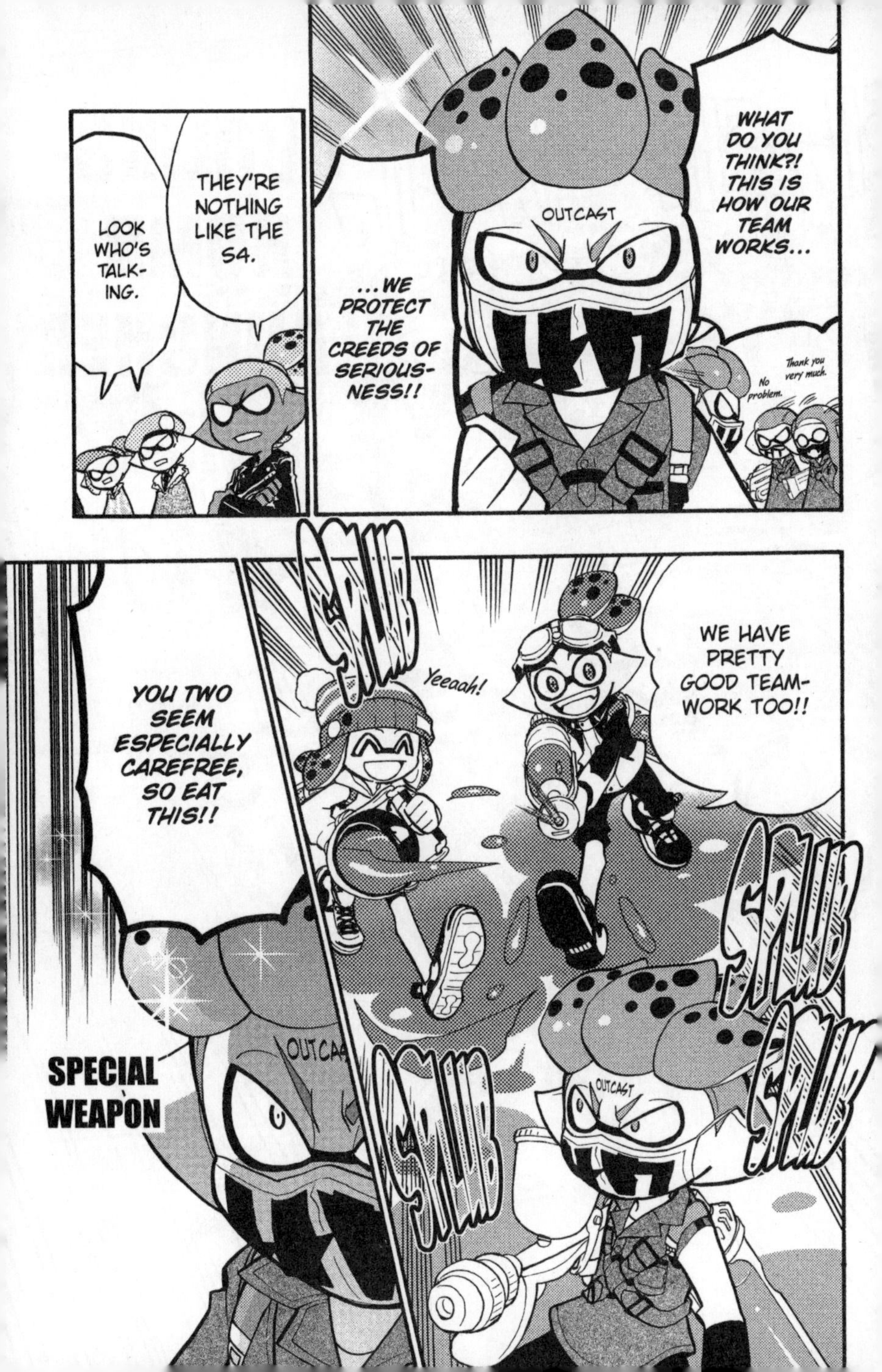
WHAT DO YOU THINK?! THIS IS HOW OUR TEAM WORKS...
OUTCAST
...WE PROTECT THE CREEDS OF SERIOUSNESS!!
Thank you very much.
No problem.
THEY'RE NOTHING LIKE THE S4.
LOOK WHO'S TALKING.
WE HAVE PRETTY GOOD TEAMWORK TOO!!
Yeeaah!
YOU TWO SEEM ESPECIALLY CAREFREE, SO EAT THIS!!
OUTCAST
OUTCAS
SPECIAL WEAPON

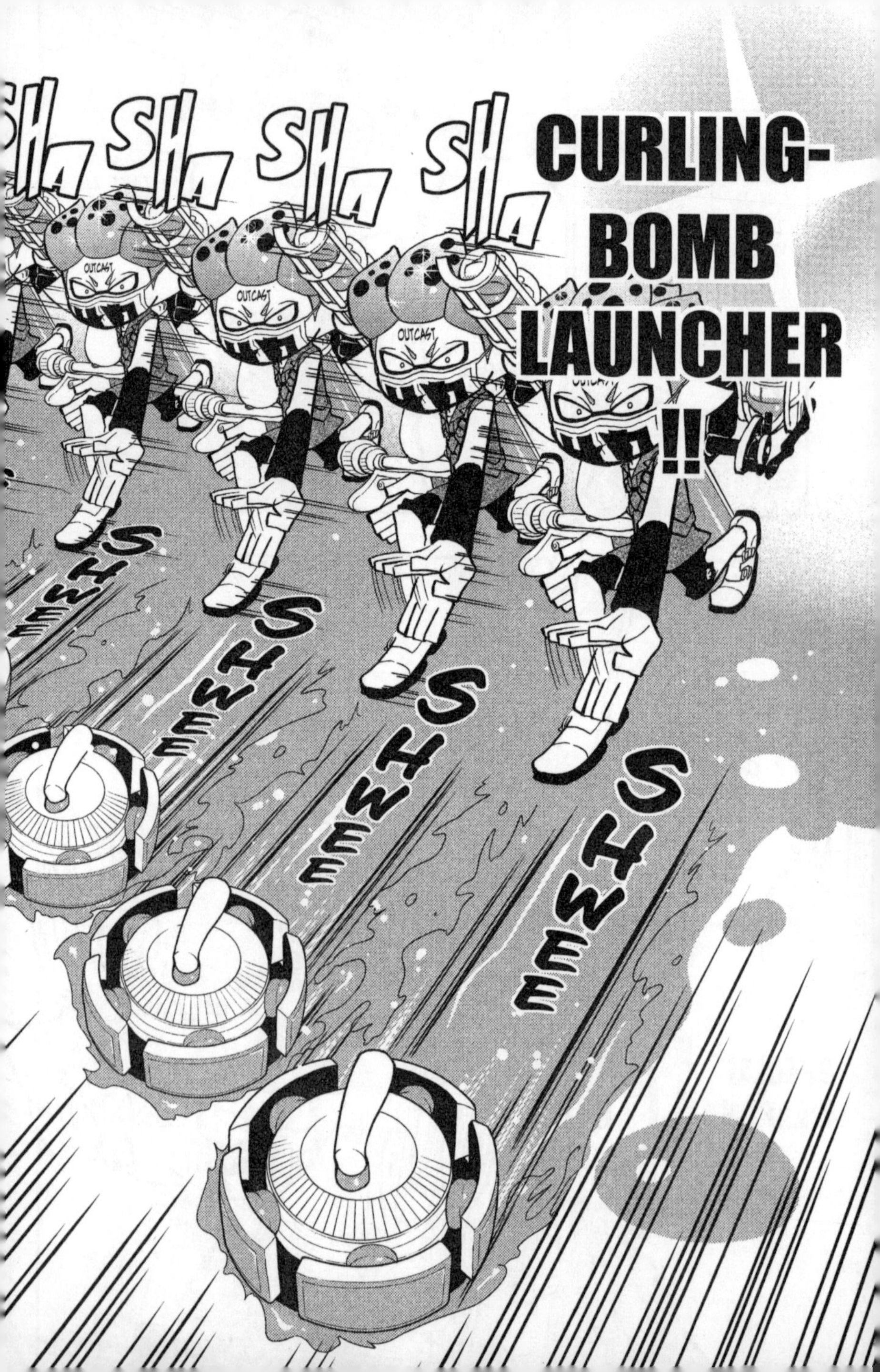
SHA
SHA
SHA
SHA
CURLING-BOMB LAUNCHER!!
OUTCAST
OUTCAST
OUTCAST
SHWEE
SHWEE
SHWEE
SHWEE

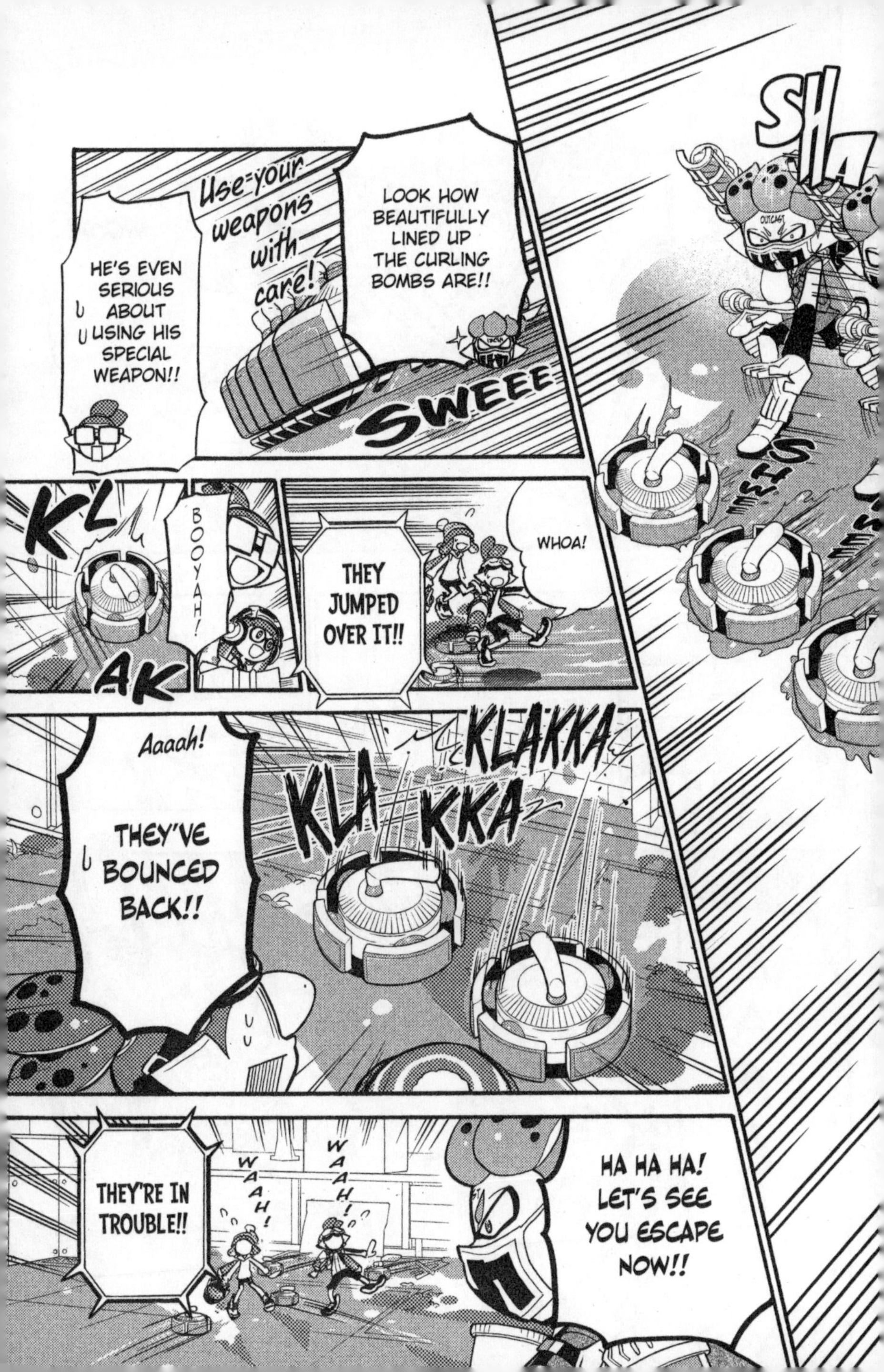
SHA
SHWEE
LOOK HOW BEAUTIFULLY LINED UP THE CURLING BOMBS ARE!!
Use your weapons with care!
HE'S EVEN SERIOUS ABOUT USING HIS SPECIAL WEAPON!!
SWEEE
WHOA!
THEY JUMPED OVER IT!!
BOOYAH!
KLAK
KLAKKA KLAKKA
Aaaah!
THEY'VE BOUNCED BACK!!
HA HA HA! LET'S SEE YOU ESCAPE NOW!!
WAAH!
WAAH!
THEY'RE IN TROUBLE!!

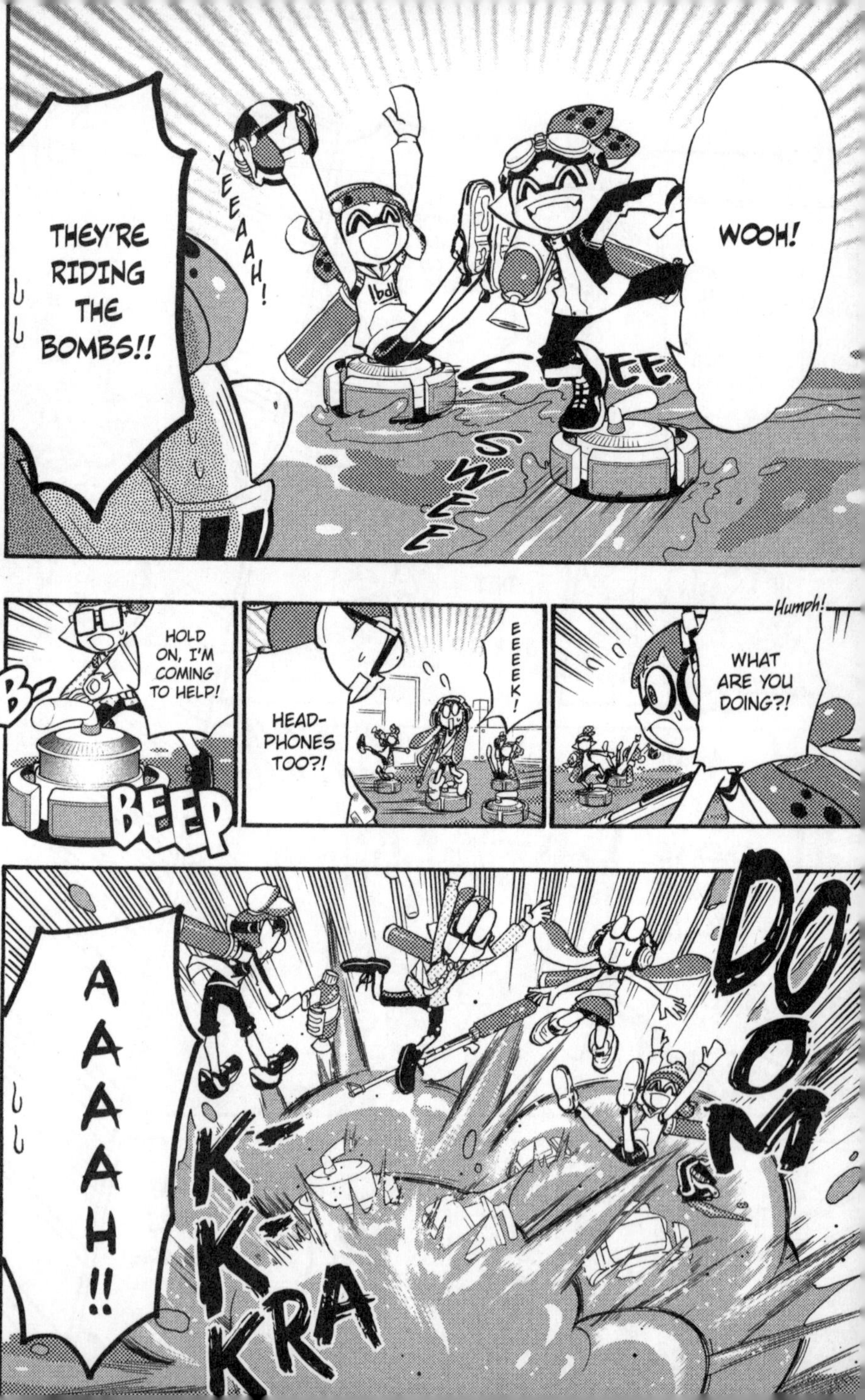
WOOH!
SWEE
YEEAAAH!
THEY'RE RIDING THE BOMBS!!
SWEE
Humph!
WHAT ARE YOU DOING?!
EEEEK!
HEAD-PHONES TOO?!
HOLD ON, I'M COMING TO HELP!
B-
BEEP
DOOOM
K-K-KRA
AAAAH!!

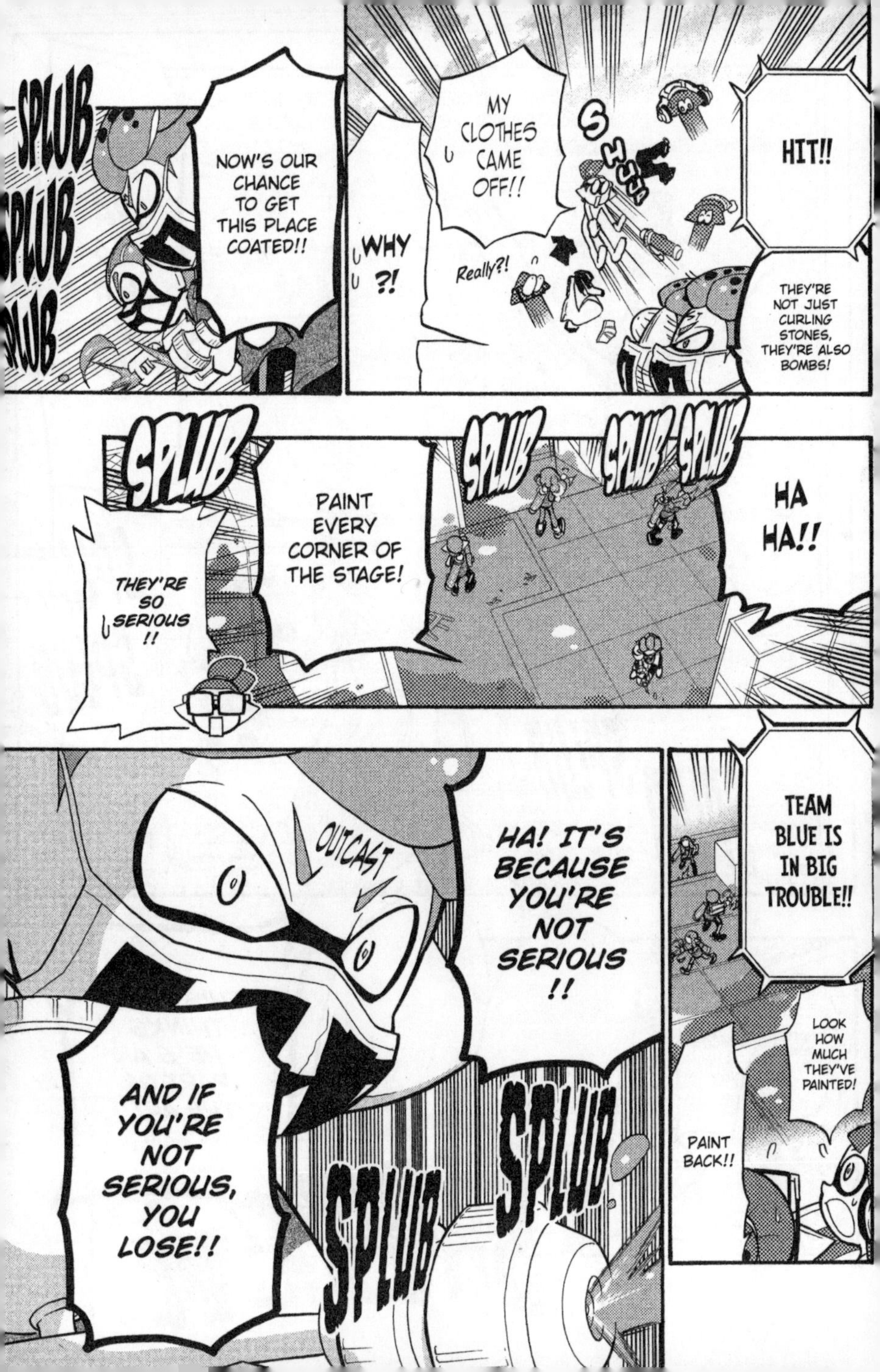
HIT!!
SHUUA
THEY'RE NOT JUST CURLING STONES, THEY'RE ALSO BOMBS!
MY CLOTHES CAME OFF!!
Really?!
WHY ?!
SPLUB SPLUB SPLUB
NOW'S OUR CHANCE TO GET THIS PLACE COATED!!
HA HA!!
SPLUB SPLUB SPLUB
PAINT EVERY CORNER OF THE STAGE!
SPLUB
THEY'RE SO SERIOUS !!
TEAM BLUE IS IN BIG TROUBLE!!
LOOK HOW MUCH THEY'VE PAINTED!
PAINT BACK!!
OUTCAST
HA! IT'S BECAUSE YOU'RE NOT SERIOUS !!
SPLUB SPLUB
AND IF YOU'RE NOT SERIOUS, YOU LOSE!!

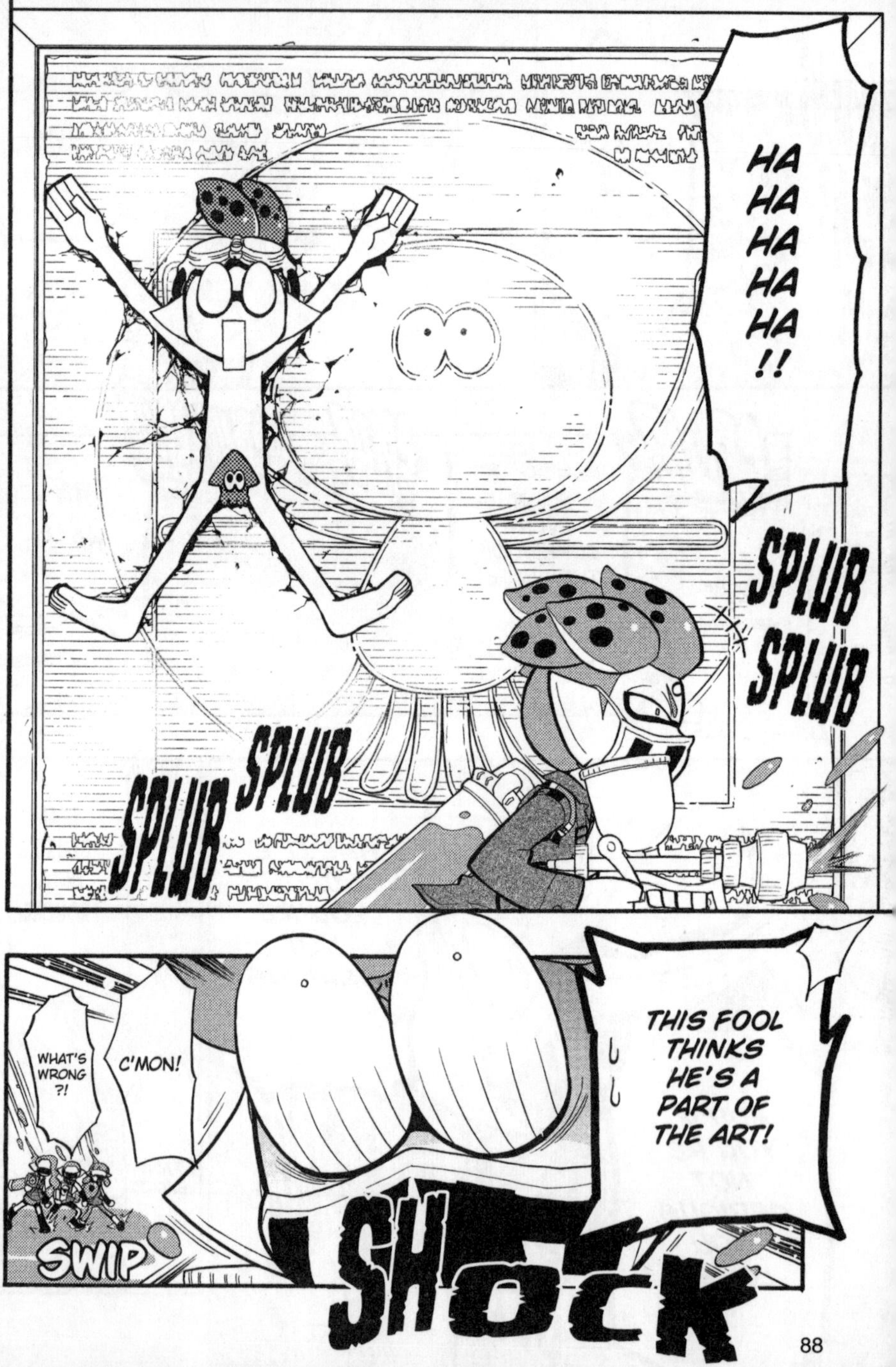
HA HA HA HA HA !!
SPLUB SPLUB
SPLUB SPLUB
THIS FOOL THINKS HE'S A PART OF THE ART!
SHOCK
C'MON!
WHAT'S WRONG ?!
SWIP

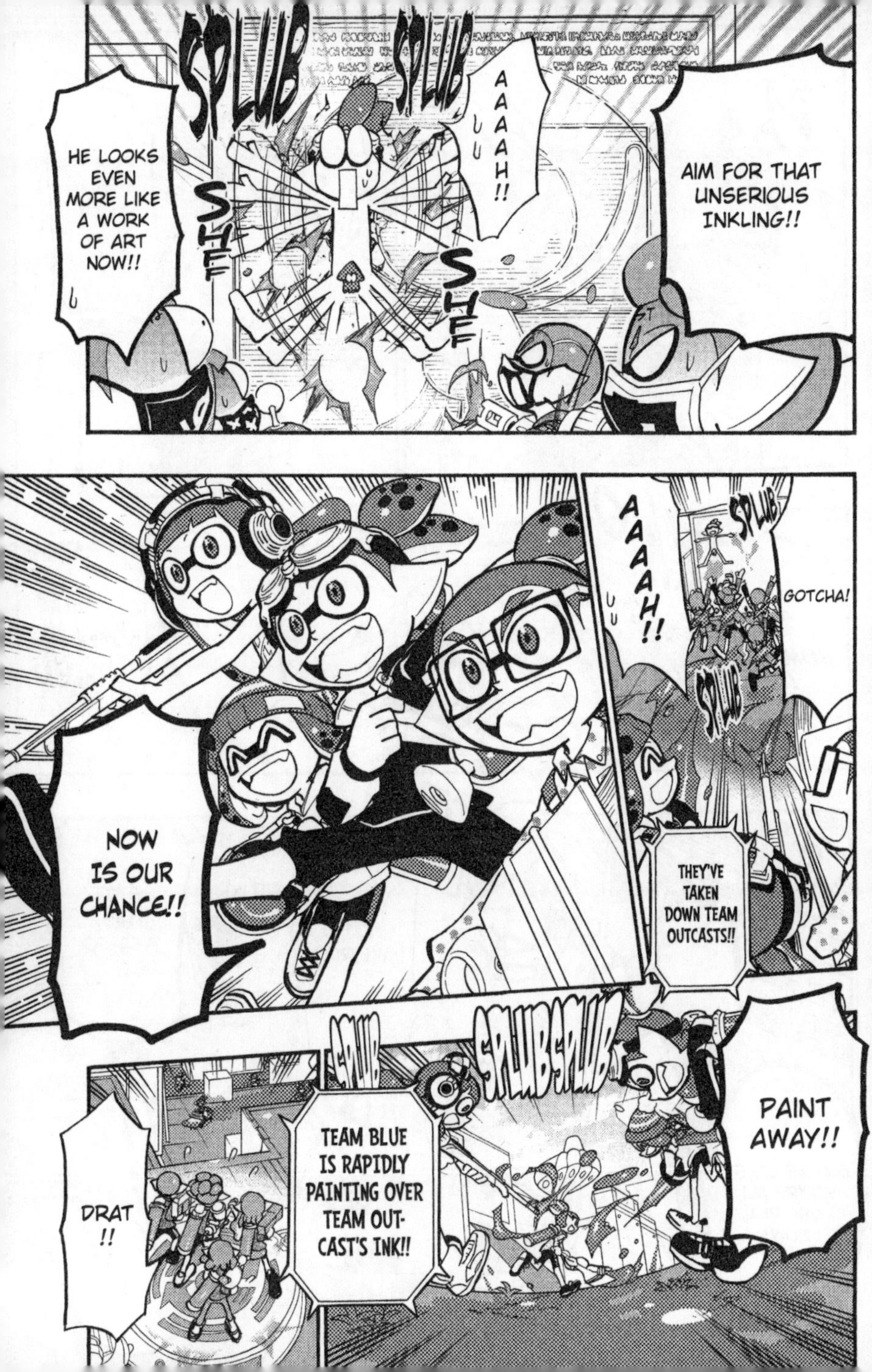
AIM FOR THAT UNSERIOUS INKLING!!
SPLUB
SPLUB
AAAAH!!
SHFF
SHFF
HE LOOKS EVEN MORE LIKE A WORK OF ART NOW!!
AAAAAH!!
SPLUB
GOTCHA!
SPLUB
THEY'VE TAKEN DOWN TEAM OUTCASTS!!
NOW IS OUR CHANCE!!
PAINT AWAY!!
SPLUB SPLUB
SPLUB
TEAM BLUE IS RAPIDLY PAINTING OVER TEAM OUT-CAST'S INK!!
DRAT!!

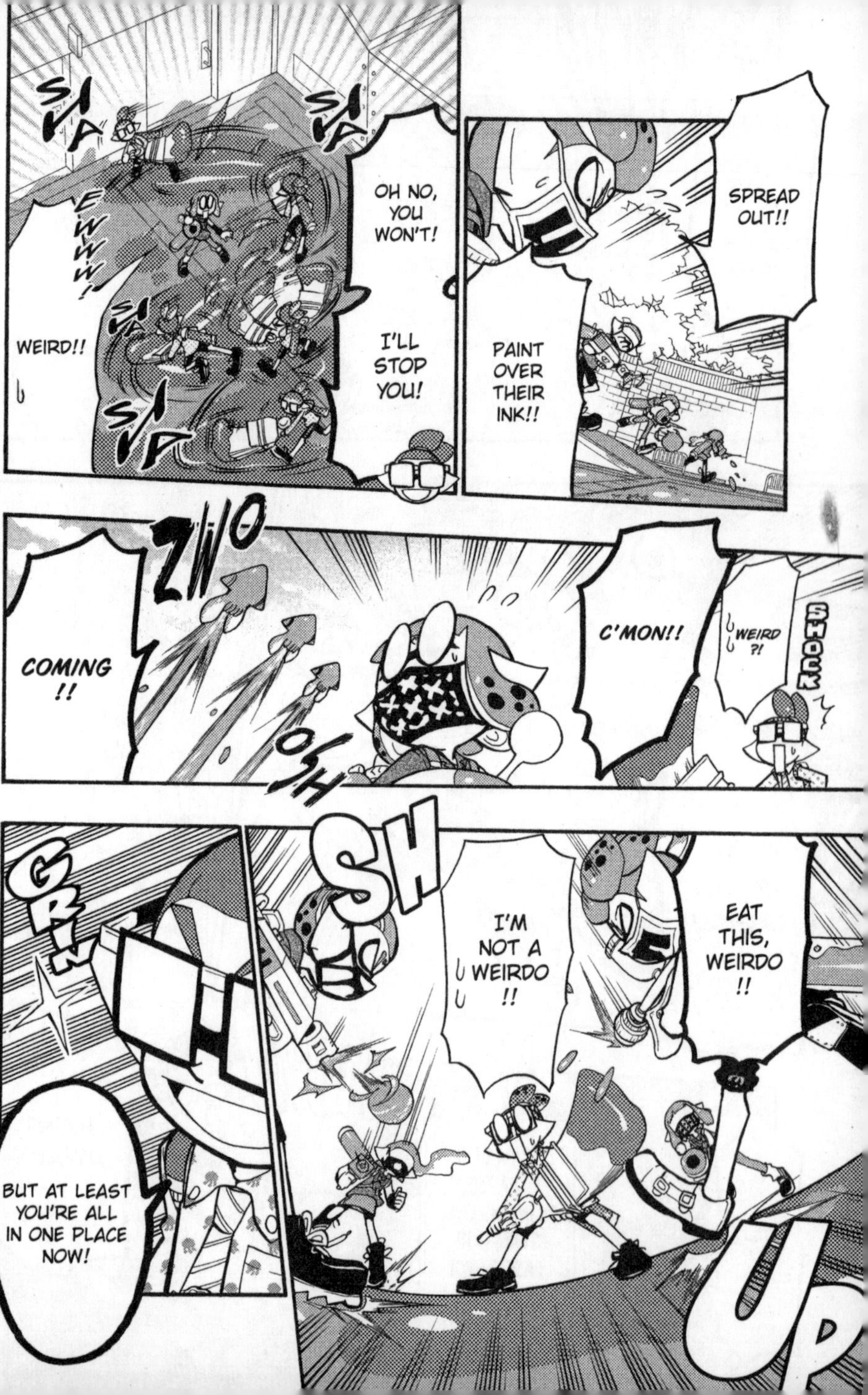
SPREAD OUT!!
PAINT OVER THEIR INK!!
OH NO, YOU WON'T!
I'LL STOP YOU!
EWWWW!
WEIRD!!
SHOCK
WEIRD ?!
C'MON!!
ZWO
COMING !!
EAT THIS, WEIRDO !!
I'M NOT A WEIRDO !!
SH
UP
GRIN
BUT AT LEAST YOU'RE ALL IN ONE PLACE NOW!

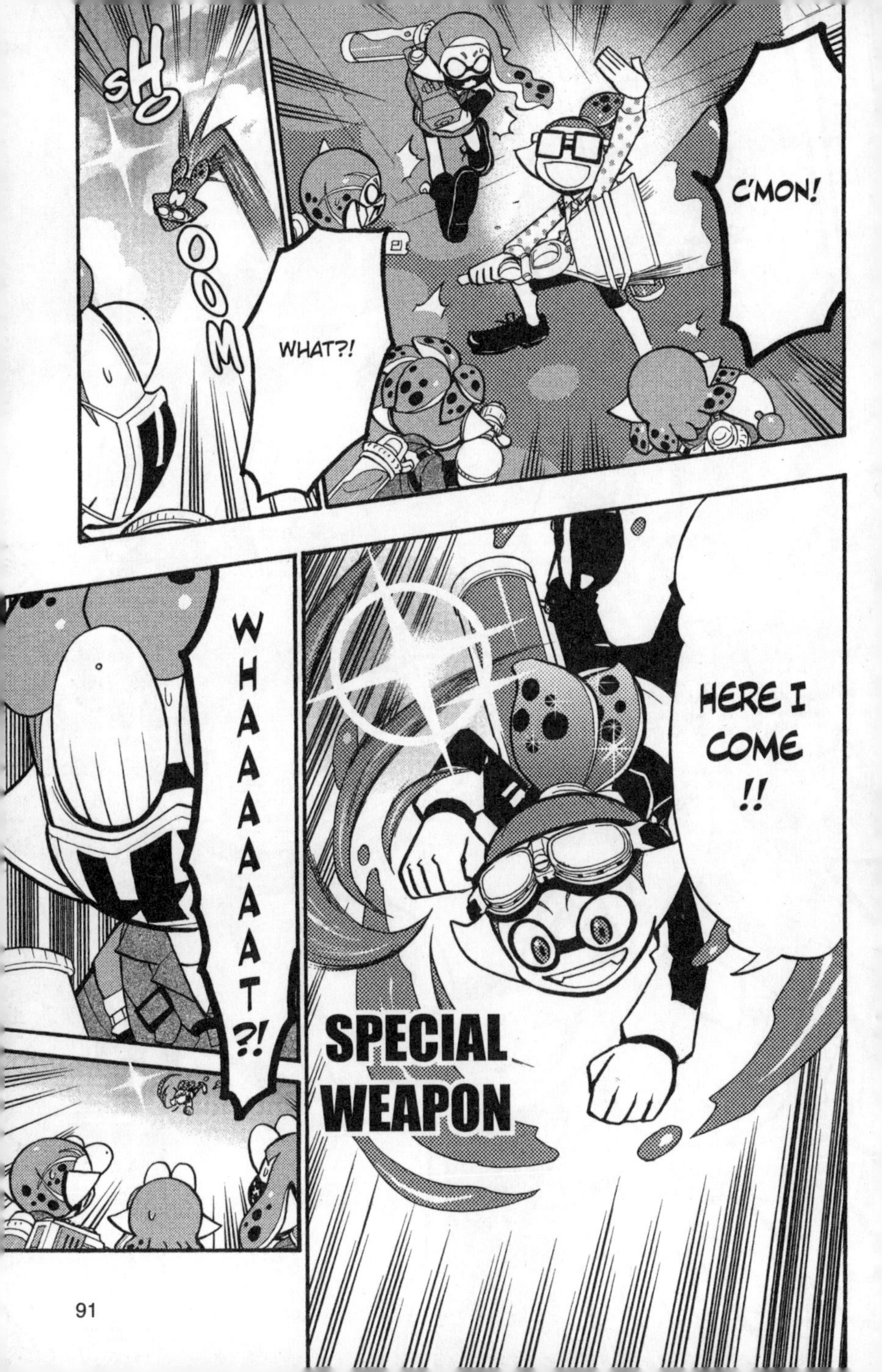
C'MON!
WHAT?!
SHOOOOM
HERE I COME!!
SPECIAL WEAPON
WHAAAAAAT?!

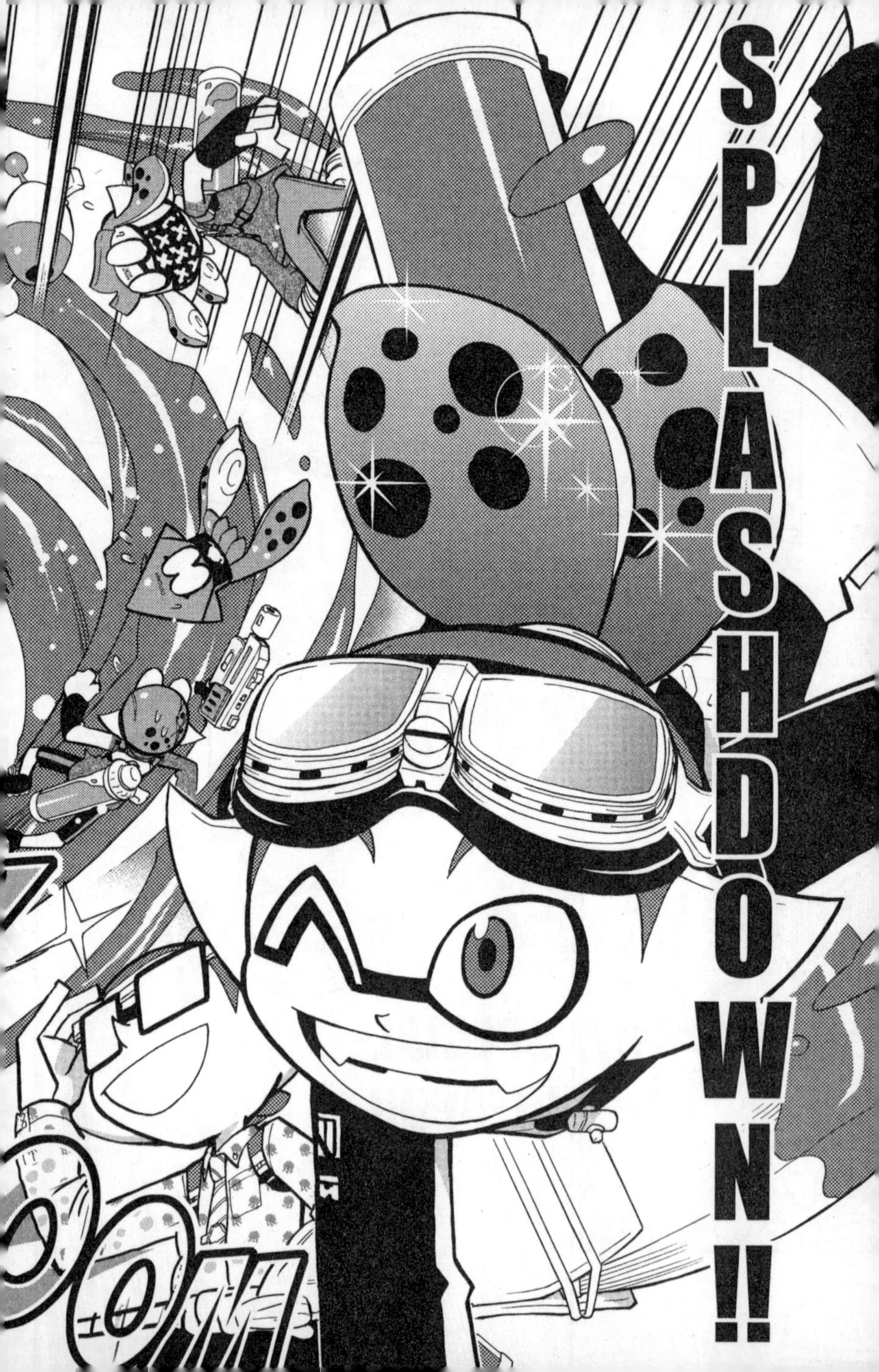
SPLASHDOWN!!

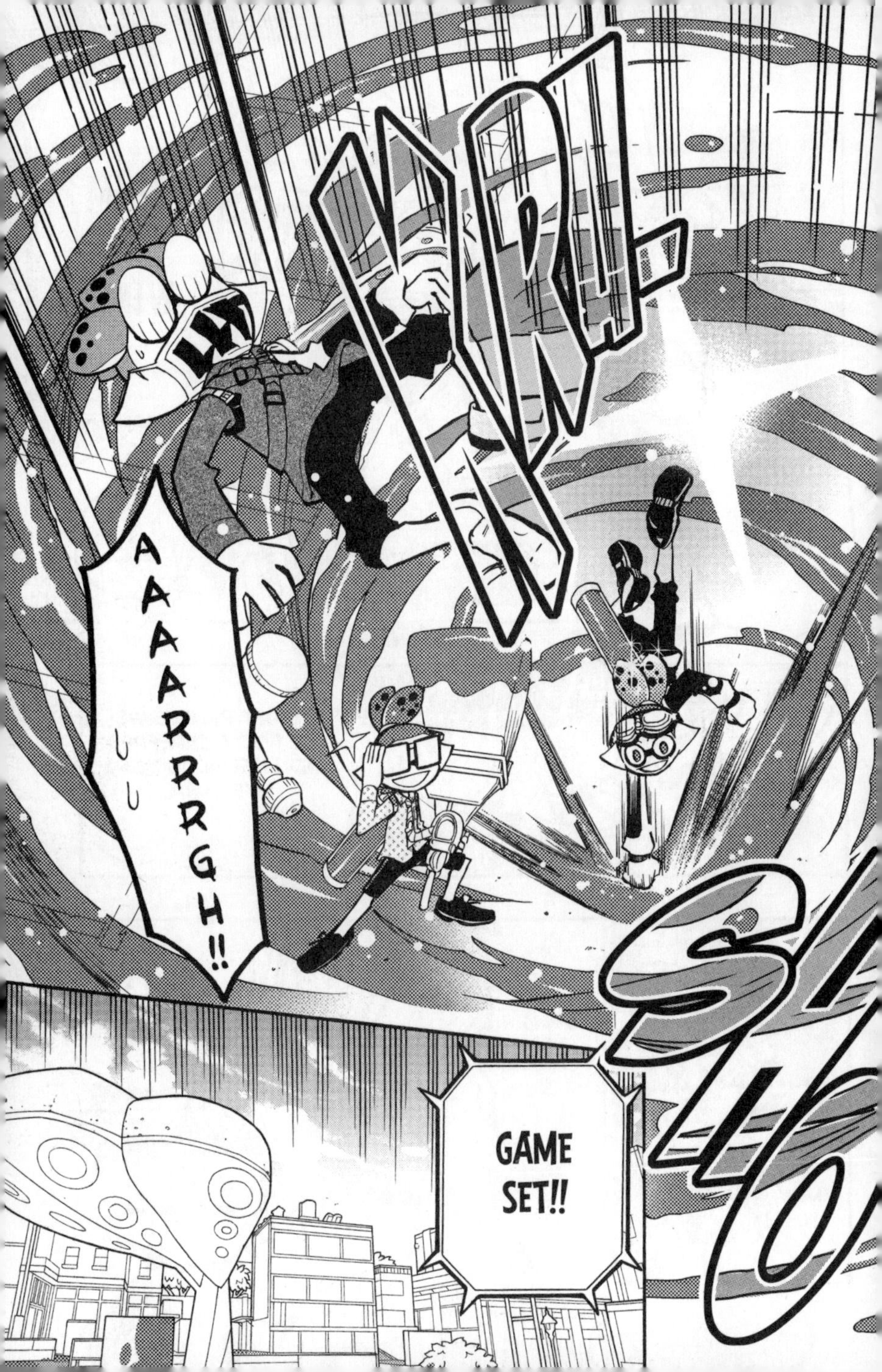
AAAARRRGH!!
GAME SET!!

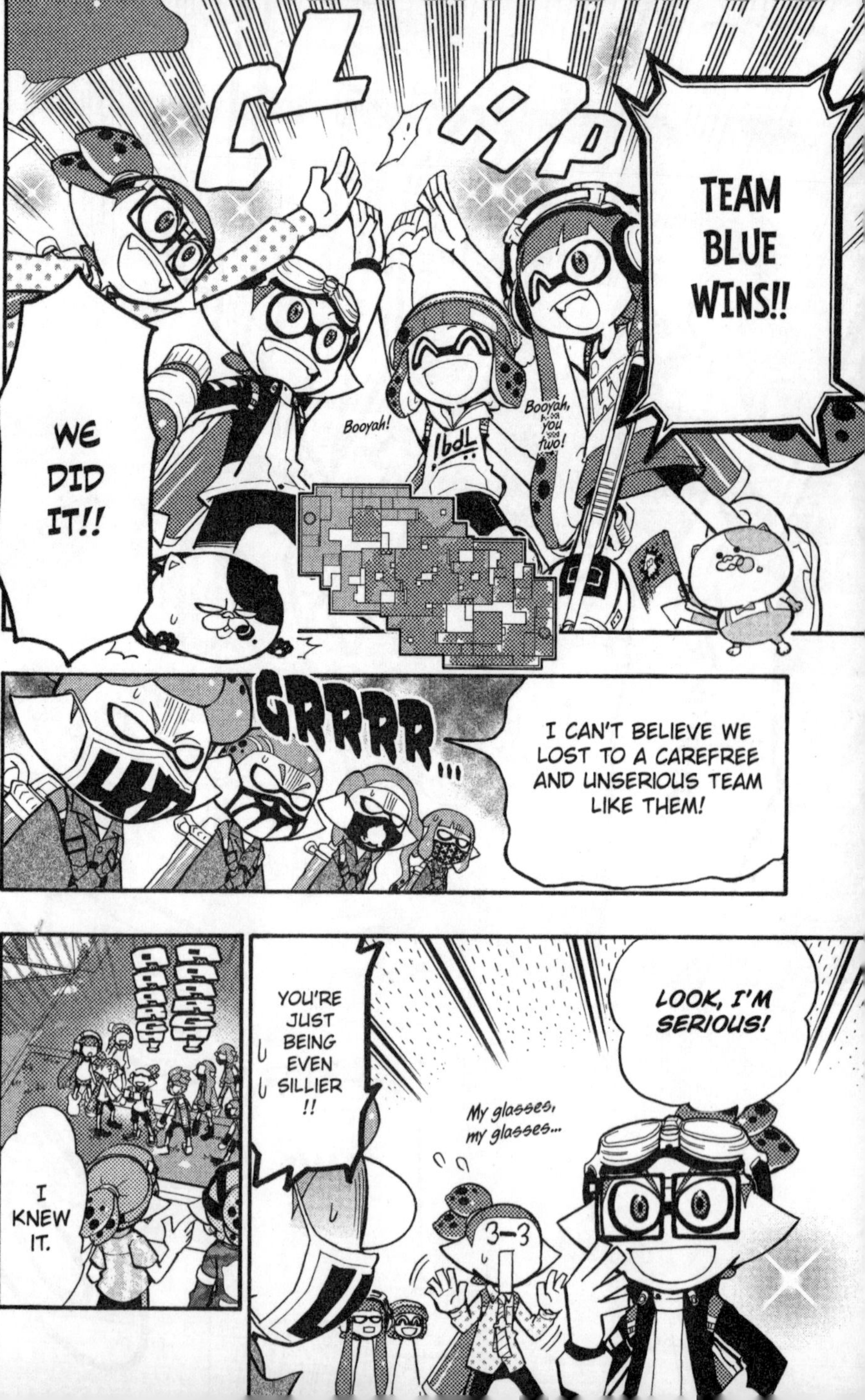
TEAM BLUE WINS!!
CLAP
Booyah, you two!
Booyah!
WE DID IT!!
I CAN'T BELIEVE WE LOST TO A CAREFREE AND UNSERIOUS TEAM LIKE THEM!
GRRRR...
LOOK, I'M SERIOUS!
My glasses, my glasses...
YOU'RE JUST BEING EVEN SILLIER!!
I KNEW IT.

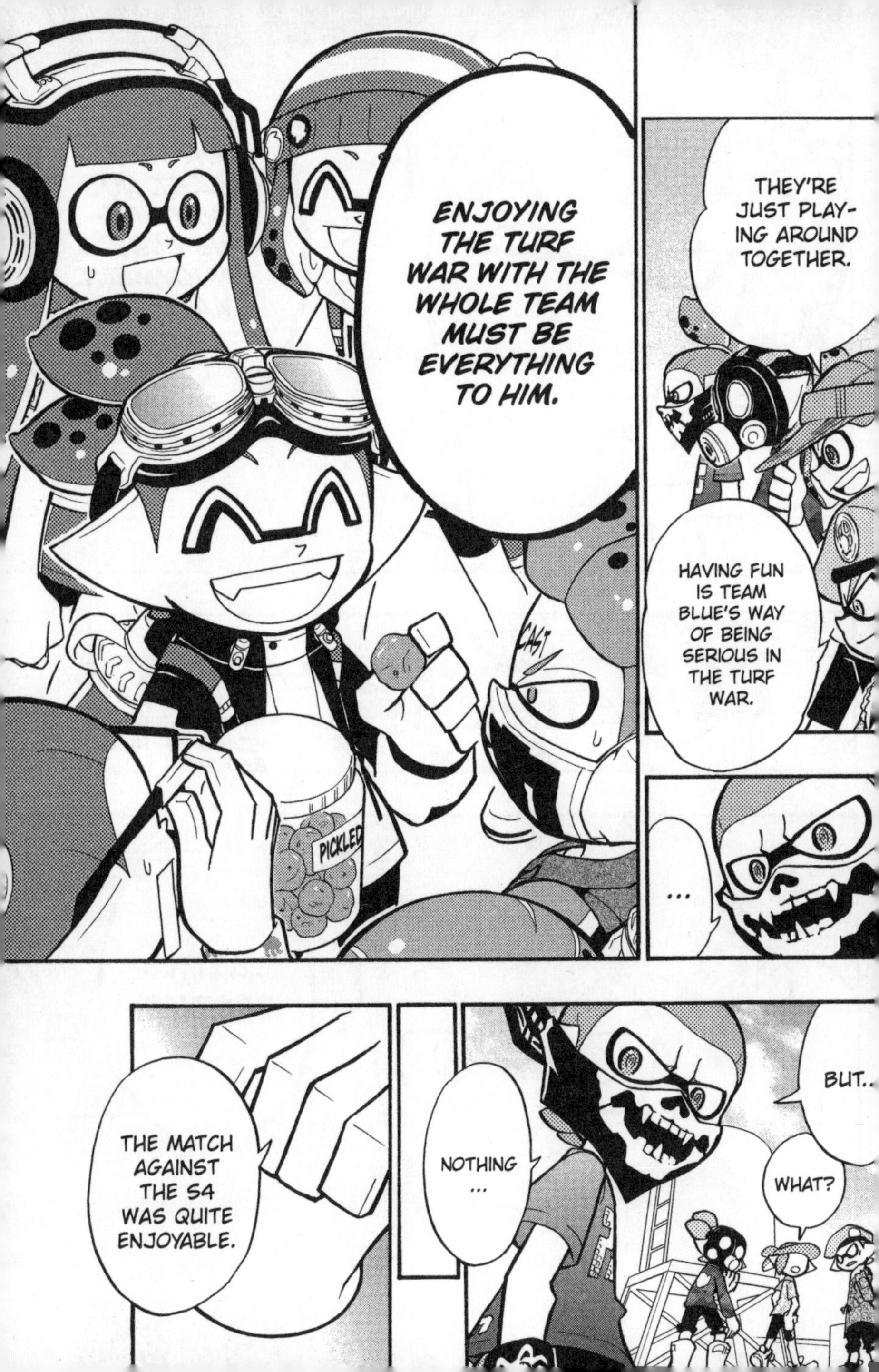
THEY'RE JUST PLAY-ING AROUND TOGETHER.
HAVING FUN IS TEAM BLUE'S WAY OF BEING SERIOUS IN THE TURF WAR.
...
ENJOYING THE TURF WAR WITH THE WHOLE TEAM MUST BE EVERYTHING TO HIM.
PICKLED
BUT..
WHAT?
NOTHING ...
THE MATCH AGAINST THE S4 WAS QUITE ENJOYABLE.

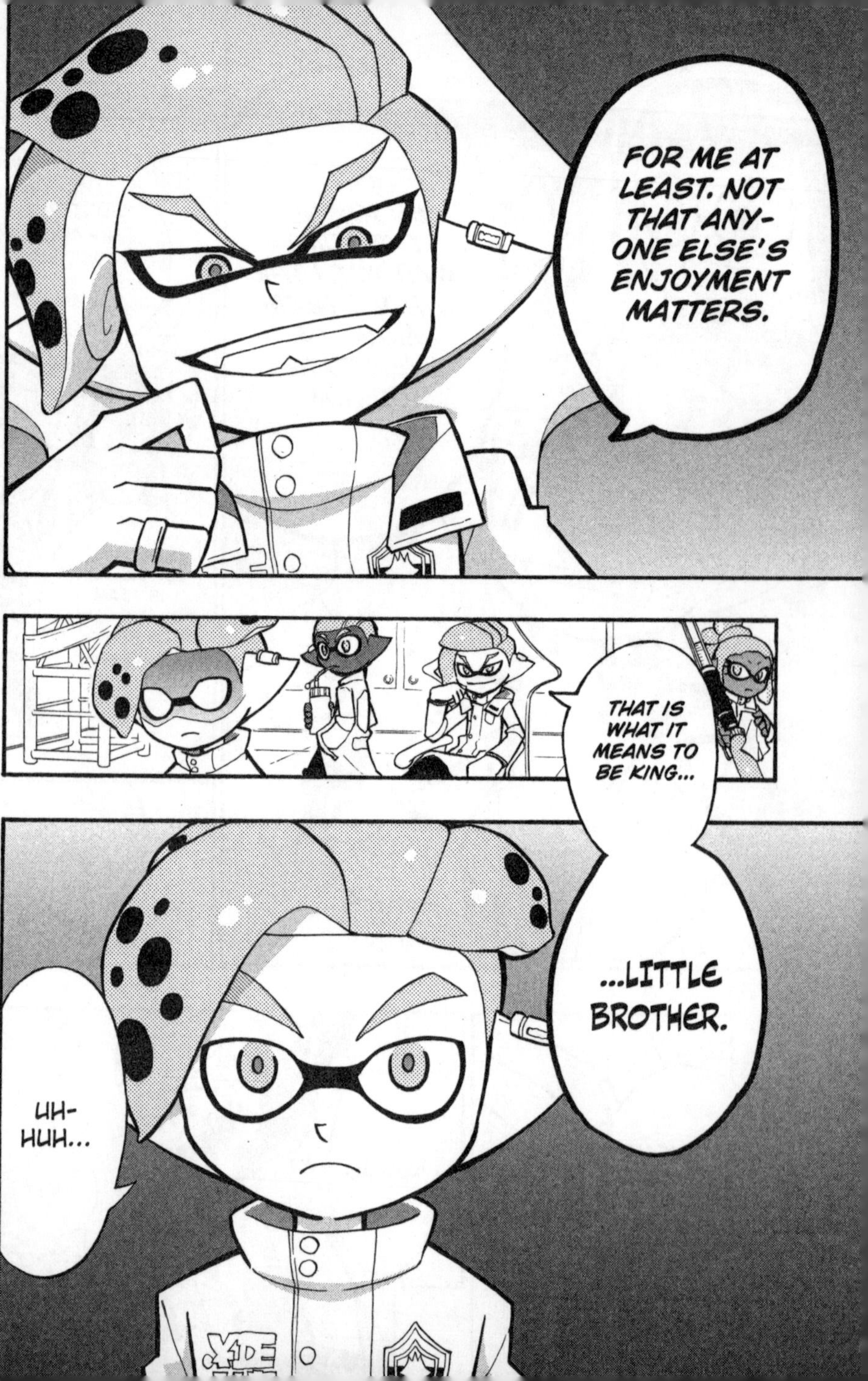
FOR ME AT LEAST. NOT THAT ANYONE ELSE'S ENJOYMENT MATTERS.
THAT IS WHAT IT MEANS TO BE KING...
...LITTLE BROTHER.
UH-HUH...

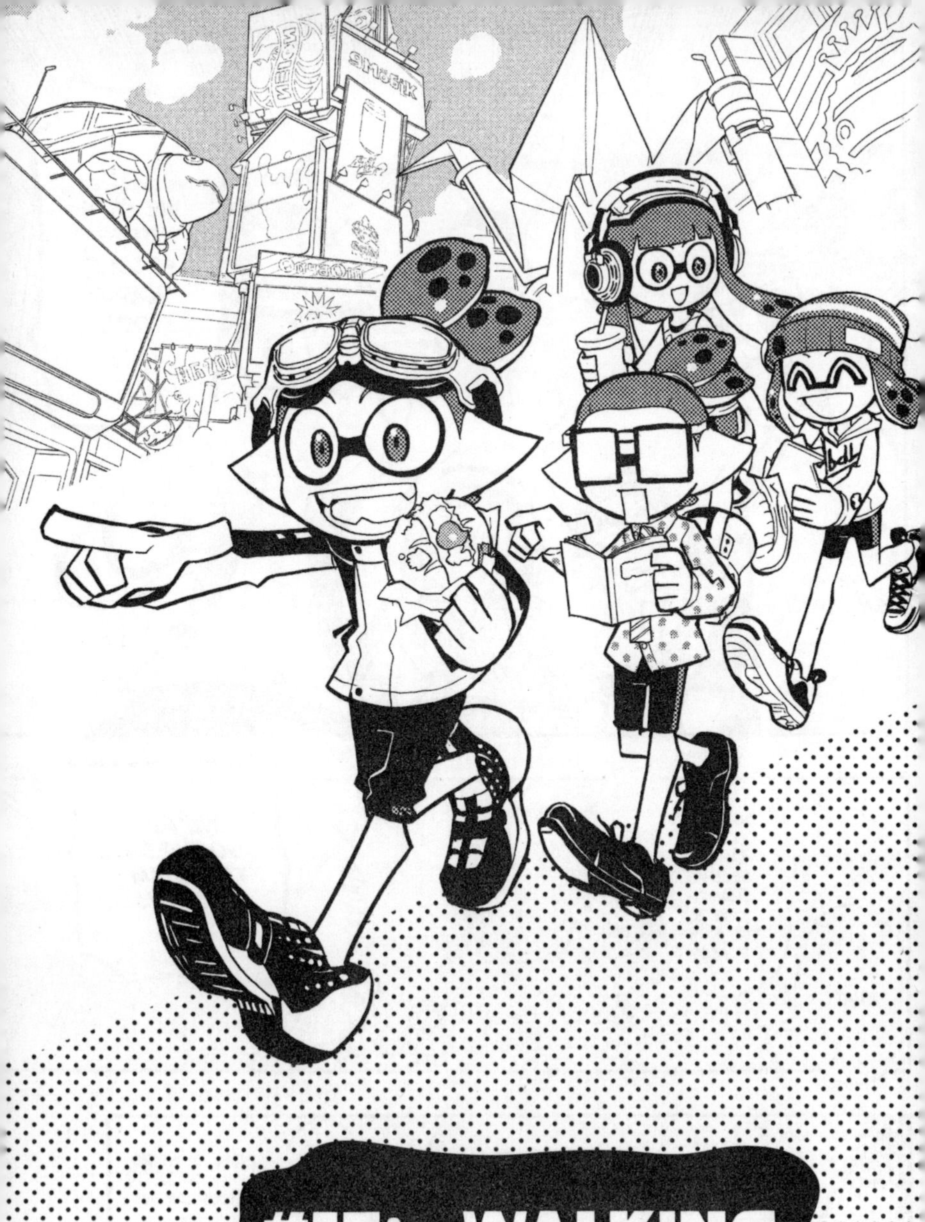

#15: WALKING AROUND TOWN

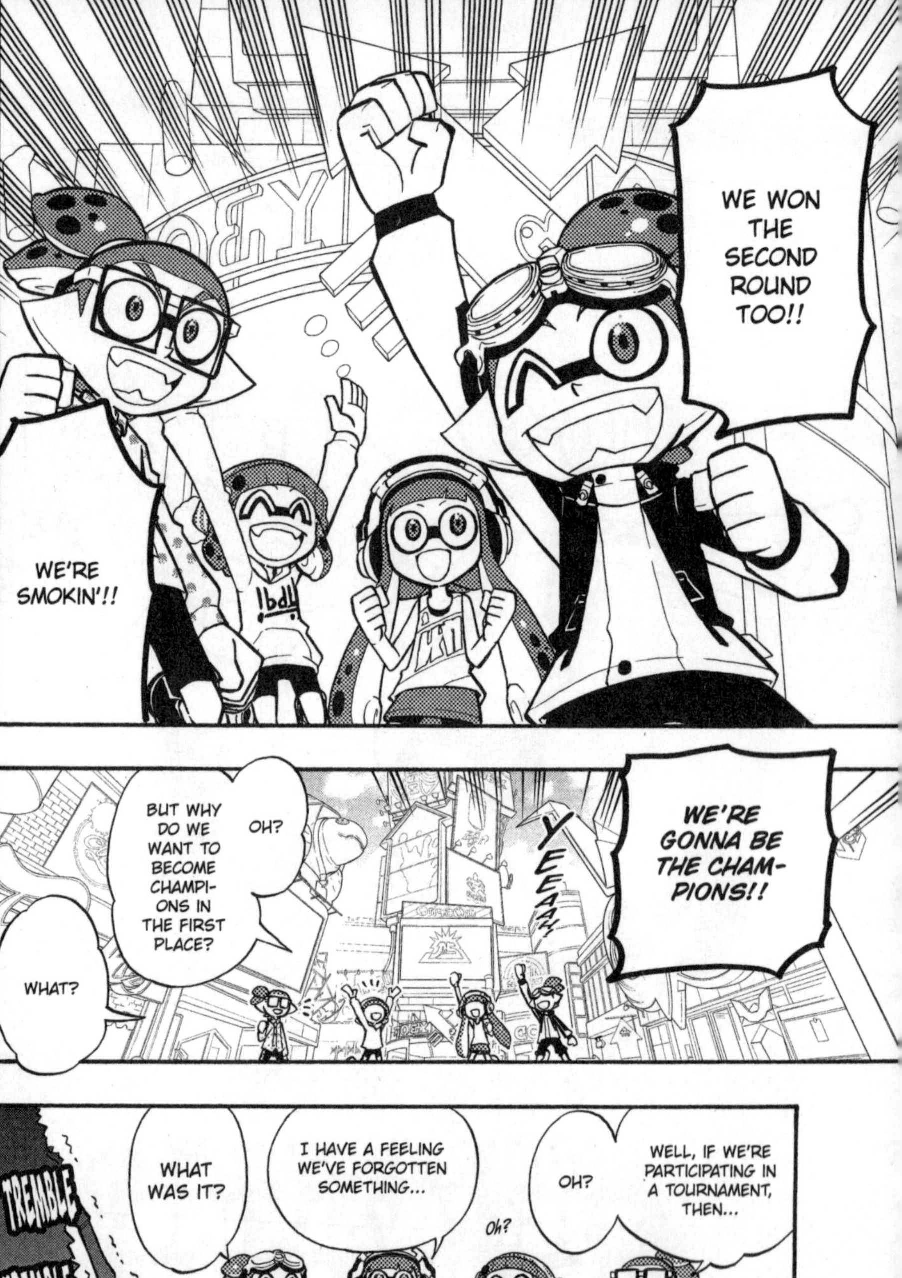
WE WON THE SECOND ROUND TOO!!
WE'RE SMOKIN'!!
WE'RE GONNA BE THE CHAMPIONS!!
YEEAAH!
OH?
BUT WHY DO WE WANT TO BECOME CHAMPIONS IN THE FIRST PLACE?
WHAT?
WELL, IF WE'RE PARTICIPATING IN A TOURNAMENT, THEN...
OH?
Oh?
I HAVE A FEELING WE'VE FORGOTTEN SOMETHING...
WHAT WAS IT?
TREMBLE
TREMBLE

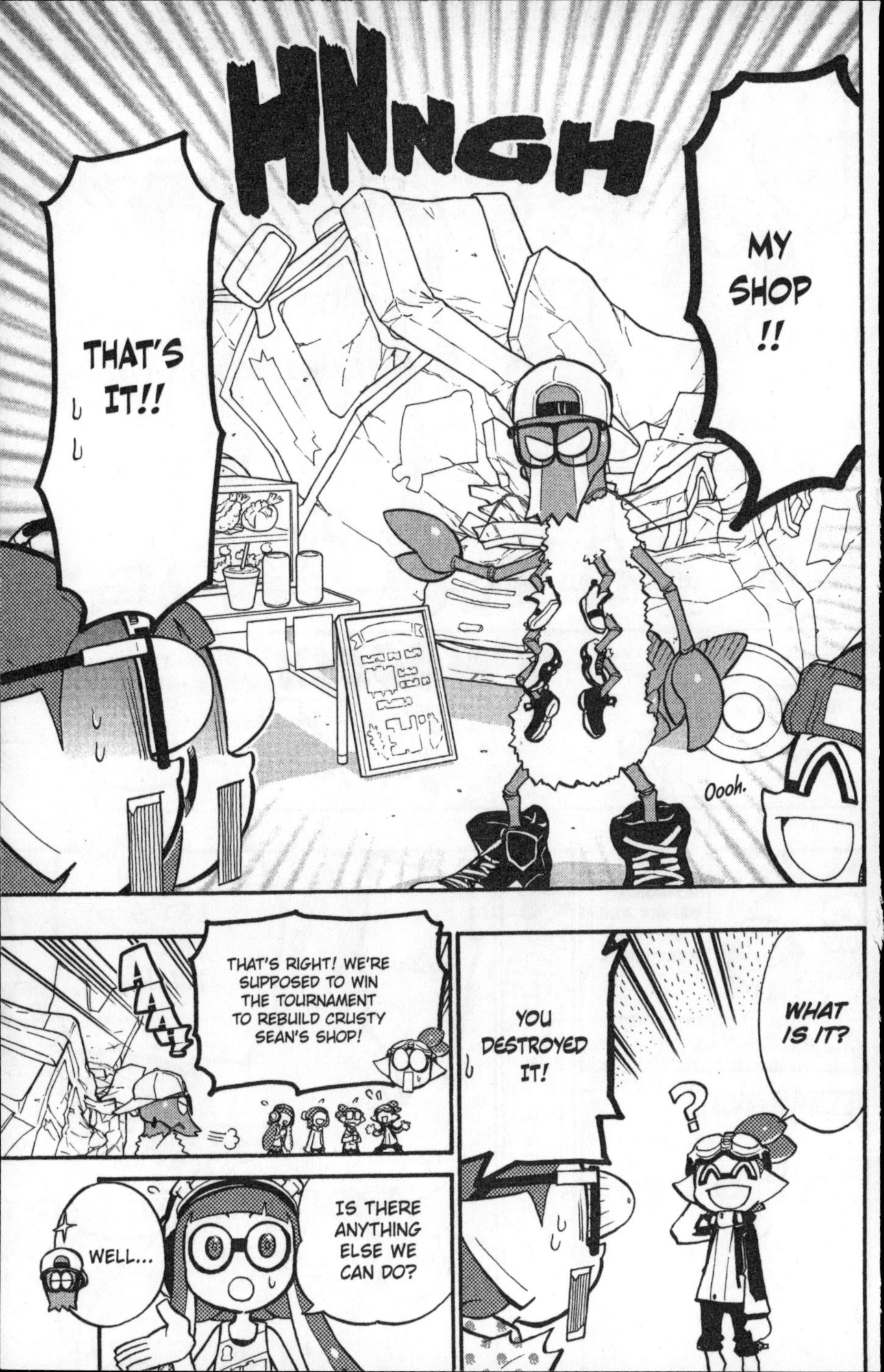
HNNGH
MY SHOP!!
THAT'S IT!!
Oooh.
WHAT IS IT?
YOU DESTROYED IT!
?
AAA!
THAT'S RIGHT! WE'RE SUPPOSED TO WIN THE TOURNAMENT TO REBUILD CRUSTY SEAN'S SHOP!
IS THERE ANYTHING ELSE WE CAN DO?
WELL...

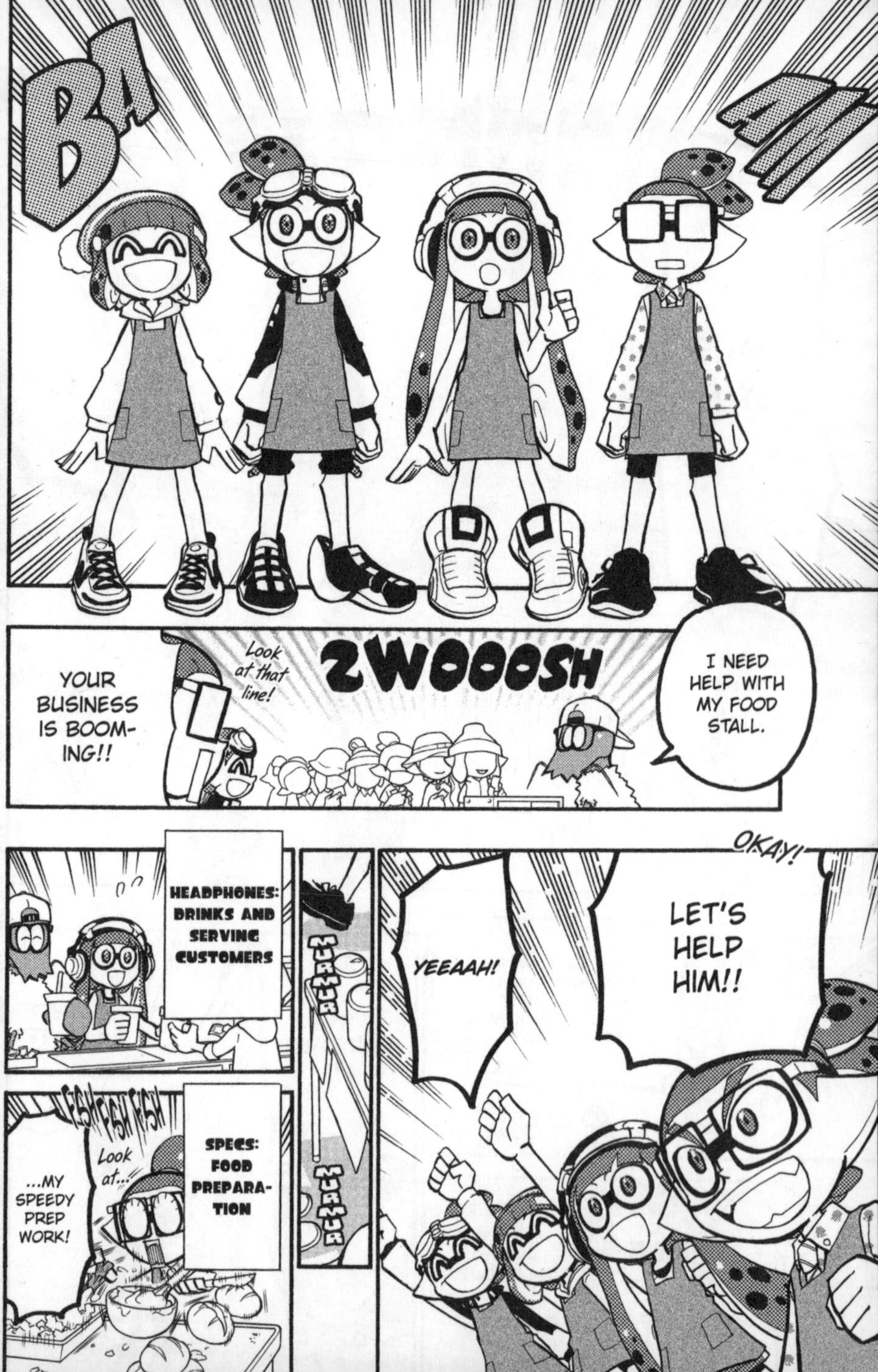
BA
AM
I NEED HELP WITH MY FOOD STALL.
ZWOOOSH
Look at that line!
YOUR BUSINESS IS BOOMING!!
OKAY!
LET'S HELP HIM!!
YEEEAAH!
MURMUR
MURMUR
HEADPHONES: DRINKS AND SERVING CUSTOMERS
FISH FISH FISH
SPECS: FOOD PREPARATION
Look at...
...MY SPEEDY PREP WORK!

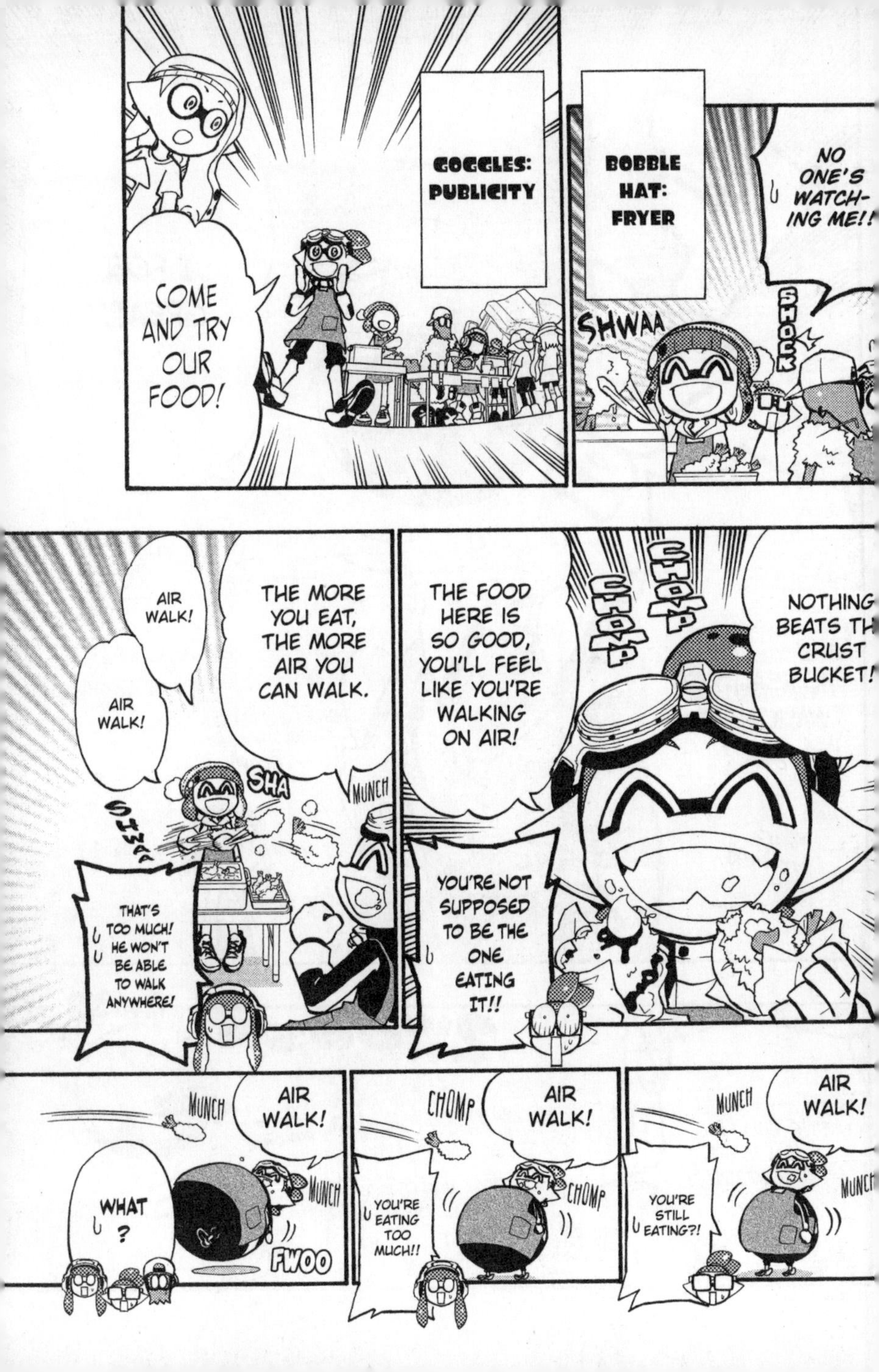
BOBBLE HAT: FRYER
NO ONE'S WATCHING ME!!
SHWAA
SHOCK
GOGGLES: PUBLICITY
COME AND TRY OUR FOOD!
CHOMP
CHOMP
NOTHING BEATS TH CRUST BUCKET!
THE FOOD HERE IS SO GOOD, YOU'LL FEEL LIKE YOU'RE WALKING ON AIR!
YOU'RE NOT SUPPOSED TO BE THE ONE EATING IT!!
THE MORE YOU EAT, THE MORE AIR YOU CAN WALK.
AIR WALK!
AIR WALK!
MUNCH
SHA
SHWAA
THAT'S TOO MUCH! HE WON'T BE ABLE TO WALK ANYWHERE!
AIR WALK!
MUNCH
MUNCH
YOU'RE STILL EATING?!
AIR WALK!
CHOMP
CHOMP
YOU'RE EATING TOO MUCH!!
AIR WALK!
MUNCH
MUNCH
WHAT ?
FWOO

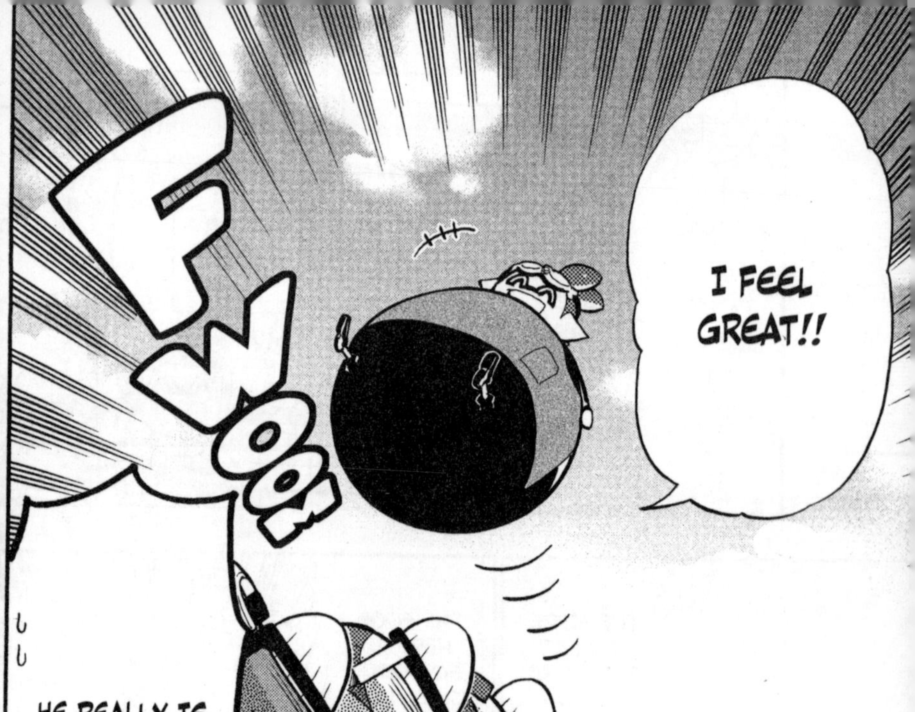
I FEEL GREAT!!
FWOOOM
Ooooh.
HE REALLY IS WALKING ON AIR!!
What's happening?!
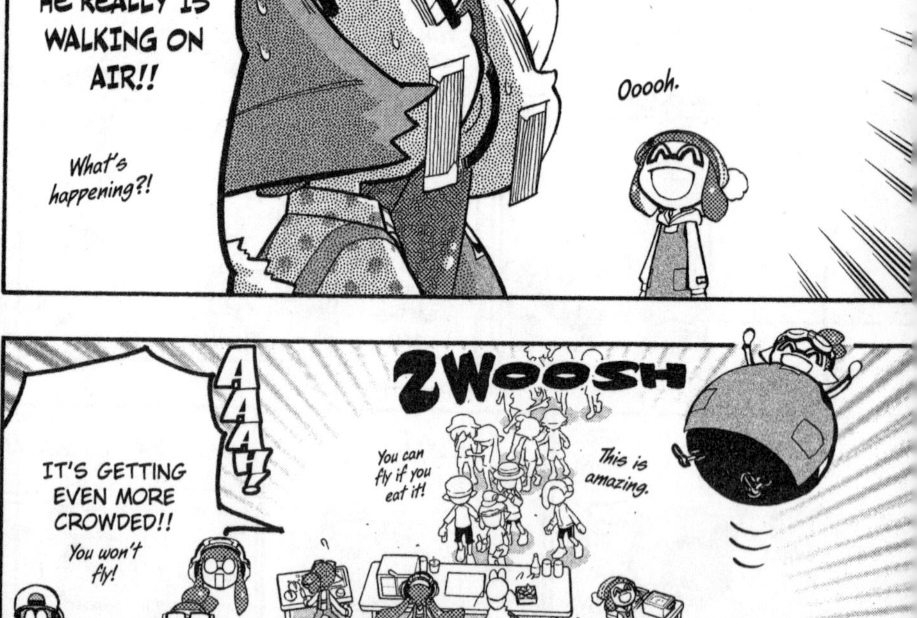
ZWOOSH
This is amazing.
You can fly if you eat it!
AAAH!
IT'S GETTING EVEN MORE CROWDED!!
You won't fly!

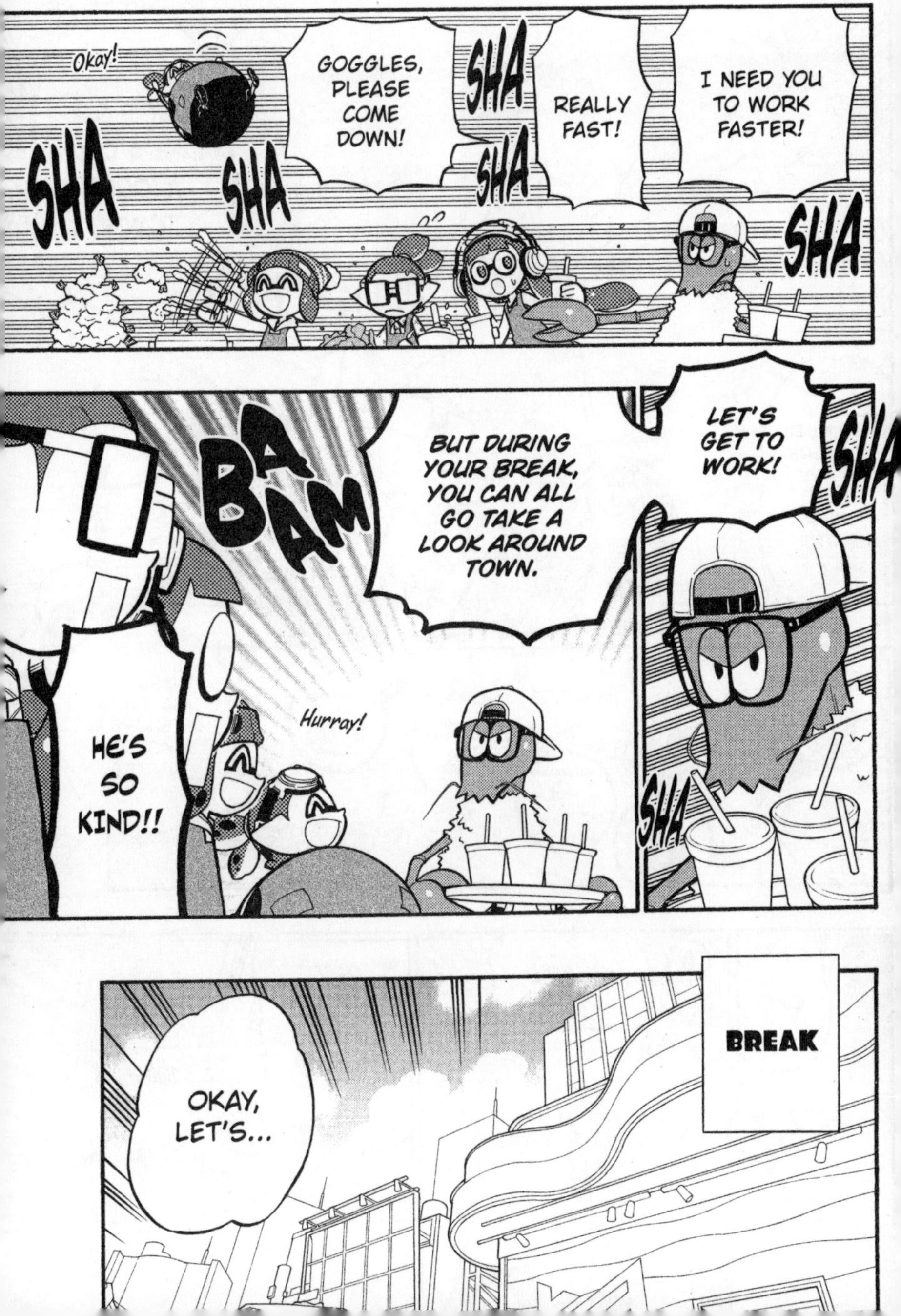
SHA
I NEED YOU TO WORK FASTER!
REALLY FAST!
SHA
SHA
GOGGLES, PLEASE COME DOWN!
Okay!
SHA
SHA
SHA
LET'S GET TO WORK!
SHA
SHA
BUT DURING YOUR BREAK, YOU CAN ALL GO TAKE A LOOK AROUND TOWN.
BA BAM
Hurray!
HE'S SO KIND!!
BREAK
OKAY, LET'S...

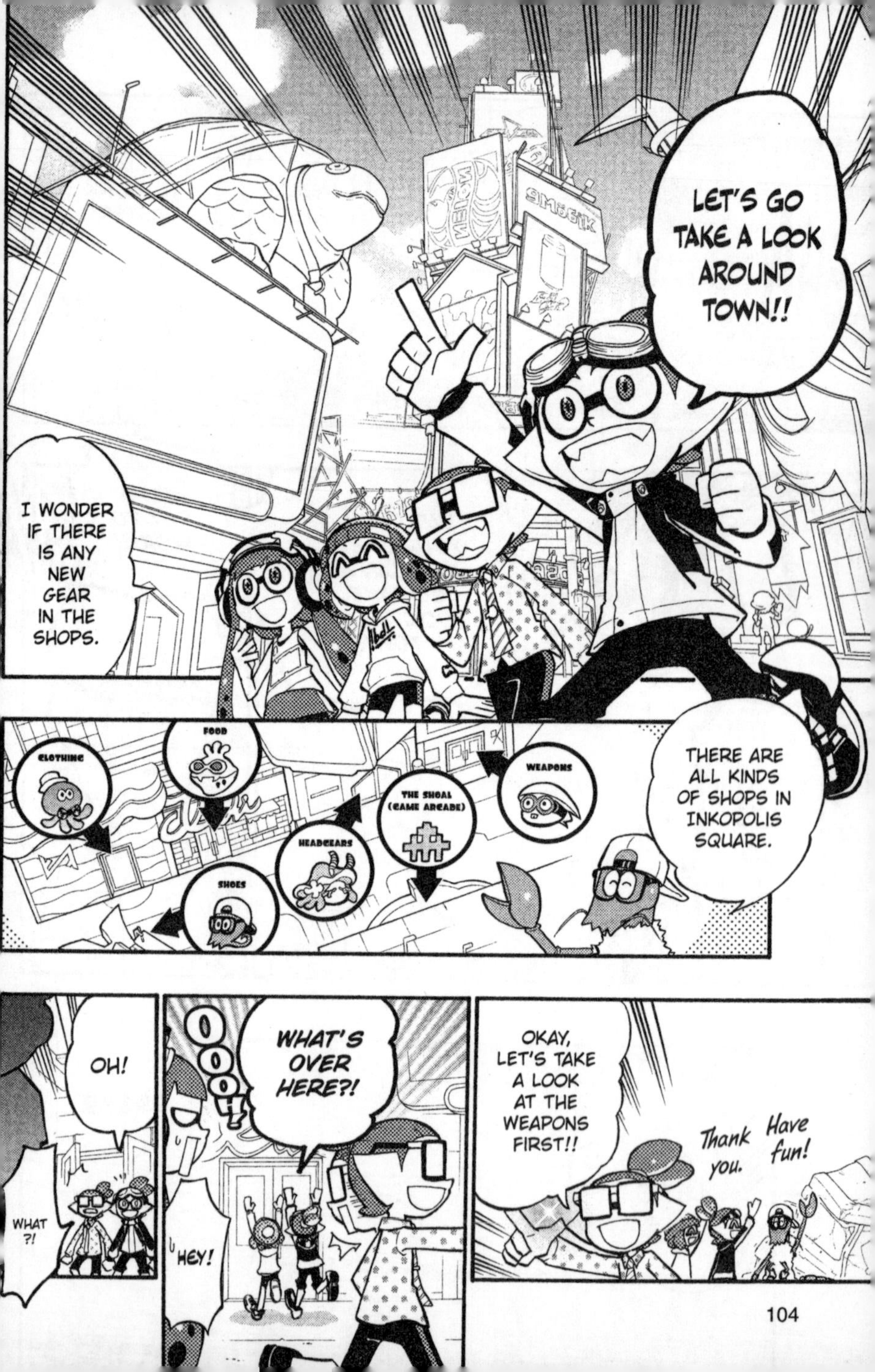
LET'S GO TAKE A LOOK AROUND TOWN!!
I WONDER IF THERE IS ANY NEW GEAR IN THE SHOPS.
THERE ARE ALL KINDS OF SHOPS IN INKOPOLIS SQUARE.
WEAPONS
THE SHOAL (GAME ARCADE)
FOOD
HEADGEARS
CLOTHING
SHOES
OKAY, LET'S TAKE A LOOK AT THE WEAPONS FIRST!!
Have fun!
Thank you.
WHAT'S OVER HERE?!
OOO!
HEY!
OH!
WHAT?!

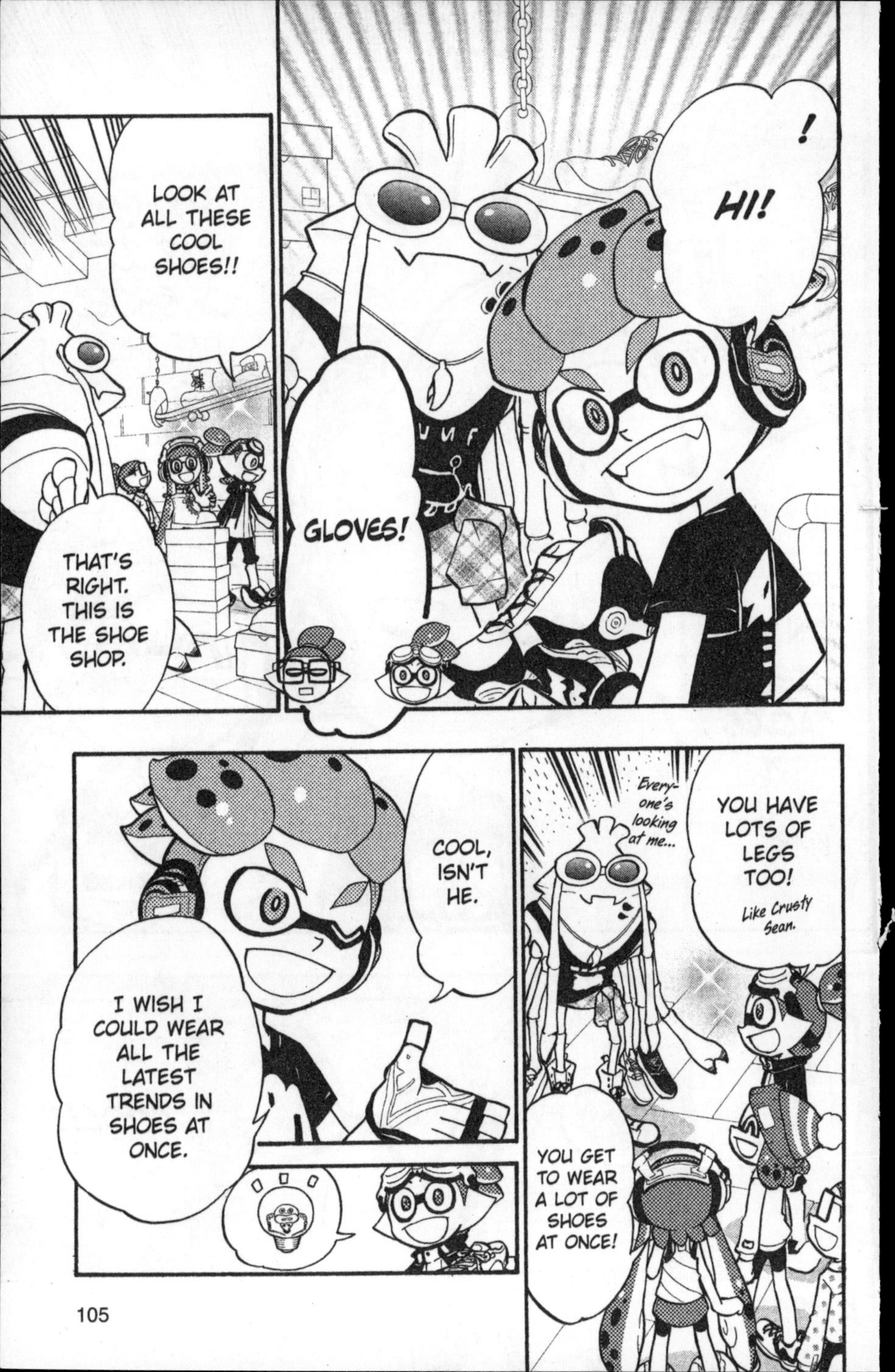
! HI!
GLOVES!
LOOK AT ALL THESE COOL SHOES!!
THAT'S RIGHT. THIS IS THE SHOE SHOP.
YOU HAVE LOTS OF LEGS TOO!
Like Crusty Sean.
Every-one's looking at me...
YOU GET TO WEAR A LOT OF SHOES AT ONCE!
COOL, ISN'T HE.
I WISH I COULD WEAR ALL THE LATEST TRENDS IN SHOES AT ONCE.

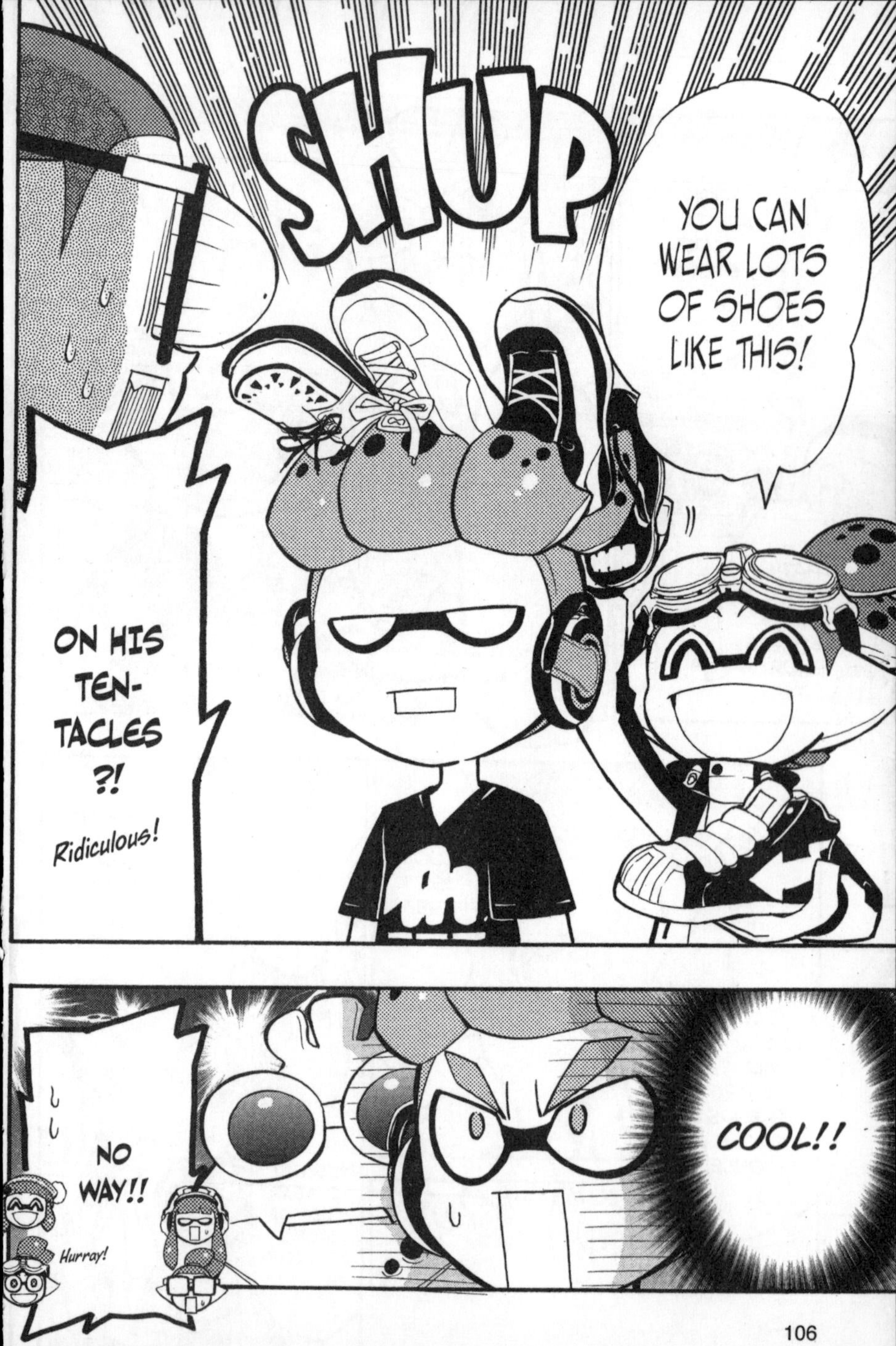
SHUP
YOU CAN WEAR LOTS OF SHOES LIKE THIS!
ON HIS TEN-TACLES ?!
Ridiculous!
COOL!!
NO WAY!!
Hurray!

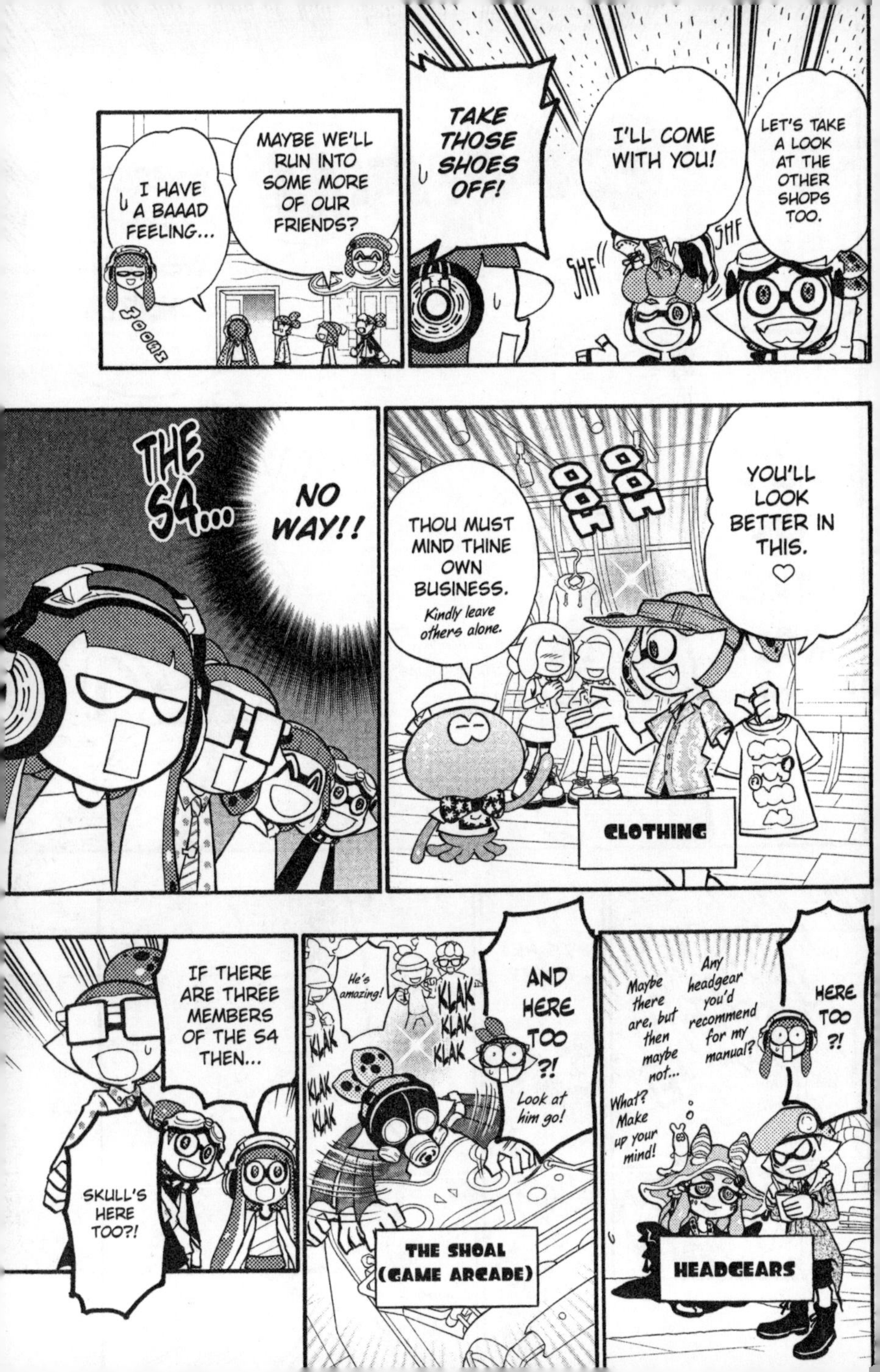
LET'S TAKE A LOOK AT THE OTHER SHOPS TOO.
I'LL COME WITH YOU!
SHF
SHF
TAKE THOSE SHOES OFF!
MAYBE WE'LL RUN INTO SOME MORE OF OUR FRIENDS?
I HAVE A BAAAD FEELING...
YOU'LL LOOK BETTER IN THIS. ♡
THOU MUST MIND THINE OWN BUSINESS.
Kindly leave others alone.
CLOTHING
NO WAY!!
THE S4...
HERE TOO ?!
Any headgear you'd recommend for my manual?
Maybe there are, but then maybe not...
What? Make up your mind!
HEADGEARS
AND HERE TOO ?!
He's amazing!
KLAK KLAK KLAK
KLAK KLAK KLAK
Look at him go!
THE SHOAL (GAME ARCADE)
IF THERE ARE THREE MEMBERS OF THE S4 THEN...
SKULL'S HERE TOO?!

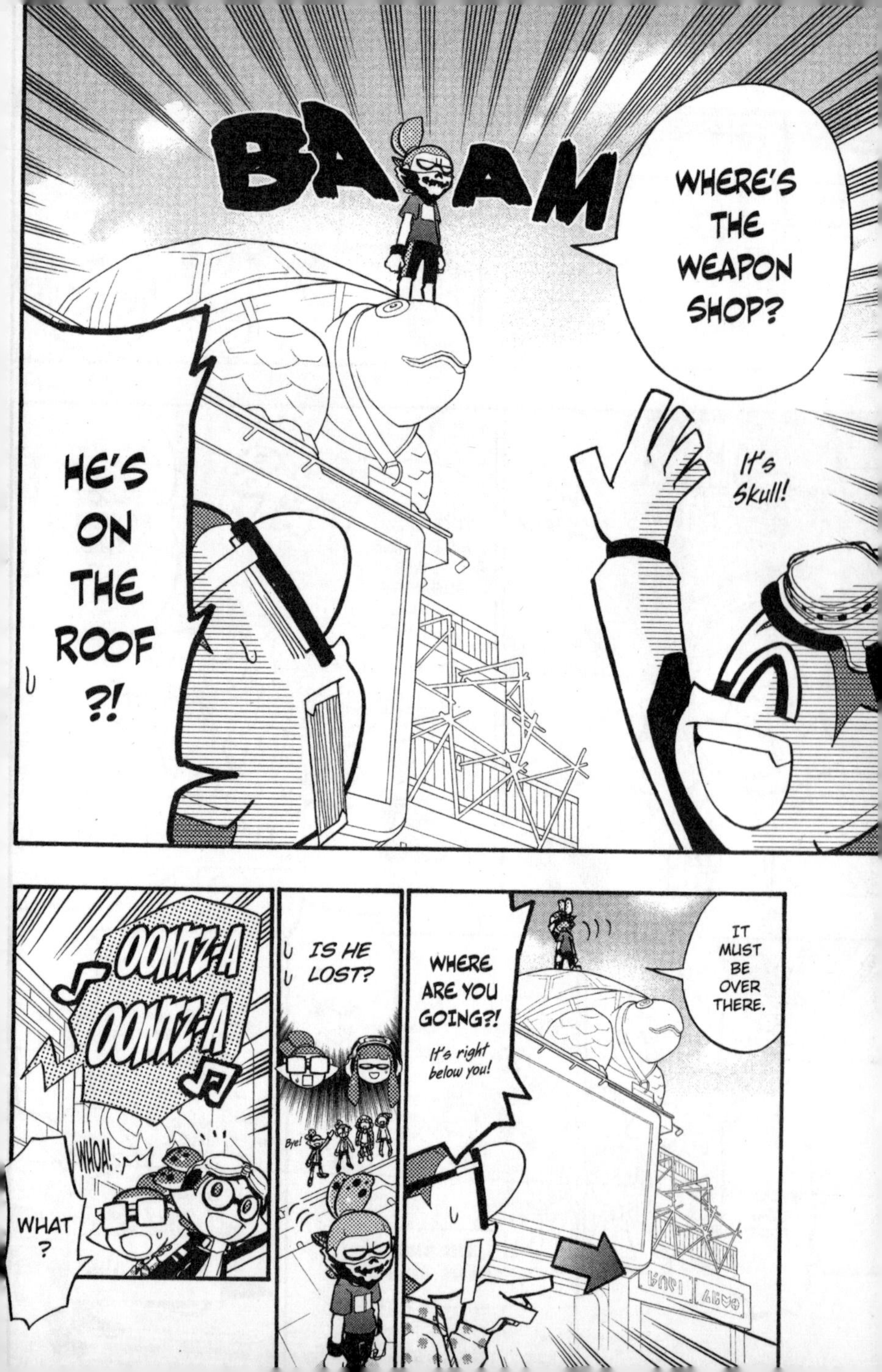
BAAM
WHERE'S THE WEAPON SHOP?
It's Skull!
HE'S ON THE ROOF ?!
IT MUST BE OVER THERE.
WHERE ARE YOU GOING?!
It's right below you!
IS HE LOST?
Bye!
OONTZ-A OONTZ-A
WHOA!
WHAT ?

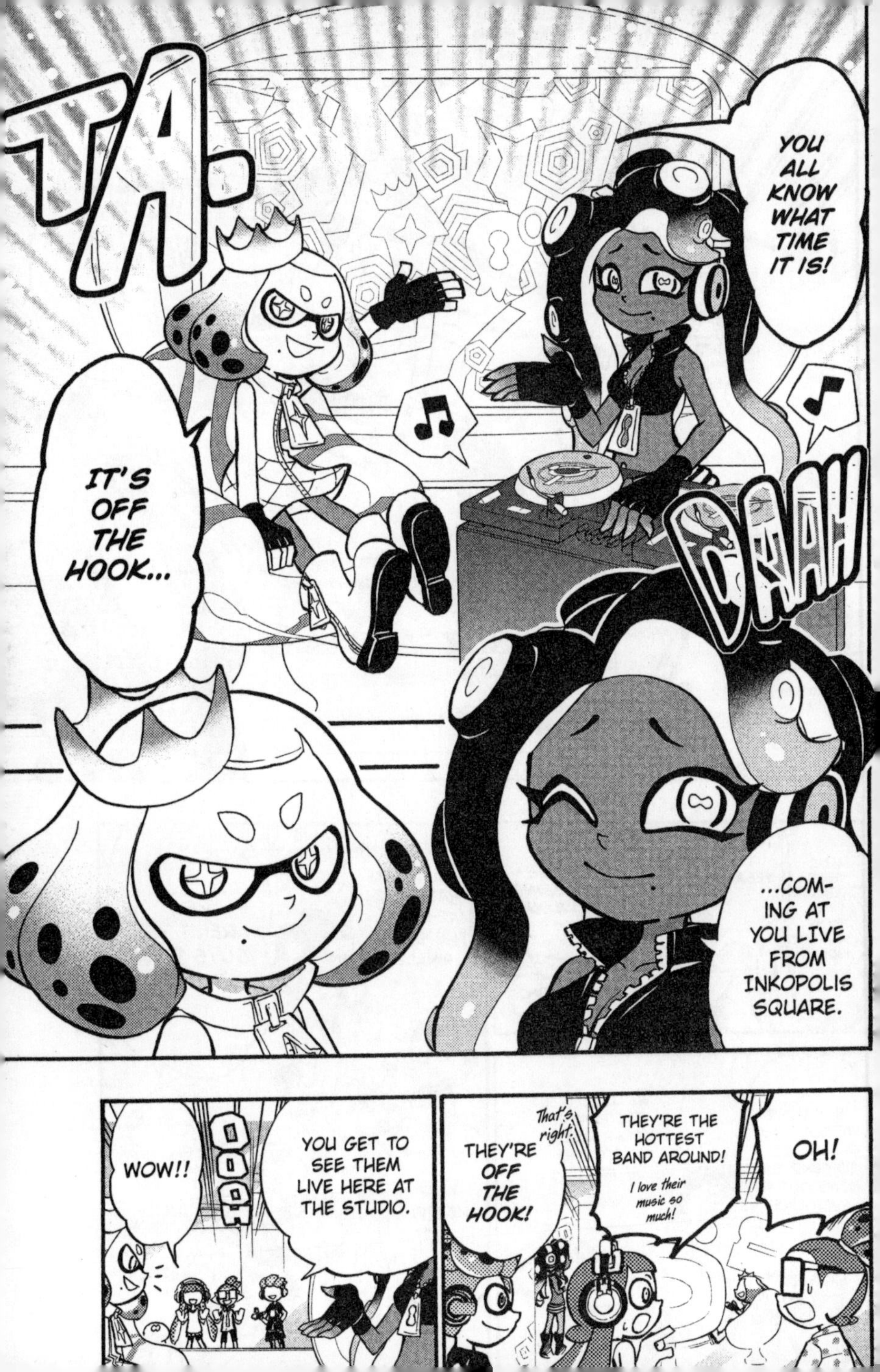
YOU ALL KNOW WHAT TIME IT IS!
TA-
DAAH
IT'S OFF THE HOOK...
...COMING AT YOU LIVE FROM INKOPOLIS SQUARE.
OH!
THEY'RE THE HOTTEST BAND AROUND!
I love their music so much!
That's right.
THEY'RE OFF THE HOOK!
YOU GET TO SEE THEM LIVE HERE AT THE STUDIO.
OOOOH
WOW!!

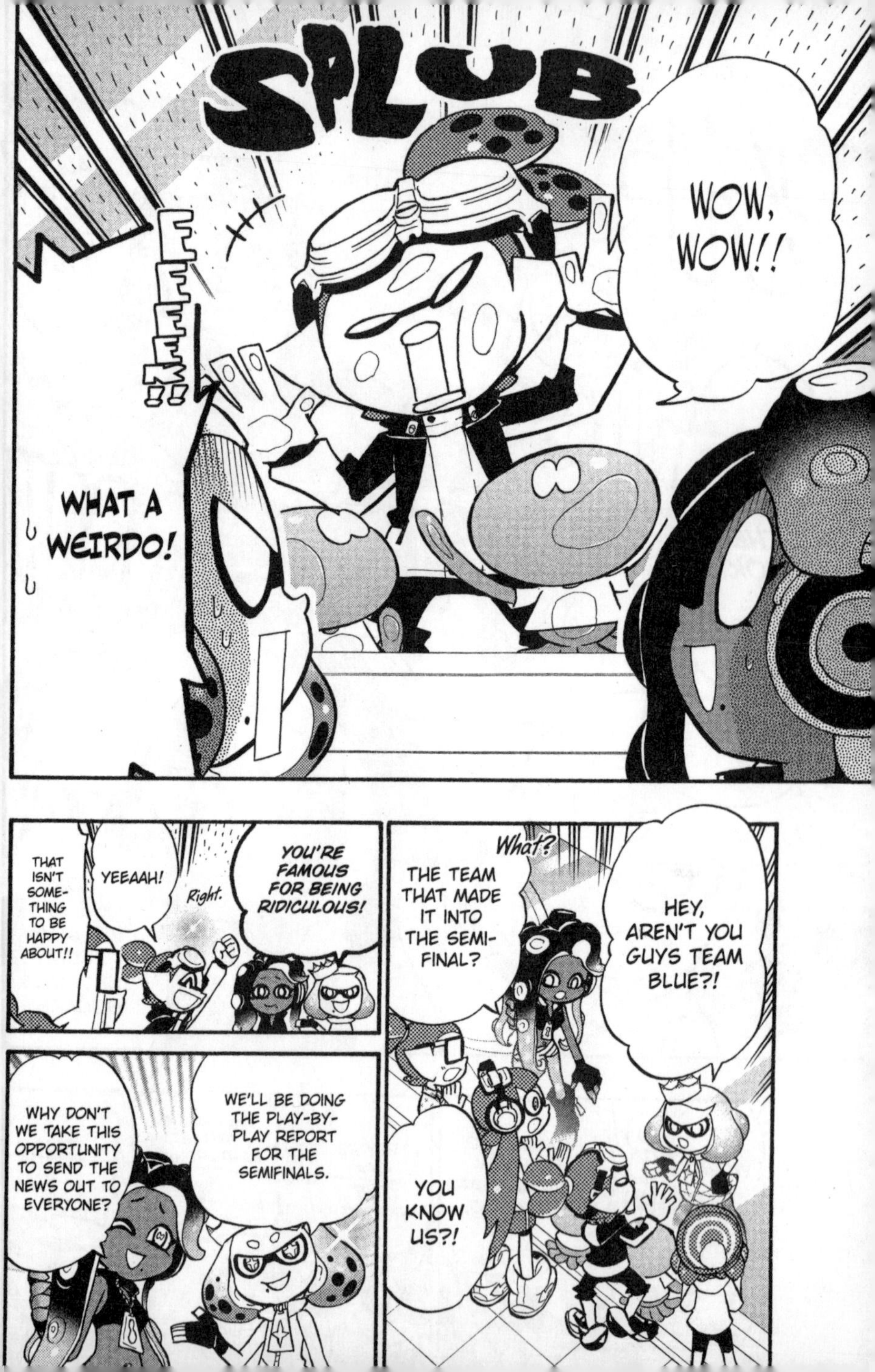
SPLUB
WOW, WOW!!
EEEEW!!
WHAT A WEIRDO!
HEY, AREN'T YOU GUYS TEAM BLUE?!
What?
THE TEAM THAT MADE IT INTO THE SEMI-FINAL?
YOU KNOW US?!
YOU'RE FAMOUS FOR BEING RIDICULOUS!
Right.
YEEAAAH!
THAT ISN'T SOME-THING TO BE HAPPY ABOUT!!
WE'LL BE DOING THE PLAY-BY-PLAY REPORT FOR THE SEMIFINALS.
WHY DON'T WE TAKE THIS OPPORTUNITY TO SEND THE NEWS OUT TO EVERYONE?

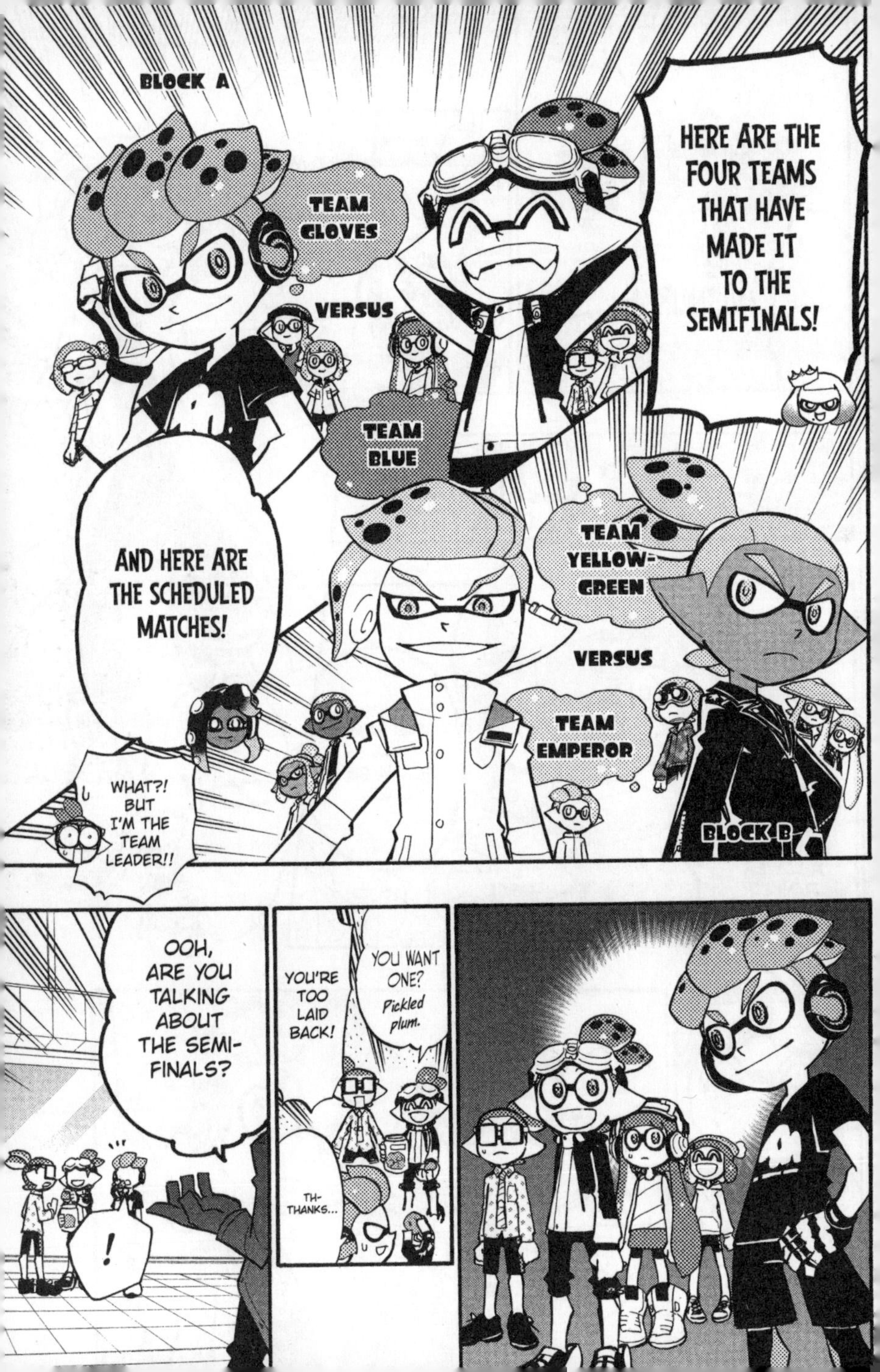
HERE ARE THE FOUR TEAMS THAT HAVE MADE IT TO THE SEMIFINALS!
BLOCK A
TEAM GLOVES
VERSUS
TEAM BLUE
AND HERE ARE THE SCHEDULED MATCHES!
TEAM YELLOW-GREEN
VERSUS
TEAM EMPEROR
BLOCK B
WHAT?! BUT I'M THE TEAM LEADER!!
YOU WANT ONE? Pickled plum.
YOU'RE TOO LAID BACK!
TH-THANKS...
OOH, ARE YOU TALKING ABOUT THE SEMI-FINALS?
!

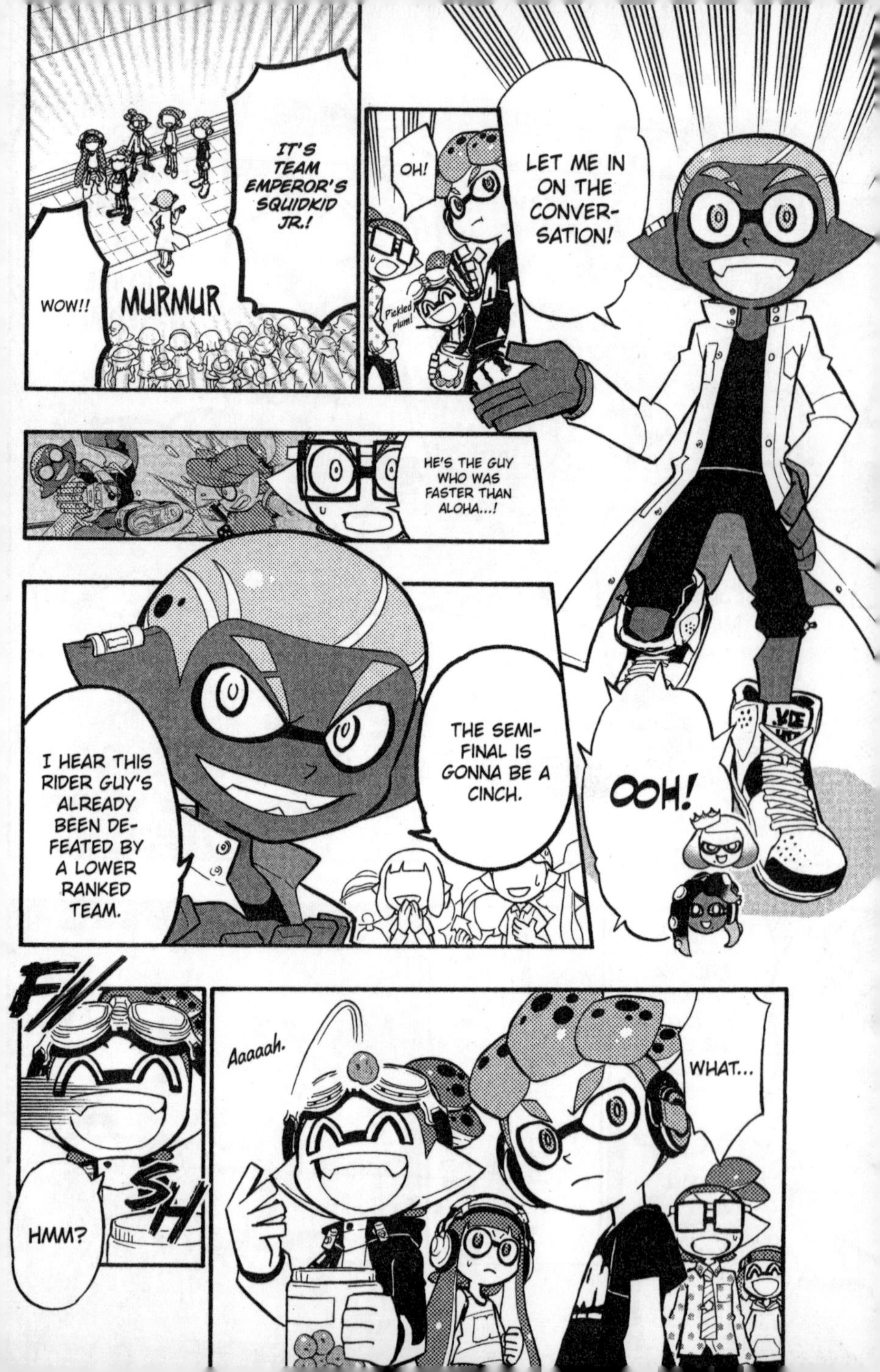
LET ME IN ON THE CONVERSATION!
OH!
Pickled plum!
IT'S TEAM EMPEROR'S SQUIDKID JR.!
MURMUR
WOW!!
HE'S THE GUY WHO WAS FASTER THAN ALOHA...!
OOH!
THE SEMI-FINAL IS GONNA BE A CINCH.
I HEAR THIS RIDER GUY'S ALREADY BEEN DE-FEATED BY A LOWER RANKED TEAM.
WHAT...
Aaaaah.
FW
SH
HMM?

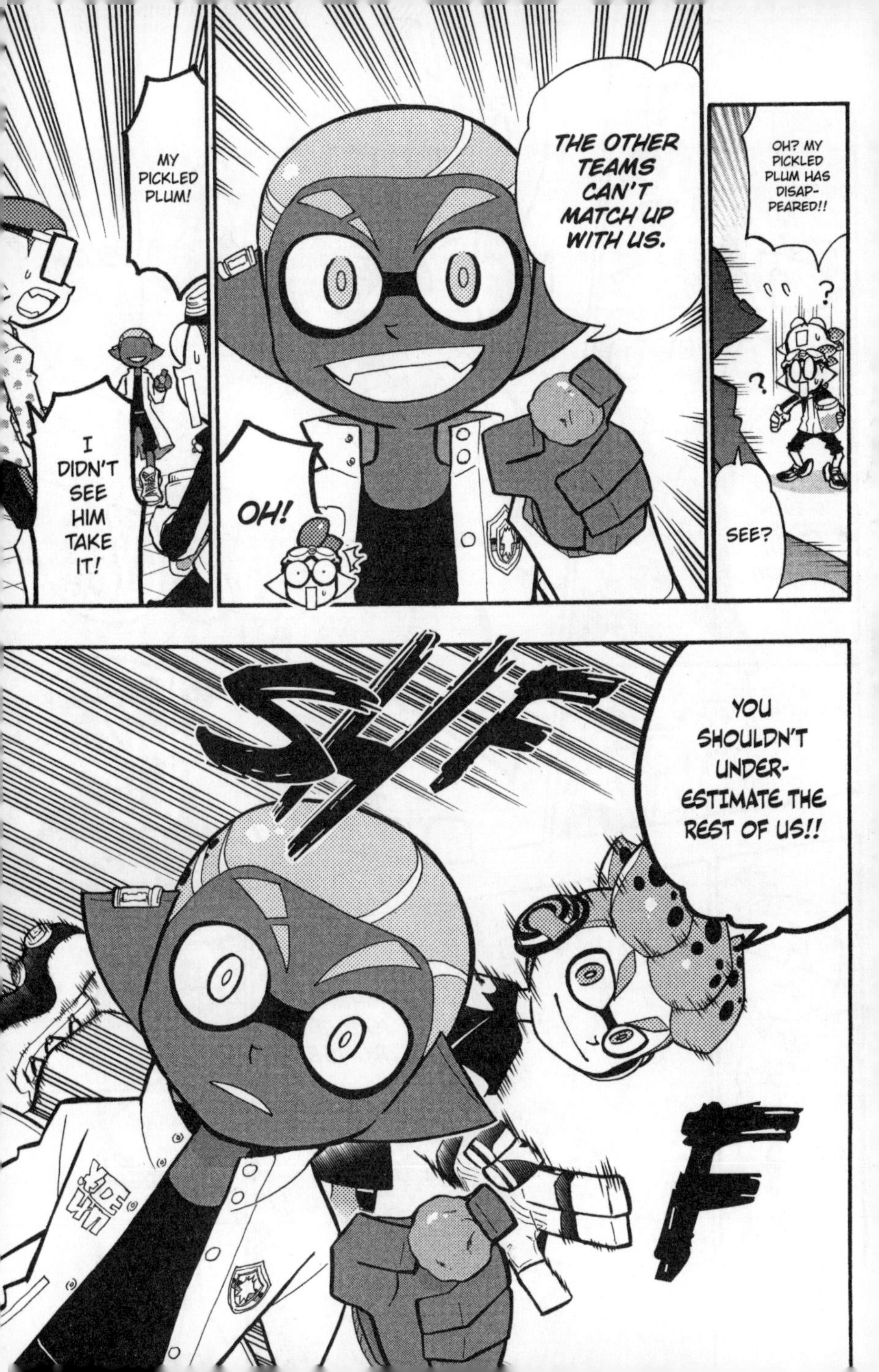

OH? MY PICKLED PLUM HAS DISAP-PEARED!!
SEE?
THE OTHER TEAMS CAN'T MATCH UP WITH US.
OH!
MY PICKLED PLUM!
I DIDN'T SEE HIM TAKE IT!
YOU SHOULDN'T UNDER-ESTIMATE THE REST OF US!!

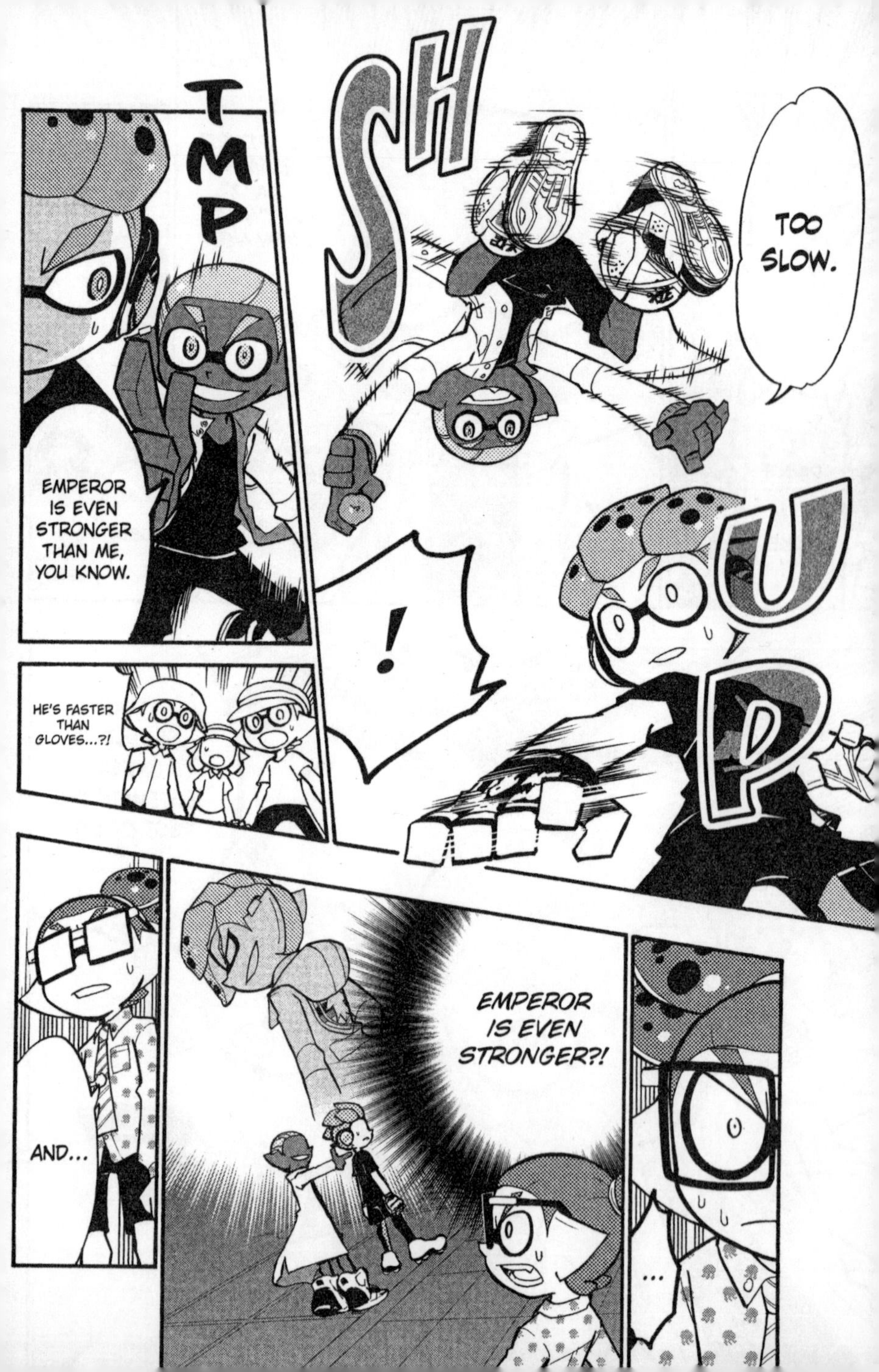
SH
TOO SLOW.
!
UP
TMP
EMPEROR IS EVEN STRONGER THAN ME, YOU KNOW.
HE'S FASTER THAN GLOVES...?!
...
EMPEROR IS EVEN STRONGER?!
AND...

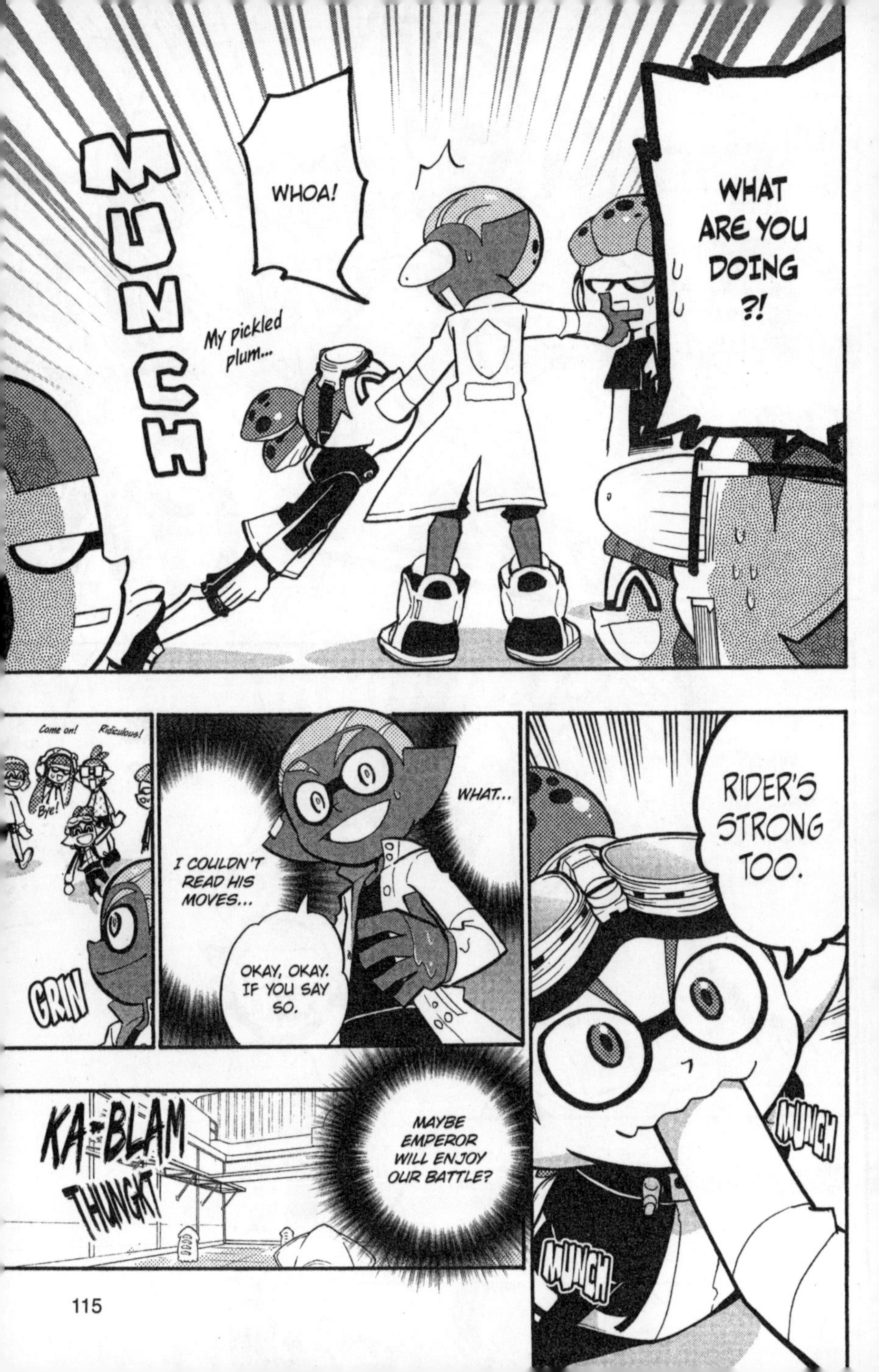
WHAT ARE YOU DOING ?!
WHOA!
My pickled plum...
MUNCH
RIDER'S STRONG TOO.
MUNCH
MUNCH
WHAT...
I COULDN'T READ HIS MOVES...
OKAY, OKAY. IF YOU SAY SO.
Ridiculous!
Come on!
Bye!
GRIN
MAYBE EMPEROR WILL ENJOY OUR BATTLE?
KA-BLAM
THUNGK!

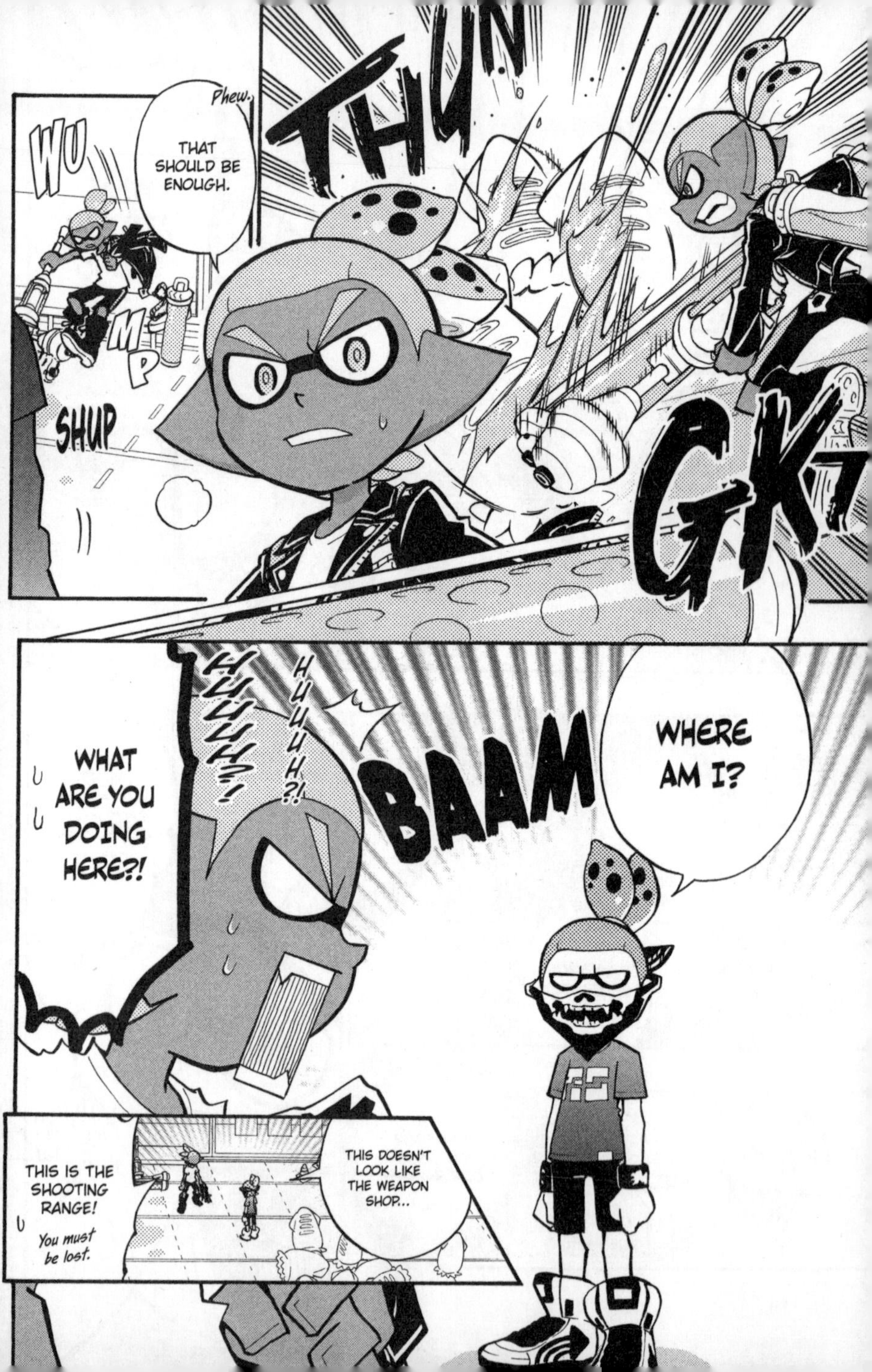
THUN
GK
Phew.
THAT SHOULD BE ENOUGH.
WUMP
SHUP
WHERE AM I?
BAAM
HUUUUH?!
HUUUUH?!
WHAT ARE YOU DOING HERE?!
THIS DOESN'T LOOK LIKE THE WEAPON SHOP...
THIS IS THE SHOOTING RANGE!
You must be lost.

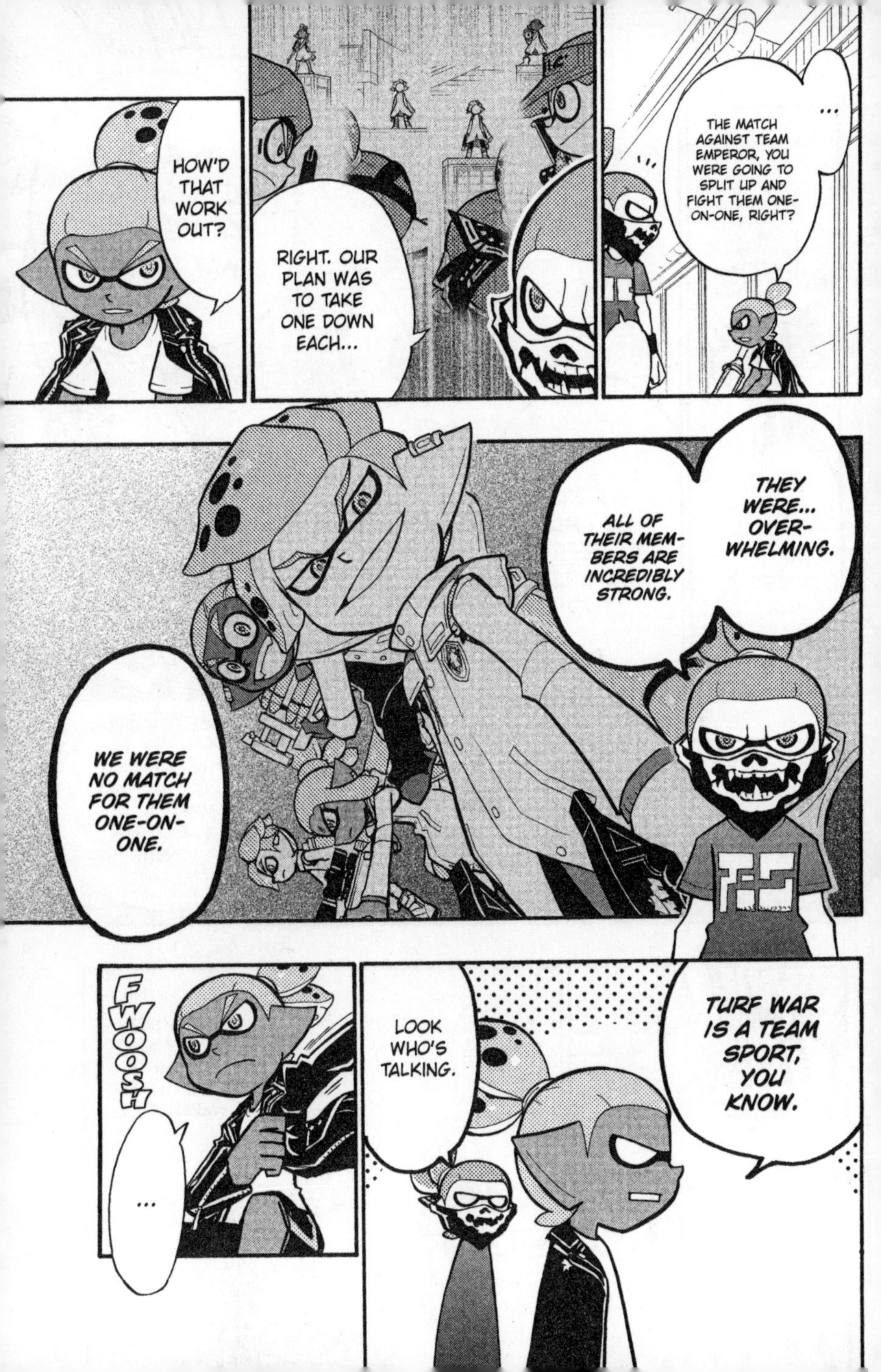
...
THE MATCH AGAINST TEAM EMPEROR, YOU WERE GOING TO SPLIT UP AND FIGHT THEM ONE-ON-ONE, RIGHT?
RIGHT. OUR PLAN WAS TO TAKE ONE DOWN EACH...
HOW'D THAT WORK OUT?
THEY WERE... OVERWHELMING.
ALL OF THEIR MEMBERS ARE INCREDIBLY STRONG.
WE WERE NO MATCH FOR THEM ONE-ON-ONE.
TURF WAR IS A TEAM SPORT, YOU KNOW.
LOOK WHO'S TALKING.
FWOOSH
...

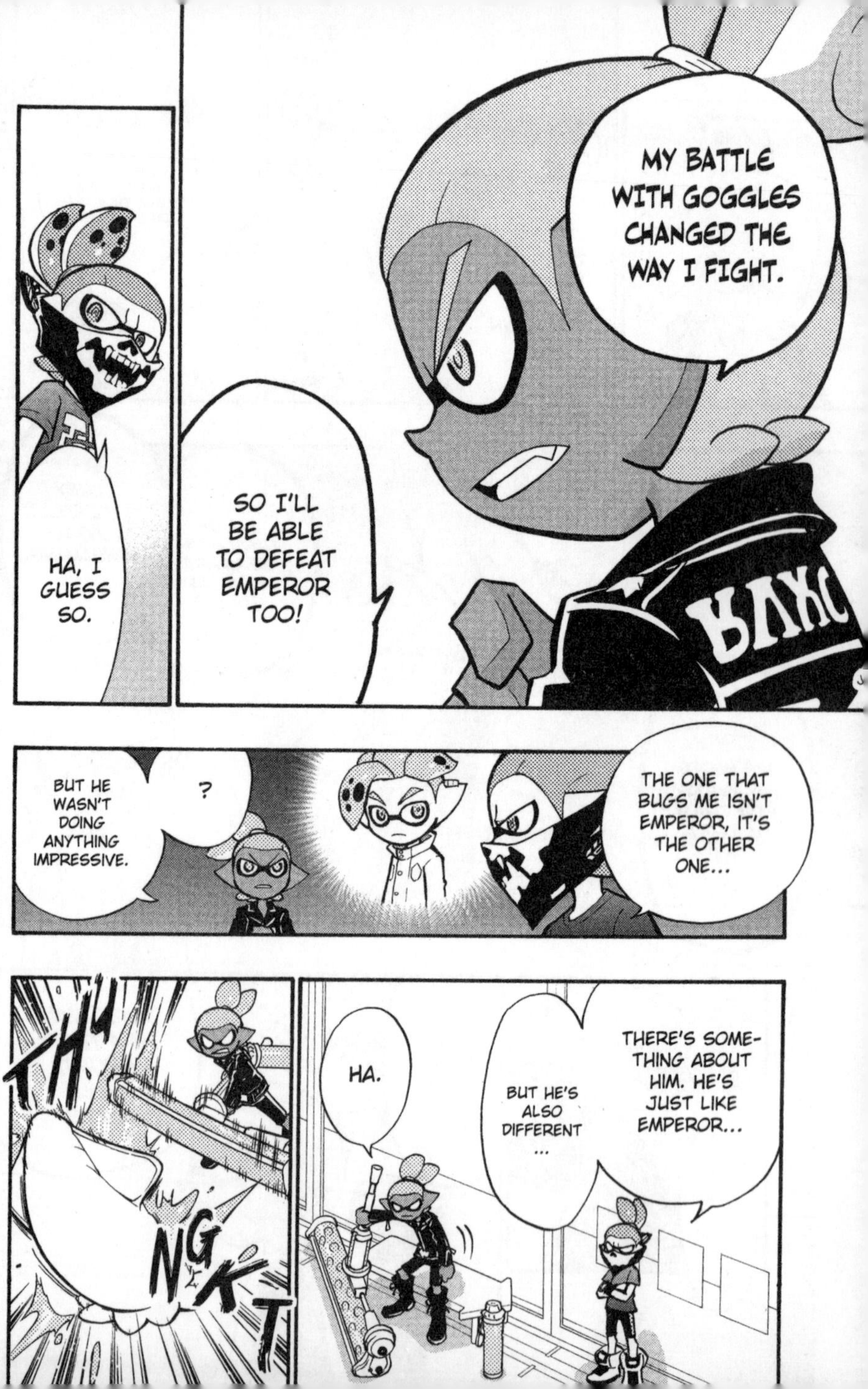
MY BATTLE WITH GOGGLES CHANGED THE WAY I FIGHT.
SO I'LL BE ABLE TO DEFEAT EMPEROR TOO!
HA, I GUESS SO.
THE ONE THAT BUGS ME ISN'T EMPEROR, IT'S THE OTHER ONE...
?
BUT HE WASN'T DOING ANYTHING IMPRESSIVE.
THERE'S SOME-THING ABOUT HIM. HE'S JUST LIKE EMPEROR...
BUT HE'S ALSO DIFFERENT ...
HA.
THUNGKT

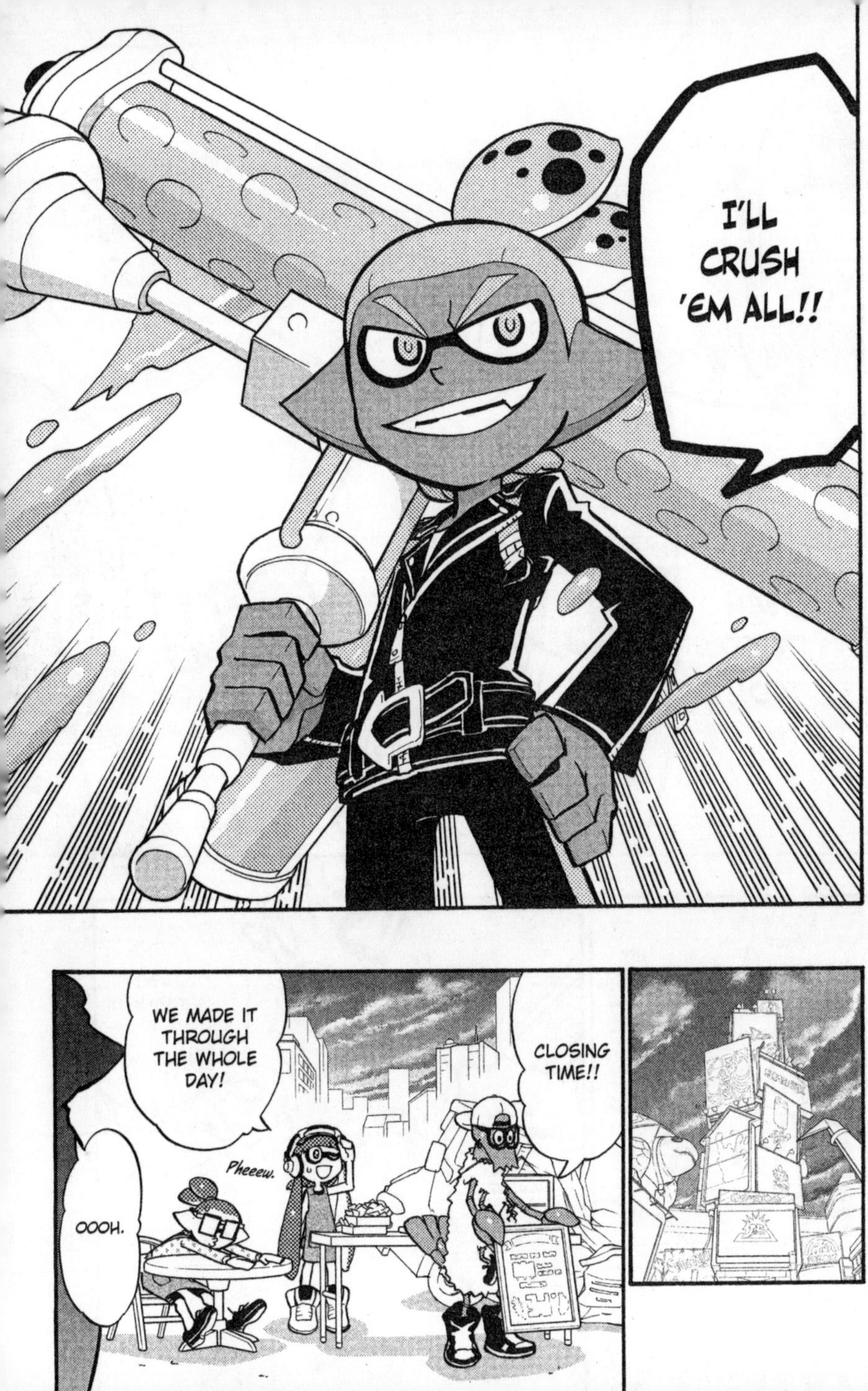
I'LL CRUSH 'EM ALL!!
CLOSING TIME!!
WE MADE IT THROUGH THE WHOLE DAY!
Pheeew.
OOOH.

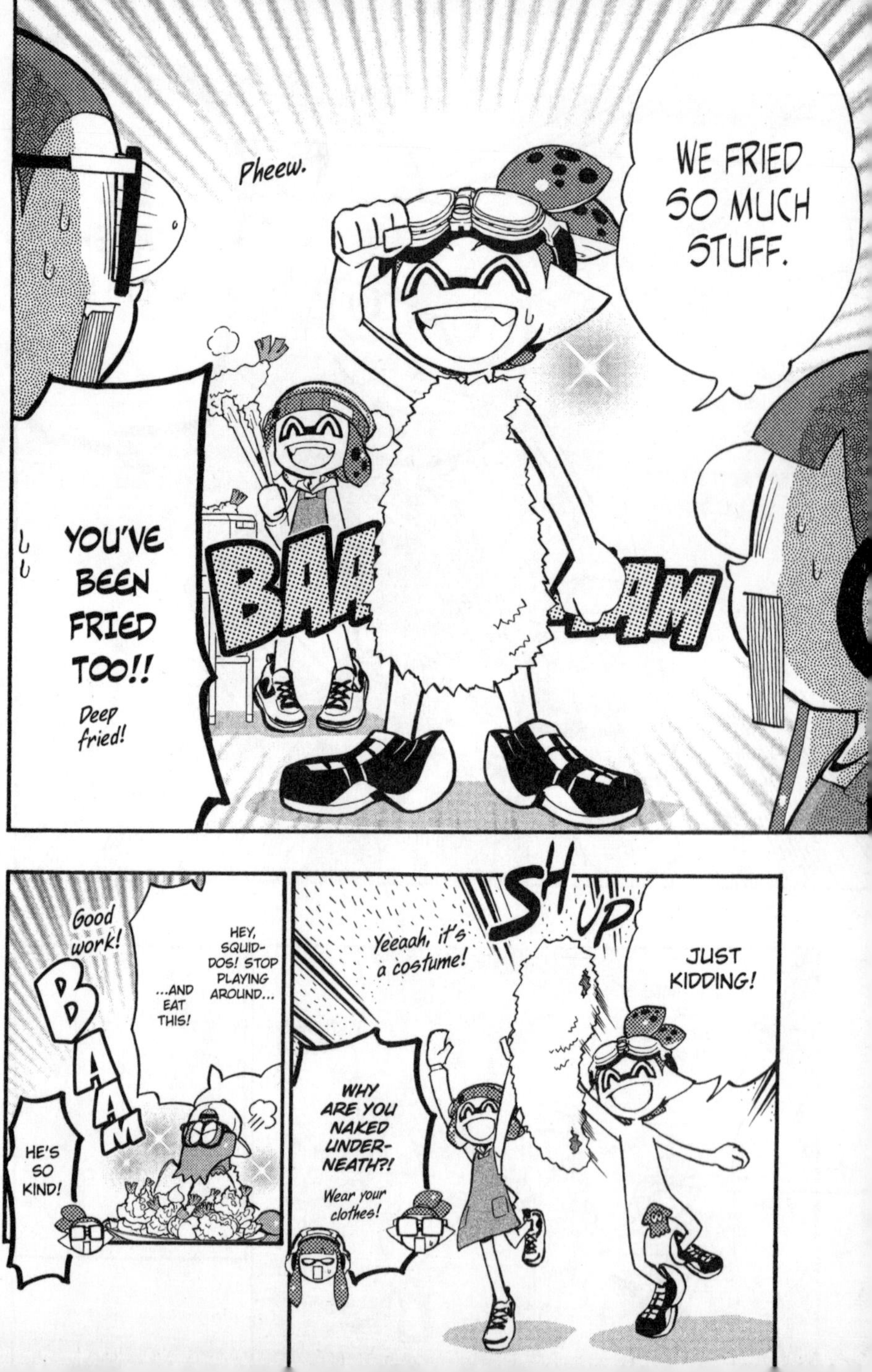
WE FRIED SO MUCH STUFF.
Pheew.
BAA
AM
YOU'VE BEEN FRIED TOO!!
Deep fried!
SHUP
JUST KIDDING!
Yeeaah, it's a costume!
WHY ARE YOU NAKED UNDERNEATH?!
Wear your clothes!
HEY, SQUID-DOS! STOP PLAYING AROUND...
...AND EAT THIS!
Good work!
BAAM
HE'S SO KIND!

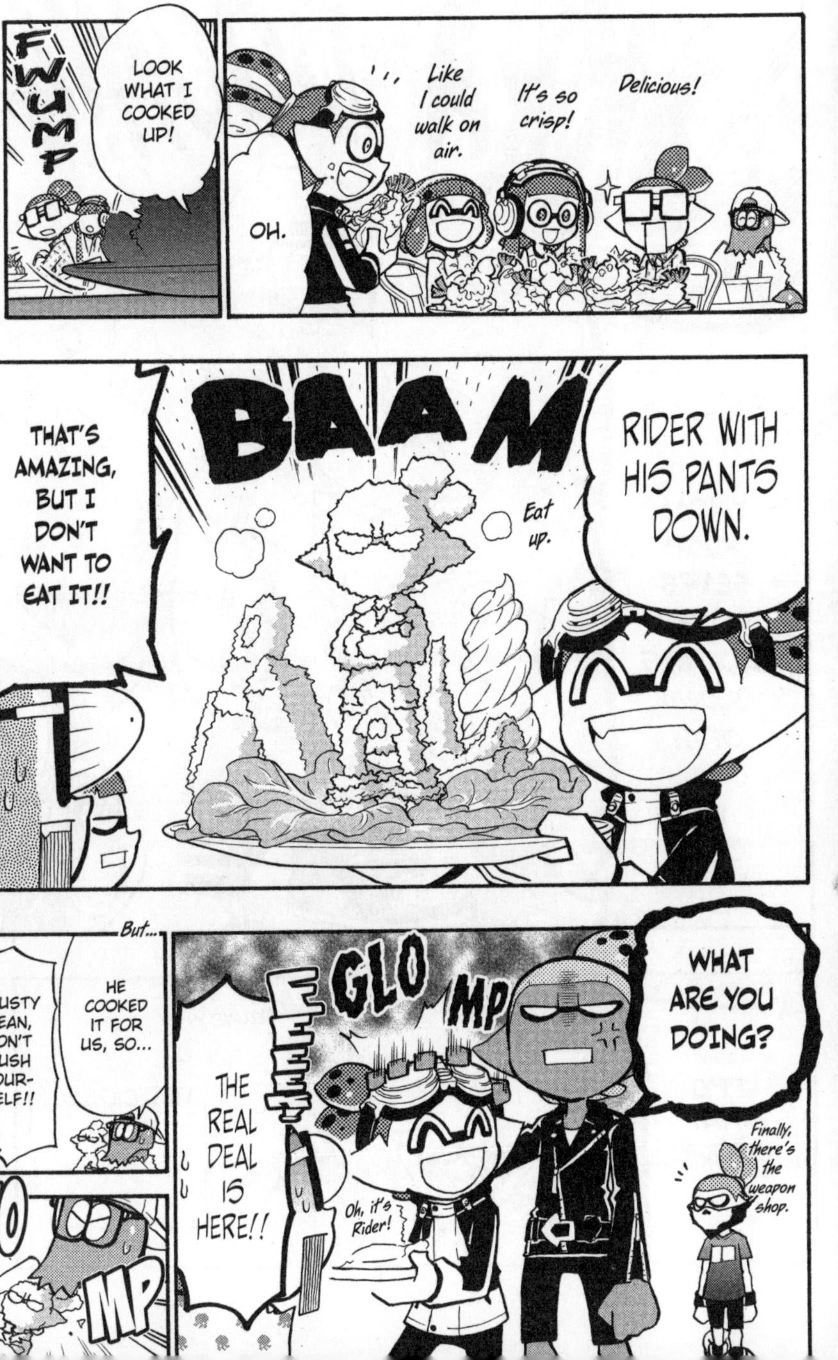
Delicious!
It's so crisp!
Like I could walk on air.
OH.
LOOK WHAT I COOKED UP!
FWUMP
RIDER WITH HIS PANTS DOWN.
Eat up.
BAAM
THAT'S AMAZING, BUT I DON'T WANT TO EAT IT!!
WHAT ARE YOU DOING?
Finally, there's the weapon shop.
GLOMP
THE REAL DEAL IS HERE!!
Oh, it's Rider!
But...
HE COOKED IT FOR US, SO...
CRUSTY SEAN, DON'T PUSH YOUR-SELF!!
CHOMP

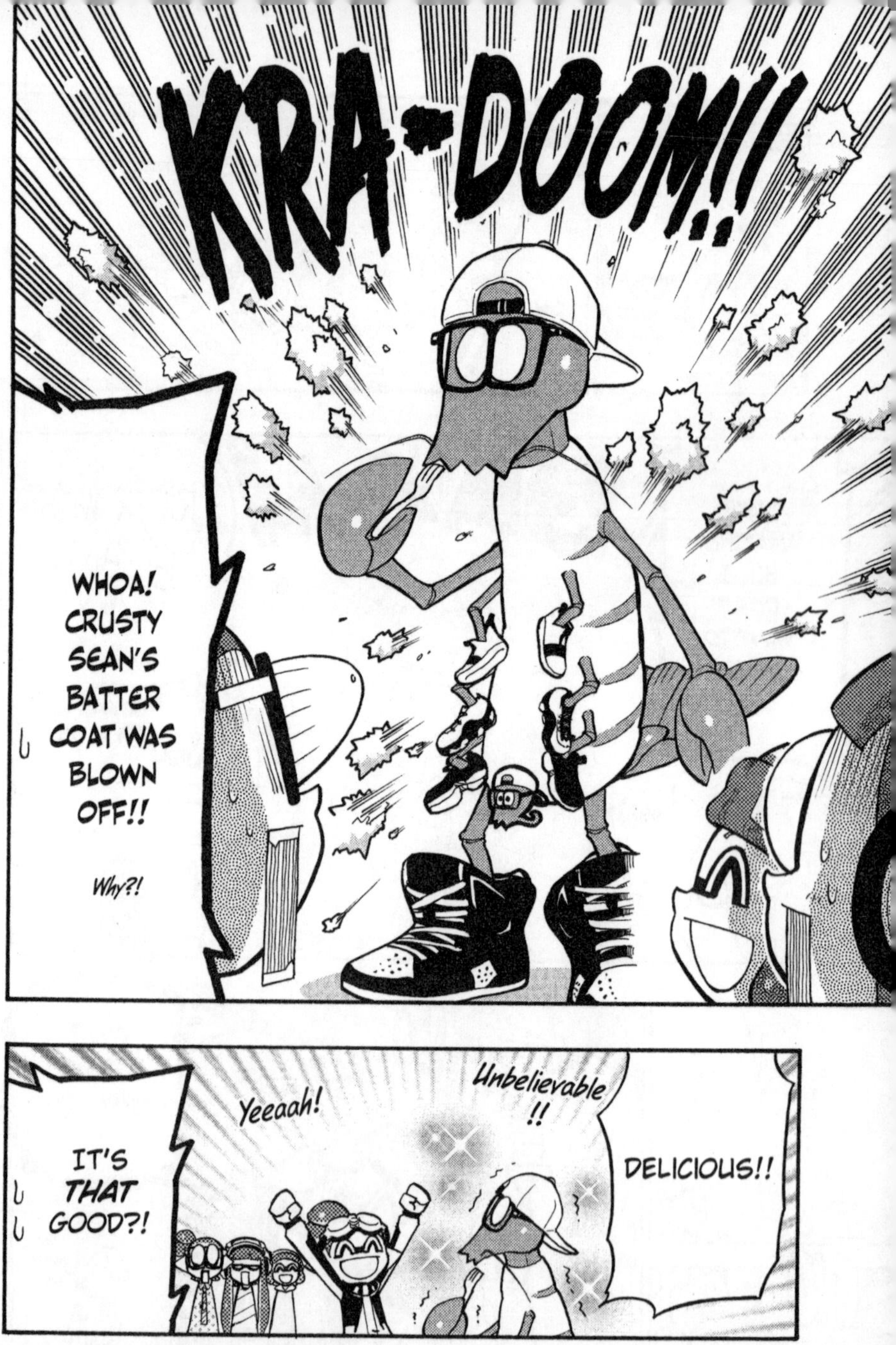
KRA-DOOM!!
WHOA! CRUSTY SEAN'S BATTER COAT WAS BLOWN OFF!!
Why?!
DELICIOUS!!
Unbelievable!!
Yeeaah!
IT'S THAT GOOD?!

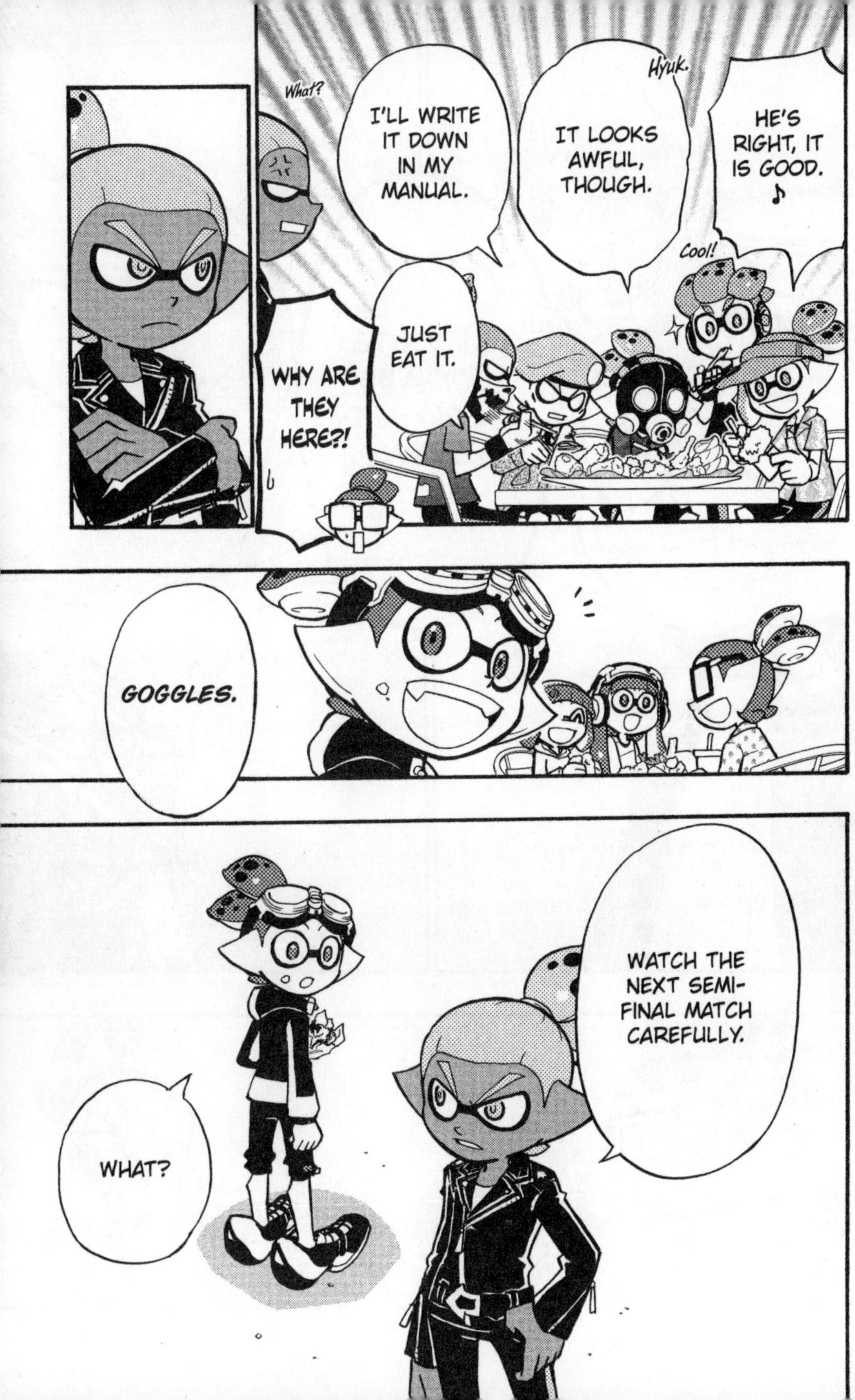
HE'S RIGHT, IT IS GOOD. ♪
Hyuk.
IT LOOKS AWFUL, THOUGH.
Cool!
I'LL WRITE IT DOWN IN MY MANUAL.
What?
JUST EAT IT.
WHY ARE THEY HERE?!
GOGGLES.
WATCH THE NEXT SEMI-FINAL MATCH CAREFULLY.
WHAT?

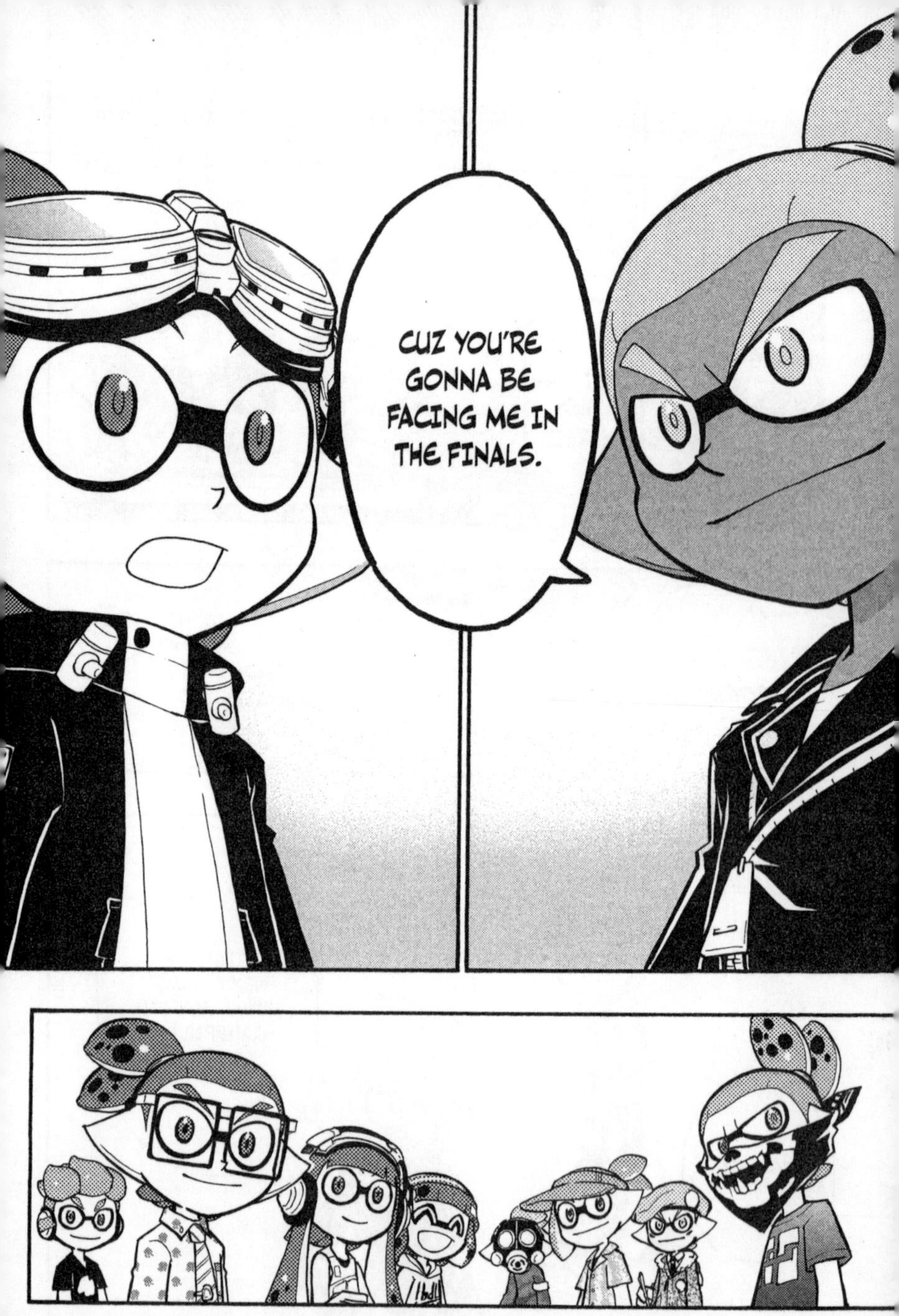
CUZ YOU'RE GONNA BE FACING ME IN THE FINALS.

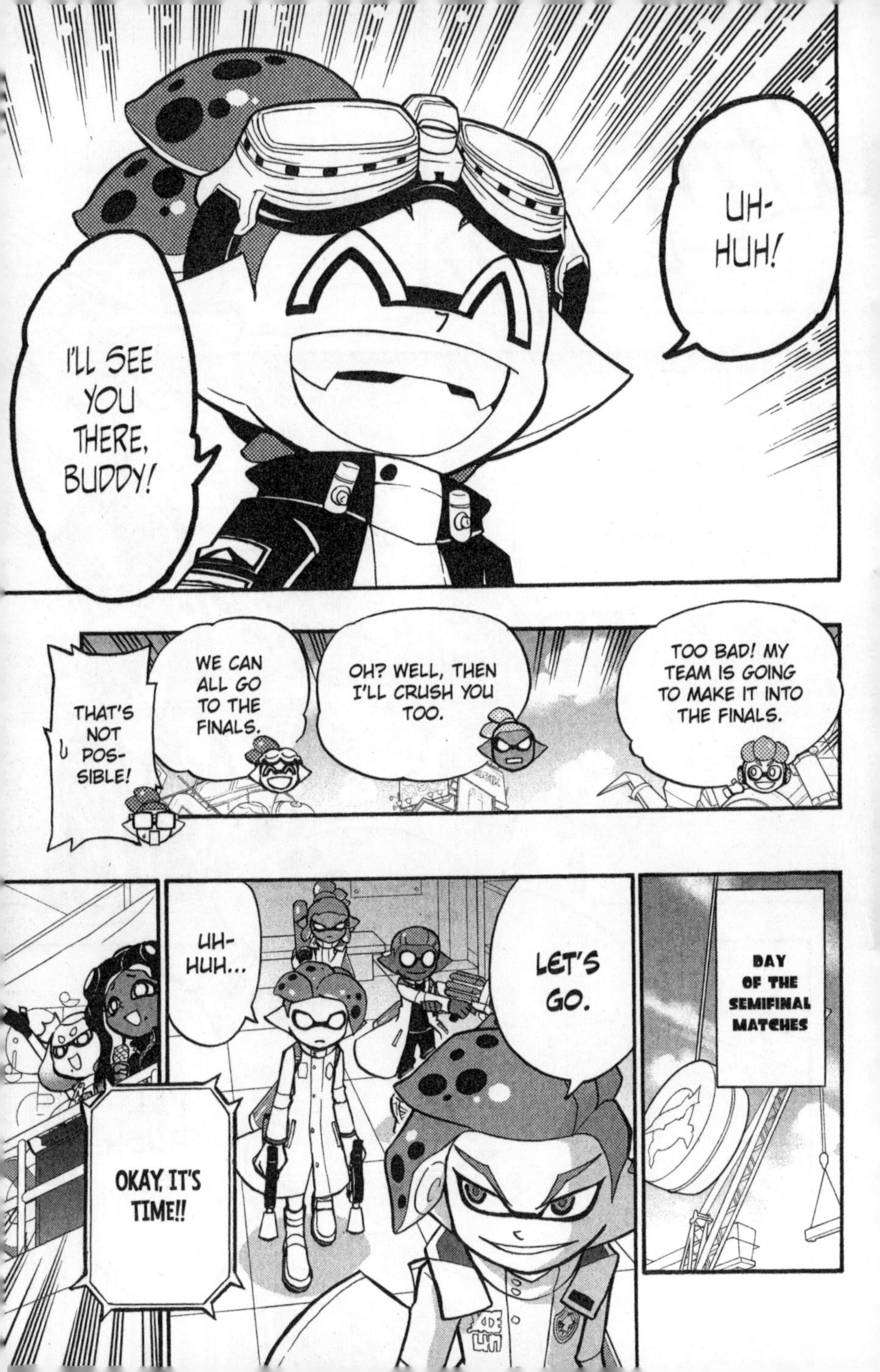
UH-HUH!
I'LL SEE YOU THERE, BUDDY!
TOO BAD! MY TEAM IS GOING TO MAKE IT INTO THE FINALS.
OH? WELL, THEN I'LL CRUSH YOU TOO.
WE CAN ALL GO TO THE FINALS.
THAT'S NOT POS-SIBLE!
DAY OF THE SEMIFINAL MATCHES
LET'S GO.
UH-HUH...
OKAY, IT'S TIME!!

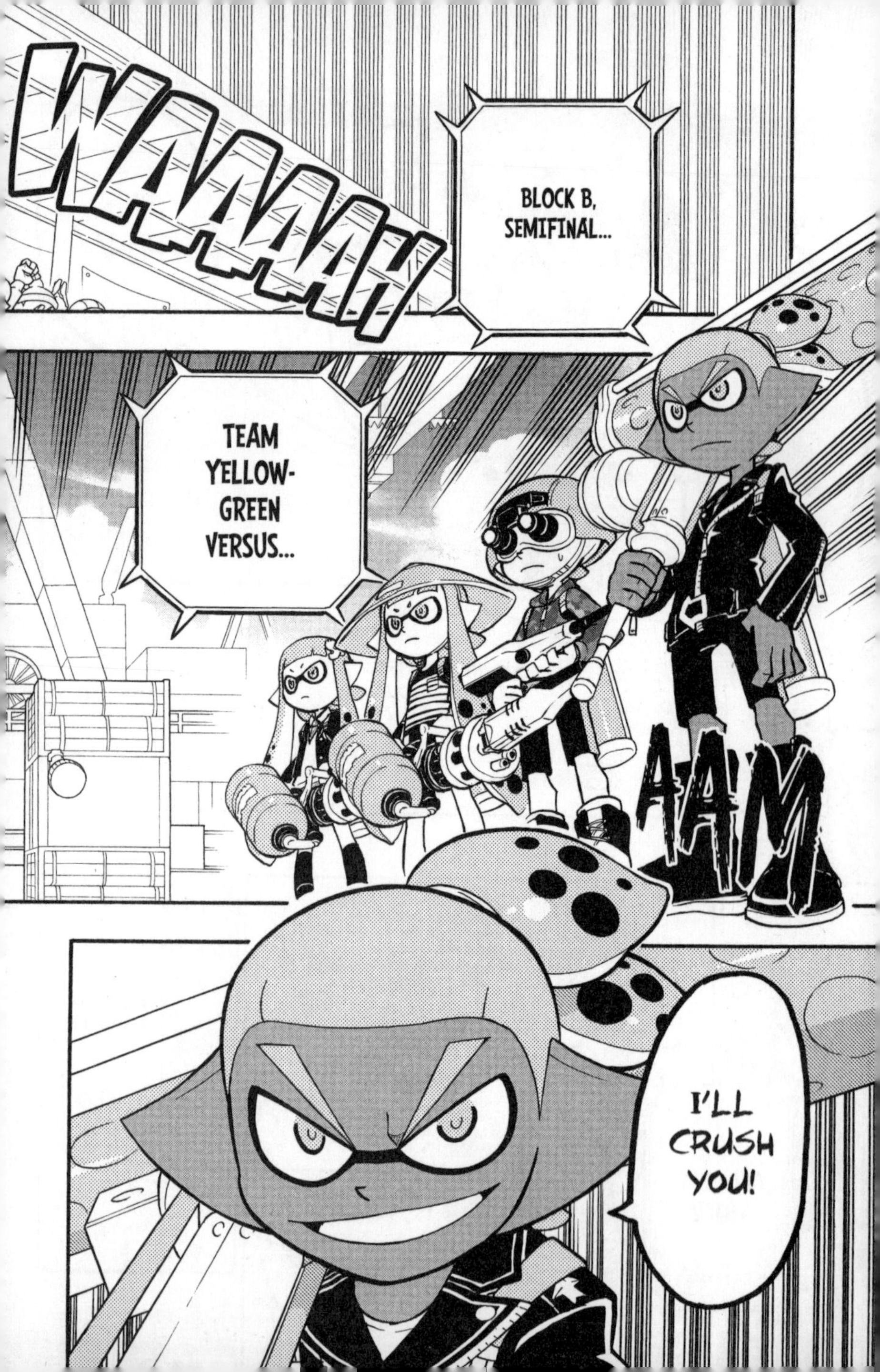
BLOCK B, SEMIFINAL...
WAAAAH
TEAM YELLOW-GREEN VERSUS...
AAM
I'LL CRUSH YOU!

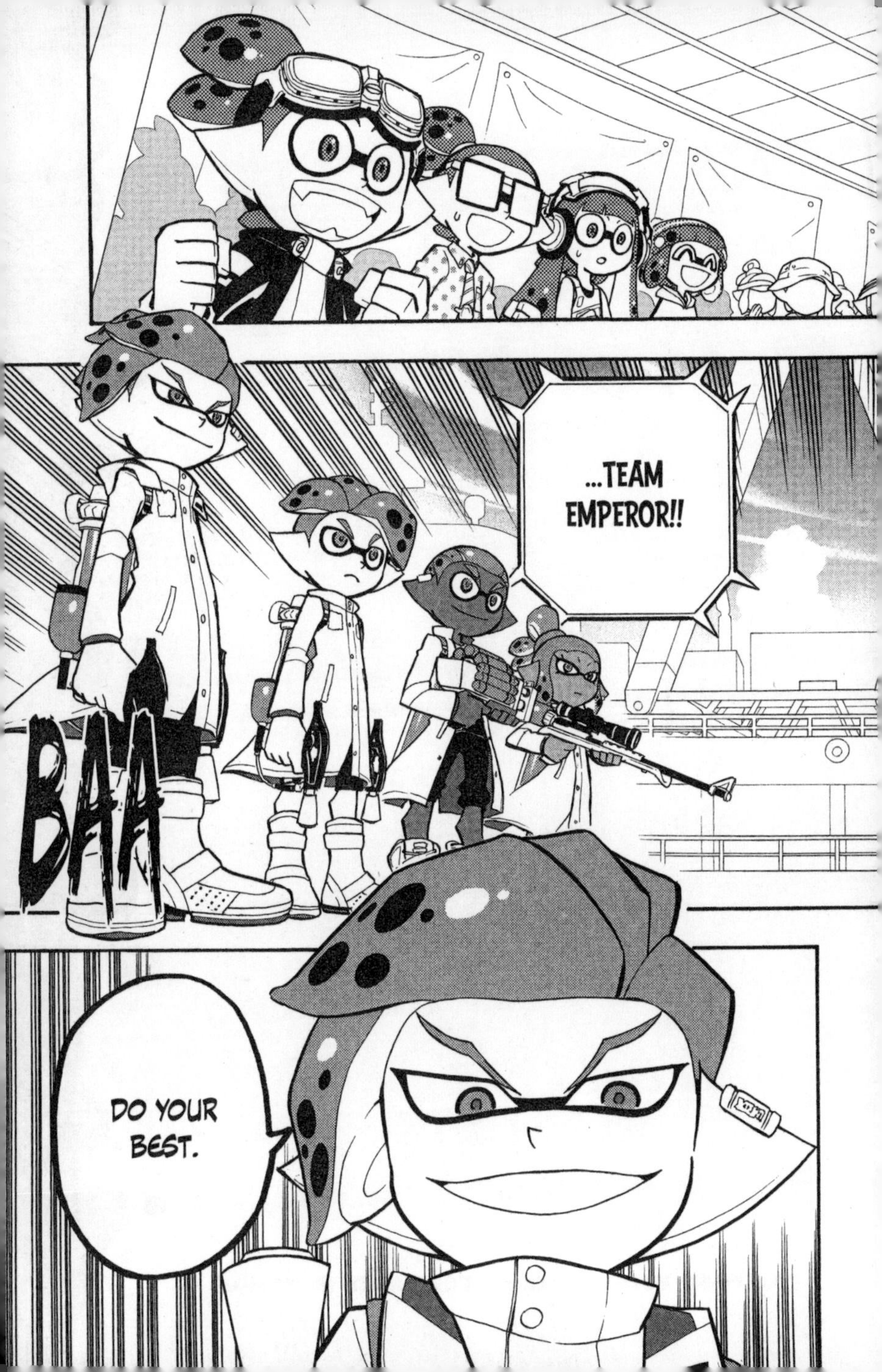
...TEAM EMPEROR!!
BAM
DO YOUR BEST.

SPLATOON VOLUME 4 END / CONTINUED IN VOLUME 5

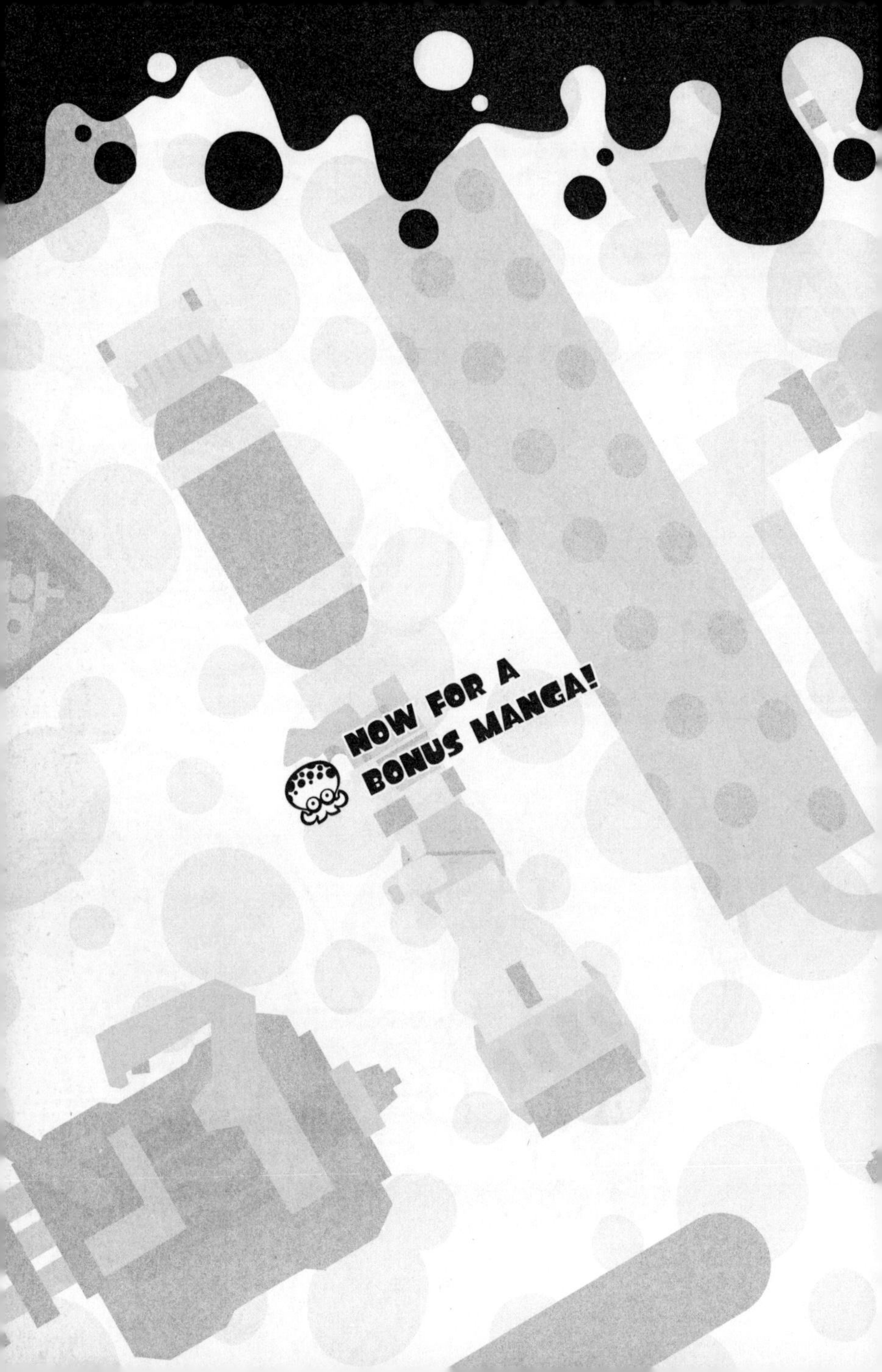
NOW FOR A
BONUS MANGA!

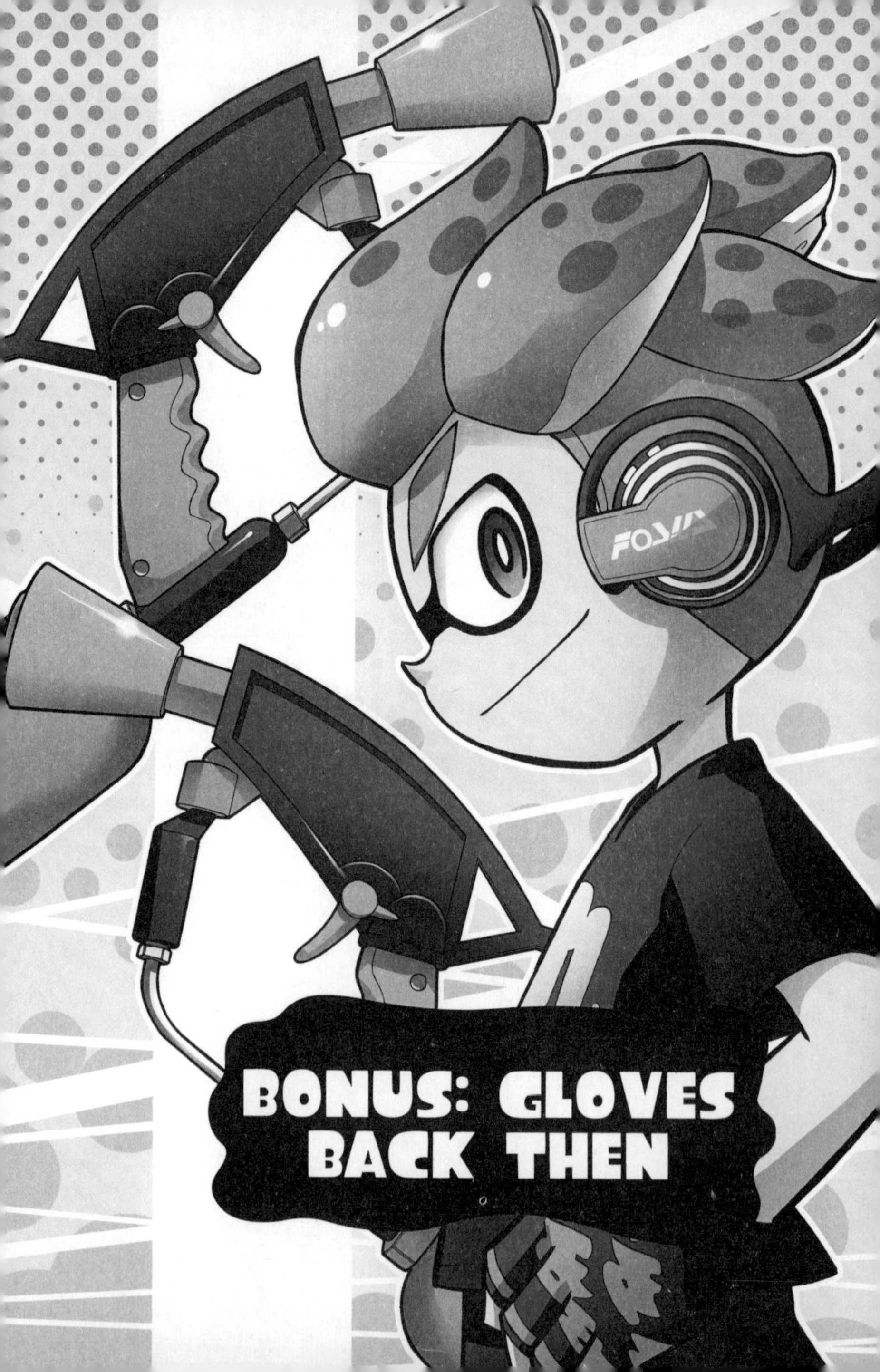
FOSIA
BONUS: GLOVES
BACK THEN

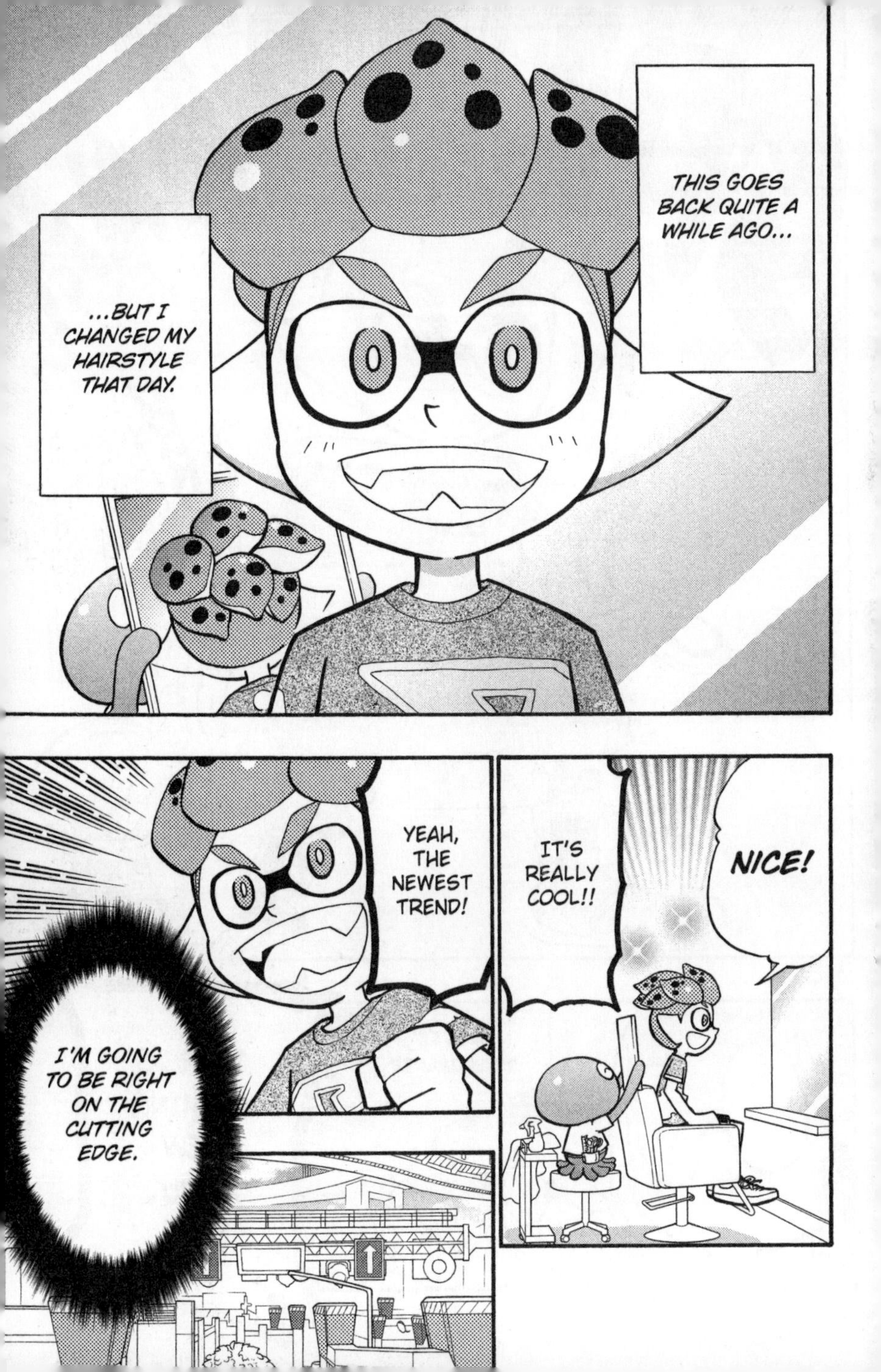
THIS GOES BACK QUITE A WHILE AGO...
...BUT I CHANGED MY HAIRSTYLE THAT DAY.
NICE!
IT'S REALLY COOL!!
YEAH, THE NEWEST TREND!
I'M GOING TO BE RIGHT ON THE CUTTING EDGE.

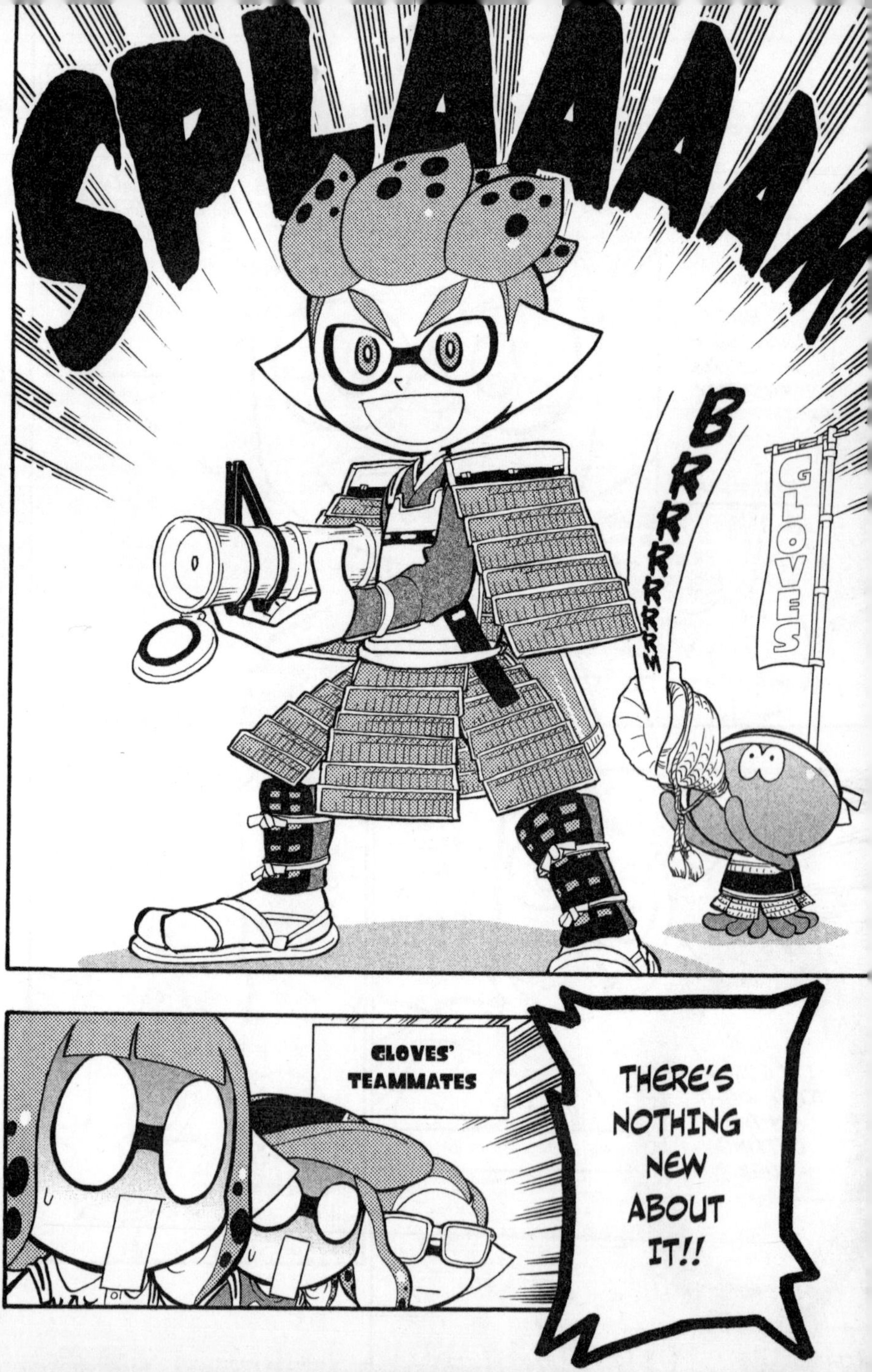
SPLAAAAM
BRRRRRRRM
GLOVES
THERE'S NOTHING NEW ABOUT IT!!
GLOVES' TEAMMATES

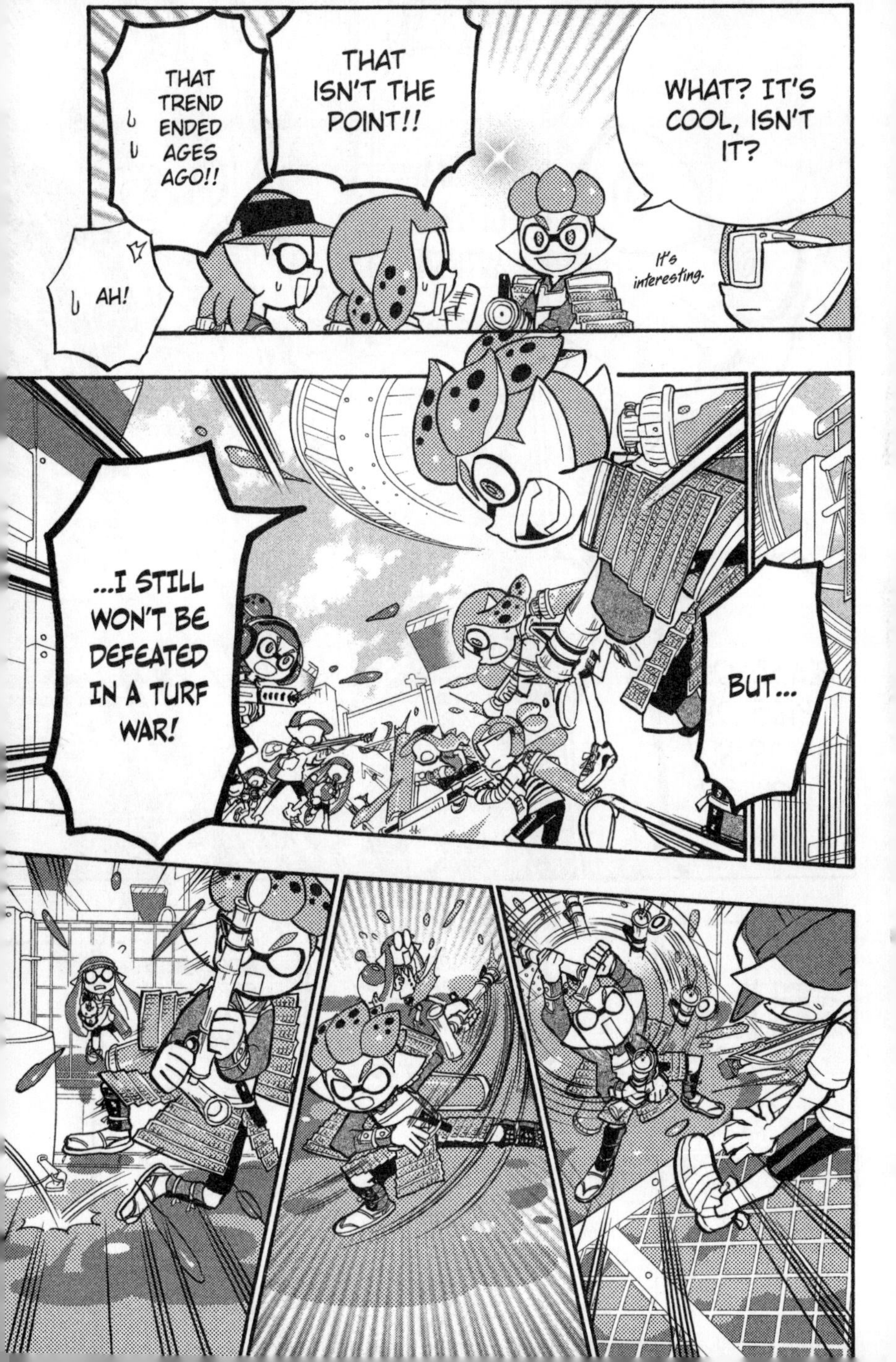
WHAT? IT'S COOL, ISN'T IT?
It's interesting.
THAT ISN'T THE POINT!!
THAT TREND ENDED AGES AGO!!
AH!
BUT...
...I STILL WON'T BE DEFEATED IN A TURF WAR!

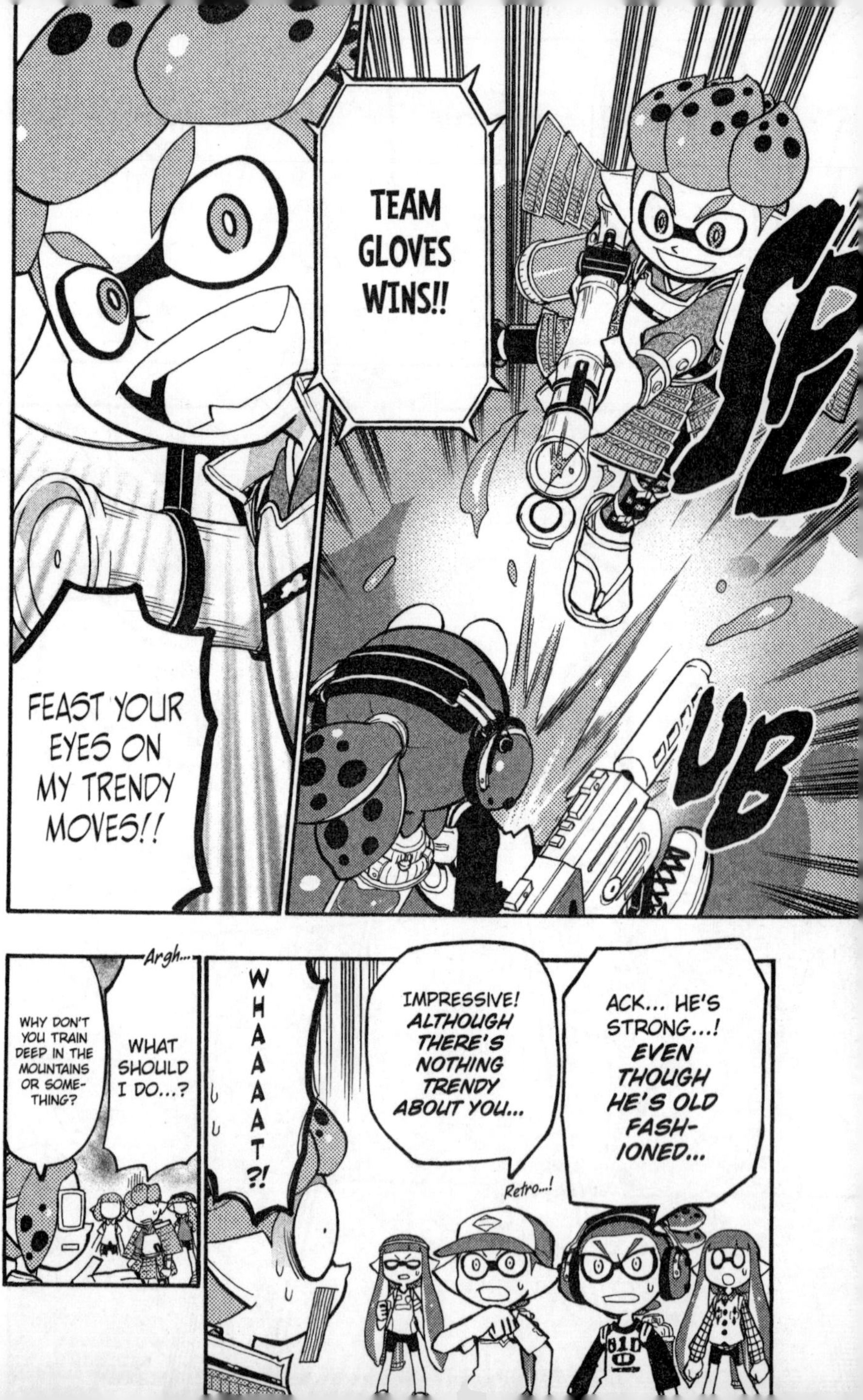
TEAM GLOVES WINS!!
FEAST YOUR EYES ON MY TRENDY MOVES!!
ACK... HE'S STRONG...! EVEN THOUGH HE'S OLD FASHIONED...
IMPRESSIVE! ALTHOUGH THERE'S NOTHING TRENDY ABOUT YOU...
Retro...!
WHAAAAAT?!
Argh...
WHAT SHOULD I DO...?
WHY DON'T YOU TRAIN DEEP IN THE MOUNTAINS OR SOMETHING?

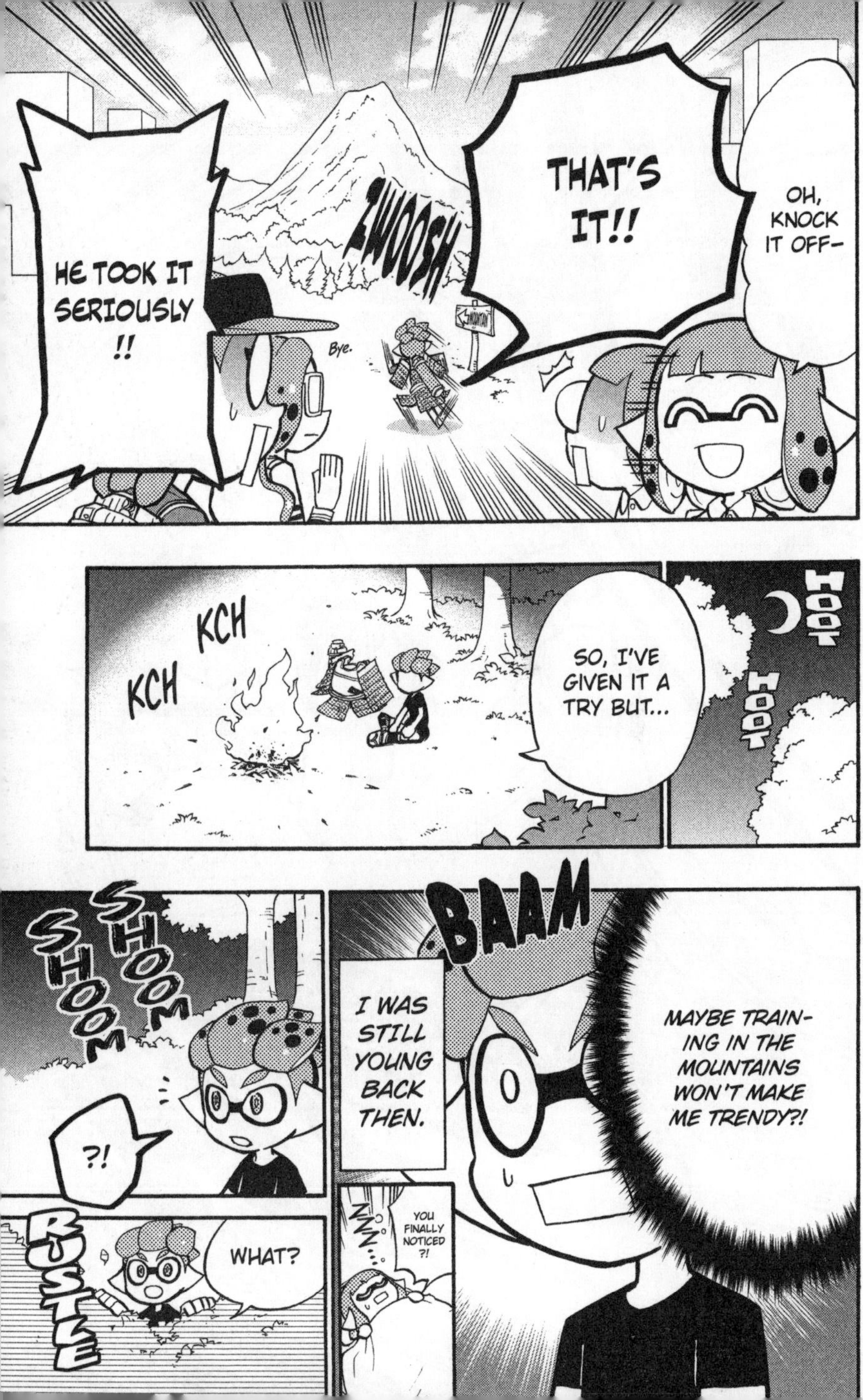
OH, KNOCK IT OFF–
THAT'S IT!!
ZWOOSH
Bye.
HE TOOK IT SERIOUSLY!!
HOOT HOOT
SO, I'VE GIVEN IT A TRY BUT...
KCH KCH
BAAM
MAYBE TRAINING IN THE MOUNTAINS WON'T MAKE ME TRENDY?!
I WAS STILL YOUNG BACK THEN.
YOU FINALLY NOTICED?!
ZZZ...
SHOOM SHOOM
?!
WHAT?
RUSTLE

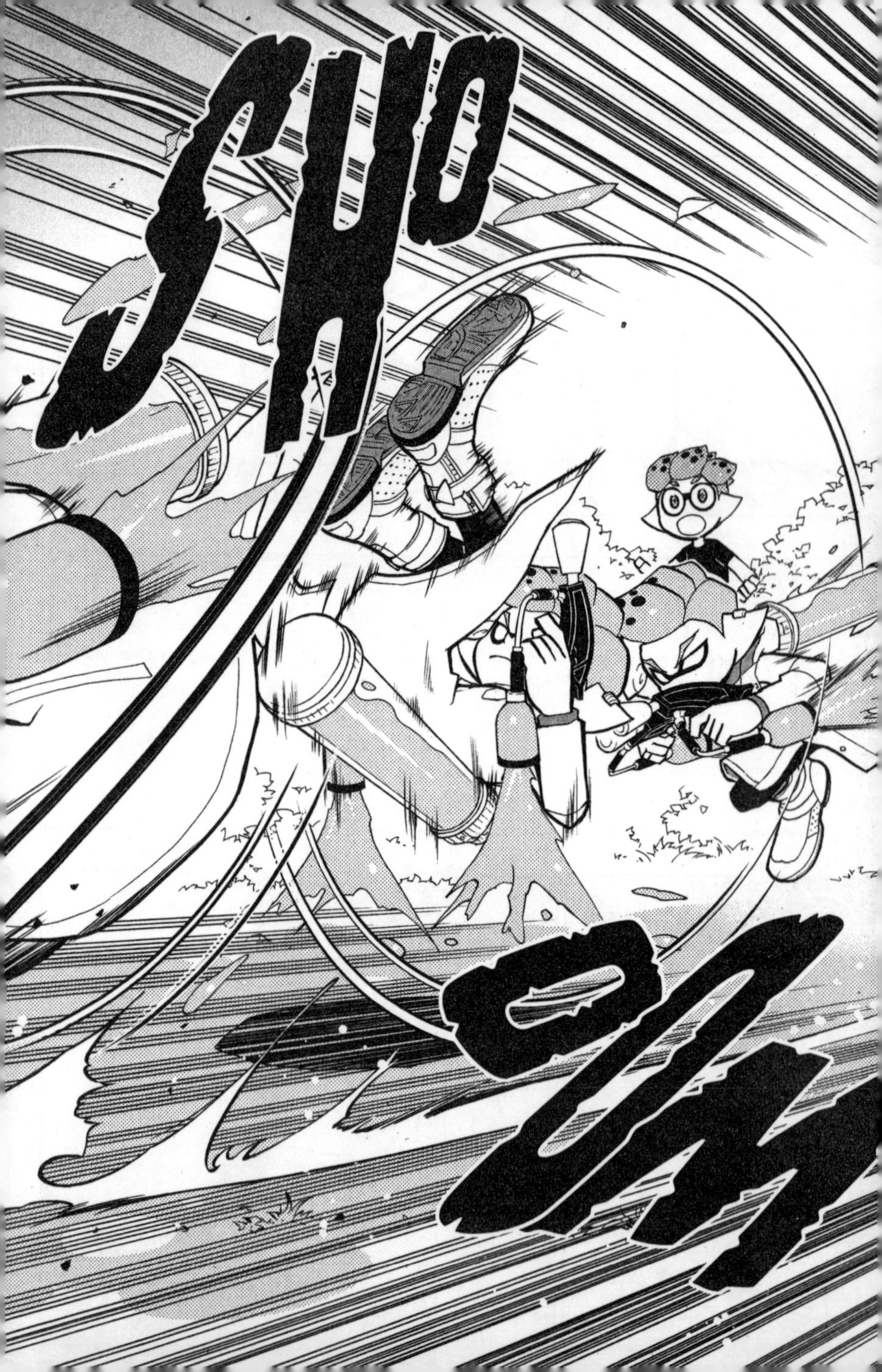

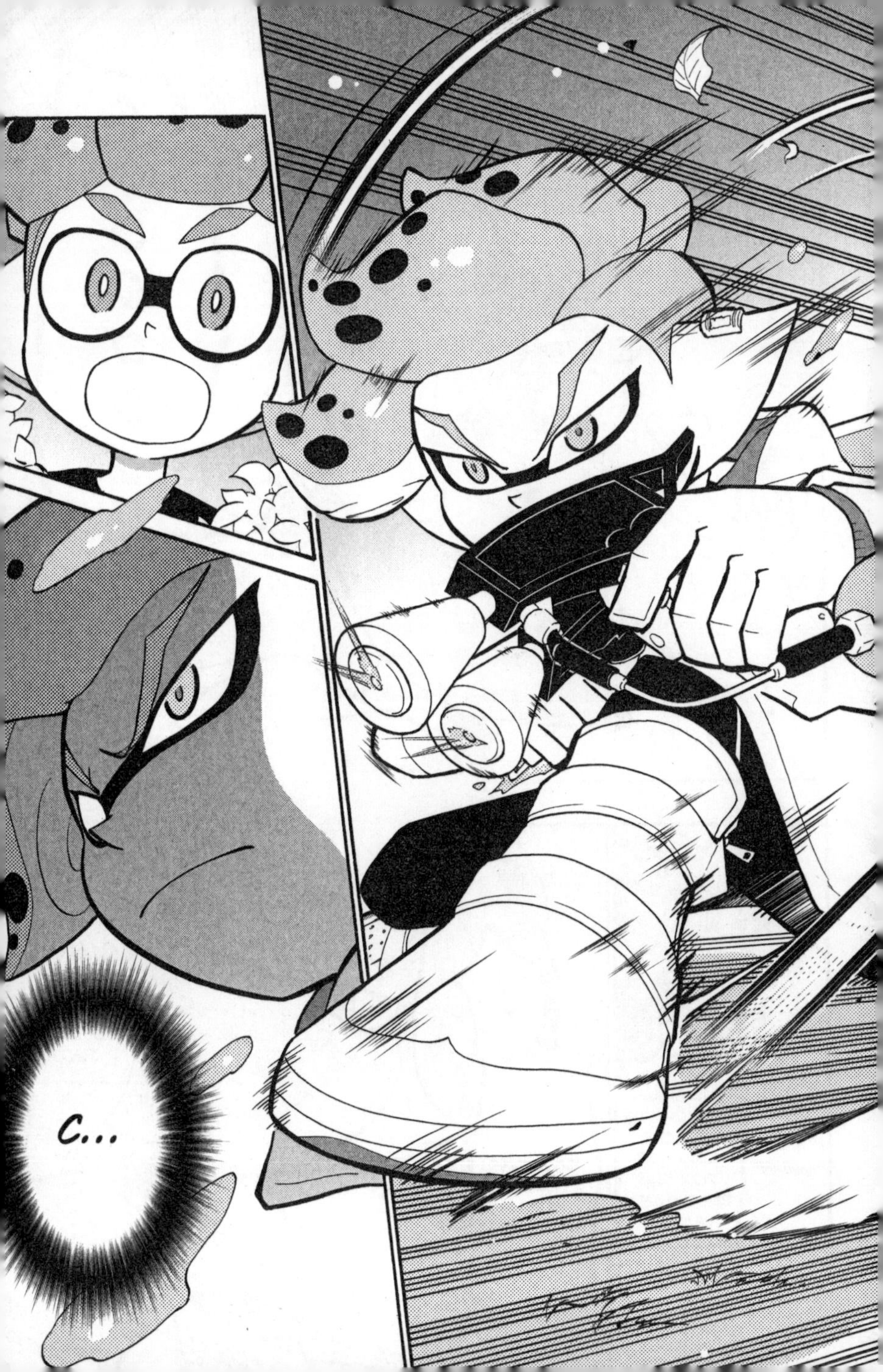
C...

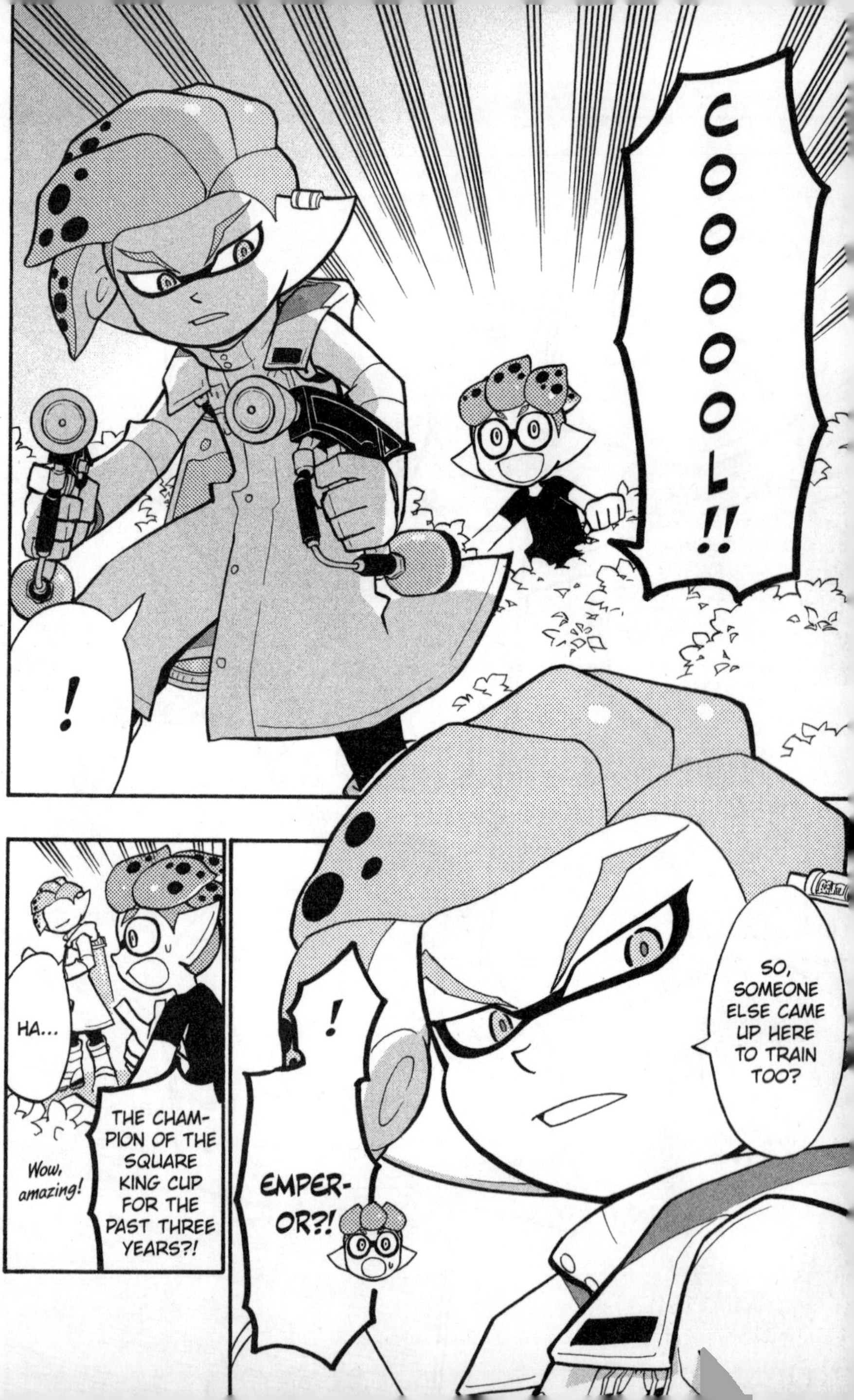
COOOOOL!!
!
SO, SOMEONE ELSE CAME UP HERE TO TRAIN TOO?
!
EMPER-OR?!
THE CHAM-PION OF THE SQUARE KING CUP FOR THE PAST THREE YEARS?!
HA...
Wow, amazing!

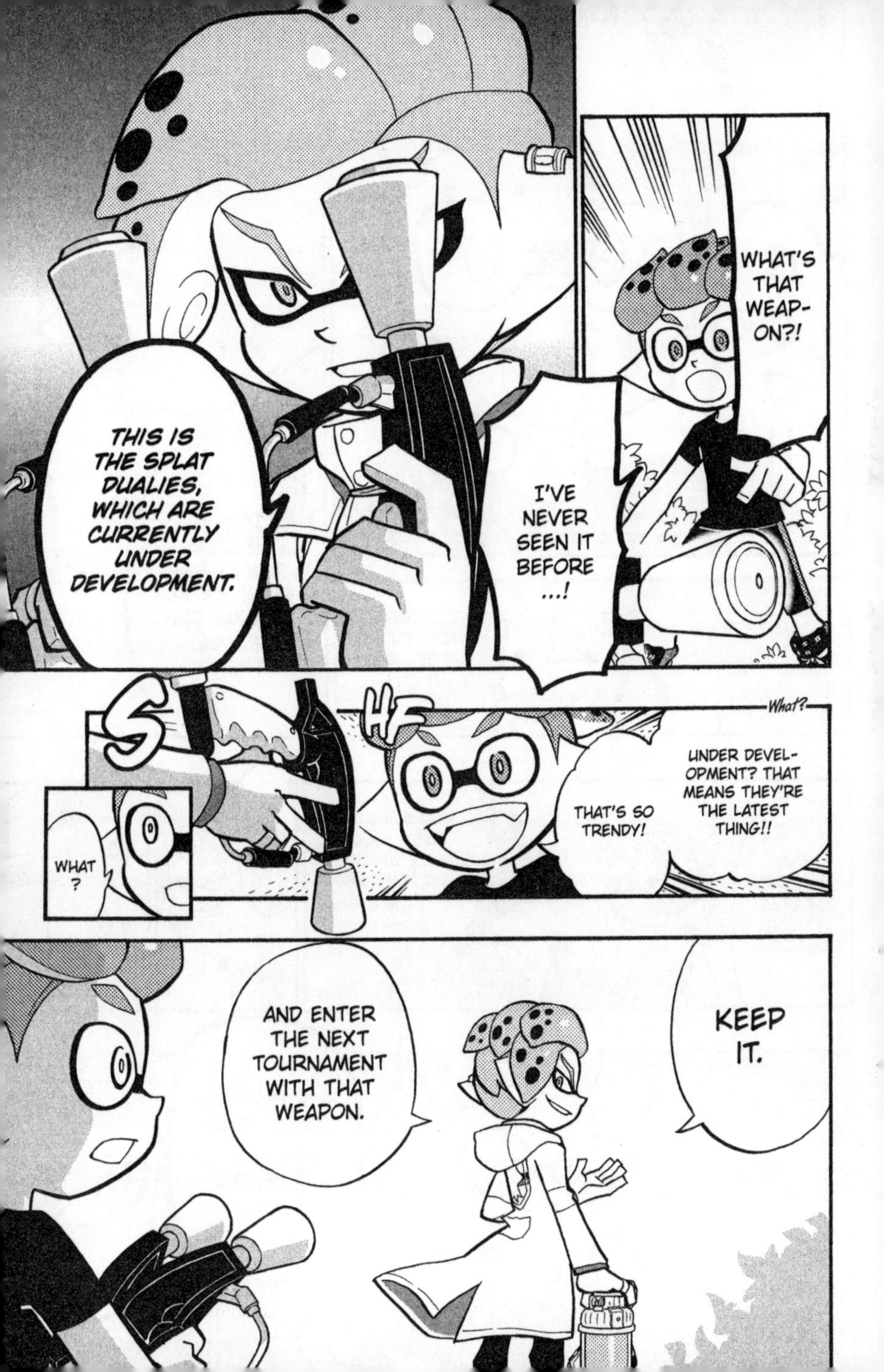
WHAT'S THAT WEAP-ON?!
I'VE NEVER SEEN IT BEFORE ...!
THIS IS THE SPLAT DUALIES, WHICH ARE CURRENTLY UNDER DEVELOPMENT.
What?
UNDER DEVEL-OPMENT? THAT MEANS THEY'RE THE LATEST THING!!
THAT'S SO TRENDY!
HF
S
WHAT ?
KEEP IT.
AND ENTER THE NEXT TOURNAMENT WITH THAT WEAPON.

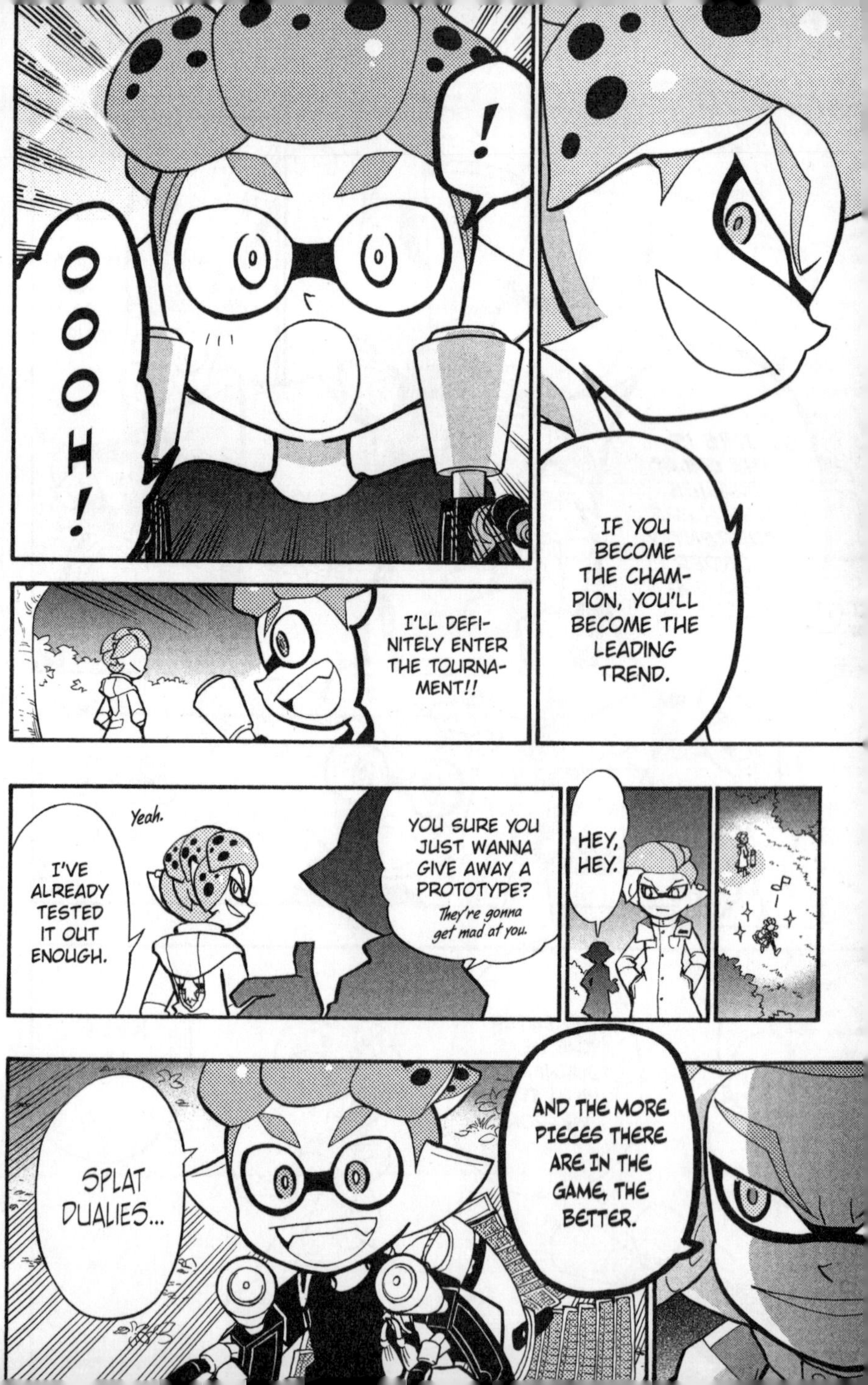
IF YOU BECOME THE CHAMPION, YOU'LL BECOME THE LEADING TREND.
!
OOOOH!
I'LL DEFINITELY ENTER THE TOURNAMENT!!
HEY, HEY.
YOU SURE YOU JUST WANNA GIVE AWAY A PROTOTYPE?
They're gonna get mad at you.
Yeah.
I'VE ALREADY TESTED IT OUT ENOUGH.
AND THE MORE PIECES THERE ARE IN THE GAME, THE BETTER.
SPLAT DUALIES...

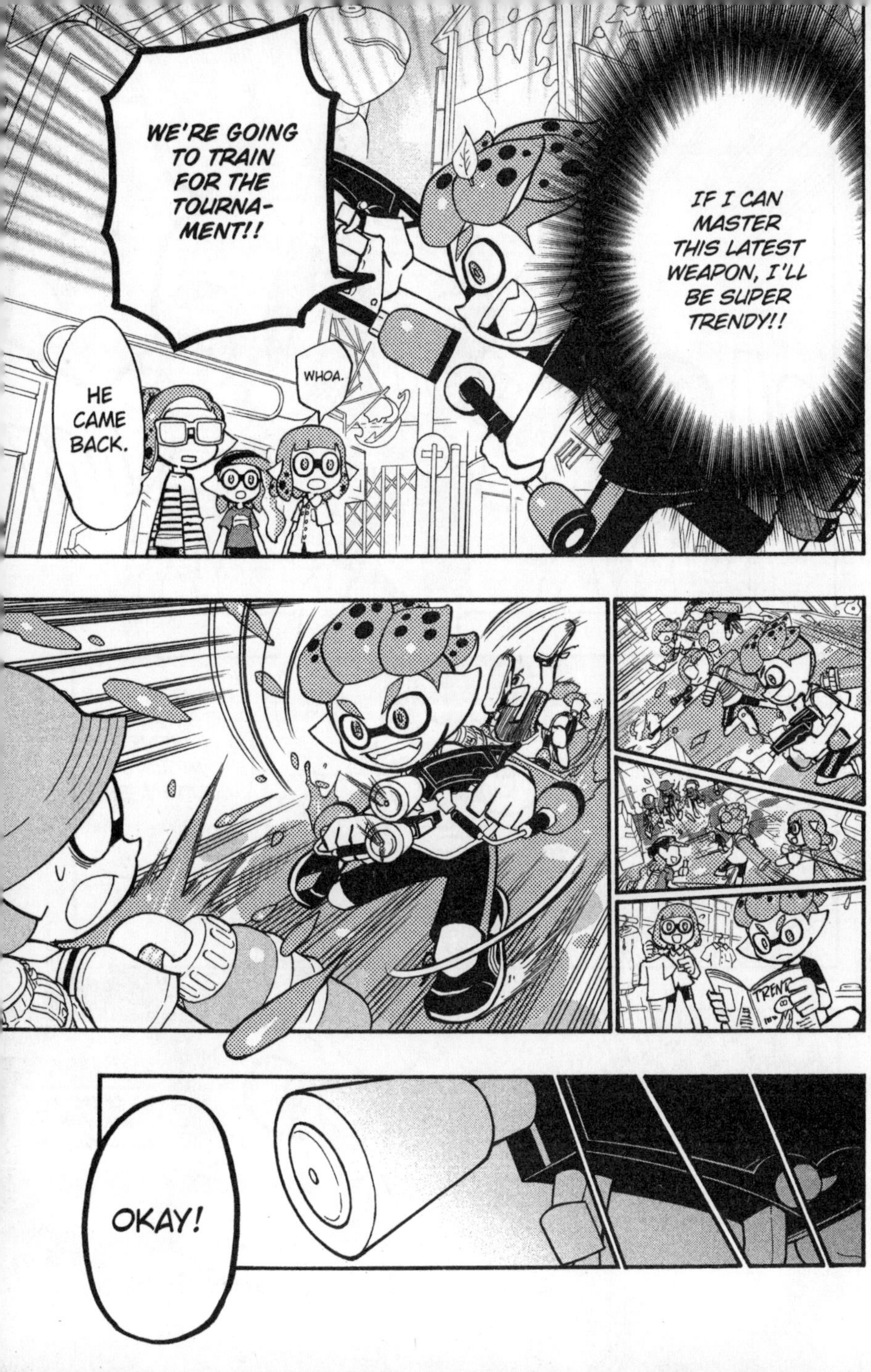
IF I CAN MASTER THIS LATEST WEAPON, I'LL BE SUPER TRENDY!!
WE'RE GOING TO TRAIN FOR THE TOURNA-MENT!!
WHOA.
HE CAME BACK.
OKAY!

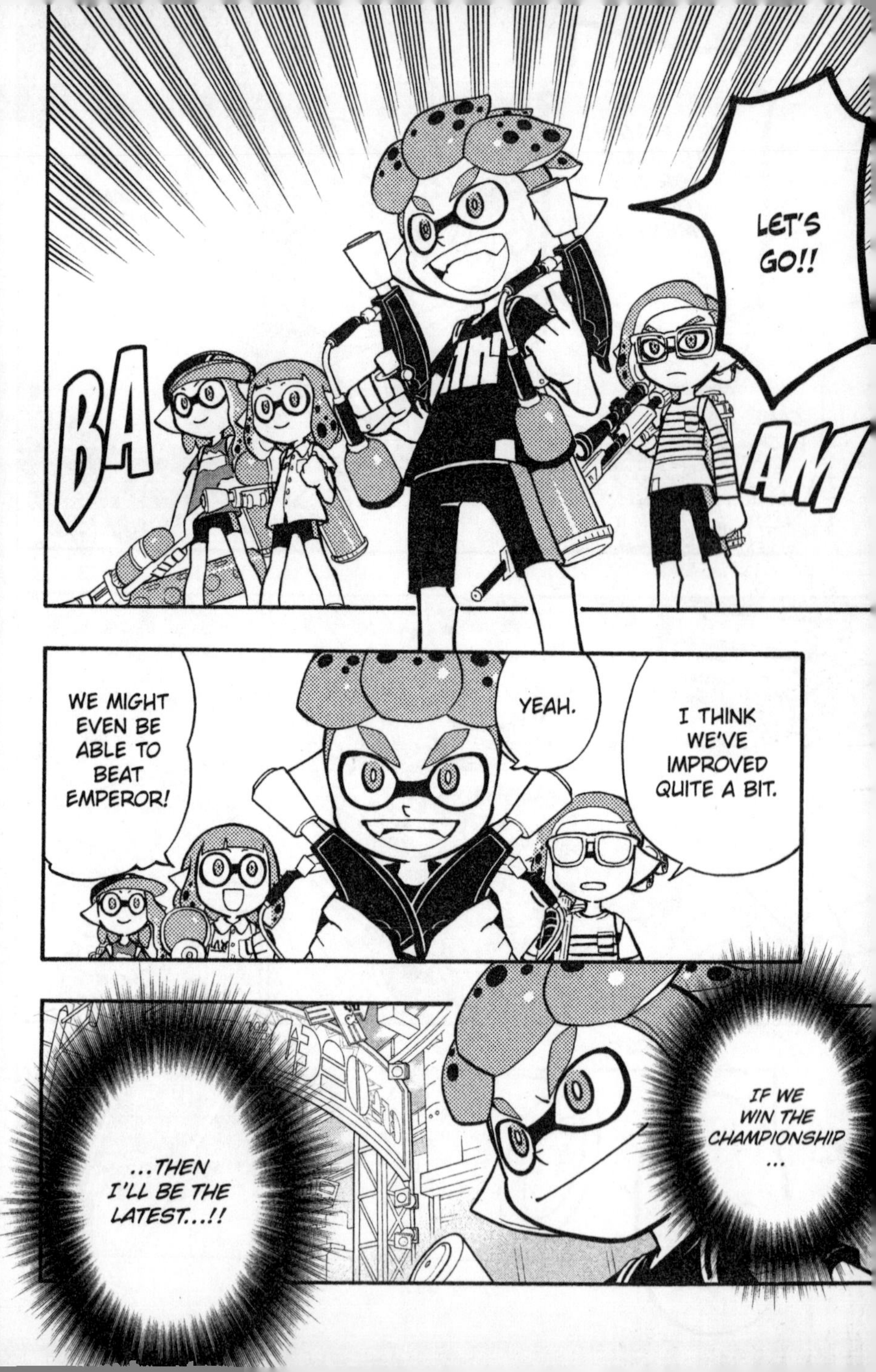
LET'S GO!!
BAAM
I THINK WE'VE IMPROVED QUITE A BIT.
YEAH.
WE MIGHT EVEN BE ABLE TO BEAT EMPEROR!
IF WE WIN THE CHAMPIONSHIP ...
...THEN I'LL BE THE LATEST...!!

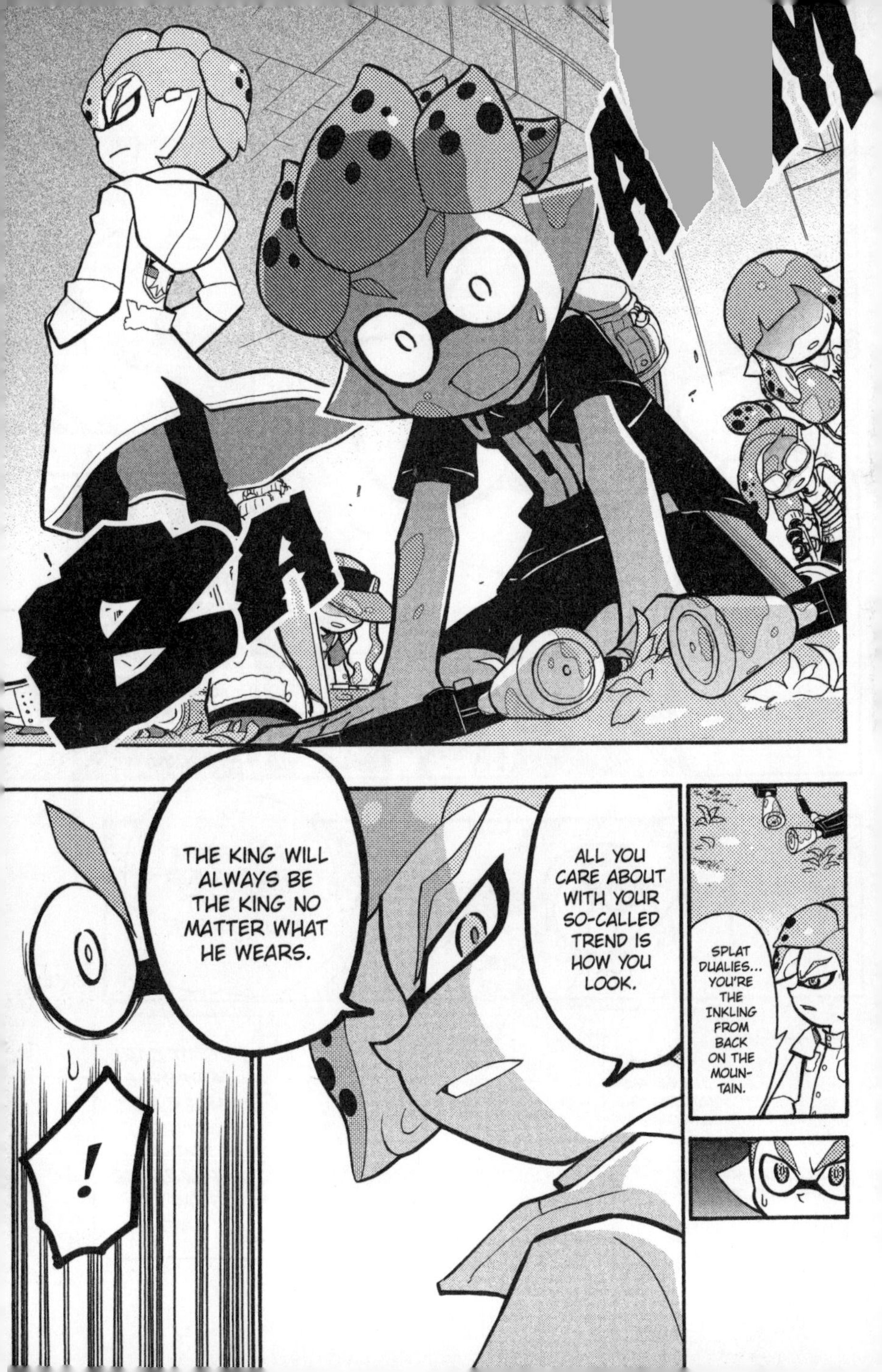
SPLAT DUALIES... YOU'RE THE INKLING FROM BACK ON THE MOUN-TAIN.
ALL YOU CARE ABOUT WITH YOUR SO-CALLED TREND IS HOW YOU LOOK.
THE KING WILL ALWAYS BE THE KING NO MATTER WHAT HE WEARS.
!

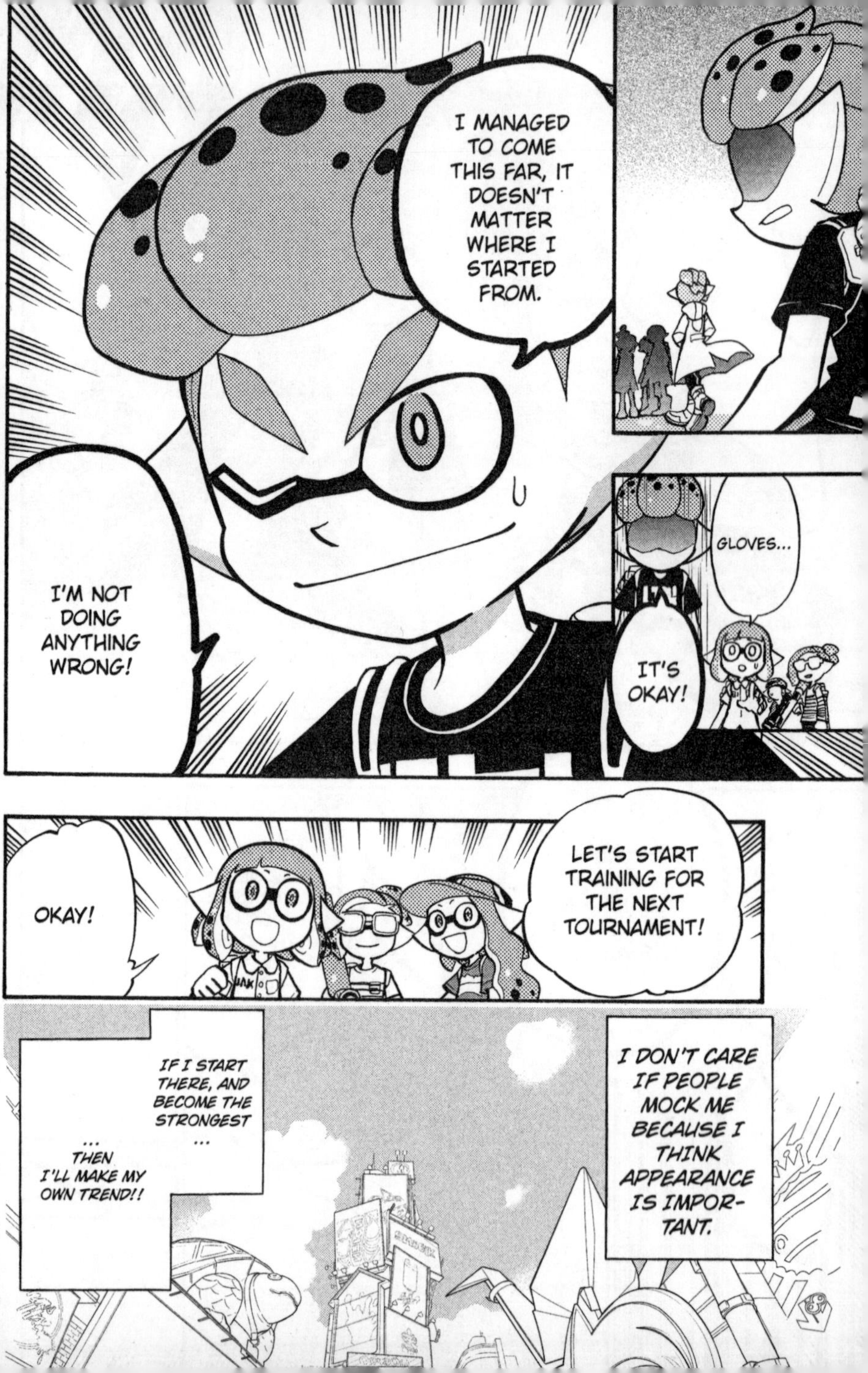
GLOVES...
IT'S OKAY!
I MANAGED TO COME THIS FAR, IT DOESN'T MATTER WHERE I STARTED FROM.
I'M NOT DOING ANYTHING WRONG!
LET'S START TRAINING FOR THE NEXT TOURNAMENT!
OKAY!
I DON'T CARE IF PEOPLE MOCK ME BECAUSE I THINK APPEARANCE IS IMPOR-TANT.
IF I START THERE, AND BECOME THE STRONGEST ...
... THEN I'LL MAKE MY OWN TREND!!

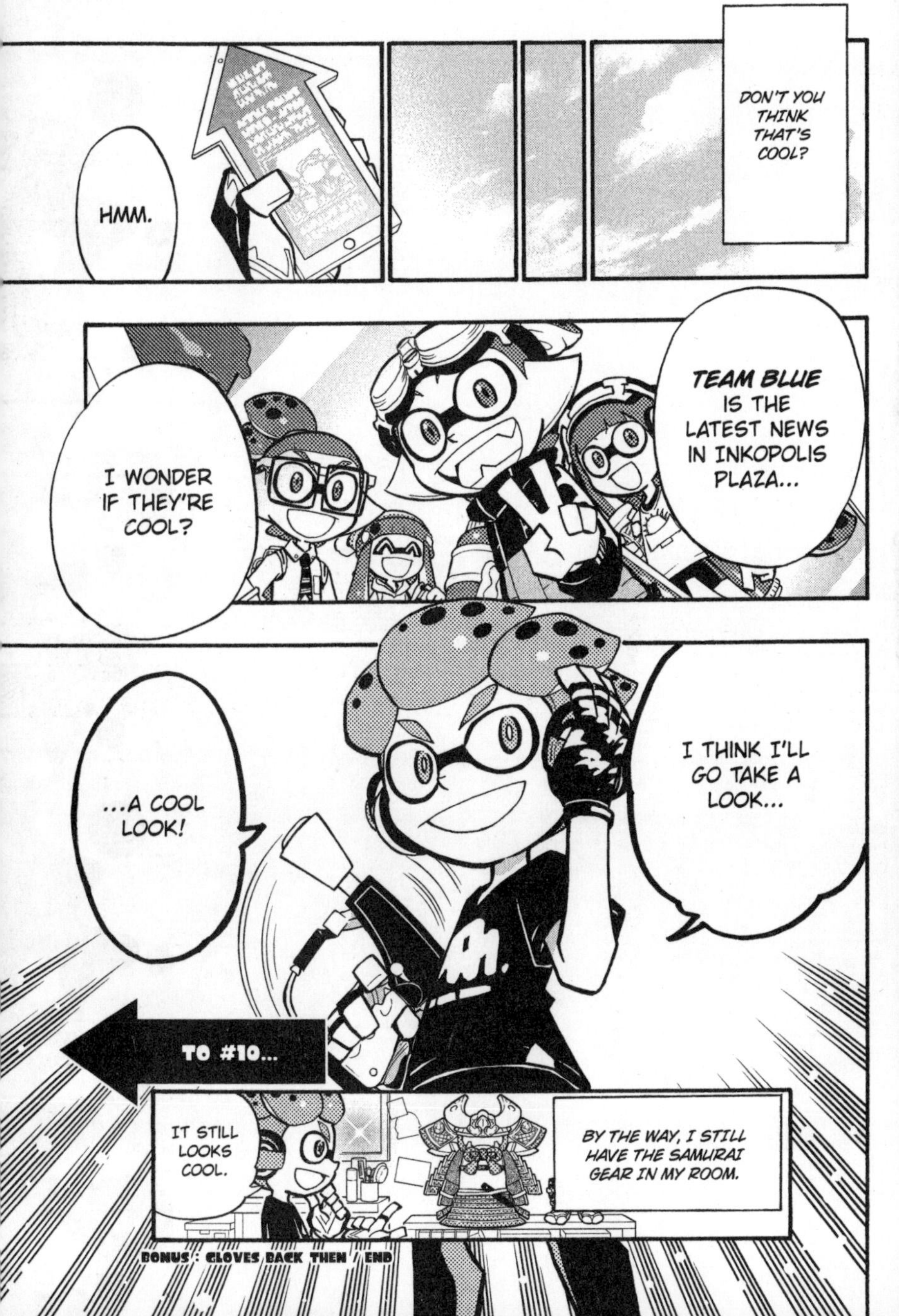
DON'T YOU THINK THAT'S COOL?
HMM.
TEAM BLUE IS THE LATEST NEWS IN INKOPOLIS PLAZA...
I WONDER IF THEY'RE COOL?
I THINK I'LL GO TAKE A LOOK...
...A COOL LOOK!
TO #10...
BY THE WAY, I STILL HAVE THE SAMURAI GEAR IN MY ROOM.
IT STILL LOOKS COOL.
BONUS : GLOVES BACK THEN / END

INKLING ALMANAC

GLOVES

Weapon: Splat Dualies
Headgear: Squidfin Hook Cans
Clothing: Black V-Neck Tee
Shoes: Yellow-Mesh Sneakers

INFO

• He spends an hour doing his hair each day.
• Every morning, he practices his cool poses in the mirror.

Hmm, really?

That's not cool.

TEAM GLOVES

(INK COLOR: NEON GREEN)

STRAPS

CLIP-ONS

HALF-RIMZ

Weapon: Splat Roller
Headgear: Takoroka Visor
Clothing: Navy King Tank
Shoes: Neon Delta Straps

Weapon: Splattershot
Headgear: Squid Clip-Ons
Clothing: Octobowler Shirt
Shoes: Mint Dakroniks

Weapon: Splatterscope
Headgear: Half-Rim Glasses
Clothing: Pink Easy-Stripe Shi
Shoes: Shark Moccasins

INFO

• After Gloves's training session in the mountains, they talked about training as a team
in the mountains too but decided to compromise by training at a camping site.

TENNIS HEADBAND

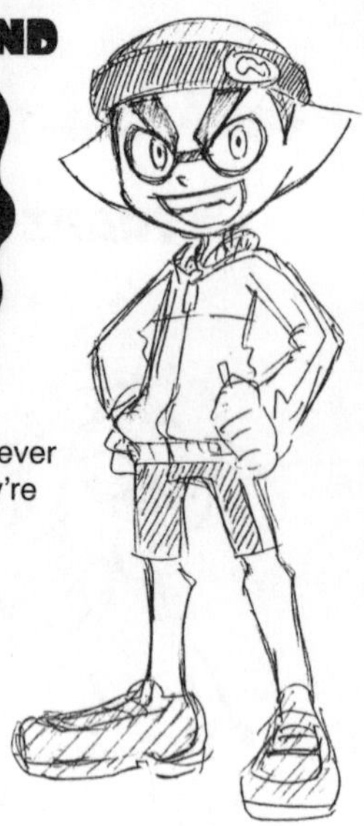

Weapon: Bamboozler 14 MK I
Headgear: Tennis Headband
Clothing: Retro Gamer Jersey
Shoes: School Shoes

JOGGING HEADBAND

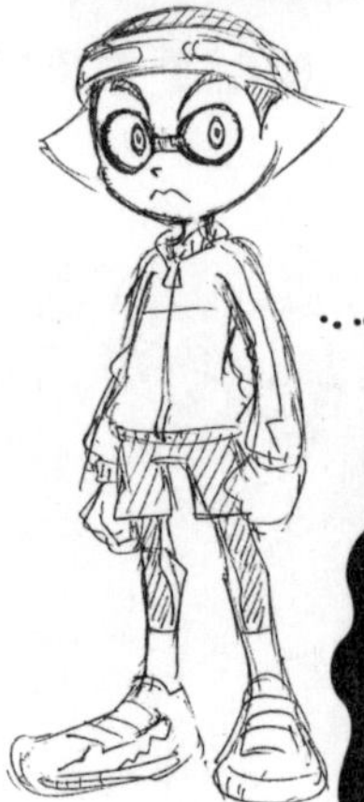

INFO

• They've wanted to use the word "cool" ever since the match against Gloves, but they're too embarrassed to say it.

Weapon: Luna Blaster
Headgear: Jogging Headband
Clothing: Retro Gamer Jersey
Shoes: Strapping Reds

SQUASH HEADBAND

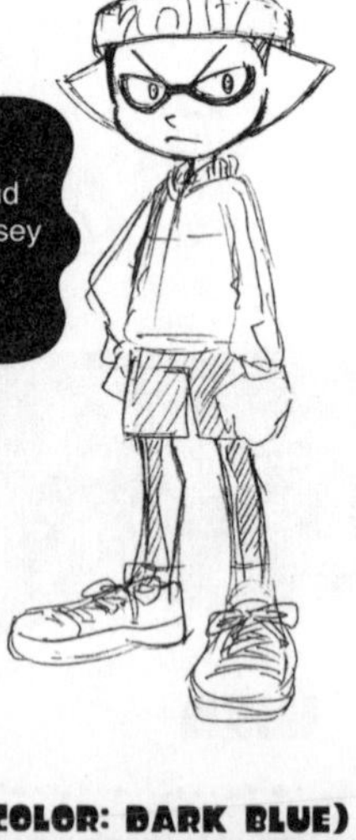

Weapon: Dual Squelcher
Headgear: Squash Headband
Clothing: Retro Gamer Jersey
Shoes: Cream Hi-Tops

B-BALL HEADBAND

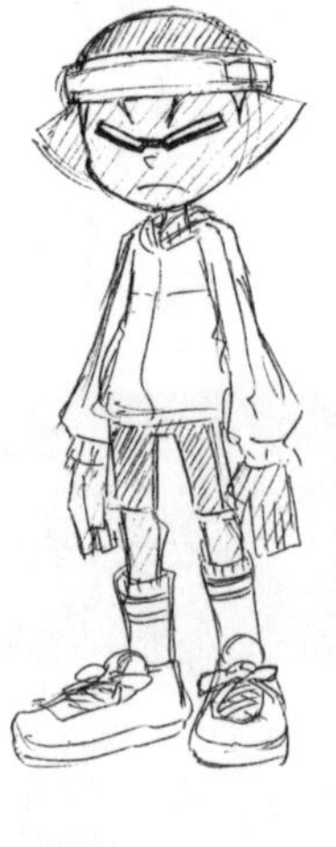

Weapon: Splattershot Pro
Headgear: B-ball Headband
Clothing: Retro Gamer Jersey
Shoes: LE Lo-Tops

INFO

• They've been thinking about inviting a girl to their training sessions, but in the end, its always these four boys that gather to train.

(INK COLOR: DARK BLUE)

TEAM RETRO GAMER

SCHOOL ASYMMETRY

SCHOOL SHORT

Weapon:	Splash-o-matic
Headgear:	Squid Clip-Ons
Clothing:	School Cardigan
Shoes:	School Shoess

INFO

• They've been training at night to make their voices sound higher.

Weapon:	Splattershot Jr.
Headgear:	Squid Clip-Ons
Clothing:	School Cardigan
Shoes:	School Shoes

SCHOOL BUN

Weapon:	Tri-Slosher
Headgear:	Squid Clip-Ons
Clothing:	School Cardigan
Shoes:	School Shoes

SCHOOL LONG

Weapon:	Inkbrush
Headgear:	Squid Clip-Ons
Clothing:	School Cardigan
Shoes:	School Shoes

(INK COLOR: PINK)

INFO

• They split up to go and buy their school uniforms.

TEAM SCHOOL CARDIGAN

TEAM INKFALL

(INK COLOR: LIGHT BLUE)

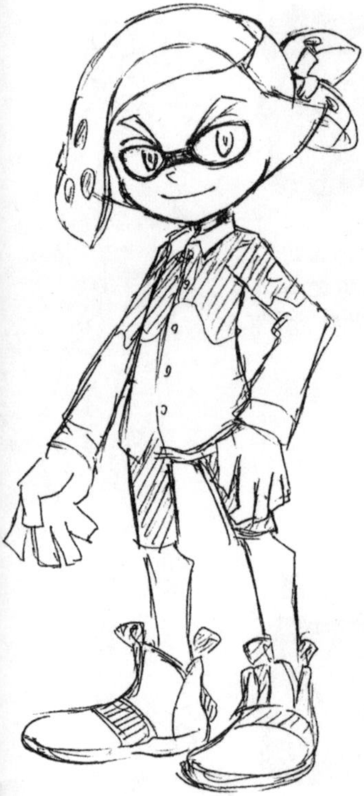

INKFALL

Weapon: Splattershot Pro
Headgear: Squid Hairclips
Clothing: Inkfall Shirt
Shoes: White Norimaki 750s

INFO

• He hates getting dirty, but he loves to eat spaghetti with tomato sauce.

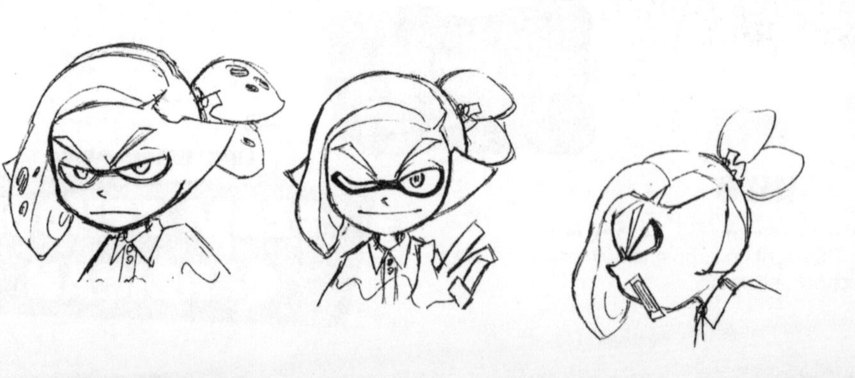

KNIT HAT

Weapon:	H-3 Nozzlenose
Headgear:	Knitted Hat
Clothing:	Half-Sleeve Sweater
Shoes:	Arrow Pull-Ons

ARROW

Weapon:	L-3 Nozzlenose
Headgear:	White Arrowbands
Clothing:	Short Knit Layers
Shoes:	Squid-Stitch Slip-Ons

VADER

Weapon:	Jet Squelcher
Headgear:	Jellyvader Cap
Clothing:	Positive Longcuff Sweater
Shoes:	Turquoise Kicks

INFO

• They are all clean freaks, so they always smell of soap.

CLAMS FACEMASK

Weapon: Aerospray MG
Headgear: King Facemask
Clothing: Crimson Parashooter
Shoes: Kid Clams

INFO

• He wakes up early every morning to do stretches with his grandfather.

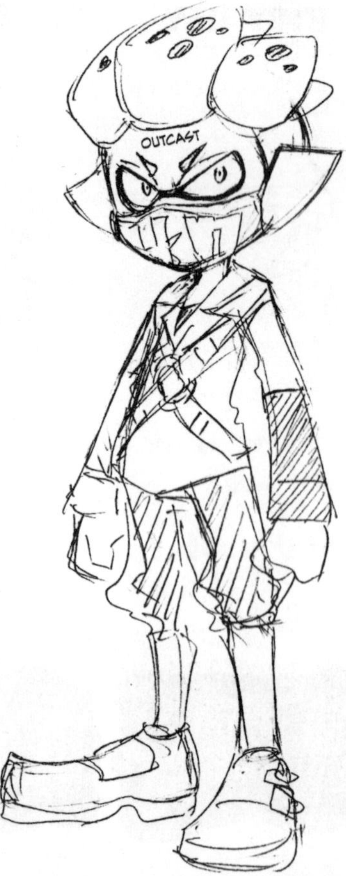
OUTCAST

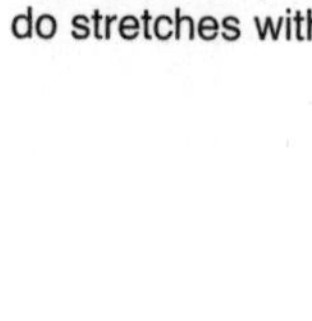
OUTCAST

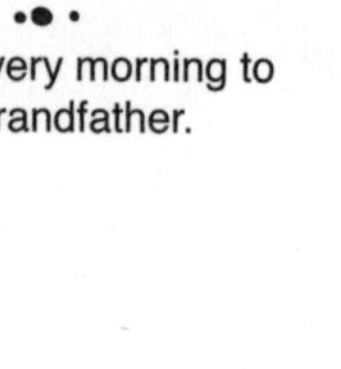
OUTCAST

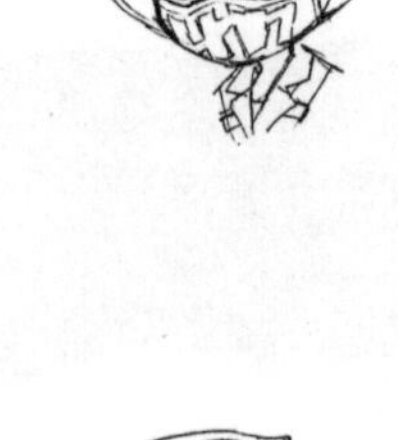
OUTCAST

TEAM OUTCASTS

(INK COLOR: DARK ORANGE)

CHOCO FACEMASK

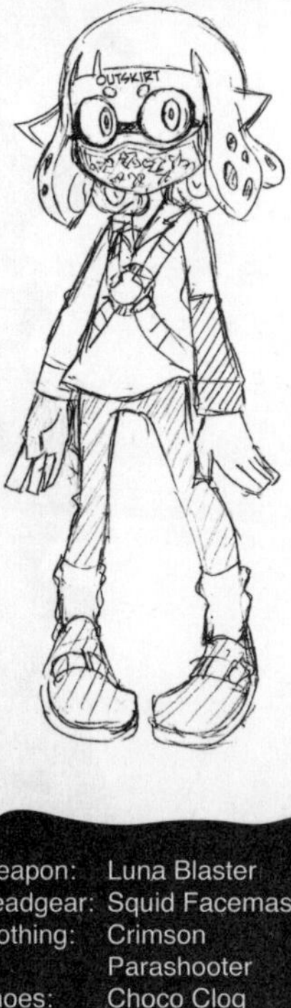
OUTSKIRT

Weapon: Luna Blaster
Headgear: Squid Facemask
Clothing: Crimson Parashooter
Shoes: Choco Clog

PUNK MASK

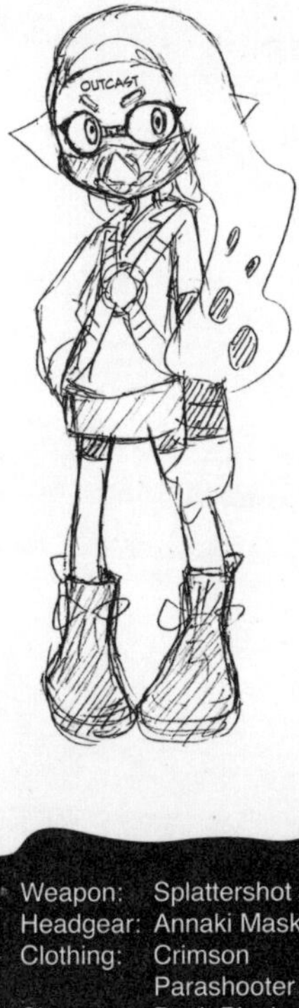
OUTCAST

Weapon: Splattershot Jr.
Headgear: Annaki Mask
Clothing: Crimson Parashooter
Shoes: Punk Blacks

PIRANHA FACEMASK

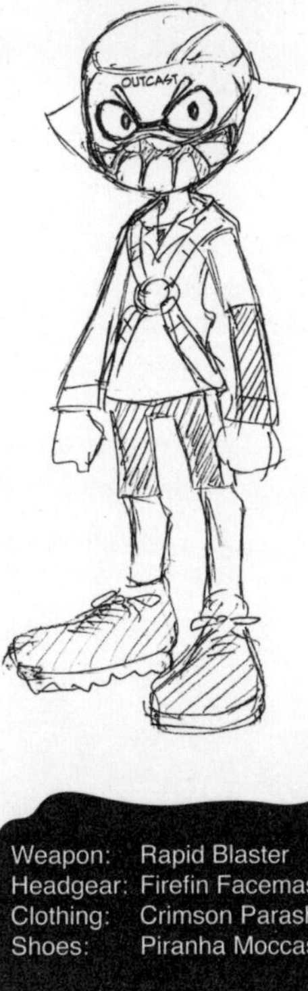
OUTCAST

Weapon: Rapid Blaster
Headgear: Firefin Facemask
Clothing: Crimson Parashoote
Shoes: Piranha Moccasins

INFO

- They have actually never seen each other's faces.

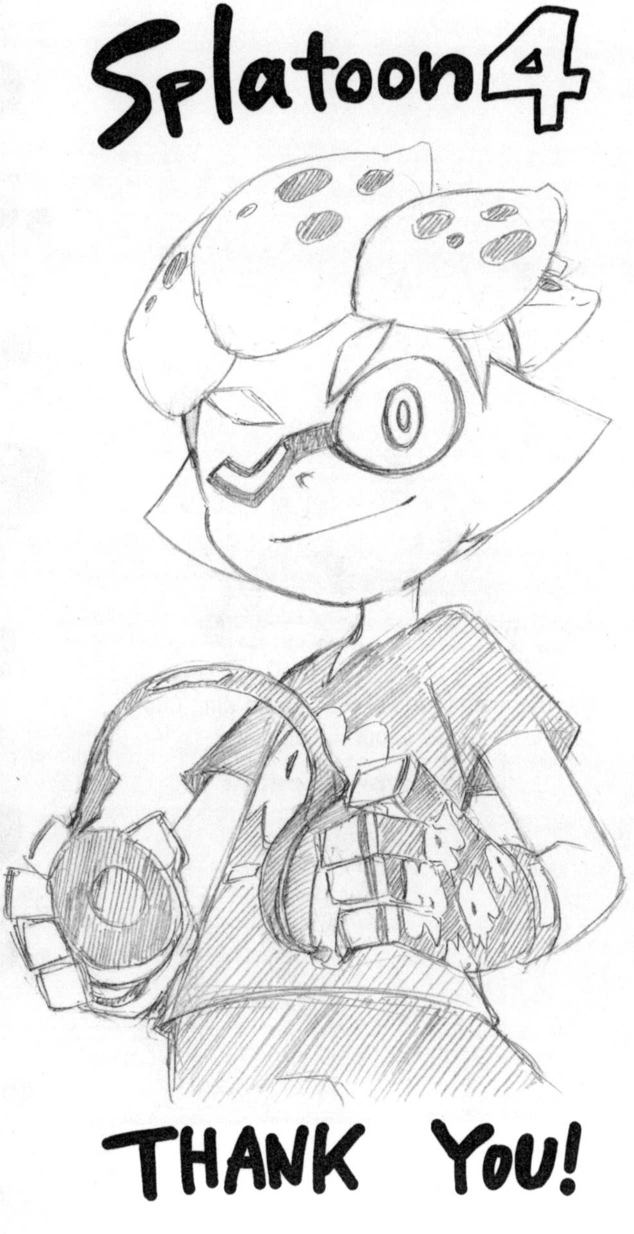
Splatoon 4
THANK YOU!

The main round of the Square King Cup
is about to begin!

Sankichi Hinodeya

Splatoon

Volume 4
VIZ Media Edition

Story and Art by
Sankichi Hinodeya

Translation **Tetsuichiro Miyaki**
English Adaptation **Jason A. Hurley**
Lettering **John Hunt**
Design **Shawn Carrico**
Editor **Joel Enos**

SPLATOON Vol. 4 by Sankichi HINODEYA
© 2016 Sankichi HINODEYA
All rights reserved.
Original Japanese edition published by SHOGAKUKAN.
English translation rights in the United States of America,
Canada, the United Kingdom, Ireland, Australia and
New Zealand arranged with SHOGAKUKAN.

The stories, characters and incidents mentioned
in this publication are entirely fictional.

Original Design **100percent**

Printed in Italy

Published by VIZ Media, LLC
P.O. Box 77010
San Francisco, CA 94107

10 9 8 7 6 5 4 3
First printing, September 2018
Third printing, January 2022

PARENTAL ADVISORY
SPLATOON is rated A and is
suitable for readers of all ages.

Splatoon reads from right to left!

This is the end of this graphic novel.